Ta... ...g... up near Ed... ...ys were spent in ...emote c... ge ... . Highlands, the region ...here her detective G...vin Macrae lives. Like her sailing heroine, Cass, she has always been used to boats, and spent her gap-year earnings on her first sailing dinghy, *Lady Blue*. She studied English at Dundee University, did a year of teacher training and took up her first post, teaching English and French to secondary-school children in Aith, Shetland. Gradually her role expanded to doing drama too, and both primary- and secondary-school pupils have won prizes performing her plays at the local Drama Festival. Some of these plays were in Shetlandic, the local dialect.

The Shetland Sea Murders is the ninth novel in her much-loved Shetland Sailing Mysteries series.

By Marsali Taylor

The Shetland Sailing Mysteries

Death on a Longship
The Trowie Mound Murders
A Handful of Ash
The Body in the Bracken
Ghosts of the Vikings
Death in Shetland Waters
Death on a Shetland Isle
Death from a Shetland Cliff
The Shetland Sea Murders

THE SHETLAND SEA MURDERS

MARSALI
TAYLOR

ACCENT

First published in 2021 by Headline Accent
An imprint of HEADLINE PUBLISHING GROUP

1

Cataloguing in Publication Data is available from the British Library

ISBN 978 1 4722 7596 7

Typeset in 11/13.5pt Bembo Std by Jouve (UK), Milton Keynes

Printed and bound in Great Britain by Clays Ltd, Elcograf S.p.A.

Headline's policy is to use papers that are natural, renewable and recyclable
products and made from wood grown in well-managed forests and other
controlled sources. The logging and manufacturing processes are expected
to conform to the environmental regulations of the country of origin.

HEADLINE PUBLISHING GROUP
An Hachette UK Company
Carmelite House
50 Victoria Embankment
London
EC4Y 0DZ

www.headline.co.uk
www.hachette.co.uk

Contents

Dedication	vii
Part I	1
Part II	45
Part III	83
Part IV	131
Part V	181
Part VI	223
Part VII	265
Part VIII	305
Acknowledgements	333
A Note on Shetlan	335
Glossary	337

For Teresa Chris, my agent, who's kept believing in me.

I

A Ring around the Moon

Chapter One

Saturday 19th October

Tide times at Aith
HW 00.32 (2.0m); LW 06.35 (0.9m);
HW 12.50 (2.0m); LW 19.05 (0.9m)

Sunrise 07.53, moonset 14.24; sunset 17.44, moonrise 19.48.

Waning gibbous moon

The Mayday startled me awake in the middle of the night, crackling through the speaker of the handheld radio in *Swan*'s aft cabin. I heard Magnie stir in the berth below me, and reach out a hand to grab it and turn the volume up.

'–day, Mayday.' It was a man's voice, heavily accented, and sounding as if he was reading from a script. 'Shetland coastguard, this is fishing vessel *Dorabella, Dorabella, Dorabella*, with thirteen people aboard. We on rocks the west side Ve Skerries, beside Papa Stour. We request immediate assistance. Shetland Coastguard, Mayday, Mayday, Mayday.'

I wriggled forward in my bunk and snicked my light on. We were all awake now, Magnie with the handheld black by his ear and Geordie, the engineer, leaning out of his berth; all listening intently as a calm voice from Shetland Coastguard requested further details. It was a struggle to get the information. *Dorabella* was a thirty-metre long-liner, registered in the Ivory Coast, but with the owners in France. No, nobody was

3

hurt. The ship wasn't in immediate danger. There was no water coming in. No apparent damage to the engines. They were still running, to keep the fish fresh. They'd been on their way to port, with a full hold. Yes, they'd tried to reverse off, but with no success, and the tide had come as high as it was going to. They were stuck fast.

Magnie came out of his berth, pulling his jeans and a jumper on over his sleeping thermals, and I wriggled out of mine, and followed suit. We went up into the stillness of the night.

We were anchored off Vementry Isle, on the westside, round the corner from Brae, and just opposite where I'd grown up. The wooden deck below our feet belonged to *Swan*, Shetland's own tall ship, a converted Fifie fishing boat which had been built here over a century ago. My friend and former sailing teacher Magnie was in charge, and enjoying skippering a proper fishing boat again. He could just remember *Swan* as a working boat; he'd been a boy when she'd left Shetland in the fifties. When she'd been rediscovered, half-sunk and rotting in an English harbour, he'd been one of the campaigners to bring her hull back and restore her as a living memorial of the Shetland fleet in the great herring days. Given his fishing experience and his skipper's ticket, he was now a valuable volunteer crew.

It was a weekend trip, a charter for a Shearer man who was celebrating his sixtieth, and later than *Swan* would normally do, because by mid–October the weather was too uncertain. It could be a golden autumn weekend or a flying gale from the north, chilling as winter, but this was when Shearer's birthday was, and he had a sudden fancy to take his sister and nieces on a three–island trip to see the guns of Vementry, the caves of Papa Stour, on the western corner of the Shetland mainland, and the cliffs of Foula, seventeen miles out into the Atlantic. It just so happened that Papa Stour was also hosting a music weekend, with a concert on the Saturday evening, so we were going to that while we were there. He was a friend of the

4

Trustees – he'd wangled the *Swan* a good insurance deal with his firm, which took some doing with a hundred-year-old wooden boat whose remit included paying passengers and school trips – and *Swan* needed all the cash she could get, so the secretary had taken the booking, and crossed fingers for decent weather.

'Besides,' Geordie the engineer had said cheerfully, 'it gets me out of all the work at home on Papa, with this music evening we're going to. Every house on the island as full as it can get, and baking and boiling all day on every cooker. I'm well clear of it.'

There were four passengers: Stevie Shearer, his sister and her two daughters. Stevie had been the first to arrive, roaring up on what even I could see was a classic bike: scarlet, with those leaning-back handlebars and the chrome of the engine polished silver-bright. He'd come over and greeted us all cheerily, then gone back and spent ten minutes padlocking the wheels and draping a tarpaulin over it. There was a touch of cliché about him: the jet-black hair sleeked back, the sleeveless t-shirt, Harley Davidson tattoos on both arms (hidden, I presumed, by his shirt when he was brokering insurance), tight jeans and round-toe biker boots. He was one of those jovial characters who was too touchy-feely for me, a bit too matey in the way he'd steadied himself on the perfectly steady gangplank by putting one arm around me. He'd apologised, of course, and added a joke: 'Why is a sailor like an uncaught criminal?' I'd remembered I was paid crew and smiled nicely. 'I don't know – why is a sailor like an uncaught criminal?'

'They both need plenty of rope!' He laughed uproariously. I did a token-gesture smile, and invited him to make himself at home on deck.

The women were not long behind him, his sister and one daughter together, and the other in a separate car. Stevie's sister was older, maybe ten years older, going by the age of the daughters, who looked to be in their late forties, and chalk and cheese: one dressed with the neat colour-coordination of a worker in the public eye, the other in a swirling patchwork skirt and cheesecloth blouse. Their mother had the look of an ageing hippy too, but it was the conventional daughter she'd come with, and I felt a bit of tension in the way she and the colourful daughter greeted each other, quickly smoothed over by Stevie's exuberant welcome to them both. I hoped it wasn't going to be one of those occasions where an attempt to patch up a quarrel by forcing people together just made everything worse.

We got them all on board, gave the safety briefing, then left the Walls pier. It was five o'clock now, and steekit mist, with the marker buoys and lines of mussels appearing suddenly from the greyness around us. The shore colours were dulled by it: ochre seaweed, charcoal rocks, olive hills with their tops hazed by cloud. The sea-stacks off the back of Vaila loomed through the mist and were swallowed again. Our passengers made themselves comfortable on deck and watched the world go by, Stevie and his sister with their backs propped against the dinghy, the two sisters one on each side of the hatch. Stevie kept coming out with awful jokes, and there was protesting laughter from the others.

Once we were out into the Atlantic, the mist thinned. There wasn't enough wind to get the sails up, but the late-afternoon sun was warm on our backs as we came through Papa Sound, the strip of water separating Papa Stour from the mainland. We crossed the south end of St Magnus Bay into the Røna channel and anchored in the bay to the back of the World War I guns on Vementry Isle.

The clear sky gave us a long twilight, with daylight on deck until well after seven. Our passengers sat around on deck chatting under a half-moon the colour of newly polished brass while I put a pot of tatties on, and Geordie cast for mackerel, using a waand with a dozen hooks. He struck lucky straight away. They came up twisting and flashing silver-bellies below their tiger-striped green and black backs. He caught each with a hand and tweaked it free; a twist of the fingers to break the gills, then he dropped them into the bucket, still flapping. We'd eaten our supper of fried mackerel and tatties around the wooden table in the main cabin that had once been the ship's fish hold, and I'd thought with a twinge of nostalgia that this was right home food. There was nothing like fresh-caught mackerel, the sweet flesh, and the oiliness of it sopped up by the oatmeal. Magnie had done an apple crumble and custard, and after that there'd been birthday cake and champagne under glittery 'Happy Birthday' banners, then we'd sat on deck watching the stars come out until the good sea air had sent our family yawning to bed.

Now the water was shifting silver in the moonlight, with the long Atlantic swell rolling over it, the hills outlined dark against the midnight sky. The wind had fallen away completely, and there was the cold tang of frost in the air. There was a ring around the three-quarters moon, sign of a warm front approaching with the changeable weather that would bring. Magnie and I stood in silence on the deck, looking at the dark headland of Vementry Isle between us and the open sea, and thinking of the boat on the rocks twelve miles beyond it.

The Ve Skerries was a horrible spot, a treachery of wicked rocks stretching out from the Ormal, the largest of them. I'd often seen the grey smudge of the white concrete tower built there far on the horizon; you couldn't see the rocks themselves, for they lay too low. If we'd been out in the Røna we'd just have been able to make out its light, flashing white twice every twenty seconds.

The men of the Aberdeen trawler *Ben Doran* had died there in the 1930s; in the seventies, the last of the men of the *Elinor*

Viking had been lifted off the same spot only ten minutes before their boat had begun breaking up. I stood there in the darkness and prayed with all my might for these men there now.

Geordie came up to join us. 'Any news?'

A clatter of the radio answered him, the Coastguard moving *Dorabella* to a working channel. We changed too, and listened as the Coastguard helicopter was scrambled, and the lifeboat. Ten minutes later we heard the lifeboat's engines as she set out from her pier down at Aith. It took her no time at all to reach us, a white wash streaming from her bows as she passed through the Røna at full speed, the roar beating out through the calm night then diminishing into the distance. *Swan* rocked to her passing, and the waves crashed white on the beach thirty metres from us.

Twelve miles, and the lifeboat's top speed was twenty-five knots. She'd be there in half an hour. The fishing boat's radio operator had said they were in no danger at the moment, and there was nothing to harm them in the weather. The lifeboat would get them off safe from that wilderness of rocks, as long as it could manoeuvre up to them. The *Ben Doran* had been unlucky; she'd steamed right in between the rocks in the days before lighthouse and lifeboat, and ended up stuck in the middle of them. She'd had no radio on board. By the time another boat had spotted her, the wind had risen, and the sea was a boiling turmoil around them. A number of other trawlers had braved the conditions to go out there. They'd seen seven men tied to the rigging in their oilskins, but been unable to get to them.

'How came they,' Magnie said, 'to go apo the Ve Skerries on so calm a night? Thirty metres long, they said. You're no' telling me a boat that size didn't have the latest sort of chart plotter to tell them within an inch where they were.'

'A chart plotter still needs someone to look at it,' I said. 'It was the lights, wasn't it, with the *Ben Doran*? They were gutting fish, and the glare of the gas lights blinded them. Maybe these men were busy hauling in their lines, and not looking around them.'

'You can get good fishing around the Skerries,' Geordie said. He was from Papa Stour, and knew the area. 'They've maybe been over-keen to get a good catch, and drifted closer than they should have, and then not been able to get their lines up in time to avoid the rocks.'

'But didn't they say they were heading for port with a full hold?' I asked.

'That wouldn't stop them wanting to take in a few more,' Geordie said.

Magnie nodded. 'Thirteen men. That's short-handed on a hundred-footer. I'd've expected fifteen.'

'The owners cutting costs,' Geordie said cynically. 'Cheap foreign seamen paid starvation wages, and no attention to health and safety once they'd got their certificate.'

The *Ben Doran* had had a crew of nine. The bodies of the last two had been found later, washed up with a great coil of rope between them. They'd been the strongest swimmers of the crew, and it was thought they'd tried to swim with a rope to the Ormal, to get the others across to the rock above the water. Their graves were in Sandness kirkyard: *Greater love hath no man, than that he lay down his life for his friends.*

I shook the sorrow away. The chopper had airlifted the men of the seventies *Elinor Viking* off. The modern Oscar Charlie was on its way. Even if the lifeboat couldn't get to them, these men would be saved.

I glanced at the time on the plotter behind us, and became practical. Half past midnight. 'Neap tides too,' I said. 'Unless they're lucky and get a big swell at the next high tide, the boat'll be stuck there until the new moon. Ten days.'

'If she lasts that long. Ten days without a gale, in the second half of October?'

I made a face. No boat would last long with an Atlantic gale washing over her.

'The forecast's good for the weekend,' Geordie said. 'They'll maybe find some way of getting the fish off, if they can keep the generator running for the refrigeration.'

'Shame to waste it,' Magnie agreed.

There was a distant thrumming in the air, like a far-off bumblebee. It grew closer and filled the air: the chopper on its way over. We waited, and listened, until the last noise of it had died away, and the night was silent again.

The stillness was broken by a ringing phone from the main cabin. It broke off, there was a muttered voice, and then there were steps on the companionway. Stevie Shearer came out, in a t-shirt and shorts, phone to his ear, and went straight to the bow without looking back at us. It was like him, I thought, to assume he was alone on deck, just because he wanted to be. His voice floated clearly aft, in workmanlike French. 'What do you mean, on the rocks?'

There was silence again as he listened. 'Okay. But the engine's still running. Can you get the fish from the hold?'

Another silence, then he said, 'I'll see what I can do. Don't make any stupid admissions. You were steaming back to port with a full hold . . . get them in, then. Cut them if need be.' He jerked the phone from his ear, and stood for a moment, looking out.

We'd stayed still by the wheel, aft, turning our shoulders to his conversation. Now, out of the corner of my eye, I caught a flash of something white moving in the black square of the main cabin entrance. I turned my head to look properly, and glimpsed a face, someone hovering at the top of the ladder. She saw my movement and ducked back, but I could still see the white shoulder of a t-shirt at the side of the doorway. She was still there, listening.

Stevie punched in a number with angry jabs of his fingers,

and put it to his ear again. He spoke in English this time. 'The *Dorabella*'s on the Ve Skerries . . . yes, stuck fast. The men are to be airlifted off. They've kept the refrigeration unit running, but we need to empty that hold . . . Yes, get on to it right away. And organise someone to meet the men. We'll speak tomorrow.' He rang off and turned to come back towards the companionway. The white shoulder vanished, but I thought I caught the soft thud of feet going hastily downwards, one metallic rattle of a bunk-curtain being drawn.

Now at last Stevie saw us standing there at the wheel, and did a double take, then came to join us. 'Hope I didn't wake you.'

Magnie shook his head. 'The Mayday did that.'

He left it at that, but Stevie rushed into speech. 'She's one of ours − I mean, my firm insured her. If they can't get her off soon she'll be a total loss.'

'But with no loss of life,' I said.

'Yea, yea,' he agreed quickly. 'That's the important thing, of course. And if it's possible to get the fish off her that should help.'

'She may be lucky and float off tomorrow,' Geordie said.

'Let's hope so.' He shrugged, turned his head quickly as if he'd heard a noise in the main cabin, stared for a moment, then looked at us. 'Well, I'll get back to my bed.' He gave a cursory glance round up at the star-filled sky, with the sickle of the Charioteer hanging above the Ward of Muckle Roe. 'A bonny night. See you in the morning.' He sketched a wave and headed back below.

'Well,' Magnie said. He looked around at the silvery water, the dark hills, and gave his shoulders a shake. 'We have these folk to give a good time tomorrow. Shall we turn in?'

'Leave the radio on,' I said.

'Yea, yea, I'll do that.'

We went below, still listening as the Coastguard directed

operations. The helicopter arrived at the Skerries just as we were back in our bunks, and began lifting the men off straight away. They could take all thirteen. The men would be landed at the Clickimin in Lerwick, would be checked out in the hospital, then handed over to Aubrey and his volunteers of the Fisherman's Mission. It must have felt an age to those men, standing on their deck in the flashes of the lighthouse, but to us on board *Swan* it seemed an incredibly short time before the chopper was reporting that they had all the men safe, and they were heading for Clickimin. The lifeboat coxswain reported that they were standing down. Soon after, we heard the chopper drone above our heads again, with those men safely aboard, and then the lifeboat heading homewards. *Swan* rocked to her wash. Magnie switched back to channel 16 and turned the volume down. 'Well, folk, I'm going back to sleep.'

He turned over and soon his snores were vibrating against the wooden walls. Geordie's joined them. I lay awake for a bit longer. My berth was stuffy compared to my own *Khalida*, the eight-metre yacht that was my home, where the hatch was right by my head, and I missed my Cat and Kitten, who'd been left with Dad and Maman for this weekend. Cat felt at home with Maman's brand of elegance, which included a glowing peat fire and a comfortable Chinese rug, to say nothing of exotic scraps from the kitchen, and Dad had installed a cat flap in the back door so that he could come and go, as he was used to. I was less sure about Kitten, who'd never lived in a house before, but given the way she installed herself on the captain's red velvet couch at every opportunity I suspected she'd make herself at home on Dad's Chesterfield. She looked frail and delicate, but there was an iron paw inside every one of those little white mittens.

I wasn't going to get back to sleep any time soon. I turned onto my back, crossed my hands behind my head, and contemplated my world. I'd done my first six weeks of life aboard

Sørlandet as an A+ Academy. *Sørlandet* was the smallest of the three Norwegian tall ships, a three-masted, square-rigged beauty. Like all tall ships she'd been funded by a mixture of grants and paying passengers, but at last she'd found financial security as a floating college for older teenagers. They'd learn regular lessons, seamanship and life skills as they helped sail her around the world, stopping at ports where they could have time off, and their parents could fly over and join them. Her crew was supplemented by qualified teachers and we had sixty trainees on board, sixteen-and seventeen-year-olds, thirty boys, thirty girls. They were divided into watches of ten, two-hour watches, and they were young and silly, and needed to play music all the time, which drove me round the bend.

I checked myself. I was being unfair. Some, of course, were already keen sailors, and fitted straight into the life of the ship; a pleasure to be with. Others, well . . . for example, the one who'd been given the choice of military college or *Sørlandet*. He was going to be trouble. Already he was moving from dumb insubordination to active malice – in his hands plates slipped, and ropes tangled, or were knotted in a way that meant you couldn't release them as fast as you might need to sometimes. Nothing major, so far, but a tall ship at sea wasn't the place for pranks. And the girl who'd been affronted, that second day on board, to find that nobody had ironed her sheets during the day; well, she was learning, and the experience of being 'the other half' would do her good.

I had an ulterior motive for being on board the *Swan*: her captain of the last ten years had just retired, which was why Magnie was officer in charge, and I'd been hauled in to help. The captain's post would be advertised in spring. Now was my chance to get to know more about her, in case I decided to apply. I had the paper qualifications and the experience in sail training ships, but I knew less than I needed to about old-fashioned fishing boat rigs like *Swan*'s, and nothing about how she functioned otherwise: generators, engine, safety procedures. The post would probably go to her current mate (the one I was standing in for, currently with her leg in plaster after too enthusiastic a tackle in a hockey game), but in that case there would be a mate post free.

The thing was, *Sørlandet*'s Academy routine was six weeks on, six weeks off while she was in European waters, and eight weeks elsewhere. I'd had a good think about Cat and Kitten, and decided that it would be best for them to come home and live with my partner, Gavin, full-time; otherwise, it would be a nightmare of passports and vet visits and flights. I'd miss them, of course, but it wouldn't be for long each time.

I wanted Gavin and me to work. He was a Police Scotland DI, and we'd met through his first case up here, the Longship murder, a year and a half ago – I paused to wonder at that. It felt now like I'd always known him. We'd managed a long-distance relationship so far, but then Gavin had requested transfer out of the national serious crimes squad and back to a local post. When his boss had offered a Shetland post at the same seniority level, we'd talked about living together. He'd made it clear that he wanted me to be part of that; otherwise, he'd hold out for an Inverness posting, near his own home hills.

I'd thought hard about it. I knew there'd be the usual adjustments, but the biggest for me was that it might mean me having to give up sailing oceans. We both wanted children, and for that I'd have to stay ashore, wherever Gavin's job was. If I got a berth on board *Swan* it wouldn't be full-time, as my *Sørlandet* post was, so I'd have to save harder during the months I was at sea, to keep paying my share of household expenses over the winter, and I'd probably need to pick up shore jobs as well, but we'd be together more. *Swan* would be busy all summer, including longer trips, but as her base was Shetland I'd be able to get home in between them, and early and late summer were generally 'hameaboot' trips: day sails with schools or charter guests, or weekends sailing round Shetland. I'd be completely away only from June to mid August, instead of the current six or eight weeks on, then the same off. I'd been asking around on *Sørlandet* about how couples were finding that rota, and getting mixed responses. My watch leader, Petter, reckoned it worked well, easier than being separated from Frederik for the whole summer; another officer, Jonas, said his wife hated it. 'She's just got used to getting along without me when I arrive and throw things out, and then we're just getting into a routine when I go again.'

Well, I'd just have to see how Gavin and I got on with it. He was used to living on his own all week, at his Inverness flat, though he went home to the family farm for weekends. His brother, Kenny, would miss his help, especially as their mother was getting less able – not that she'd admit to it. If I was home all winter, if a job came up for him in Inverness, we could open up his cottage further along the loch, and commute between the flat and his loch together, or I could stay at the loch and help about the farm while he worked in town. I knew that he'd want to go home eventually. He'd be based in Shetland for now, but his hills would call him, just as the sea called me.

Meantime, once this trip was over, I needed to get on with getting our rented cottage ready for Gavin moving up here, in three weeks' time. It was going to be strange living together on land.

I yawned, and went to sleep.

Chapter Two

There was only the faintest of ripples along *Swan*'s green hull when I woke. I turned onto my side and squinted at my watch. Ten to six. Magnie was still snoring, and Geordie joined in with the occasional snort. The air was sour, in spite of the open hatch at the top of the ladder. I pulled my jeans and jumper over my pyjamas and climbed quietly up, socks and shoes in hand.

Yes, it was very still. Up here on deck the first clear light was a milky streak above Weathersta. As I watched, it spread along and began to brighten over Linga, to the south of east, where the sun would rise. A seal came up five metres from the side of the boat, turning his dog profile from side to side to get a good look at me and sculling with spotted flippers.

The generator cleared its throat and rumbled into life, breaking the silence. Magnie must be up, and our trainees soon would be. I headed down into the darkened main cabin and crossed it to the galley. A cup of tea all round would go down well. I kept my face turned away from the cabin as sighs and curtain noises signalled people getting up. Stevie's sister was the first, trailing past me to the heads in a glory of patch-work dressing gown. It took me a moment to remember her name. Amitola, that was it. She gave me a friendly smile as she passed. She had long, curly hair, dark but streaked with grey, which made her brother's gleamingly black head even more implausible. It was held back from her face by a headscarf tied like a hairband. She had that weathered complexion of someone who's spent a lot of time outdoors, her brother's prominent beaked nose, and startlingly white brows above her dark eyes.

I tried to remember Magnie's character summary. 'One o' these causes folk, you ken. Women's causes. She was one of the ones making a fuss for equal pay in the council, and she volunteers for the Women's Aid folk, that kind o' thing. She's a regular at the Alting debates. Believes a better world can be made by working for it.'

'If we all really worked at it, maybe it could,' I'd said. 'Particularly if the men worked at it too.'

'Yea, maybe.' He gave me a sideways look out of his pebble-green eyes. 'You're young yet. She's retired now, but she had a peerie café in Sandwick for a while, home-baked bannocks, fancies, and everything made with goat milk, for folk who hae allergies.' His tone was vaguely approving, so I gathered her baking passed muster. 'She does this "wild swimming" too. You ken, going off in the sea in wetsuits to commune wi' seals and the like.'

'She's never thought of standing for the council, if she wants to improve things?'

Magnie snorted. 'As if that would do any good. You'd need more women than four or five to make any impression on that lot. She bides in a peerie house just out o' Sandwick – well, it used to be out o' town before they built all those new houses around her.'

I made a face at that, and sympathised with Amitola, who'd moved to the country and found the town catching up with her. I hoped she'd enjoy the weekend away from it.

'Aye aye,' Amitola said on her way back. I heard the creak as she clambered back into her berth, then more creaks as she got dressed inside it. Within five minutes she was back, just as bright in a rainbow-striped knitted waistcoat over a loose white top and red cord trousers. She sat down on the edge of the bench seat to do up her DMs, then came into the galley. She might have been seventy, but her movements were brisk and sure. 'What can I do to help?'

'Thanks. Can you set mugs out for everyone? Magnie was talking pancakes for breakfast, but a cup of tea first thing always goes down well.'

'Mugs.' She did a quick head count. 'Four of us and three crew?'

'Right.'

She began taking the *Swan* china mugs from the holder above the sink, a brisk, accustomed movement. 'Today we're going on to Papa Stour, aren't we?'

'We'll go ashore on Vementry first, and have a look at the guns, then head on for the Papa caves, and finally into Housavoe for the night.'

'I lived on Papa, oh, for nearly five years, back in the seventies.' Her face was wistful. 'I loved being there. It was so quiet – you'd pause while you were working, and just stand for a moment and listen to the silence, and there was the smell of the flowers, and the stars in the winter nights, so bright I used to tell the girls they were made of diamonds from the Sky Goddess's broken necklace.' A shadow came over her face; for a moment her eyes were dark with what looked like anger. 'Well, that was then. I hope it's not a mistake going back.' She shook off the bleakness and spoke cheerfully. 'But Stevie was so keen on this trip that he got me persuaded. I've never seen the guns either, nor landed on Foula.' She set the last mug down, reached into the fridge for a carton of milk, and moved into the cabin, shaking the curtain of the bunk above hers. 'Moon? Cup of tea for you.' She turned to the next bunk. 'Sky?' There was a muffled protest from within the bunk. 'Sorry. Kirsten. Cup of tea.' She turned back to me. 'I'll just go up on deck, give other people room to get dressed.'

I watched the red trousers and green boots climb upwards. *Back in the seventies* . . . Papa had had a colony of hippies living there then, and I'd have taken no bets on whether Amitola had been one of them. That explained her daughters' names: Moon and, apparently, Sky. Moon was the colourful one; her sister, every inch the sober council employee, in trousers coordinated with her jumper, sensible shoes and a contrasting scarf at her neck, had introduced herself firmly as Kirsten. I didn't blame her. I'd shortened my French Cassandre (Maman had been singing in *The Trojan Women* while she was pregnant with me) to Cass on my first day in Primary 1.

I poured three mugs, added the milk and sugar of preference for Magnie and Geordie and headed upwards into the air. Amitola was sitting on the foredeck hatch, singing softly to the seal in a bonny alto voice; Magnie was up and leaning over the wheel, pebble-green eyes surveying the last wisps of mist on the Brae hills. I passed him his mug.

'Thanks to you, lass.' He jutted his chin downwards. 'Are they rising?'

'I'm leaving them to it. Amitola woke her daughters.' I set the tray down and called below, 'Geordie, cup of tea for you.'

'The smell o' breakfast'll soon get them on their feet.'

'Nothing like sea air,' I agreed. I was beginning to feel peckish myself. Breakfast on board *Sørlandet* was at half past seven, and it must be getting on for that now.

'I'll go and start these pancakes,' Magnie said. He drained the last of his tea and headed below. I nipped down and dressed properly, washed my face, managed to coax a comb through my hair and replaited it, then came back on deck and watched as the grey bands of cloud at last flushed pink from below, and then the sun shone silver between them, even further to the south-east than I'd been looking, almost over the cottage we'd rented, too bright to look at. A good omen for Gavin and I?

I was just reflecting that I was being ridiculously nervous, looking for good luck in the position of the rising sun, when Stevie came up on deck, stretching. The smell of pancakes drifted after him.

'Good morning, good morning!' he sang cheerfully. 'Here's a morning joke for you, Cass: What's the best thing about Switzerland?'

'The mountains?' I guessed.

'Don't know about them, but the flag is a big plus!'

I groaned obligingly, and headed below to help.

Everyone was up now. Kirsten's short hair was neat above moss green jumper and jeans, Moon's long hair was in wild curls around her shoulders. You'd not have taken them for sisters from a distance, but close up there was no missing the resemblance: the family bony nose, and their mother's dark eyes. Moon's skin was weathered to a brown tan, Kirsten's was soft and pink, as if she lived an indoor life. The biggest difference in their faces was the expression. Kirsten was office-worker brisk and competent, Moon dreamy, as if she barely saw the world around her.

I put maple syrup and bananas on the table, then squeezed past Magnie and began doling out cutlery, followed by the platefuls of pancakes, passed to the nearest person then handed round the square table with the sun, in traditional fashion. By the time everyone else was served, my stomach was rumbling. I joined the others at the table, squished a banana over my pancake and helped myself to maple syrup.

'Any more news of the *Dorabella* this morning?' Stevie asked.

I shook my head. 'Nothing on the radio.'

'We should try SIBC,' Magnie said. He gave the ship's clock a glance. 'Nearly half past eight. Snick on the radio, would you, Geordie?'

Geordie rose. 'It's the weekend,' he objected, as he reached up to the dials above the chart table. 'I doubt they won't have updated their news broadcast yet.'

Nor had they; we got a local teacher winning a national Physics award, the fencing team doing well in Birmingham and a lost dog, but no mention of the trawler. Geordie switched it off again, and Stevie explained to everyone else.

'But they got all the men off safe,' Magnie said, 'and that's the main thing. You never know, if they can lighten the hold she may just float off, good as gold.' He rose. 'Who's for more pancakes, before we go and explore the guns?'

We ferried them ashore in *Swan*'s inflatable, leaving Geordie aboard as anchor watch. There was still a scar on the hill above us where the heavy barrels had been winched up from the naval ship that brought them, a hundred years ago. It had been a feudal world then, I reflected, with crofters still dominated by the laird, and women in long skirts and cartwheel hats asking for 'votes for women'. It was a bonny walk upwards on the soft turf, with the last yellow hawkweed still bright against the green grass. We came at last up onto the plateau of the hill, and stood looking around.

I only knew the Vementry guns from sailing below them. From the Røna, the hill they sat on looked as if a giant had taken a bite out of the top of it, and you could just make out the gun mountings and the long barrels pointing seawards. They'd been put there in World War I to defend the fleet, which had lurked in St Magnus Bay and come into Swarback's Minn, the hand-shaped piece of water between Aith, Voe and Brae, to anchor and refuel. There had been a coaling station at Weathersta, and the admirals of the fleet had stayed at Busta House. They'd gone from here to the Battle of Jutland.

The guns were impressively large this close. There were three of them, the two covering St Magnus Bay mounted on a wide concrete platform with a little parapet around it, and the third on its own, barrel pointing over the Røna. The firing ends on the platform were well over my height, their cogs and levers red with rust, and the projecting barrels were a good four metres long. They could fire shells a distance of twelve miles, Magnie told our passengers, and fire accurately at six miles. A step on each side of the workings showed where the men had stood, eyes narrowed against the bright light coming through the lookout slit. Below the platform were grassed-over foundations where their accommodation hut had been. I had a vague notion the actual hut had been transferred to Aith to become part of the old school buildings.

Our guests scattered out around them. Stevie climbed up on top of one of the gun mountings and stood there, turning slowly round, jokes temporarily and mercifully stopped, face alight with interest. Amitola and Moon clambered onto the barrel and balanced on it; Kirsten watched them from a distance, then shrugged and complied as they called her over to take photos. If you hadn't been photographed doing it, you hadn't been there. She leaned against the gun below them while I took several photos of all four of them with her camera. Amitola and Moon gathered round her to look at my efforts, laughing. When Stevie wandered over too, all ready with another joke, I headed swiftly to the look-out post by the third gun.

It was a basic concrete turret, with a wide slit at head-height, and no protection against the elements. Just past it were dark lines in the grass where the soldiers had cast their peats. I scanned the pale blue water, the near red cliffs of Muckle Roe and the far-off grey of Eshaness through the slit, then came out and walked over to the third gun.

It couldn't have been a fun posting, I reflected, sitting down on the soft turf with my back wedged against the parapet, and the sea spread dazzling below me, out here for weeks, in all weathers; but then, the alternative was the trenches. By comparison this was a cushy number. That led me on to wondering how they'd felt when they'd gone home. They'd have heard about the scale of the slaughter, of course they would have, in newspapers and letters from their mothers, sisters, sweethearts. I wondered if they'd really believed it until that last boat had come to take them off, kitbags over their shoulders, and they'd returned to their villages to find most of their contemporaries gone and those that were left walking like old men on staffs, maimed almost beyond recognition, or crippled by gas. Had they felt guiltily grateful for the windswept island that they'd cursed as a hellhole for those four years?

I was about to stand up when there were voices behind me, softly confidential, as if the speakers had come over here to be alone.

'Have you thought any more about what I was telling you about?' It was Moon's voice. There was something childish about the way she spoke; her voice was high in pitch, and level in tone.

They were standing on the gun parapet right above me. If they'd looked down they'd have seen me. I was just easing my legs forward to stand up when one calf locked into cramp. I gritted my teeth and leaned back, stretching the muscle out.

Above my head, Kirsten replied, her voice soft but sharp with exasperation. 'You're going to ruin this weekend if you start going on about it.'

'Now you're pretending you've forgotten again!'

Kirsten's voice hardened. 'There's nothing to forget. I'm older than you, remember.' She paused, as if she was looking round to make sure nobody was listening. Her voice went from anger to coaxing. 'Uncle Stevie was a cool uncle. Remember all the funs we had with him. Going swimming from the Sands o' Sound, and having water fights, and that time we went camping and made a real fire.'

'You didn't like the camping,' Moon said. 'You said there were creepie crawlies.'

'But you liked it.' She sounded like she was trying to reason with a four-year-old. 'You loved it. And remember the time he brought you that talking doll for your birthday.'

23

'But maybe he was grooming us.'

'Oh, for goodness sake!' Kirsten abandoned persuasion and went into big sister mode. 'Moon, will you just get it into your head that just because some half-baked therapy has you "remembering" God knows what doesn't mean it actually happened. Induced memories, they call it. Their questions suggest what they want to hear, and your hypnotised state makes you want to be helpful, so you give them what they want. Haven't you heard about people being persuaded they've been abducted by aliens, or reincarnated from being an Egyptian princess, or nonsense like that? Uncle Stevie never groomed us, or did anything he shouldn't have.'

'He babysat us.' Moon's voice was stubborn.

'Of course he did. He was our uncle, helping Mum out.'

'And he took videos of us.'

'Look, what I'm saying . . .' Kirsten's breathing was ragged above me. The cramp had gone, but there was no way I could come out now. I hoped she wouldn't look down. 'Listen, Moon, you've just taken a notion in your head. You've been listening to all these child abuse revelations, and they're getting you confused. Of course I remember him taking videos of us.' Her voice rose, then was clamped down. 'Video was exciting back then. It wasn't like now when everyone's making films on their phone all the time. We did a dance routine to Kylie Minogue and he filmed us, and then we watched ourselves. I remember that. I'd have been maybe eight, so you'd have been six. I even remember us showing the video to Mam when she came home, and us all laughing.'

'You make it sound like it only happened once.'

'That's the time I remember.'

'But you've blotted out the other times.'

Kirsten snapped, 'I haven't blotted out anything. There was nothing else. *Nothing*.'

There was a long pause. I waited, hoping they'd move away,

24

but there was no sound of footsteps on stone above me. At last Moon said, 'There was another girl. A neighbour . . . no, her father was your teacher, and his wife didn't go out much, but when she did you used to babysit for her. Don't you remember?'

Kirsten's voice was wary. 'I remember babysitting from time to time. I was glad of the money.'

'And one time I came along too, because you'd already fixed up the babysitting, then Mam had to go out, and Uncle Stevie came and visited. He rang the doorbell while we were all watching telly, and said he'd come along to make sure we were okay. The girl was in P1, with blond curls, she was really sweet. There was a peerie brother too, but he was in bed, asleep. Her name was . . . was . . . it began with a S . . .'

'I don't remember anyone.'

'According to you, it's all my imagination.' Moon's voice sounded like she was pouting. 'Maybe this girl will remember better. S . . . no, G . . . Gina . . . Ginny . . . Jane . . . Jenny – Jen, that was it.' Her voice was triumphant. 'Jen. We danced with no clothes on. He shouldn't have got us doing that.'

'We didn't dance naked!'

'We *did*. When we were peerie, after we'd had a bath. We came down wrapped in our towels to have a cup of cocoa before bed. And this time, with that peerie lass, Jen, you wouldn't do it, but she and I did. Do you really not remember?'

'It didn't happen.'

'He encouraged us to dance like that, and he videoed us.'

Kirsten gave an angry laugh. 'You're just making this up.'

'You know I'm not.' Moon paused then added defiantly. 'I went to visit a lawyer, to tell him all about it. It wasn't right.'

'You did what? Oh, Moon, that was silly.'

'I didn't actually make a statement though. I told the secretary what it was about, and then I wasn't sure if it really was something I remembered, when you were so sure it wasn't, and I said I'd save it for another day, and went out again.'

Kirsten gave a long sigh of relief. 'Good. Now, listen to me, Moon.' Her voice coaxed. 'How about you forget about it all for this weekend, huh? We'll talk about it, really talk about it, once we get home. We'll have an evening together, you and I, and talk about it. For now, though, how about remembering all the fun we had with Uncle Stevie when we were wee. Listen to his jokes. If he'd done something bad to us, he wouldn't joke with us all the time, would he?'

Moon thought about that. 'S'pose not,' she agreed.

'He wouldn't.' Kirsten's voice was firm. 'And like Mum said, it's his birthday. You don't want to spoil that for him. Remember the jellyfish fight?'

Moon began laughing. A voice from behind made us all jump. It was Stevie. 'Having fun, girls? If it's a good joke, I want to hear it, or I'll have to tell you one of mine.' I heard his steps coming towards me. 'Isn't Cass about here somewhere? I thought she came this way. No? Come and pose again at the gun for me.'

I waited until I was sure they'd gone before I moved cautiously in the other direction and eased myself upright behind this gun turret, so that they wouldn't see me if they looked back. I didn't feel ready to go out and be sociable yet. I leaned my back against the gun and looked out over the Røna, thinking.

There was something not right about Moon. Too easily persuaded. I remembered that air she had of living in her own head. No doubt the *Sørlandet* teachers would have a term for it; I'd been astonished, these last weeks, how laziness or stupidity or just plain awkwardness could all be diagnosed as something on a spectrum. 'A lack o' mother wit,' Magnie would call it; not necessarily a lack of intelligence, but a lack of the ability to read people and situations. A fool who jumped on a bandwagon and rushed blindly in where angels feared to tread.

It was funny she'd come on this trip – no, maybe not. She seemed able to hold two things in her head at once, her jokey

Uncle Stevie and the dodgy man she said had filmed them naked as children; not as two facets of the same personality, as an adult would, but swinging from one to the other, not sure which was the 'real' Stevie. Her mother had reminded her of the fun uncle whose birthday she mustn't spoil, but being with Kirsten seemed to remind her of his more sinister side – if he had one. Moon herself didn't seem to be sure of it, and Kirsten said it was all therapy-induced nonsense. I'd have sided with Kirsten if there hadn't been something defensive in her denials, but I thought that if she kept saying nothing happened, Moon would probably believe her – unless, of course, some malign providence made her run into the other possible check on her memory, the Jen she'd mentioned.

Jen. It wasn't a common name here. She'd be easy enough to trace, if you knew her school year. *You used to babysit her.* Kirsten had been, say, mid-teens and Jen had been P1. Seven or eight years younger, in her early forties. There'd be school year books, or even a visit to Dennis Coutts in the street would do it. He'd have done the Bell's Brae and Sound Primary School year photos back then. It would be easy enough to make up some excuse to get a print, and then ask around. Or back issues of *The Shetland Times*, in the Archives. We'd still done prize-givings when I was at school, ten years later, and they were listed in the paper, all our names with the commendations we'd achieved in various subjects. Jen's name would be there.

It could all get very unpleasant. I just hoped we'd get the weekend over before a row blew up.

Chapter Three

We set off just after eleven and headed for the back of Papa Stour. It was a bonny day to be out, more summer than autumn, with the blue sky fretted with high cirrus, and the hills smooth green. Only the colour of the water betrayed the season, a cold steely-blue. The wake gurgled under *Swan*'s forefoot and shushed along her sides.

I brought up a tray of tea mugs and the biscuit tin as we chugged gently across the six miles of long Atlantic rollers towards the northern side of Papa. Our passengers were all up on deck, clustered comfortably around the main hatch. Stevie and Kirsten were leaning back against the grey rubber dinghy, legs stretched out on the warmed deck, and Moon and Amitola sat upright on the step beside them, admiring the view and trying to work out where the West Burrafirth opening was. You'd never have thought, from Kirsten and Moon's faces, that they'd just quarrelled over whether their uncle had taken dodgy videos of them as children.

Then I glanced aft and caught the expression on Stevie's face, as he looked forward at Moon. He looked very far from being a loving uncle. Then, like the wind changing, the hard face was gone, and he was leaning towards Kirsten. 'Here's one for you, Kirsten: Did you hear about the mathematician who had a phobia about negative numbers? He'd stop at nothing to avoid them.'

'Ouch!' Kirsten protested. 'Stevie, you missed your vocation. You should have been writing jokes for Christmas crackers.'

Amitola laughed. 'How do you think he can afford his bike?'

'Okay,' Stevie said. 'Moon, here's one for you: why do we tell actors to "break a leg"?'

Moon looked puzzled, and shrugged.

'Because every play has a cast!'

She thought about it for a moment, then her face lit up and she laughed. I took myself out of earshot below.

I was just heading to the wheel with tea when there was a throb of engines behind us. I looked over Magnie's shoulder, and saw the orange superstructure of the lifeboat between two plumes of foam.

'She's going back to the Ve Skerries,' Magnie said. 'A watching brief on the trawler as the tide comes in, and a try at getting her off with the Coastguard tug. It was on the wireless while you were below.'

Moon lifted her phone as *Charles Lidbury* passed by us and headed at speed towards the Ve Skerries. I wasn't sure if we'd be able to see them at work on the trawler from the back of Papa, not from on board anyway. I started working it out. For someone standing at sea level, the horizon was 2.9 miles, and the Ve Skerries were three miles north west of Papa. The Papa men had seen the men of the *Ben Doran* through spyglasses, but that had been from the cliffs on Papa. The *Swan* would give us at best an extra metre of height. Horizon distance equalled the square root of 1.144 x your height above the water in feet. It took me a moment to do the arithmetic, but I reckoned somewhere around 3.5 miles. Yes, we might be able to see what was going on.

I'd just finished washing up the tea things and was back on deck when we reached Papa: earth-brown cliffs, fissured vertically, with long lines of white where generations of sea-birds had nested. This side of the island was riddled with natural arches continually being made and destroyed by the sea, islet to arch, arch to stack, then the stack itself destroyed in a winter gale.

'Is that the Ve Skerries?' Stevie asked, at my shoulder.

He was pointing to a smudge on the horizon, low, grey shapes like cloud on the surface of the water, and the upright of the Ormal light, glinting white as the sun caught it. I nodded, and reached for the spyglasses. 'You should be able to see what's going on with these.'

He snatched them from me and raised them to his eyes, fiddling with the wheel in the centre to get the best possible focus. As we came closer I could see the orange of the lifeboat at the southern end of the skerries, and the white control tower and navy hull of the Coastguard tug. There was a reef above water beside her, and I could just make out the trawler's white superstructure jutting above it. I glanced at the chart. It looked like she'd gone ashore on the southernmost skerry, Da Clubb. She might be intact now, sitting on the rocks in this calm, but unless she could be floated off soon she'd be battered into pieces by the next Atlantic gale.

Stevie's knuckles were white on the glasses. If she couldn't be salvaged, she'd be an expensive loss for his firm. He watched until we came around Fogla Skerry, and the Ve Skerries were out of sight, and then handed the glasses back to me without a word said.

We anchored in the bay behind Lyra Skerry, wallowing gently in the swell. It was a bonny lunch spot. A rectangular stack jutted out of the water; beside it, on a skerry white with guano, shags sat upright like penguins on an iceberg. Foula lay to the south-west, twenty miles away, its three steps sharp against the sky, close enough now to see the contours within the outline, a cliff curving inwards from the right, and another, mistier, in the centre. Above it, the striped clouds glimmered pearl-grey.

We served up filled rolls for lunch, and Magnie did a bit of yarning while we ate. 'Right here where we are now, folk, was the scene of the Aith lifeboat's most dramatic and dangerous rescue, back in 1967 – the *Juniper*, who went aground just below that cliff there. It's gone now, but there was a stack jutting up in front o' the cliff, the Snolda, that means a spindle, and the *Juniper* had steamed right up between the stack and the cliff. There were twelve men aboard. It was a cold February dawn when the lifeboat was called out. John Robert Nicolson, he was the coxswain of her then, and he brought her around Papa and around the outside of Fogla Skerry there. The Coastguard chopper was in attendance, but the *Juniper* was too close to the cliffs for it to get the men off, so it was up to the lifeboat. Well, the tide was ebbing away, so that the trawler was sitting on the bottom, and there was barely enough water for the lifeboat to get in. The engineer, he was below, and he told me later that the depth sounder registered just the same as if she was on the slip in Aith. Well, the *John and Frances* – that was the lifeboat, the *John and Frances Macfarlane*, after the folk who owned Macfarlane's Biscuits, they used to visit regularly – the *John and Frances* crawled into the passage. There was a big swell, so she was lifting up and down, and the trawler was lifting too and being dropped with a clang on the rocks, and all the men were ready on deck, soaked with the spray, waiting. They managed to get two of the lifeboat men aboard, with ropes, and then they just had to wait for the swell to bring the two boats level enough for each man to jump, one or two at a time. The lifeboat crew aboard the *John and Frances* stuffed each one below as they caught him, and when the last man was off they waited for a good big wave and swept out forwards between Lyra Skerry and the wreck. There was a bit of damage to the lifeboat, from bashing against the trawler, but the men were all safe, and the crew were decorated for that rescue. One o' them told me that coming home he could hardly believe what they'd just done. The sun was coming up, and the wind was behind them, and it was so peaceful away from the noise of the trawler on the rocks. It had all been done so quickly: they'd gone out, they'd got the men, and now they were bringing them safe home.'

Our guests made appreciative noises. 'I mind the *John and Frances Macfarlane*,' Stevie said. 'She lay off, there was no pier then. And then the next boat, she was the *Snolda*, after that rescue.'

Magnie nodded. 'A Barnet, she was, the *John and Frances*, a good seaboat, but she could be capsized. It was anxious waiting on bad nights when the lifeboat was out. You'd look down the voe to Aith and see the lights still on in all the houses until she came home again. The *Snolda*, she was an Arun, and the first of the self-righting classes. This one, she's a Severn class and that bristling with gadgets that John Robert, the old coxwain, would hardly recognise her as a lifeboat.'

'We went to see her being christened!' Moon said, her face lighting up. 'The *Snolda*. Prince Charles and Lady Diana came up for it.'

Kirsten nodded. 'I remember that too.' She shot her a sideways glance, as if she was going to add something, then closed her lips. Sisterly squabbling over memories was for when they were in private.

Magnie saw the glance too and came in smoothly over it. 'Now, folk, if you're all finished, Geordie'll take you to explore the caves.'

We left Magnie to clear away and squeezed everyone else into the inflatable, sitting around the edge on the grey rubber tube. This was a new one for me too. I'd never seen inside the Papa caves, though I'd spotted the dark mouths often enough from out at sea. We went through the arch in Lyra Skerry first, below chunked black boulders with bird guano like dripped

32

paint. The rock tunnel surrounding us was the green of mermaid's hair. We came out into the light again and ducked into another cave mouth, leading into blackness this time. I slid my thumb onto the torch switch. From ahead of us there was a low moaning sound, echoing eerily in the darkness, then a splash, and the boat rocked slightly as if something had passed it. One of the women squealed.

'Shine your light forrard, Cass,' Geordie said, 'and we'll see who's oobing.'

The circle of brightness lit up a sandy beach at the end of the cave, with several indignant seals turning their snouts towards us. A second one splashed into the dark water.

'Look at those eyes!' Amitola said. 'You can see why people thought they were half human.'

Geordie backed the boat out again, into the light, and putted landwards, towards a rose-red beach with a great rectangular boulder like an abandoned wardrobe. There was a lifebuoy and an orange buoy washed up beside it, just above the tideline; I wondered if they'd come from the *Dorabella*. He cut the motor to ticking over, and we drifted into another dark mouth. This cave was perhaps twenty metres long, with the rocks inside coloured a soft rose pink, as bright as if it was newly painted.

'Gorgeous!' Amitola said. 'Look at that colour.'

'And how clear the water is,' Kirsten said.

We all looked down. A metre below the boat was a floor of green-furred boulders, magnified by the cold water. Something moved among them, a flick of long, sinuous tail. 'Did you see that?' Kirsten asked. 'Long and skinny.'

'A conger eel,' Stevie said. 'That was a big one, he must've been three metres long. Here's one for you, Kirsten: Why's a conger eel like a councillor?'

'Go on then,' Kirsten said.

'It wriggles its way out of sticky stuations.'

33

Moon looked into the water and shuddered. 'Horrible. Let's get out of here.'

'Now for the big one,' Geordie said, as we reversed out. 'Torches at the ready. Hang on, I'm going to open the throttle.'

He gunned the engine and we roared half a mile along the coast, bouncing on the waves, then turned and stopped dead in front of another gaping mouth. 'The Hol o' Bordie, this is,' Geordie said. 'Hang on, aabody.'

We came in slowly, the swell lifting us up to within a metre of the roof, then sinking us down again. It was like coming into an Aboriginal painting, terracotta and ochre, marked with black curves and spots, the colours so fresh it was hard to believe someone hadn't created it. As we went further, the metre above the water was embossed with cream-coloured barnacles.

Geordie kept the motor ticking gently. The light dimmed, darkened. 'Torches now, folk.' I switched mine on, shining it forwards on the black water, and Amitola did the same for a moment, then turned her torch upwards. The beam lit up gold flecks in the black roof. There were more ooohs from the passengers. I moved my beam to centrally in front of the RIB. The tunnel narrowed, narrowed, until the wall on each side of us was close enough to touch with a stretched arm.

'You're sure there's somewhere to turn?' Stevie asked from behind me. His voice sounded rougher, and I wondered if he was claustrophobic.

'Don't worry,' Geordie said. 'We're no' needing to turn. A bit more darkness and then we'll come out on the other side o' the headland.'

I didn't much like the darkness myself. The two torch beams only emphasised the utter blackness of rock walls and water. I'd never been afraid of depths but these inky waves made me think of what lay beneath them, more sharp-toothed conger eels, and tentacled octopus, and dead things rotting. I swallowed and focused on shining my light ahead. Geordie wouldn't bring us in here if there was any danger.

The tube of the inflatable under me shifted as someone moved. Suddenly a cry broke the silence behind me. There was a scuffling noise, the wind of a flailing arm, and then a scream abruptly cut off by a splash. Geordie cut the motor instantly. Both torch beams swivelled round onto white faces, open mouths, and then, descending, onto Moon, struggling in the water, lifejacket inflated like a great collar around her. She was already ten metres behind us and panicking. I shoved my torch at Amitola, grabbed the boat's paddle and began manoeuvring backwards while Geordie picked up a long pole and held it out towards her.

'Moon,' he said. 'Stay calm now. Just let the lifejacket keep you afloat. We're coming.'

I kept paddling. Five metres – two – now Geordie's pole was within her reach. 'You just take hold of that pole now.'

She was too busy struggling to listen. I backed the boat until we were alongside her, and Geordie and Stevie were able to reach over the side and haul her back aboard. She collapsed in a heap on the fibreglass floor, struggling for breath. Amitola and Kirsten leaned over her, making fussing noises, and helped her to sit up on the floor. I pulled off my jacket and laid it round her shoulders. 'Huddle into this. We'll get you straight back to the boat for a hot shower.'

'Torches forward, folk,' Geordie said. We crawled in the dark for what seemed like an age, with Moon still sniffing, and Amitola making comforting noises, and then suddenly there was a slit of golden light ahead of us and colour in the walls. The sea turned blue below us, and we were out in the fresh air once more. I stowed my torch back in the steering column and turned to Moon. 'Are you okay?'

She didn't look okay. Her face was bone-white, her hair

35

damp against her skull. Her teeth were chattering. She nodded. 'I'm not hurt. It was just the shock of falling in, and the cold.' She shuddered. 'And those eels. Scary.'

'But what on earth were you doing?' Stevie asked. 'How come you fell in?'

Moon bit her lip and shook her head. 'I just felt myself going and before I knew it I was in the water. I s'pose I wasn't holding on properly.'

'A warning to you to think what you're doing,' Kirsten said.

'You were lucky not to get chopped up by the propellor,' Stevie said. Amitola gave a squeak of horror, and Moon shuddered, and hugged the jackets closer to her.

We didn't need that kind of image. 'Well, hold on now, everyone,' I said briskly, 'and let's get back to *Swan*. A hot shower will do you good, Moon. We'll get the kettle on again, and I was planning a cinnamon apple cake to fortify us for going round the rest of Papa.'

Geordie roared us back to the *Swan*, and Moon and I climbed aboard, followed by Stevie and Amitola, still fussing. 'Moon, you get dry straight away. A shower first, to warm you. D'you need any help?'

'*Mam*,' Moon said, in that teenage voice, and shrugged away her mother's hand on her shoulder. She clattered downstairs. Amitola stood for a moment, looking hurt, then visibly gave herself a mental shake and turned to Stevie.

'I brought my swimming gear,' she said. 'My old wetsuit too, if anyone wants to join me exploring the kelp forest.' She called after her daughter, voice husky, as if she was uncertain. 'A swim, Moon?'

Moon paused in the cabin doorway, then shook her head and disappeared downwards.

'She's had one,' Kirsten pointed out.

Amitola looked down into the RIB at her. 'How about you?'

Kirsten shook her head. 'Not me, with eels that size about. What I'd like to do, if Geordie'll take me, is go through that cave again.'

'No bother,' Geordie assured her.

'Can I try and see if I'll fit in your wetsuit, Ami?' Stevie asked. 'These clear waters will be worth seeing. D'you have a spare snorkel too?'

The big bag Amitola had brought on board turned out to be full of gear: two wetsuits, snorkels and several sets of flippers. She and Stevie kitted up while Geordie rigged a ladder for them. Stevie clambered down first; Amitola hesitated beside me. 'I won't go far. Just around the boat. If Moon wants me, just come and call.'

'I'll do that,' I said.

'I'm a bit worried about her just now,' Amitola explained. 'She's – well, she's always been a bit imaginative. Easily influenced. She – ' Suddenly she seemed to remember she was talking to a stranger. 'Well, never mind, but if she wants me, please just shout. Please.'

'I will,' I promised They sped away, flippers waving like a dolphin's tail. Once they were safely clear, Geordie, Magnie and Kirsten roared off cave-wards. I went below and began slicing apples and mixing cake while Moon showered.

I wasn't happy. The boat had been inching along in the dark tunnel, and I couldn't see any reason why even letting go of her hold on the rubber tube would make her fall in. Stevie could easily have overheard her quarrel with Kirsten. *A warning to you to think what you're doing.* If there was any truth in her memories, that would be a motive for stopping her talking about them. There had been a couple of historic abuse cases in Shetland recently, and both men had gone to jail, even though the offences were thirty years earlier, and they were now in their seventies. There was Kirsten too. If she really wanted to keep what happened in her childhood buried, she'd have to stop Moon digging it up. Then there was their mother, Amitola . . . *always been a bit imaginative*. I wondered if that was what had caused the tension I'd sensed between her and Moon, that Moon was accusing her own little brother of abusing them. Kirsten had said Moon's therapy had planted false memories. Perhaps that was what Amitola believed too. *Easily influenced*. Maybe she and Kirsten had hoped that this family weekend would remind Moon of the 'real' Uncle Stevie, the cheery wee brother with the awful jokes who'd been good enough to babysit them for her when they were young.

Of course it wasn't likely Moon would have been killed just falling off the RIB like that. She'd had her lifejacket on, so no matter how she'd panicked she wouldn't have drowned. She'd have had to be very unlucky to have been chopped up as Stevie had gruesomely suggested – or had he been trying to underline the warning? Equally, if somebody had pushed her, I thought, spooning the cake mix over the apple slices and putting the dish in the oven, she wasn't admitting to it. *I just felt myself going and before I knew it I was in the water.*

I tried to think about it. Amitola and I had been up in the bows with the torches. Stevie had been beside me, and Moon past him, with Geordie and Kirsten on the other side. Stevie could have pushed her from beside her, or Kirsten could have leaned across and either pushed or lifted her feet to tip her over. Stevie was closer for force, but at a more awkward angle; Kirsten was further, but pushing in the right direction.

I was uneasy about the whole thing. I was still turning it over in my mind as Moon came out of the shower, one towel as a sarong, another round her hair. 'Moon,' I said impulsively, 'if there's anything you're worried about –'

She gave me a blank look, but I persevered. 'If you want to talk to someone, Magnie's the skipper.'

I'd thought for a moment that there was an arrested expression in her eyes, as if something I'd said had struck home, but she was already shaking her head and turning away from me. 'I'm not worried about anything.' She reached into her bunk for her bag and began pulling out clean clothes with hands that weren't quite steady. 'If you don't mind, I'm getting dressed now.'

I retreated into the galley and left her to it.

Chapter Four

I was getting a dab hand at this, I reflected, as I served up mugs of tea and steaming, cinnamon-fragrant apple cake. I hoped Gavin would be pleased. Our guests certainly were; every last crumb was taken, and fingers licked. Moon's misanter hadn't dampened anyone's spirits; Kirsten had enjoyed her second foray through the Hol o' Bordie, and capped it by going in and out of the spread-down fingers of Fogla Skerry. Stevie and Amitola had had a curious seal accompany them exploring the kelp forests of the sea bottom, and Amitola had brought up a complete scaddiman's heid, a sea urchin, in shades of purple.

Magnie finished his tea and rose. 'Well, folk, I think it's time we weighed that anchor and headed around into Housa Voe for the night's entertainment, that concert in the kirk. I'm sure you'll all a' heard the North Ness Boys already, but they're aye a treat.' He paused and gestured towards the headlands with a hand. 'And we're a bit late in the year, but in the summer all this hill is covered wi' sea pinks, and that was how the Papa men knew they were coming home, by the scent of flowers that guided them to the island. If the boys sing "Da Sang o da Papa Men", an' I hope they will, for they do it most beautifully, then you'll hear that mentioned.'

It was a bonny run round the lower half of Papa. For the first bit we were running alongside rugged red cliffs, with fanged reefs stretching long fingers out into the water, then the cliffs lowered to pebble beaches, the hill moorland greened to pasture. We came past a bay Magnie named as Joanie Queerie's Hol. 'It was this way,' he said, 'the men o' Papa were being pestered by a Press Gang ship – the Shetland men were known to be good seamen, so the Press Gangs were especially active up here, taking men for the Dutch and Napoleonic wars. They set two red lights on the mid-sound baa to wreck the ship, but their trap caught a Dutch brig instead. The first body ashore had been a Johan Wheeri, so this bay's still kent as Joanie Queerie's Hol, and there's a Dutch Loch up there too.'

I kept an eye on Moon. I thought she was quieter, subdued, and I noticed she was keeping well away from the side of the boat. When she and Kirsten sat down against the rubber dinghy, she was quick to insert herself to the inside, wedged securely against the cabin hatch. Stevie came back to join us aft, and Magnie put him on the helm. Amitola remained at the guard rail, looking out at the passing land. You could see she was remembering as her eyes dwelt on the Dutch loch, the headlands: picnics with the children, perhaps, or long walks away from them. When we came to the mouth of Hamna Voe, the scene of several shipwrecks, Amitola drew a long breath. Her face was intent on the houses below the kirk, two traditional cottages in a line just above the beach. 'That's where we lived,' she said. She turned to me and smiled. 'I'm glad I came now. Look, it's hardly changed at all – the line of the hills, and the green parks, and the sweet smell of the air. The things I loved, they're all still here.' She looked out again, and added softly, 'The happy times.'

There were maybe a dozen houses in view now, Papa's main settlement. 'The Manse and the Primary School,' Geordie said, suddenly chatty as he pointed them out. 'That's me Alma Mater, as they say. I was in Lerwick for the first years of my life, then we came home to Papa, where me mam grew up, and after that I was a Papa man. We still hae a house here, that white een apo the hill there, and we come out for weekends and the holidays.' His head was up, his eyes bright, and there was a little smile curving his lips. 'Once we're around this headland you'll see the houses properly. That's the kirk, where we're going this evening, a fifteen-minute walk from the pier. Now, a bit above it, can you see, that square log building wi' no roof, that's the Stofa, and there's a good story goes with that too. Back in 1299, a woman called Ragnhild Simmunsdatter took her landlord to court. Sir Thorvald Thoresson, he was. Her case was that they'd never had to pay rent on their croft, Bragister, she called it, and she said he was taking rent from them and no' passing it on to his masters in Norway. He was governor of Shetland at the time, Sir Thorvald, and the case was heard at Easter at the Alting, you ken, the law court on the promentary at Tingwall loch. It found in his favour.'

'Not a surprise,' Kirsten commented sourly.

'Well, no. And just ahead of us now, the tallest of those brown stacks there, between us and Housa Voe, where we're making for, well, that's Frau Stack, or Maiden Stack,' Geordie said. 'Sir Thorvald, that we were just speaking of, well, his son's daughter fell in love with a man he didn't approve of, the son, that is, he was Thorvald too, but they called him Tirvil, well, he didn't approve o' the young man, so he built a little house on the top of the stack and put his daughter in it while he went off on a voyage to Norway. There were ruins on the top of the stack, but it lost a part o' itself last winter, and the ruins went with it. The archaeologists say they're more likely to be a hermit's dwelling, a nun, maybe, since the story of a woman living there was handed down. Papa Stour is the big island of the priests, after all.'

There was a reef running out across the entrance of Housa Voe, but Papa had a tricolour light in a little white shed on the shore. Magnie motored gently parallel to the entrance while it showed red and turned at last when it shone white. Now the houses of Papa were spread out in front of us, dotted along the rich land that came up from the bay and dreaming peacefully in the golden afternoon sun. Most of them were traditional houses, low, whitewashed cottages after the Norse pattern, with a few taller new-builds among them. The isle's only road began at the pier, followed the shape of the bay southwards, then curved over the headland to Kirk Sand and continued on to the airstrip, hidden from us by the rise of the low hill.

The Foula folk had insisted their ferry needed to be based on Foula. The Papa Stour folk had to be content with one based at West Burrafirth on the Shetland mainland, a forty-minute journey away. You could get in in the morning and out again at teatime on Wednesdays and Saturdays, in either direction, and there was an evening ferry on Fridays and Sundays for school bairns and mainland workers. I supposed that most Papa residents had a boat as well, capable of taking them to the nearest point of mainland at least, the pier at Sandness.

'Tammie's tenant has arrived then,' Geordie said to Magnie. He nodded over to a pair of white cottages above the start of the long pebble beach that made the south half of the bay. 'The low cottage there, with the red phone box in front of it. The last Button A and B in the country,' he added, to me. 'There's smoke from the chimney.'

'What's he doing on Papa? Artist, writer, naturalist?'

'Just a retired body, I think, who wants peace and quiet. I ken nothing about him except that he was coming. A Roberts man coming home from Leeds, and arriving on this morning's ferry. Tammie was that pleased to have got the place let so soon. He wasn't expecting anyone until the summer.'

'I suppose coming for the start of the winter gets the worst over with,' I said.

Geordie's eyes went to the pier. 'We're got a reception committee. Me mam's come to take our lines.'

I glanced ahead, saw the main pier empty, remembered the

teatime ferry, and looked back at the older pier jutting out from the shore. Standing there on the concrete was the best type of crofter wife: little and tough, with a flowered headscarf, pink checked nylon apron on under her navy parka, and a square tweed skirt coming down to meet serviceable rubber boots. She was planted squarely a metre back from the pier edge, one hand held out for the lines. Geordie threw his to her, and she caught it neatly and held it while he sprang ashore after it. Magnie did a text-book demonstration of how to manoeuvre an unwieldy fishing boat in a tight space, ending up with her broadside on to the old pier. I followed Geordie ashore, and in no time we had *Swan* tied up alongside.

'An hour to explore, folk,' Magnie said, 'and back here for 6.30, then we'll set out for the concert. It's at seven, and there are serious eight o'clocks to follow, so we'll no' try to eat afore it.'

I opened up the break in the guard rail to let our passengers ashore, then went forward to where Geordie's mam was standing to make a final adjustment to the mid fenders. One look, and the cheery 'aye aye' died on my lips. Some US president had once said that you had the face you deserved by the time you were sixty. I'd never seen anything so bitter as Geordie's mother's face under the bright flowered headscarf. Resentful lines were scored between her brows and at each side of her thin mouth, as if her life had been a struggle, and she blamed the world for it. Her dark hair was pulled back in a bun, tightening her cheekbones, and narrowing her eyes.

She hadn't noticed me. One thin hand was on Geordie's arm; she was speaking rapidly up at him. I caught only the end of it, my head bent over the lines. 'You need to come at once,' she said. 'You and Kenny. I'm said nothing to Jen. We need to speak about what we're going to do about him.'

My movement backwards caught her eye. She turned away, but the breeze swirled her last words to me. 'He's no biding here. He's got to be made to go.'

II
Cirrus Clouds

Chapter Five

Geordie went off with his mother, and Magnie said nothing was needing done aboard, so I gave the saloon a quick tidy, then went for a tramp to stretch my legs. Our guests were walking along the road. Amitola had tried to stride ahead, as if she wanted to be alone with her memories, but Moon had held her back by sliding her arm through hers. 'Come on, Mam, show us where we were born!' They'd gone off in a group after that.

I cut across seaward of the ferry waiting room and toilet block and headed through the field parallel with the shore. Geordie and his mother had already reached what I presumed was her cottage, a peerie white traditional croft house, built low to withstand Shetland weather, with a porch sticking out in front with the door in the middle, and a window on each side. They were standing at the door, Geordie leaning back a bit, and his mother gesticulating angrily. I raised a hand to them, and strode onwards.

Five hundred metres more, and I'd come level with the house Geordie had pointed out, with the post-office scarlet phone box outlined against the cream wall behind. I'd come across Buttons A and B in old detective stories: you put your money in and pressed button A to speak, or button B to get your money back if nobody answered. Although the chimney was smoking lazily, there were no lights on in the house behind it, so I could probably go and look without disturbing anyone – and besides, if it really had been the last phone box with buttons A and B still working, the owners of the house were likely used to visitors posing for photos.

I tramped up through the long grass towards it, and made as much noise as I could on the last piece of tarmac road in front of it, so that nobody inside felt I was sneaking up on them. It was plain that any historic phone was long gone; the shelf inside was empty, the phone-box door missing, and there were a couple of fencing posts propped up against one corner. Droppings on the floor suggested that sheep had been using it as a handy shelter.

The cottage by the phone had presumably once been the shop/Post Office, and had now been refurbished with a new door and windows and a corrugated roof. A retired body wanting peace and quiet, Geordie had said.

A growl from behind me made me turn. It was a black and white collie, with raised hackles and bared teeth. He followed up the growl with a volley of barks which bounced off the cottage wall. I straightened myself up and looked around for an owner, hoping that a really savage dog wouldn't be allowed to run loose, and wondering if I could take one of the fence posts to fend it off until I got back off its territory.

At first I couldn't see anyone, then I heard a shout from behind me. The dog stopped barking, but kept its gaze on me. I glanced round and saw a man halfway between me and Geordie's mother's house. I thought at first that it was Geordie, and called out a relieved 'Aye aye.' Then, when he came close enough to see, I realised I'd been mistaken; this was a much older man, into his seventies, with his dark hair liberally streaked with grey. He said, 'Here,' roughly to the dog, went past me and opened the cottage door. 'Get in there.'

The dog obeyed, and the man turned to me, voice smoothed to friendliness. 'I hope he didn't give you a fright.' His voice was a mixture of Shetland and south, as if he'd spent a long time away.

'I'm sorry if I was trespassing,' I replied. 'I was curious about the phone box.'

He smiled at that. 'Yea, yea, the button A and button B. Long gone now, but I mind using it when I was younger.' He looked at me more closely. 'Did I see you coming ashore from the *Swan*?'

I nodded. 'Cass Lynch, from Muckle Roe.'

'Paul Roberts.' He had eyes of a blue so dark that it was more like faded navy. His intense stare made me feel uncomfortable. He smiled and turned away to lean against his doorway, giving a long look round at the rose colours of the sunny bay below us, the light glinting on the water. 'I'm come home to settle down after a lock o' years away.'

Geordie had said he was from Leeds, but he made it sound as if he had been bred here. 'Are you a Papa man?'

'Na, but both me bairns are here, and me grandchildren an' all.' He nodded up towards the big white house on the hill above us, three hundred metres away. 'A boy and a lass, just got to the secondary stage. They're on the mainland, of course, for the week, but they come back to Papa at weekends. I'm fairly looking forward to spending more time with them. Biding south, you never really get to ken them. Visits are no' the same as being right on the doorstep.'

He had that straight-at-you look that I associated with someone telling me a lie. I was just trying to think of an answer to that when he gave me that charming smile again. 'Do you have bairns yourself now?'

The question sent a pang through me for the baby I'd lost. I shook my head, and tried for a light tone. 'I'm plenty young yet, and having fun sailing the world.' I glanced down at the *Swan*. 'I'd better get back. I'm mate on this trip.'

'But you're coming up to the concert in the kirk?'

'Oh, yes, we're looking forward to it.'

'I'll see you there, then.' He raised a hand and went into the dark cottage, shoving the dog inwards with one foot as he opened the door. A light sprang up inside. I saw him crossing the kitchen to the sink, and turned away, not wanting to be a window-watcher.

I'd mistaken him for Geordie, and he'd said he had children here, and grandchildren, a boy and a girl just got to secondary age, who came home for weekends, and the house he'd indicated was the white one on the hill that Geordie had pointed out as his. Geordie's father.

I glanced up at Geordie's mother's cottage as I passed, and saw her still on the doorstep, upright and bitter, her head turned towards Paul Roberts's lighted window. Geordie's mother, and Roberts's ex-wife. What had Geordie said on board the *Swan*, that they'd left Lerwick when he was a bairn and come to bide on Papa, where his mother grew up? That presumably was when the marriage had broken up, and not amicably either, if his mother's face was any guide. She'd not let him near her grandbairns – if she could stop him.

I had a notion, though, that she couldn't. I had a feeling there had been some court case, oh, way back, when I was at secondary school. I delved in my memory. Yes. It had been when we'd done talk for English. Talk was a third of your final mark, three solo talks (all of mine had been linked to sailing) and three discussions, with the teacher listening in and grading you for your comments. One topic had been on whether parents should always be given access to their children. It hadn't been an inspired discussion, as I remembered over the distance of fifteen years, and Inga, filled with her history project on women's suffrage, had sidetracked us with a long history of how women had had to fight for access to their own children, and quoted with emphasis a case where two little girls had been assigned to their violent father in spite of their mother's

50

protests, and one had died. The laws that reckoned a father was the obvious guardian had only changed when married women were allowed at last to own their own property, and were able to maintain their children. She'd got brownie points for her research, but been docked for monopolising the discussion, to her vociferous indignation. Grandparents, grandparents, they'd come into it somehow. Suddenly I had a flash of the quiet, fair, boy, Ian? – no, Duncan, that was it. He'd said there'd been a court case saying grandparents should have access too, unless the parents could come up with a cast-iron reason why not. Grandparents were important to a child. I'd thought of Mamy and Papy on their smallholding in France, and Granny Bridget and Da Patrick in a welter of aunts, uncles and cousins in Dublin, and agreed, with the reason that they might not be here in Shetland, but they gave me a glipmse into the different cultures I came from, which raised my mark from 6 ('No contributions') to 3 ('Agreed with others, with reasons').

He's no biding here . . . There was trouble brewing.

The sun slipped down behind Mauns Hill in a glory of amber sky that turned every moor, rock and beach with the slightest hint of pink in it to glowing rose. The ferry came into the big pier, ramming up against the car slip with a clunk, and three cars and a cheerful chattering of folk came off it, laden with bags from the Saturday trip to Lerwick. The walkers were met by more cars; the older vehicles residents saved for Papa while the newer, road-worthy cars waited at the West Burrafirth terminal across on the mainland. Suddenly the road was busy with headlights.

We set out for the kirk as soon as everyone had gathered. Stevie was still overflowing with bonhomie that felt slightly overdone. Amitola was quiet, thoughtful, but I thought there was a softer look, a sense of release in her dark eyes and around her mouth, as if coming back had been less painful than she'd feared. Kirsten was sharing memories of childhood beach-combing with Moon, the pair of them looking friendlier than I'd yet seen them. I fell in beside them. 'Memories of your old home?'

Moon shook her head, then paused, and shrugged. 'It's strange, but though I don't remember it, I do remember too. The beach, running down to the sea, it's like I remembered it in my dreams all these years. Almost like somewhere I've been searching for – somewhere I wanted to return to.'

'I was five when we left,' Kirsten said. 'But you know what I remember most vividly arriving at Granny's? How clean every-thing was there, and it all smelt of flowers, not earth and animals. And the bath!' She laughed at her childhood self. 'It was like magic. Taps that turned, and hot water just came out, and Granny put bubble bath in it. And a bedside light with a switch. I thought I'd arrived in fairyland.'

'What sort of house do you have now?' I asked, curious at the picture she'd conjured up of that little girl enthralled by civilisation.

'All mod cons,' Moon said. 'Don't you, Sky? Beautifully dec-orated in shades of cream, perfectly posed pot plants, not a magazine out of place. And a bath every night if you want one.'

'I've moved up from bubble bath to bath bombs,' Kirsten agreed.

Magnie had brought torches, but it was too bonny a night to use them, with the stars gradually coming out above us, and a gold glow to the east where the moon was rising. There was enough light to see the tarmac road, and we tramped cheerfully up the short hill, past where the three standing stones stood dark and sinister against the sky, and the light glimmered still on the water of West Voe beyond them; past Geordie's house, with only a hall light showing; past another up to our right, behind a hedge of low trees, and then on down to the fork where the kirk was. It blazed with lights, gold rectangles

52

making the twilight black, and Magnie switched on his torch and threw the beam before us as we came through the gate.

'There's no path here, folk, can you see your way? Cass, you go ahead and shine your torch back on the ground.'

I hardly needed to; the open door spilled light outwards in welcome, and Geordie was coming out to guide us in. 'Come in, come in. You've got the choice of stalls or balcony, take your pick.' He spoke cheerily, but there was a troubled frown between his brows, and a grim look about his mouth. I opted for balcony and motioned the others before me upstairs.

'Keep me a seat,' Stevie said to Amitola. 'I'm just spotted someen I want to have a word with.'

He slipped sideways into the dark of the graveyard, where a man was standing. 'Now then, boy! How's it going?' I heard him say, then he slipped his arm through that of the other man, and led him into the dark, talking earnestly, with a couple of glances over his shoulder. I couldn't hear the words, but I thought the name *Dorabella* drifted back to me. Of course everyone on Papa would know all about the stranding, and given that Stevie probably insured their boats, Land Rovers or crofts, they'd know about his connection with her.

The rest of the party had gone in, and I followed them up the narrow steps. There were two rows of pews, with plenty of room for all our party at the front. I slipped in beside Magnie, and looked around.

Papa's was a typical Shetland kirk, a simple white box of a building with lower walls and a higher roof than was usual. Old-fashioned lanterns sent triangular shafts of light down the walls, and pendant bulbs high above our heads lit the vee-lined ceiling. The woodwork glowed with polish, and there were pictures between the windows, including a lovely etching of flying swans.

The gallery we were in was at the west end, facing the altar. The light darkened the rich reds and blues of the stained glass above it, but I could make out a boat, and Christ's outstretched arms. There was writing below it, a list of names. The altar and the organ top were decorated with flowers on red velvet cloth, and there was a pulpit below the stained-glass window, with railed steps on each side. The sanctuary was filled with excited youngsters holding instruments; I looked for two that might be Geordie's Cathy and Andy and found two dark heads of the right age among the fair ones.

I'd looked up my statistics before the trip. Papa had eight full-time residents, and twenty-five weekenders, mostly Papa-bred folk like Geordie who had to live on the mainland for work or for their children's schooling. In Geordie's case, he'd told me as we were getting *Swan* ready to sail, he'd worked as engineer on the Papa ferry along with shifts on a whitefish boat, and they'd managed to stay on Papa full-time until Cathy reached secondary age. Then they'd moved to Bixter, on the west side, so that the children could go to the Aith school. His wife had got a job with a solicitor in Lerwick, but they all came back to Papa on the Friday evening ferry, and away again on the Sunday evening one.

It looked like the whole population had come home for the weekend, and more besides, their mainland friends and relatives joining in the spree, for the pews at ground level were filling up, and more folk had come up to join us on the balcony. Every bed on the island would be in use tonight. Geordie's mother was down at the front, along with a couple of about the same age – her neighbours, maybe, Tammie who'd rented the phone box cottage to Paul Roberts. She'd taken off her head-scarf and pinny. Her dress was the same iron-grey as her hair, and there was no sign of relaxation in her expression as she turned to glare behind her at a middle pew below us, where Paul Roberts was ushering a couple of latecomers in before him, smiling that same intent smile he'd used on me. *He's to be made to go . . .* but how could she make him go if he didn't want

54

to? If he'd decided that what he wanted was to be home with his children and grandchildren around him?

The concert was in aid of the restoration of the church. The leader of the community buy-out came forward, moving awkwardly, one hand on the pew end, the other on her rounded belly; there would be a new baby in Papa in a couple of months. She spoke a bit about its history and the work that was needed before she handed over to the young musicians. I sat back and prepared to enjoy myself. Youngsters in Shetland took their music seriously, with a range of instruments taught in the schools from primary upwards, an annual schools music festival to show off their skills, and music at school prizegivings and fundraisers, village teas and concerts. This lot came forward confidently, and launched straight into 'Amazing Grace': the tune first, on fiddles, guitar, flute and saxophone, then Geordie's Cathy singing in an impressively rich voice, like an American gospel singer. They got the applause they deserved, and invited us to join them in two hymns: 'And don't say you don't ken the words,' Cathy said, 'for we'll no' believe you.' They were the good old Shetland seafaring staples, 'Eternal Father' and 'Will Your Anchor Hold', sung at every lifeboat service and funeral, so we sang out with enthusiasm, Magnie roaring out the bass line beside me.

After that the North Ness Boys came forward: three brothers, with Aubrey, the oldest, taking a good deal of ribbing about his arm in a sling, which meant he couldn't play: 'So the sound might be improved!' his siblings promised us. They did several Gospel numbers, then as Magnie had said they might, let the instruments hang from their straps and launched a capella into 'Da Sang o da Papa Men'. It told how the haaf fishermen rowed some sixty miles out to sea from Papa until three-shelved Foula with its high cliffs had gone down below the horizon, 'rowing Foula doon', before letting out the long lines their wives and children had coiled and baited for them. The song listed all the things they'd take with them, and ended with them coming home, following the Moder Dy, the underswell which always went shorewards, and led by the scent of the island flowers. They sang it beautifully, and to hear it here in Papa's own kirk brought a lump to my throat.

They ended with 'The Loard's my Hird', the Shetland version of the 23rd Psalm. We were still clapping vigorously when the committee lady rose to thank everyone, and invite us all along to the school for eight o'clocks and more music-making. 'Just two hundred yards further along the road,' she assured us, 'and we hae cars for anyone that doesn't feel able for walking.'

It was still a bonny night for walking, with the moon turned from brass to silver, and the stars bright on the other side of the sky in the cloud ribbon of the Milky Way. The church gradually emptied below us, and we balcony folk followed along the dark road and into the school playground, where the light was streaming out of the doorway and windows. A flock of children dodged in the darkness, giggling and calling to each other.

I followed the adults into the main schoolroom. Chairs had been set out in a double circle and along one wall of the room was a table groaning with best Shetland eight o'clocks: black cauldrons of fragrant soup, filled rolls, sandwiches, trays of fancies and an urn of hot water for tea or coffee. The urn was presided over by Geordie's mother while an older lady wielded the soup ladle. The other woman was serving a family group with cheery comments; Geordie's mother was standing upright as if she'd swallowed a marline spike, mouth thinned to a hard line, dark eyes fixed defiantly on the man in front of her.

It was Paul Roberts, entirely at his ease, holding out his cup to her as if it was the most natural thing in the world. 'Tea, please, Betty,' he said, in a casual voice, as if she was the merest acquaintance, and gave her the cup. He picked up another fancy while she was filling it, and added, still in that throw-away voice, but with an undertone of black fury that the words didn't seem to justify. 'I see you're still wearing long sleeves.'

She drew in her breath with a hiss. Her lips parted, then closed again, trap-tight. She handed him the cup with hands that were trembling with suppressed fury. He took it, turned away and walked to a seat in the corner, genial smile back in place.

Betty's hooded eyes followed every move. It might have been thirty years ago, but whatever lay in their shared past, she'd neither forgotten nor forgiven.

Chapter Six

'You're Cass, aren't you?' said a woman's voice from behind me. I turned quickly and saw the committee lady. 'I'm Geordie's sister, Jen.'

Now she said it, I saw a resemblance to Geordie, although she was fair where he was dark; she was the right age to be his sister, and there was a similarity about the features. She turned to make sure the door was secure. 'In case of a stray sheep,' she explained, smiling. There was a muttering noise from the man with her, which included the word *fences*. Even Papa, I took it, had the perennial falling-out about fence maintenance. Jen laughed and took his arm. 'How was your trip round the back of the island?'

Jen. I'm said nothing to Jen, Geordie's mother had said. 'It was great,' I replied. 'Have you seen the caves there?'

'I'm ashamed to say I havena, or no' gone inside them from the sea like that. It's mad, they're the first thing visitors go to see, but here I am, a native, and never gone.'

'It's always the way,' I said. 'If you bide in a place you're the last to go and see the sights.'

'We could have a scoit in them one day in the dinghy, if you'd really like to,' her husband said. 'Only maybe no' right now. Next summer.'

Jen laughed again. 'No, no' right now.' She turned her head to me, and patted her stomach. 'Our baby's due in two months.'

She turned her head back to her husband, voice warm with affection. 'Kenny's fussing over me like a mother hen.'

'You won't fuss over yourself,' he retorted.

They moved from the dim hallway into the main room, and now I saw Jen's face properly. I'd never seen anyone who looked so happy. No, happy was too ephemeral a thing; joy shone from her face, softening her dark eyes, the thin mouth that was the shape of her mother's. She could have posed for a Madonna, one hand below her swollen stomach as if she was cradling the whole world. She was Geordie's older sister, so it had to be a late baby, and there were no other children around her to suggest it was a tail-end Charlie, unless they were old enough to be causing the delighted shrieks which drifted in the open window. She saw my glance at her stomach, and smiled. 'Ridiculous, isn't it? Here I am, after hoping through all those years, and having given up, and suddenly, at forty-two – ' The hand below her stomach curved upwards to caress the baby. Her smile lit the room.

'And shouldn't be doing all this running around,' her husband said firmly. 'Come on now, Jen, come in and sit down. You're been on your feet long enough this day, baking and doing the flowers in the kirk and good kens what else.' He set a chair for her. 'Be at peace now.'

Jen gave me a rueful look, and obeyed.

'You just sit,' Kenny said. 'I'll get you soup and a fancy, and no nonsense about eating sensibly. You can manage a million-aire shortbread for once.'

Jen smiled. 'I likely can, at that. Go you and get yourself something, Cass, it's all good.'

I didn't need urging. I started with mutton soup, thick with chunks of tattie, a cheese roll and a tuna one. It took a bit of deciding between the crisp sugared shortbread, the butterfly cakes and the marshmallow tiffin; I compromised on two of the three, reflecting that if I was going to come to live on land

59

I'd need to watch what I ate. Perhaps conventional housework might use up a few calories, but it wouldn't be as many as mast-climbing did. I was about to go and sit down beside Jen again when I saw Moon had forestalled me.

'Hi,' she said. 'I'm Moon. Did you say your name was Jen?'

There was no sign of recognition on Jen's face. She looked up, smiling. 'Jen Wishart. You're from the *Swan* too, aren't you?'

Moon nodded. 'I'm Stevie's niece. Moon.'

Jen smiled. 'Moon! That's pretty.' Then her eyes narrowed, thinking; there was a sudden flare of awareness in them. 'Oh, *Moon.*' She sat up straighter, animated. 'Moondancer? Did you grow up in Lerwick? I was at Bell's Brae primary school, and you were up among the big ones. You had a big sister in secondary, called Skywalker. I was always envious of your bonny names.'

A look of satisfaction crossed Moon's face, like Cat when he'd finally put his paw over an elusive fly. 'Yes. Sky's here too – ' She indicated with one hand. 'Over there, in the green jumper. She calls herself Kirsten now. Didn't she used to babysit you, when you lived in Lerwick?'

Jen's shoulders tensed. The hand holding the plate jerked, tilting it forward, and Moon leaned quickly to straighten it. Jen brought her other hand up to steady it. 'Sorry, so clumsy of me. Thanks.' She smiled and began chattering, voice slightly high, words tumbling out too fast. 'I don't really remember much about living in Lerwick. It was so long ago, and when we came out to Papa that kind of overlaid those memories.' She gave Moon a sideways glance. 'My mam and dad split up, you know, and it was a difficult time, those last years in Lerwick.' She took her fancy in her hand, set the plate down, and curved her free hand around her belly. The serene joy returned to her face. 'That's all behind us. It doesn't matter now.' She glanced down at her belly, and smiled. 'All gone.' Then her face hardened. She gave Moon a determined look, lips tight, and for a moment I saw her mother in her. 'Not to be remembered.'

I flicked a glance over at Paul Roberts, chatting to one of the visitors, and hoped with all my heart that he wasn't going to destroy her happiness by bringing those past years back.

Someone else was watching him too, an old man with a fringe of white hair sticking out from a dark skull-cap, and circular black-framed glasses. Maybe it was the skull-cap that made him look foreign, or the round head. He was sitting at the side of the room, slightly apart from a family party, and looking at Roberts with eyes narrowed, as if he was trying to remember where he'd seen him before.

I flicked my eyes round to check our passengers were enjoying themselves. Stevie was chatting away to the older man I'd taken to be Tammie, and Kirsten was speaking to a woman of her own age who looked as if she might be a colleague. Amitola was laughing with the musicians, but even as I glanced over she shot a quick look at Roberts. She'd know him, of course, if Kirsten had babysat his children. It wasn't a friendly look: dislike, tinged with surprise, maybe, at finding him here.

'Hi,' a voice said in my ear. 'You're Cass, aren't you?'

I turned. A woman in her late thirties was smiling at me. She looked like an office worker, with short, streaked-blond hair in a neat bob, a slick of lip-gloss and blue eyes outlined by mascara. She had a smart black top, and a silver necklace like a Bronze Age torque curved round her neck. She wasn't pretty, exactly, with a bony nose and eyes that slanted slightly downwards, but her smile outshone them, and she'd packaged herself to look smart. 'Isla,' she said. 'Geordie's wife. He's been telling me all about you. Nice to meet you.'

That placed her. She'd recently got a job as a secretary in a law firm in Lerwick, Geordie had said, which explained the slicker presentation than was usual out here in the country.

61

She'd make a welcoming receptionist, with her warm smile, and her low voice would sound good on the phone.

'It's great to be aboard with Geordie in his home waters,' I said. 'He's been telling us all the isle's stories. Are you from Papa too?'

She nodded. 'Born and bred – I was Geordie's childhood sweetheart.' She laughed. 'Well, maybe he didn't have a lot of choice when they came here. There was only him, me, Jen and my wee brother in the school, but I made sure he stuck to me once he hit the wide horizons of the Anderson High School.'

'I don't suppose it was difficult,' I said. 'He looks like one who doesn't go for change.'

She shook her head. 'He'd had change enough, in his early life.' Her eyes flicked to Roberts, hardened, then returned to me. She gave a forced laugh and spoke jokily. 'If he'd not been forced to go to secondary school I think he'd never have left Papa again.' She brushed that away with a gesture. 'I've managed to persuade him onto the mainland, for the bairns' sake. They're loving being at the big school in Aith.'

'Your daughter's got a wonderful voice, really mature for someone so young.'

'Yes, she's taking singing lessons in Lerwick now, and her teacher thinks she has real potential. She organises the band too.' She made a deprecating gesture. 'But I'm just her proud mother.'

'Plenty to be proud of,' I said. 'And you're enjoying your work – for a lawyer, isn't it?'

She nodded, eyes lighting up. 'I'm loving it. Oh, it's not that I didn't enjoy being at home with the bairns, and running the croft, but – ' She paused, catching air with one hand. 'Suddenly I feel grown up, you know? I get up and out and go to work, and it's serious and challenging and important. Geordie doesn't quite get that. He thinks I'm doing it for the extra money, and right enough we couldn't have two houses without it, but really I'm doing it for me.' She laughed. 'My own pay packet, instead of this stupid feeling I have to justify buying things that are just for me with Geordie's money.'

'I'm moving in with my partner,' I confessed, 'and he's a policeman on the kind of salary I've never even dreamt of. I'm going to find that hard too, especially if we have children, and I have to give up work completely.' I'd been financially independent since I'd been sixteen, hand-to-mouth, but always scraping by. I wasn't sure how I was going to like being well-off on money I hadn't earned myself. I changed the subject quickly. 'What sort of things do you do in your law firm?'

'Oh, all sorts: receptionist, and typing up letters and statements of people when Tony's preparing a case – that's all confidential, of course, but it's fascinating. Horrid sometimes.' She wrinkled her nose. 'What people get up to. You hear one side of the story, and then when you read about the case in the *Shetland Times* sometimes you'd never think it was the same one, and I'm hard-pushed to keep my mouth shut.'

Behind me, Moon rose, scraping her chair. Isla's eyes flicked in that direction, and froze. Her glossy mouth opened and then closed again, and she turned her eyes back to me, talking rather too quickly. 'Lovely you all managed to get here for the music evening. I hope you enjoyed it, and there's a treat still to come, the Papa Sword Dance. See you later.' She raised a hand and moved quickly away, leaving me thinking. *Statements.* Moon had said she'd gone to a lawyer to make a statement, then changed her mind, and Isla was in a lawyer's office taking statements. It was obvious she'd recognised her.

It didn't touch her at the moment; it was work. But if Moon persisted, if she dragged Jen into her suit, how would Isla feel then?

Suddenly there was a stir and bustle at the door, a boy's voice calling 'Oyez, oyez, oyez, hear ye, gentles all!' and Geordie's Andy came in. There was a chorus of oohs and a bustle of excitement. He was dressed in a white shirt and black breeks, with a blue sash diagonally across his breast, and he brandished an aluminium broadsword. He gave us a moment to quieten down, then continued declaiming:

'Come forth into the pleasant night,
Where all the welkin's starry bright,
And there it will our pleasure be,
To show our martial dance to thee.'

I'd heard of the Papa Stour Sword Dance, but never seen it performed, even though there were a couple of boys at the Brae school when I was there who were Papa-bred and took part in it. We all squeezed out into the school playground, where an outside light shone down on a row of seven men, each with a different colour of sash, and with a pair of fiddlers beside them. Each man stepped forward in turn to introduce himself in poetry as archaic as Andy's had been, and the names took the dance back to before the Reformation: St James of Spain, played by the older man I'd guessed to be Tammie, St Denis of France, St Andrew, played by Andy, St David, St Patrick, St George, played by Geordie, and St Anthony of Italy. Between each introduction there was a short solo jig by the speaker, holding his sword level above his head, and then they all danced together, setting in and out, clashing their swords so that the blades flashed under the light and finally weaving them into a seven-pointed star, which they held triumphantly aloft. It was skilful and thrilling, the swishing and clang of the blades in the night, the swirling of the white-shirted dancers, and they got a hearty round of applause at the end.

I'd been almost first out, so I was last back in, or almost last. Paul Roberts was behind me. He hesitated for a moment on the threshold, then I heard his feet scrape as he turned. I looked behind me, surprised, and saw him striding off into the darkness.

Chapter Seven

Something had woken me; some movement on board or in the water around the boat. A guest who couldn't sleep, maybe, going up on deck to look at the stars. I lay for a moment, listening. There was a creak, a slight suggestion of the boat quivering, then nothing. Silence, apart from Magnie's snores. All the same, I was sure there had been something.

The cabin was hot, and smelled of diesel. I lay for five minutes, listening, then got up, hauled my clothes over my thermals, and went up on deck.

The Papa folk were taking full advantage of having houses filled with friends and family. The squares of windows glowed gold in the darkness all round: a light on in the little cottage on the other side of the pier; another up at Geordie's house, another in the house with trees beyond it. The nearest house, Betty's, was in darkness, but there was a light in the one beyond it, Paul Roberts's house, making a rectangular patch of light on the grass. Now what was he awake for? He hadn't been involved in the party atmosphere.

My musings were interrupted by a flash on the road. Someone was walking by torchlight; going home from a party, maybe. I couldn't see whether it was one person or more, just the moving circle of brightness that dimmed everything around it. It had just reached the corner of the road where the track led down to Paul Roberts's cottage. The pinprick star flashed left and disappeared behind the line of long sheds that led up from Roberts's house roadwards.

I sat down on a coil of rope and waited. In a few minutes the torch light reappeared at the cottage, shining a circle of light on its white wall, and was as quickly dimmed. The cottage door opened, the light inside snicked off, and the dancing light began making its way back up the road. It disappeared behind the sheds again, then reappeared, moved upwards for the last bit of the turn-off track, a pin of light dancing in the darkness, then turned left and right again. They were going away from me, onto the narrow neck of land between the road and the West Voe, the sea inlet on the north side of the island.

Now what was Paul Roberts doing heading into the hills at this time of night? I watched the dancing torch, realised I was wide awake now, and let my curiosity get the better of me. I swarmed quickly down the cabin stair to change my seaboots for trainers, swung myself off the boat and set off up the moonlit road as quickly as I dared. If they looked back they'd be too blinded by their torch to see me, a dark shadow in the moonlight. I could move quickly along the road, with the tarmac firm under my feet. When the torch disappeared over the slight rise between the jetty and the nearest point to West Voe I broke into a soft-footed jog to lessen the distance between us.

At the top of the rise I stopped abruptly, heart thudding. There were three tall, dark figures on the horizon, standing like sentinels. For a moment I thought the middle one had turned its head and was moving towards me, and then I remembered the three standing stones, right on the top of the rise. My heartbeat slowed back to normal. Of course that was what they were, black and sinister as they looked, like shrouded watchers in the moonlight. I set off across the hill towards the furthest one, moving carefully across the rocky turf, and realised now that I should have left a note for Magnie. It would be a long way to crawl back if I broke an ankle.

Suddenly I thought I heard a noise behind me. I stopped and listened, and felt that prickling down my back-neck as if I was being watched, but however I strained my eyes I couldn't see any movement behind me. I shrugged and went on.

The light had almost reached the shore. Now they were shielded from the houses they were less cautious. A second torch blinked on, a proper searchlight this time that swept across the shifting water, bleached the pebbles of the shore and cast dark shadows from the rocks, then swung around towards the smaller light picking its way to the shore. The two walkers stood out briefly as silhouettes in its light, then the searchlight was turned downwards. It was in a small RIB, an inflatable with a fibreglass bottom like our Brae rescue boats, maybe five metres long, the sort of thing a decent-sized fishing boat might use as a tender. There was one person in the boat, looking up impatiently towards the walkers feeling their way towards him.

All this messing about with torches would ruin their night sight. I came down the hill parallel to them but more to the east, crouching low to keep below the skyline, and got to where the land rose to a curved headland, then dropped down on the ground. Even after a dry summer it was still damp; I raised my front up on my elbows, and felt the ground water soak cold through my jeans and jumper. I wriggled forward to the edge of the hill until I dared go no further.

Below me, the men were getting into the boat. The searchlight showed me silhouettes: one medium-height, solid-built man holding the boat, a medium-height, medium-build one and Paul Roberts, tall with broad shoulders. They were all dressed for a night excursion, with the neon strips on waterproof jackets and trousers lighting up, woollen hats blurring the hair. The torches flickered then switched off as they clambered aboard and settled themselves on the grey rubber tubes. I heard the engine start. The boat's steaming light switched on,

67

a bright white light on the boat's metal frame which was no doubt visible at the two miles specified by the Col. Regs. The blaze of it stopped me seeing any more details of the men.

They had a straight run out of the voe, but after that they'd disappear behind the headland on either side. I stood up, feeling a cold breeze I hadn't noticed chilling the wet part of my jeans, and looked around. The land rose on each side of me, but it was a good deal further to the cliffs of the west, and I had the impression it would be rougher going. There was a rise to the north east here, the North Ness. The moon outlined a stone cairn at its highest point. I tried to visualise the map. The Ve Skerries were well clear of Papa to the north, and the north coast of Papa ran east-west, with only a slight slant westwards at the western corner. I thought I should be able to see all this side of Papa and clear to the Skerries from this hill.

The going wasn't as bad as I'd feared once I struck inland. The heather had been grazed right down and razed by the north winds, so that I was walking on short stems and flattened peat, with the occasional scatter of stony ground or squelchy bits. Below me, the boat putted steadily out of the bay. I'd almost reached the cairn when the engine note rose to a roar. I looked around and saw the white light speeding up and turning left to head in a north-westerly direction. Beyond it, as I watched, came two white flashes on the horizon: the Ormal light. The boat below altered its heading slightly, so that it was going straight towards the Skerries.

I kept walking upwards. My eyes were well accustomed to the dark now, and I could stride out on this level going, so it was only another ten minutes before I got to the cairn at the top of the rise. I stood on the leeward side of it, arms on the top to lean my chin on, and was able to really look round. Out to sea, where the Ormal light blinked its double flash every twenty seconds, something was going on.

Dorabella was lit up, her steaming light plainly visible and, smudged below, her deck and cabin lights. Beyond her there was another vessel, larger, over fifty metres, for two mast lights shone into the darkness, one higher than the other. If I listened with all my ears I thought I could just distinguish the rumble of machinery faint on the wind.

I thought about tides. It felt like it might be around midnight. Within an hour it would be high water again. With the moon waning gibbous towards the neap-bringing crescent, every tide would be slightly lower than the one before, meaning the chances of getting her floated off diminished. It was perfectly reasonable that they would try again now, even in the darkness, instead of waiting another day.

But then why the secrecy? Why had the men come out at night by torchlight, crossing the island? The answer to that, I supposed, was that West Voe was much handier for a small boat from the Ve Skerries to pick them up at, rather than the boat coming right round the east of the island to the pier.

My soaked knees were cold, and my bed was calling me. I was just about to turn away from the cairn when a hand on my shoulder spun me around, and a blazing torch shone full in my face.

I jerked my shoulder free. 'Hey!' I protested.

The torch fell. 'Oh, it's you.'

It was a male voice, Shetland, and sharp with anger. All I could see, with my eyes still dazzled, was a dark shape looming over me. 'Who's that? Get that light out of my eyes.'

The torch moved upwards to show his face, suddenly sinister with up-lit shadows. 'Kenny. Jen's man, you were speaking to us earlier, in the school.' He made an effort and calmed his voice, but I could still feel the anger coming off him like waves pounding at a shore. 'I'm sorry if I gluffed you. I just saw someone standing up here and I thought you were up to no good.'

'You're lucky I didn't have a heart attack on the spot,' I said, still furious myself at the fright he'd given me. 'I coulda been just stargazing, or enjoying the quiet.'

'No harm done, though,' he said.

I shrugged away my annoyance. 'None,' I agreed more civilly. 'What were you doing out here anyway at this time of night?'

'Oh, just checking on the sheep. It aye has to be done, you ken.'

It did, but not at midnight in mid-October. 'You didn't see the lights then?' I persisted. He'd turned his circle of torchlight onto the hill, ten metres ahead of our feet, and was starting to stride briskly after it. I followed. It took a moment before he answered me.

'Lights? No, I saw no lights. Was that what brought you up here?'

'A couple of men with torches,' I said. 'They got into a RIB in West Voe and headed for the Ve Skerries.'

He was silent again, as if I'd been too blunt, revealed too much information. I felt all my suspicions rising. Either he'd followed them too, and then seen me on the height of the hill and decided to investigate, or he'd been the walker who'd gone to fetch Roberts. He'd seen Roberts into the RIB, then come to investigate me. I remembered that feeling I'd had of eyes on my back. Whichever, he was leading the way back to the *Swan* at a good lick, so it seemed he had no sinister intentions. All the same, the way he'd crept up on me wasn't a normal reaction to seeing someone else on a dark hill. You'd usually try to reassure them, not go out of your way to scare the living daylights from them.

He spoke at last, slowly, as if he was thinking it out for himself. 'They'll be trying to float the trawler off again. They might manage it, there's still the same height of water as when she grounded, but it'll be dropping the next couple of days.'

'If they could empty her hold, that would lighten her.'

The circle of light jerked on the ground, as if this was something he hadn't thought of, or didn't want me to think of. 'Aye, likely.'

He'd brought me the quickest way down, and we'd reached the road, closer to the pier than where the two men had struck out over the hill. 'There,' he said. 'You'll see your way now.'

I didn't retort that I'd seen it fine before. 'Thanks.'

He stood there watching while I got back on board, then the light turned away and swung up the slight rise. I stood a moment on deck, looking around at the dark bulk of the Maiden Stack on the glimmering water, the house on the left-hand headland of the bay dark on the skyline, and the sweep of middle of the bay.

My gaze stopped there. Someone was sitting on deck, half-hidden against the column that held the compass. I went half the distance towards them and spoke softly. 'Hello?'

The shadow moved, and turned so that the pier light fell on a pale face. It was Moon. 'Hello yourself. Fine night.'

'It is,' I agreed. I sat down on the step. 'The stars are much clearer here than in Lerwick – is it Lerwick you stay in?'

She shook her head. 'I'm not really permanent on Shetland. Just home for a visit. I'm renting a place in Quarff.'

'D'you live down south then?'

There was a touch of uncertainty in her voice as she answered. 'I don't live anywhere really. I just go wherever sounds interesting and find work there.'

'I used to be like that,' I said. 'Find a ship, and work my passage to where it was going.'

'It sounds an interesting life.'

'It was.' But I was thirty now, and going to settle down.

'Where were you just now?' she asked. 'Partying, or out for a walk?'

I laughed, and avoided an answer. 'I'm not a party girl. What about you?'

71

'I was partying, but now I'm not sleepy. I thought I'd just sit and enjoy the stars. Mam's not back either.'

'She's likely found old friends from her time here on Papa, and she's yarning.'

'Very likely,' Moon agreed. A touch of malice crept into her voice. 'Wasn't that someone with you? What would your policeman say?'

I wasn't even going to begin explaining what had been going on, or try and defend Kenny bringing me back. I turned a deaf ear, and made a show of a yawn and a stretch. 'Well, time to get back to our berths.' I stepped back, and made a gesture towards the cabin, but she didn't move. 'Tomorrow's the big day – off to Foula, the island west of the sun.'

Moon shook her head and stayed put. 'Oh, I'm not sleepy yet, and the stars are so lovely. I'll sit on deck a bit longer. G'night, see you in the morning.'

I couldn't order her to bed. 'Good night,' I said and headed below, yawning in earnest now, sleep flooding over me. I took off my clothes, squirmed into my berth and was out like a light.

Chapter Eight

Sunday 20th October

Tide times Aith
HW 01.20 (1.9m); LW 07.21 (1.0m);
HW 13.39 (1.9m); LW 20.03 (0.9m)

Sunrise 07.55, moonset 15.23; sunset 17.41, moonrise 20.26.

Waning gibbous moon

There had been a frost in the early hours of the morning; the dew of it gleamed cold on the deck. I stood on the mat to get my feet clad, then sat on the step looking out. The water was lighter than the land, a pale grey-blue circle around us. There was a blue rim above the eastern hill, which gradually lightened to milky white, then flushed palest gold, darkening the hills below it to a black silhouette where every rock, every house roof and chimney, every telegraph pole, stood out sharp and clear against it. Now I could see the land reflections in the water. Slowly, much slower than in summer, the textures of the land became visible, the knobbled brown of heather and smooth grass, then the houses sharpened into focus, white against the green parks. The air was chill, with just a breath of wind from the south on my cheek, and the sheep were still huddled down against the cold, a scattering of white ones up around Paul Roberts's house, and one dark one, a tethered ram maybe, lying ten yards below the houses, and halfway between the phone box and Betty's house.

I'd slept soundly until Magnie had woken me at seven. Geordie arrived just as I reached the deck, raised a hand in greeting, and disappeared below to start the engine. He looked tired, red-eyed, face drawn, as if he'd had a sleepless night of worrying about what to do. When I went through to the main cabin to put the kettle on, Stevie's curtains were drawn, and Moon's, but Amitola and Kirsten were up, and by the time I'd got the big teapot on the table, Moon was stirring, and Stevie came out yawning. There were tired lines drawing down the corners of his mouth, but he spoke cheerily. 'Well, folk, are you all set for today's treat, a close-up view o' the cliffs o' Foula?'

'It fairly will be a treat,' Magnie agreed. 'They're something special to see. Have you been out there yet, Cass?'

I shook my head. 'I've only ever gone up north closer to Papa. I'm looking forward to it.' I began pouring out mugs of tea. 'Help yourselves to milk and sugar.'

They were all up now. Amitola was warmly dressed in a thick wool jumper in shades of red and different pattern knobbles, but her face looked pale above it, as if returning to her former home hadn't been so easy after all; as if she'd spent the night fighting demons. Kirsten was trim and neat as ever; I couldn't read her face at all. Moon was bright and breezy, as though the sleepless night had invigorated her, turning her mug round in her hands and smirking into the brown tea. 'A bonny day for it,' she said. Stevie gave her a quick look, as if he mistrusted this good mood, too sunny to last, like a child waking up too bouncy: tears before bedtime.

Once tea was drunk, everyone rose to get on jackets and hats. The first sun had come through at last, picking up the autumn colours on land, the chocolate hills, the rusty sword leaves of iris in the ditches, the tinted flowering currant bushes around the houses. The orange lobster buoys glowed on the water. Over in the park, the white sheep had risen and were grazing, but the dark ram was still lying in his place. There were high cirrus clouds fretting the blue arch above us. *Mackerel skies and mares' tails, Make tall ships carry small sails.* When I filled in the log, I noticed that the pressure had dropped a point.

We motored into the centre of the bay to put the mainsail up. Once we'd got the sail ties off and loosened the heavy folds of tan canvas, we formed three teams. Magnie took Stevie and Amitola on the heavy throat, Geordie had Kirsten and Moon on the peak, and I controlled the topping lift. It was a laborious business even with the capstan to take the weight. *Swan*'s great telegraph pole gaff which held the top of her mainsail up and out to catch the wind had to be hauled right up to the top of her mast. The wishbone-shaped throat went up the mast, and the peak, the other end, was hauled separately at the same time until, after fifteen minutes' worth of moving from one rope to another, hauling our hardest, the tan striped sail was stretched high above our heads. Magnie handed me the helm and headed below to do breakfast. I turned the wheel until *Swan*'s nose was heading seawards. The sail curved, even in that slight breeze, and I heard the water ripple along our sides as we went round past Maiden Stack and Forwick. A gannet cut us, snow-white against the grey water.

Gradually Papa Stour faded to a low hump behind us. Foula lay etched ahead like an island on a stained-glass window, mist blue. Amitola and Moon propped themselves against the dinghy and sat there looking aft at the rolling sea. Kirsten went forrard to sit on the aft end of the bowsprit. Stevie commandeered the other side of the main hatch from Amitola and Moon, back against the hatch cover, legs stuck out in front of him.

We had eighteen miles to go: a three-hour motor, for the mainsail wasn't doing us much good in terms of propulsion, though it would steady our motion once we got near the Shaalds o' Foula, the rougher patch of water over the shallows between the mainland and the island. The *Titanic*'s sister ship, *Oceanic*, had been wrecked on a reef there back in World War I. Hoevdi Grund, the rocks were called, and I'd checked our course took us well away from them.

Magnie gave a shout from the hatch. I handed over to Geordie, and went to help. He'd done the full Sunday fry-up, with bacon, eggs, sausages, mushrooms, tomatoes, fried bread and even slices of best Stornoway black pudding. I began serving it upwards through the hatch in a clatter of plates and juggling of oven trays and frying pans. It was all very nice, I reflected, but it did create a lot of washing-up, especially when you were making for this many people. That didn't stop me doing justice to it once I slid down beside Stevie by the main hatch. Magnie did a mean fry-up.

'Are they going to try and float the *Dorabella* off today?' I asked Stevie once I'd demolished one of my sausages, half my bacon and a slice of black pudding. 'High tide's around half one, isn't it?'

He nodded. 'The plan is to empty the fish from the hold into another vessel this morning. There's a buyer waiting for them. We're hoping that will lighten her enough for the Coastguard tug to get her off.'

'No damage to her?' Magnie asked.

Stevie shook his head. 'No water coming in that they can see. Of course there may be a hole plugged by a rock, but we'll only find that out once she's clear.'

'You weren't tempted to try last night,' I said casually, 'with those extra few inches of tide, and such a fine night?'

He shook his head decisively. 'Not in the dark. No, they're waiting for daylight.'

I was tempted for a moment to mention the lights I'd seen, but decided that there was no need to stir that bilge water.

What an insurance man didn't know, his heart wouldn't grieve over. I remembered his phone call the night the trawler had struck. He'd been talking about *lines*, getting them in, or cutting them. That meant she'd still been fishing when she'd gone on the rocks, even though someone had mentioned a full hold. She'd probably run into a shoal and been unable to resist taking more cod or haddock over her due allowance. It could've been covered up during a normal landing, but if the fish had to be transferred to another boat, that boat would weigh what they'd taken on, and would report any extra over *Dorabella*'s quota. Rather than being a rescue attempt, last night's little excursion could have been taking off the illegal catch. The quotas were strictly controlled, and there were huge fines for landing more than your boat was allowed.

I looked up to find Stevie's brown eyes watching me. I managed a smile. 'Good luck to them. I hope they manage it – a boat's an expensive thing to have to jettison, quite apart from the pollution threat.'

'Ah, well,' he said, 'she's like a serving of good whisky.'

I reminded myself yet again that he was a paying passenger. 'Go on, hit me with it.'

'You can't guess? She's on the rocks.'

We all groaned obligingly. Moon turned to Kirsten, still with that air of triumph. 'I met an old friend of yours last night. A girl you used to babysit for.' She shot a quick glance at Stevie. 'A peerie lass with blond curls. Don't you remember? Jen, she was called.'

Stevie's cheery grin didn't waver, but I felt him tense up.

'I don't remember babysitting,' Kirsten said. Her mouth was stone-hard.

'It wasn't often. Her mam hardly ever went out. Mam let you go a few times, then they asked you again and you'd already said yes, but Mam said it had to be the last time, wasn't that right, Mam?'

Amitola looked startled. 'Babysitting. Goodness, Moon, that must be well over twenty years ago, if not thirty. How do you expect me to remember that?'

'Moon's got a great memory,' Stevie said. His voice was casual. 'She can even remember things that didn't happen. Here, Moon, I've got another actor joke for you. Did you hear about the actor who fell through the floorboards? He was just going through a stage.'

Moon gave him a venomous look. 'It was when we lived in Lerwick,' she insisted. 'I can't remember the family's name, but the father was one of Kirsten's teachers.'

Amitola's eyes flared in recognition. She froze for a moment, then shook her head. 'Far too long ago, Moon. Was this girl at the concert, then?'

'Hardly a girl now,' Moon said. 'She was the woman who introduced it all, the pregnant one. Jen. She remembers you, Kirsten. She remembered our names.'

Kirsten shook her head. 'Too long ago.'

'As the actress said to the bishop,' Stevie said cheerfully.

'I don't remember,' Amitola said. 'Has everyone finished?' She rose without waiting for an answer and began collecting plates. 'No, sit still, Cass, I can do these. They won't take a minute with all the hot water you have.'

'No, no, just pass them down to me. You stay on deck and enjoy the view.'

She shook her head and followed me below to the galley, where we soon got a chain of washing, rinsing and drying going. She was abstracted, eyes far away, mouth moving as if she was arguing with herself. I remembered her look at Roberts last night. Whatever memory was being resurrected, the thoughts troubled her.

We finished the dishes and she gave me a brief, blank smile, then headed up on deck. I was just making a mid-morning pot of tea when the radio crackled and burst into life: someone on

Papa requesting the lifeboat. I went over to listen. It was a woman's voice, familiar, but distorted by the radio.

'We're needing a doctor on Papa. There's a woman in her sixties had some kind of heart attack.' I knew the low timbre and efficient tone now: it was Isla, Geordie's wife. 'Betty Tammason, my mother-in-law.'

The coastguard officer moved her to a working channel, and I followed. It took me a moment to remember how to move the controls, and by the time I joined them Isla was in full flood. '. . . down by the shore, well, not on the shore, just above it, along from the cottage wi' the phone box. She had some kind of attack right there. They got her to her house, and laid her down. She's breathing easier now, but I think a doctor needs to look at her. Her colour's awful and her heart's thudding away.'

'Have you tried NHS 24 for the duty doctor?'

'I thought you'd get through to them quicker,' Isla replied.

'They'll need to talk to you. You get on to them, and we'll get the lifeboat on standby, either to bring the casualty off or to get a doctor to her. It's planning to be out your way anyway, to stand by at another attempt to salvage the trawler, once they've got the hold empty. Let me know how you get on with NHS 24.'

They signed off, and I went back to my tea-making. Betty had had an attack down below Paul Roberts's cottage. I wondered what she'd been doing there when she was so violently against him – and if something had happened to cause the attack.

When I went up on deck there was no sign that any of our passengers had heard the conversation. The sun had edged out from behind the mist, and the water had the shining smoothness of pearly-gray silk, shot with dancing sickles of light. Stevie and Kirsten had moved to the bows, and were watching Foula edge closer, the two shelves of cliff cutting down from the north side, the peak rising in the centre, lit green by the sun, the land falling away to the south. Moon was dozing gently against the dinghy, a pleased-with-herself expression on her face, and Amitola had gone aft to the wheel with Geordie and Magnie, who was in full yarn mode.

'There a lock o' names like that, that came into Shetland wi' a shipwreck. Grains, now, that came from a shipwreck in Nesting, a ship wi' grain aboard, and the Polesons, that was a ship with poles, and the Woods, that was a wood ship on Muckle Roe. The Wattersons, that was a Faroese ship blown into Dale o' Waas just back there with a Watter man and his son aboard. They were stranded there for months. The son, he fell in love wi' a local lass, and that's where that name came into Shetland from.'

'That's fascinating,' Amitola said.

'There were the Stickles too,' Magnie said. 'That's a good one. It's an Unst name. It was in Norwick, the folk woke up to see this man sitting on a seachest on the beach. He was very well dressed, an aristocratic family. Freide von Steikle, he was called, and he'd been in trouble back home, so his family deported him, and I doubt he was maybe a bit of trouble on board the ship too, for they'd just dropped him and his gear off on the beach there and left him. He married a local lass, and they had no family, but he had an illegitimate boy, and that's where the Stickles come from.'

'Isn't history interesting!' Amitola said to Moon, who opened one eye, spotted me with my tray of mugs and rose to take it from me. 'Thanks, Cass. Just what I'm needing, with all this sea air.'

I dished the mugs out, put the tray back below and checked my mobile. No signal, of course; whatever was going on back on Papa would have to wait until we got back to the mainland. I waited until Amitola and Moon had moved forward again, and then went back to lean against the aft hatch.

'Something up, lass?' Magnie asked.

I nodded, and tried to think of the fewest possible words to frame the information Geordie needed. 'Geordie, your mam's fine now but she had a bit of a turn.'

His head jerked towards me. 'A turn? A heart attack?'

'She's lying down now and breathing easier, but they wanted a doctor to look at her. I heard Isla calling for the lifeboat to fetch one.'

'An attack?' Geordie repeated. 'What happened, where is she?'

'She's at her house. Lying down.' I paused, then added, 'It seems to have happened just outside Paul Roberts's house.'

Geordie paled under his tan, and his head jerked backwards.

'You could take the RIB,' Magnie said to him. 'If you want to get back to Papa now, rather than waiting for the evening.'

I could see he was tempted by the offer, but then he shook his head. 'No. We hae this folk aboard. I'll stick wi' you. I'll go and give Isla a call on the VHF, find out what's going on.' He headed off down below, leaving Magnie thoughtful.

'How bad did it sound, lass? Betty, I mean?'

'Isla did sound more reassuring once she'd explained that Betty was lying down, but it didn't sound good. A bad colour, she said, and her heart racing.'

'Aye aye.' Magnie set the wheel to autopilot and leaned back against the stay, calculating. 'The Papa ferry's at six from West Burrafirth, and he'd need time to drive there from Walls. Twenty minutes, would you say?'

'But she'll be on the mainland by then, likely,' I pointed out. 'They'll take her to the hospital. And Geordie's work's there too, and Isla's. They'd all be coming off on this evening's ferry anyway, if they don't come with Betty.' I realised, saying it, that of course going in the ambulance with Betty would strand them in Lerwick with their car at the ferry terminal in West Burrafirth. Life got very complicated for island-dwellers with cars. 'If they do that they'll need to wait at the hospital for Geordie to come and get them. Or I suppose the ambulance could drop the bairns off at the house as it passes, or all of them if Jen went in with Betty, rather than Isla, as I suppose she might. I was thinking Isla because she was at their house, but Jen would want to go with her mother, you'd think.'

'True enough,' Magnie agreed. 'Well, Geordie can take his car from the pier at Walls to wherever they need him. We're aiming at being back there at five, so he has plenty of time to catch the Papa ferry if he needs to.'

'How soon can they get a doctor there, do you think?'

Magnie pulled a face. 'A friend o' mine tried to phone NHS 24 to get a doctor, and by the time she'd spoken to this een and spoken to that een and they'd finally agreed to send the doctor on duty it was a good hour later, and then he had to come the thirty-five-odd miles from Sandwick up to Brae. If Betty's at all fit to be moved they'd be better to get her on the lifeboat and meet her wi' an ambulance at West Burrafirth or Aith, whichever the lifeboat can get her to faster.'

Geordie came back then, face still pale. 'I'm managed to speak wi' Isla. They're taking Mam into the Gilbert Bain as soon as they can manage it, and Isla'll go wi' her, and the bairns. It was shock. She found a dead man.'

I felt my throat contract. That dark huddled shape, the ram that hadn't moved with the others, just along from the phone box cottage, where Betty's ex-husband had come back to stay. Paul Roberts. Her words rang in my head. *He's no biding here.* Someone had taken steps to make sure he didn't.

Geordie was still speaking. 'Jen's no able.' He paused, swallowed, and finished, 'The body Mam found. It was Kenny, Jen's man.'

III

A Drop in Pressure

Chapter Nine

Kenny! I gaped at him in disbelief. Magnie moved forward. 'You sit down, boy, you've had a shock. Cass, get him a cup o' tay, three sugars.'

Geordie made a 'don't bother' gesture, but I nipped below. By the time I came back, Magnie had got him sitting down by the wheel. None of the passengers seemed to have noticed anything: Amitola and Moon were forrard now, sitting on the pulled-back bowsprit and watching Foula come closer, Kirsten was by the main hatch, legs stretched out, head tilted back, eyes closed, and Stevie was by the life raft. The cheeriness had given way to fatigue; he looked every one of his sixty years.

'We'll get you back to Waas for five,' Magnie was saying, 'and that'll let you go back to Papa to be wi' your sister.'

Geordie nodded. I pressed the mug into his hands and he grasped it, clutching the warmth of it to him. Shock. As he drank, the colour came back into his face. He lowered the empty mug, looked over his shoulder to make sure no passengers were near before he spoke. 'Jen said – she said Mam said – she said someone'd killed him.' He shook his head as if the idea was too strange to credit. 'I thought, when they said down by the auld post office – ' He broke off short, as if he was saying too much. 'But why, why would anyone want to kill Kenny? He was a fine soul, and he and Jen were that blyde, wi' the baby coming. Poor Jen. I wish she coulda been spared all this.'

'We'll get you back to her as soon as we can,' Magnie repeated. He gave the ship's clock a quick glance. 'Yea. We'll be at Foula by eleven. Too early for lunch, after that brakfist they're had, so I was planning to go around the outside first, that'll take an hour and a half, and then moor up and let them have the same time again on shore, leaving at two. If you make that fish soup you were speaking aboot, we'll hae that in mugs wi' buttered bread to dip in it on the way home.'

'I'll do that,' Geordie said. He rose abruptly, as if he was glad to have something to do, and disappeared below. Soon a most savoury smell of smoked fish frying in butter began to rise up from the hatch.

I went forrard to where Kirsten was sitting and eased myself down on the deck beside her. 'Have you been to Foula before?'

She shook her head. 'I'm looking forward to it. My whole office was really envious. The cliffs are supposed to be spectacular.'

'I'm told so. I haven't been close up to them either.' I made a vague gesture towards Papa. 'When I have my own boat in these waters, I'm usually going from Brae to Scalloway, or the other way round, so I go through Papa Sound, and if I'm going further north from Scalloway, I go closer to the back of Papa, to keep well clear of the Ve Skerries.'

'The rocks where the boat Uncle Stevie was talking about are?'

'Yes.'

She turned her head to look at me properly. 'Do you spend your whole summer aboard the *Swan*, just taking folk like us on trips?'

I shook my head. 'I'm second mate aboard the Norwegian tall ship *Sørlandet*, you know, a real old-fashioned three-masted square rigger. She's a beauty.'

'Second mate!' She thought about that for a moment. 'I'd have thought the men would grab all those jobs.'

'Not nowadays. Our First Officer, that's second in command to the captain, she's a woman as well.'

'And that all works okay?'

'There's no problem at all about it in Norway. It's a lot more equal than the UK.' I wrinkled my nose. 'But I do remember one obnoxious American man who wouldn't take even the simplest order from a woman. What's your job?'

'Finance.' She gave a wry smile. 'I'm one of the third of island adults who works to the Council. When I started, oh, way back in the early nineties, I had to work extra hard to prove to them that a woman could actually handle complicated maths. Now I'm deputy director.'

'You showed them.'

'I did, but I get tired of it, you know? I don't see why we still have to be constantly proving ourselves. You know it's a hundred and fifty years now since the first women officials, on school boards? Men believed women couldn't have the vote because they couldn't organise things, but they got away with that because it was a nice, womanly occupation involved with children. Good grief, they ran those huge Victorian houses with a dozen servants and everything done by hand. I bet the school board was a rest cure after that. Though it was just a blip at first, women on the school boards here, two on the Bressay one for a couple of years in the 1870s, and then no more until 19 . . . 1911, I think it was, that was Christina Jamieson, have you heard of her?'

I shook my head.

'She was an author and folklorist, and a red-hot women's suffragist. She got on the Lerwick school board, the primary schools one, and then in the war she got on the secondary school board and chaired it.' She sat up, warming to her theme. 'Otherwise, the only women officials in the isles were the truancy officers, you ken, they chasted the bairns up when they weren't at school, and even then for a good few years around the turn of the century there was only one woman. Mary Jessie Abernethy, she was. There's a photo of her in the museum archive as a bonny young lass. She was right tall, so that she was known as "Long Jessie". There's a good story about her: she was a great reader and had a quick tongue, and when an overdressed visitor drawled at her, "Oh, Jessie, don't you ever want to get away and see the sights?" Jessie gave her a look up and down and replied witheringly, "No, I just wait till the sights come to me."'

She laughed. 'Good for her! She was the westside Compulsory Attendance Officer for years, there are people alive who remember her, going round on her bicycle.' She turned to me, flushing and eager. 'You know my ambition? I want to be the first female Convenor of the Council. We've got a female Chief Executive now, and there have been female heads of department, but the nearest anyone's got to the top job was Florence Grains. She was Vice-Convenor for a number of years, but she retired, oh, over ten years ago now.' You could have struck sparks from the flint in her voice. 'It's time there was a woman at the top. I'll be fifty next year, and I'm going to go down to working part-time. I'll stand for the Council, and we'll see how fast I can climb up the ranks.'

'Good luck,' I said. I glanced forward at Moon. 'And your sister, is she ambitious too?'

Kirsten looked surprised. 'Moon?' She shook her head. 'Moon's a funny one. She's like a child, too easily bored. She works in one place for a bit, then says it's "not for her" and goes off to something else. She's never trained for anything – she tried several college courses, but she never finished any of them.' She shrugged. 'It's how she wants to live. She sees herself as being adventurous and spiritually enlightened. A free spirit. She reckons my sort of life is no fun.'

I glanced sideways at her, and wondered what she did for

fun. I couldn't imagine her at discos in her young days. 'I'm discovering there's a lot to be said for a regular wage packet.'

'I don't like Moon's sort of fun. I go to the cinema. The lectures in the museum are good too, and I read a lot.'

It was very respectable for a future SIC Convenor, but I wasn't sure it sounded more fun than drifting about and being enlightened. I supposed that future Convenors had to be Caesar's wife.

Kirsten took the words out of my head. 'Future Convenors need to be squeaky-clean, especially if they're female. Stuff that the men would get away with, like getting blind drunk at Up Helly Aa and waking up in your drawers in a skip, all that ridiculous male behaviour which shows what a good bloke you are really, would rule a woman out straight away.'

'And all the fuss about what you look like,' I agreed. 'Too smart, you must be dodgy; too dowdy, you're boring.'

She nodded. 'Nobody ever says a black suit's boring – not when a man's wearing it.'

'I suppose they'd comment on, say, a sixties velvet one, Austin Powers style.'

'If the man wearing it was standing against a woman, they'd say it showed the kind of individuality that makes for a strong leader. On a woman, of course, it would be hankering for the past, and lack of forward vision.' She brooded for a moment. 'And whatever colour it was, it would be the wrong colour.'

'It's a funny world,' I said.

Kirsten's eyes snapped. 'It would be funny if it wasn't so serious. Even in our nice, civilised, equal, developed Europe and USA, half the world, *half the world*, are living with the default setting being male. Even in something as simple as offices. Being smaller in general, women need a slightly warmer temperature, but it's usually men who maintain the boiler and adjust the thermostats, so the women look silly huddled in jumpers while the men stride about in shirtsleeves. Shelves are put up by men too.'

'At the right height for them?'

'Bang on. The men who design the offices and car parks don't think about worrying dark areas that any woman would automatically steer clear of. And did you know that if you're in a car accident, you're nearly fifty per cent more likely to be injured, just for being female?'

I gaped at her. 'How come?'

She scowled at the waves, as if it was their fault. 'Crash dummies are male. Average male, 5'10", weighing eleven stone. I'm 5'4", eight stone. If I don't get strangled by the seat belt across my neck my chest'll be crushed by the force of the airbag. Of course that's in the passenger seat. They haven't done tests on a female dummy in the driver's seat.'

I was horrified. 'What, none at all?'

She shook her head. 'None. And even the female crash dummy is a scaled-down male shape. Just like the women police riot gear. Just like nurses' protective scrubs.' She turned her head towards me and gave a surprisingly impish smile. 'One last fact, then I'll get off my soapbox. Drugs, even drugs designed for women, are tested on male mice. No pesky fluctuating hormones to skew the results, even though men and women react completely differently to some drugs – and need different dosages too, but you never see that on the packet.'

It was true; you didn't.

Foula was getting closer. I gave Magnie a 'will I take over?' look, and he nodded. 'I'd better go and do ship things,' I said. 'Magnie's going into yarn mode, I can feel it.'

I took the helm so that Magnie could go forward to the main hatch and yarn about the places we were passing. He'd steered so Foula was to starboard, for you couldn't possibly go around it against the sun. The island was no longer the three shelves we were used to seeing from the mainland, but two, one each side of the opening into the pier, with the Sneug rising steeper on the right, and the Noup to the south. As we came around, the Noup separated itself into two, divided by a wide gully. The catspaw of the South Ness was scrabbled with rock embedded in grass, separated by an undulating rock face, fissured up and across so that it looked like a wall from the time of giants. Lichen was smeared yellow across it, like a handprint, and the sea had cut into it from beneath, so that it hung out perilously above the snatching waves.

We crossed the bay and came under the lee of the Noup. Magnie's voice floated back to me: 'Old red sandstone with igneous intrusions.' It was the colour of the desert, a pyramid shape of slanted rock cut with upright niches, like an Egyptian temple. There were dark fissures behind sheltering rocks at sea level; the next cliff face, as we came a little further round, ran black with peat from burns. We were seeing birds on the water now, toadstool-brown bonxies with white-banded wings, pirate predators as graceful in flight as an eagle.

The next headland, the first outcrop of the Sneug, was sheer rock, still on a steep slant, sliced diagonally, cement-grey with veins of cream. Another burn had created a black splash, as if a giant had left a paint pot on its side, and the layers were banded in different colours nearer the water, the cement grey shading to warm pink. Close to, the creamy white was bird guano from the thousands nesting there. The last few kittiwakes were small as barnacles on the rock face. The creamy point gave way to a curve where the giant's children had been having a play day, daubing the concave rock face with black, ochre, terracotta, olive green. There were gannets now, the white of a new snowfall, jet-black wingtips, lemon heads, cross-shaped in flight. A breath of cloud clung to the top of the hill.

Up around Magnie our passengers were staring, silent and wide-eyed. It was so big you lost all sense of perspective. Those

91

dots were goose-sized gannets, that low stack probably fifty feet high. Now we came along to the north-west face of the Sneug, a long, straight piece carved like an Assyrian bass-relief, four veiled women plodding forward in line with bowed heads and dangling hands. You could see how steeply the Sneug rose until it was abruptly sliced away by whatever long-ago tectonic shift had cut it in half. After the thrust-up peak, the cliffs continued level, 1,220 feet above sea level, I heard Magnie say, then as suddenly swooped down in a graceful curve to end in a flat spiral knob, like the end of a grand staircase. The line of cliffs became a jumble of sea-stacks, teased into arches shaped on the face of the cliff, elephant gray now. One was exactly the proportions of the Arc de Triomphe, and following it was a real arch, square and open as La Défense in Paris, feet in water, sand brown with a stripe of black. I gave a last look back as we forged forwards, and saw Foula returned to its familiar three-shelved outline.

The spell was broken. Our passengers spread out along the boat again, chattering about how amazing it was. Kirsten was asking Magnie if there would be time to climb the Sneug. 'Now we've seen it from below, it would be amazing to look down from above too.'

'If you're a quick climber,' Magnie said. 'It's over a thousand feet, not quite as high as Rønas Hill, if you're been up that, but steeper going.'

'Easy for coming down again,' Stevie said beside her. 'Just sit down and slide.'

Magnie came back to take the helm and give directions for going into the pier. We got the mainsail dropped and loosely stowed, ready for the journey home, then putted gently into the narrow opening and berthed behind a black RIB squeezed as far forward as it could go.

'Now, folk,' Magnie said, 'that fine smell coming up from below is Geordie's best fish soup, which'll be ready as soon as we're under way again. We're set to take you back to the Waas Pier for five, so we need you all back on board for two. Have fun exploring the island west o' the sun, and go carefully near the banks.'

They all trooped off. Magnie and I straightened up the lines and added an extra spring to help us get off the pier. A couple of seals watched lazily from the far end of the geo. 'Well,' Magnie said, once the lines were to his satisfaction, 'I'm off to have a yarn wi' one o' me whaling cronies, in that house joost along there. Go you and explore too, lass, if you're never been on Foula afore. There's no harm coming to the boat in here, and Geordie'll be aboard.'

I took him at his word and headed off ashore, feeling rather strange without Cat at my heels; he'd have liked this. I hesitated for a moment at the T-junction up from the pier, then decided to head north. Kirsten and Moon were ahead of me, striding up the road towards the easiest way straight up the side of the Sneug. There was a slight distance between them, a prickly feel, with Kirsten slightly ahead of Moon, as if she hadn't wanted her tagging along. I followed them at a steady pace, keeping well behind.

It was a bonny place, Foula. The road divided the parks from the hill. On my right, the land around the houses was green and fertile, made that way by generations carrying kishies of seaweed up to spread on it each spring. On my left, amber moorland led to the steep rise of the Sneug. The sheep on the scattald were coloured with fawn or grey blotches on a white ground. A red and white pony lifted its head to watch me for a moment, then went back to grazing. It was most blissfully quiet, with even the hushing of the waves silenced by the long slope of parks between the road and the shore banks; all I could hear was the wind on my eardrums, and a sheep bleating on the scattald. Even this late in the year the air was sweet with the scent of flowers.

I walked as far as the school, and paused to admire it. It was a large, new building clad in navy planking, only one storey high in the side walls, but with a pitched roof that gave another floor. The road side had a high double window, projecting out like the bow of a ship, that let you see the classroom below, with a jumble of pen pots on the teacher's desk in the nook, and a library up above. The playground had a grassed area with two flowertubs bright with orange marigolds, and a picnic table. Past it was a climbing frame and a slide set above a grassy bank, so that a careless child couldn't fall too far. I betted that when nobody was looking they'd have fun falling off on purpose, and rolling down the grassy bank.

I went through the gate, climbed up the slide steps and sat for a moment looking around me. Across the grey water, the Shetland mainland swam through the mist like a giant turtle, humped back and head. It looked very remote; living here would be like being permanently at sea, with all the petty kerfuffle of the land world left far behind: boxes to unpack, bedding to sort and pots and pans to inspect. Except, I reflected, looking down at the houses below me, that they were their own mainland, and had their own troubles too, fighting to keep their island viable, to say nothing of troubles from outside: smallpox and measles had hit the island folk hard, with no resistance to them.

I rested my chin on my hands and brooded. Leaving my *Khalida* to overwinter at Brae, where she was moored right now, meant taking my mast down. The crane was arranged for the end of the week. It was the first time I'd had to take *Khalida*'s mast down since I'd put it up in the Med, just after I'd bought her, and I was dreading it. It wasn't just the physical things, like unhooking all the electrics, which was always a pain, and knowing that one of the eight wire stays that held up her mast was bound to be seized solid; it was having my white wings taken off me. Without her sails she'd just be a motorboat with a small, slow engine and no backup for engine failure out at sea. I'd be confined to land until April, when the marina's insurance said masts could go up again.

Confined to land; more specifically, confined to our rented cottage. Oh, of course if Gavin and I didn't work out I could go back to living aboard; I'd still have gas for cooking and warmth, and I'd bought a little oil-filled radiator to run from the marina's shore power. I'd be on *Sørlandet* for between six and eight weeks at a time, depending on where she'd sailed to. And Gavin was Gavin, and I loved him, and he loved me, and though there'd be all the teething problems of first living together, there would be all the fun too. It would all be okay. I thought it would be okay – except that I was used to being my own boss, just as he was, and a ship could only take one captain. What would happen when we wanted different things, and a decision had to be made, and we both thought we were right?

I sat there looking out to sea and felt panic curl within my belly until I could sit there no longer but had to leap up and stride along the road again. Moon's scarlet jacket was well up the side of the Sneug now, but I couldn't make out Kirsten's green against the hill. I stayed on the road, walking with quick strides until I was breathless, past a close-by house on my right and another further back on my left, and around the lower flank of the Sneug. I was walking westwards now, with the sun in my eyes. Another two hundred metres and I'd come to the end of the road, with a sizeable farm blocking my way. High above me, Moon and Kirsten had made it up to the top; I could see the two figures dark against the sun-dazzle. I glanced at my watch. Half past one. I'd sat brooding longer than I'd thought. The lasses would need to get a move on to be back at the boat for two.

I hoped that climbing together like that might have shelved yesterday's argument, though I knew nothing about being a sister; it might equally have ignited it again. I could see now why Kirsten was so determined to talk Moon out of accusing Stevie of taking dodgy videos of them as children. She had her sights set upwards, and being smeared in a child–abuse case would do her no good. Oh, of course the names of the victims wouldn't appear in the paper, but everyone would know they were her and Moon; and *The Shetland Times* would print every last detail of what Moon alleged had been done to them. It would do serious damage to her career. Abused as a child; she'd have all kinds of hang-ups attributed to her, and that would get the blame every time she did something the male establishment didn't like, especially if they were friends of Stevie's. Oh, not to her face, but I could just hear them gossiping over a pint behind her back. 'Ah, well, she was the wife that shouted about child abuse, brought that case, d'you mind? His own niece. Said he'd filmed them naked as bairns, well, there was nothing unusual in that then a days, it's only recently everyone's got so finicky. Not quite right in the head, if you ask me. Nothing wrong wi' Stevie, but the Sheriff has to be that careful these days.' Then the old boys' network would get going and it would just happen that promotion would pass her by.

No, denying everything was her only hope of the high office she was determined on.

Chapter Ten

I pushed the thoughts away, and headed back at a more moderate pace. I'd just reached the turn-off when the RIB we'd parked behind spun neatly backwards, turned on a sixpence and roared off, leaving a wash that ran into the narrow bay and sloshed up the beach. The seals bobbed up and down lazily on it, unperturbed.

There was nobody aboard when I arrived back, but I'd barely begun to set the mugs out when Geordie reappeared and gave his soup a stir.

'Any news from Papa?' I asked.

He nodded. 'The lifeboat brought a doctor, and then took her off to the hospital and she's hitched up to a dozen machines. Isla said she'd phone again once the doctor there gives her an update.'

'That's good news.' I nodded at the soup. 'It smells great. Anything I can be doing?'

'Na, na, it's all under control.'

Five to two. I headed up on deck to see where everyone had got to. Magnie was striding along from the south, with another man beside him, the crony he'd been visiting, an active-looking seventy-year-old with a pair of dogs at his heels. Amitola was coming from that direction too, but nearer the sea, as if she'd taken a walk along the banks. There was a green jacket on the road I'd just come from: Kirsten, but not

Moon's scarlet jacket behind her. I looked up the Sneug and saw no sign of it coming down. There was a pair of spyglasses tucked just inside the aft cabin hatch. I got them and began a careful sweep, the road first, and then the hill. Nothing. No scarlet jacket, no walker with a bright jumper, nobody. The dotted-colour sheep grazed peacefully, without lifting their heads to stare at anyone in their territory. I swung around. Maybe she'd come down separately, on the left flank of the hill. There was nothing moving there either.

There was a cold feeling in the pit of my stomach. I clamped it down, and put the spyglasses away. They'd all be here soon enough. In the meantime, I drank my soup, put the mug back below, and began stowing all but the essential lines. I'd just finished that when Magnie arrived and stood chatting to his crony on the pier. Stevie passed them and came aboard, scarlet-faced now with exercise.

'There's soup down below,' I said. 'Help yourself.'

'Lead me to it,' Stevie said. 'I could eat a whole pony after all this hill work.' He turned his cheery grin on me. 'I'm climbed the Noup o' Foula now.'

'Not the Sneug?'

'I did that years back. I thought I'd tick the Noup off. There's life in the old boy yet.'

He went below, whistling, and shortly reappeared with a mug of soup in his hand. The heat still radiated off him, and his t-shirt had damp sweat-patches across the chest. 'Where are the women?'

Kirsten was almost at the pier turn-off. She lifted her head to watch Amitola coming from the opposite direction. Amitola obviously asked where Moon was, for she gave a wave of her hand indicating backwards behind her, and then, when Amitola asked a question, Kirsten went into persuasion mode, every gesture of body and hands eloquent. *No, really, it's nothing to worry about.*

Stevie was still standing beside me, watching, eyes narrowed in concentration. Then he saw me watching, and turned to look over the hill.

'No sign of Moon yet,' I said.

'Late as usual,' he said, unfazed. 'Moon aye needed another ten minutes. Hey, here's a good one. What d'you call a European in a hurry?'

I wasn't sure I wanted to know.

'He's Russian!' Steve chortled, and slapped me on the back.

I swung down onto the pier, and spoke to Magnie. 'No sign of Moon yet.'

'She should be back by now,' Amitola said. Her breath came in short gasps. 'Should we send out a search party?'

'Now, Ami,' Stevie said. He put an arm round her shoulders. 'You ken Moon. She'd be late for her own funeral. She'll be here any minute and most surprised that she's kept us waiting.'

'Don't fuss, Mam,' Kirsten joined in. I could see from her expression that she thought it was just like Moon to be drawing attention to herself by keeping everyone waiting.

'Where did she go after leaving the boat?' Magnie asked. 'She's maybe fallen and twisted an ankle.'

'She went up the Sneug,' Kirsten said.

I remembered the two figures I'd seen at the top, and felt an uneasy twist in my belly. 'Didn't you go up with her?' I asked Kirsten.

She shook her head, and gave a fastitious look at her boots. 'The grass was wet. I decided not to bother. But she went up all right, you couldn't miss that jacket against the hill.'

I opened my mouth to protest that I'd seen them, and closed it again. There was a sick feeling in the pit of my stomach.

'She might have slipped,' Stevie conceded. 'The Noup wasn't good going.'

Magnie turned to his crony. 'Well, Jeemie boy, you'll get

the chance to show us what your dogs can do now. Cass, can you fetch the lass's sleeping bag from her bunk?'

'I'll do it,' Amitola said. She went below and came back with Moon's bag bundled in her arms.

Jeemie took it from her, and held it out to the dogs to smell. 'Find, Moss. Find, Laddie. On you go, find!'

I watched the two black and white backs head off on the pier with scepticism which changed to reluctant admiration as they went to the head of the road and turned right without hesitating.

'That's the way we went,' Kirsten said.

'We'd better follow,' Magnie said. 'Geordie, your legs are younger as mine. You go wi' Jeemie. Stevie, you and I'll be the backup party. We hae a stretcher on board, we'll take that. Cass, you get on the radio to the Coastguard and explain what's happened. We've plenty of daylight left, but they might want to send the chopper to help us look.'

'Take the hand-held,' I said, grabbing it from its place. 'You should be able to report back with that. Channel 8, like at the regattas.'

Magnie nodded, and put it in his jacket pocket. He leaned in to me, and spoke softly. 'Keep them calm, Cass.'

I gave him a thumbs-up gesture, and turned to the others: Amitola, looking anxious; Kirsten, calm and matter-of-fact. 'Since they don't need us, let's have some soup.' I held up a hand as Amitola began to protest. 'Let's get ourselves ready to deal with whatever they find. If they have to carry her off the hill with a broken ankle, they'll need us to be fit and ready to get the boat going homewards as fast as she can steam.'

Reluctantly, Amitola nodded. 'That's good sense,' Kirsten agreed. 'Sit down, Mam. I'll help serve up.'

It was an anxious meal, made the more anxious by our attempts to make conversation. We were all too conscious of the black dogs leading the search party along the road and up the hill. Kirsten hadn't felt like climbing, she said; she'd waved Moon upwards and taken the fork to the right, down to the north-east corner of the island, and sat there a bit, looking out at the sea, and Shetland in the distance. Amitola had gone in the other direction, and sat on the rocks, meditating to the sound of the waves. I didn't mention the second climber I'd seen; if need be, and I was beginning to fear it would need be, I'd tell that only to the police. It could have been either of them I'd seen, or Stevie. Kirsten could have gone up with Moon. Stevie and Amitola had come back from the other direction, but I'd bet you could climb up the Sneug from that way too. I urged them to refills of soup, brought up a plateful of appetising-smelling cheese toasties cut in little triangles, and waited for the radio to speak.

Now I could make out two figures at the top of the rise, with the dogs moving around them. One of the figures turned and signalled to the two below, Magnie and Stevie following at a slower pace, then began descending. Amitola half rose, one hand rising to her throat. 'Have they found her? Do you think they've found her?'

I was just searching for words when the radio crackled. 'Shore to *Swan*, shore to *Swan*. Cass, are you there?'

I hurried down the steps and grabbed the microphone. '*Swan* here.'

Magnie's voice came out clear in the empty cabin. 'Cass, we're found her. She's in the sea.' He hesitated, conscious that the others would be listening. 'There's no sign o' her being living. Jeemie's biding up here to keep watching her and we'll come back down and take the RIB round to pick her up. Can you get on to the Coastguard? I'm no' sure what the procedure is, but they'll maybe have to organise a doctor to meet us in Waas.'

'Understood,' I said. 'I'll get on with that.'

I climbed the ladder with heavy steps. Amitola was slumped on the deck with Kirsten crouched beside her, an arm round her shoulders. I looked at Kirsten. 'I'll just radio the Coast-guard, and then I'll get you to help me launch the RIB.'

I went back below and passed the responsibility on. 'The lifeboat's still at the Ve Skerries,' the officer replied, when I'd explained. 'How long has the casualty been in the water?'

I tried to think when I'd seen those two climbers. 'Getting on for an hour, no, a bit over.'

'When do you think you can get to her, with your RIB?'

'Less than half an hour, but we'll not be in Walls before six now.'

'I'll talk to the lifeboat coxswain, and a doctor, see if getting her back sooner might do any good. Keep on this channel.'

I listened while they talked. The lifeboat couldn't get to Moon as quickly as we could, but it would meet the RIB on its way back to the pier and transfer her. It wouldn't do any good though, I thought drearily. Falling from that height onto water was like falling onto concrete. We had a rigid stretcher aboard, and we'd get her onto it with all the care we could, but her in-juries were likely to have been fatal, if she hadn't drowned first.

I went back up on deck. Amitola was still sitting on the deck, rigid, silent, her eyes fixed on the horizon. She didn't say any-thing, but there were tears rolling down her cheeks. Kirsten was crouched beside her, one arm around her shoulders. I crouched down too, and explained what we were planning. 'I'm sorry to ask it of you,' I finished, 'but I'll need you to help me.'

'You stay there, Mam,' Kirsten said. 'Just keep counting your breaths. I'll help Cass.'

We managed to manhandle the RIB between the two of us, and slid it over the side. When we'd done that, Kirsten laid a hand on my arm. Her breath came in little gasps. 'There's no hope, is there?'

I wasn't sure what to say, and she read my hesitation. Her shoulders slumped, and she went back to her mother, huddling close to her, seeking comfort as well as giving it. Amitola began to cry, tearing, gulping sobs, and Kirsten put both arms around her and shushed her, as if she was a child.

I went on board the RIB and checked everything was ready to go, then fought the rigid stretcher out from its corner in the engine room. By then Magnie and the others had arrived. I looked at Magnie with some anxiety; for all he was very fit, he was well through his seventies, and he'd just climbed a serious hill at speed, then descended again. His chest was still heaving with the effort.

'If you want,' I said, 'I could go with the RIB and leave you to take charge with the Coastguard.'

He flicked a glance at Amitola and Kirsten, and gave a decisive shake of his head.

'You keep in charge here, Cass, and talk to the lifeboat,' he said. 'I'll take Geordie and Stevie. She'll no' be light to get aboard.'

The men climbed into the RIB and roared off. I reported that to the Coastguard, and shortly heard Magnie's voice confirming that they were on their way. By then the lifeboat was on its way too; another ten minutes and we saw the white plume of water as she hurtled towards us.

Amitola lifted her head. 'I want to go with her.' I nodded. I was sure that would be okay.

'I'll come with you,' Kirsten said.

'No,' Amitola said sharply. Kirsten's head jerked up. They stared at each other for a long moment. 'No,' Amitola repeated. 'If we'd listened to her, been more sympathetic, then maybe – ' She made a pushing-away gesture.

Kirsten put an arm about her shoulders. 'We did listen, Mam. We did our best.' She turned her away from me, and I only heard the last murmur as I moved away myself. 'Let's not mention any of that to the police.'

'I'll tell the lifeboat,' I said in their direction, and went below again to relay that on. While I was down there, Magnie came on to confirm to the Coastguard that they'd arrived and were beside the casualty. She was floating on her front, and there was no sign of life. They were floating her on the stretcher now, and then they'd take her directly to the lifeboat.

'Amitola wants to travel with her,' I said, 'and Kirsten. Her mother and sister.'

There was a bit of consultation, and then the lifeboat said they'd come and pick the women up from the *Swan* first, then meet with Magnie. They went below to pack up their things and Moon's while I organised fenders. Soon we heard the life-boat's roar. It curved round the end of the pier and stopped beside *Swan* as gently as a feather falling. I helped Amitola and Kirsten cross the gap between the boats, handed the bags over, and watched the lifeboat go again, heading for its rendezvous with Magnie.

Suddenly I felt very tired; but Magnie was far older than me, and had been up and down hills, and hauling Moon from the water. I needed to stay alert. *Swan* was ready to go as soon as we got the RIB back aboard. In the meantime I made more tea and rested until I heard the RIB coming towards us, and saw it rounding the pier. All three men looked white and drawn as they climbed aboard.

'We'll get this boat aboard,' Magnie said, 'and then make our best speed for Waas.'

It was a silent journey. None of us felt like talking. We got away from the pier and set the boat's autohelm, then spread over the boat, thinking our own thoughts. Magnie and Geordie stayed at the helm, while I went up and down with soup mugs and cups of tea, and began cleaning up below;

Stevie huddled by the main hatch. I went and sat beside him, but it was obvious he didn't want to talk. His face was pinched under his black toorie. He spoke only once: 'I wish I'd never had this idea.' I nodded sympathetically, and remained with him in silence for a few minutes, then nodded again, and rose.

The mainland came closer. The water was still bright around us, but the land colours had begun to dim, flaring out again when the sun touched them, but darkening the moment it moved away. There was a winter feel in the air, a sense that the day was drawing to a close, even though we had a good two hours of daylight yet.

Geordie's face was anxious, and he kept trying his mobile for a signal. As soon as he got one he spoke for several minutes, face lightening, then did another call, this time trying to persuade someone to something, by his tone of voice, but without success. He sighed, put his phone away and came over to sit down beside me. 'Cass, you're no' doing anything in particular this next couple of days, are you? I was wondering if I could ask you a bit of a favour.'

'Sure.'

'I'm spoken to Isla again. She and the bairns are at home now, our house at Bixter, that is. They're keeping Mam in for observation this night, but she should be fit to go home wi' Isla for tomorrow night, and the nurse at the surgery'll give her another check-over on Tuesday, then she can come home again, back to Papa, on Wednesday.'

He paused there, and I nodded.

'What I'm worried about is Jen. I dinna want her to be left alone. She had friends biding, but they all work, and she's insisted they go off on this evening's ferry.' He glanced at his watch. 'I should make the one going across, if I don't meet anything on the Hummalees. I can bide with her tonight, and then I'll take me own boat across to West Burrafirth in the morning, and get in to me work. I'll try and persuade Jen to come with me, but I doubt she won't. She doesna ken − ' He broke off, and gave me a shy sideways look. 'You heard Mam on the pier.' I nodded. 'He − me faither − what's he calling himself, Roberts, he's a violent man. Jen doesna ken about any o' this. She doesna ken it's him, that he's there on Papa. I dinna want to leave her alone wi' him on the isle, but she's insisting she wants me to be there wi' Mam. Well, she's no' completely alone, you ken, there's Tammie and Ruby, they're the older couple down in the house beside Mam's, and Uncle, he bides up above the pier, but I dinna want to leave her alone in her own house like that. She needs another woman with her, someone her own age.' He gave me another smile. 'No fear of anyone hurting her with you to look after her. You'd see Roberts off.' His face twisted suddenly. 'He'd be all smiles to you. It's only family he's − ' He cut himself off with a gesture.

'But will Jen want me?' I asked.

'She'll be glad o' you. And I'm free from Wednesday. I'd have asked for time off, under the circumstances, but there's a big job on and it would leave us shorthanded. I was pushing my luck to get away on Friday afternoon for this trip.' His face was relieved. 'Thanks, Cass. I'll let her know you're coming.' He gave a sideways grin. 'And it'll give you a last good sail before your mast comes down.'

Chapter Eleven

We were almost at Vaila when Stevie's mobile rang in his jacket
pocket. He fished it out and looked at it as if he'd forgotten what
it was, then his gaze sharpened. He put it to his ear. 'Stevie here.'
There was a pause while the caller talked and Stevie nodded.
'Mmm ... yea ... and they managed to get all the fish off?'
They must have done, for his face lightened momentarily. 'And
the crew? ... Yes, we'll need to keep them here another couple
of days. The cost'll be worth it if we can get the boat off. We can
try again tomorrow, maybe have better luck if she's been lightened. Yeah, right, speak to you later.'

'Good news?' I asked.

He spread his hands. 'Mixed. They've managed to empty the
hold, but by the time they'd done that the water was going out
again, and she wouldn't budge. The Coastguard tug'll try again
tomorrow. It's in nobody's interests to have a wreck floating
loose.'

I agreed wholeheartedly with that one. 'Good luck,' I said.

Once we were within the shelter of Vaila Sound it became a
bonny afternoon again. The setting sun was warm on our backs,
and the parks running down to the shore were summer green.
The light caught up every hint of yellow: a painted door, a patch
of flowers against a white wall, the scrolled name of a boat on a
trailer. By the time we reached the pier I was sweating in my
jacket.

I might have known there would be a police car to greet us. It squatted in its white and neon visibility by Stevie's carefully-covered motorbike. PC Macdonald, the young policeman, who'd tried to keep me off my own boat in the longship case, was standing beside it, looking harrassed. I smiled at the reason: Maman, her long white wool coat chic against Dad's black 4x4, looked like she was interrogating him on why he was waiting for us. His hands went up in apology, and he cast a glance backwards at his partner, sitting in the car and obviously not hurrying to get out to help him. I looked thoughtfully at Maman. Her body language suggested she was pouring on her best French charm, which would explain why even the tips of his ears had gone scarlet, Shetland men not being used to it. I supposed it would be kind to save him. I raised a hand. '*Salut*, Maman. Home safe and sound this time.'

PC Macdonald scuttled forward to take our lines and fastened them to the bollard competently enough. His cohort came out of the car to help him, and Maman stood back, waiting for me to come ashore. I gave her a double kiss on the cheek, keeping my sailing overalls well clear of her coat. 'Did Cat and Kitten behave?'

She waved one hand. 'Of course. Cat was pleased to be home, and Kitten, ah, she is a little tyrant, that one. She has him twisted round her tiny paw.'

'He lets her,' I said. 'First to his bowl, and no getting up when she's sleeping on him.'

'I had to feed them separately, or he would have had no chicken at all.'

I betted it was best breast of chicken too. It would be hard work getting Kitten to take cat food again; she believed she was born to a life of luxury.

Maman flicked her eyes towards the police officers. 'What's wrong?'

I pulled the corners of my mouth down. 'One of our passengers fell off the cliffs of Foula.'

Maman's scarlet mouth became a horrified O.

'She's dead. The lifeboat brought her body in.' That was as much as I felt I could say. Maman laid her gloved hand on mine.

'Then you had better see what they want.'

'I'll just get my stuff from below. D'you want to come on board?'

She glanced at the seawashed black deck, the oiled precision of the capstan, and shook her head. 'I'll wait in the car.'

The police just wanted names and addresses of everyone on board, to contact us for a statement. Geordie gave his first, waved us a hasty goodbye and bolted for the gangplank, hand fumbling in his pocket for his mobile. I glanced at my watch: five to six. The ferry was at ten past. Yes, if he had the luck not to meet another car on the winding, narrow Hummalees road, and if they knew he was on his way, he should make the Papa ferry. Stevie gathered up his gear, began to thank Magnie for the weekend, and broke off, face twisting. Magnie clapped him on the shoulder, and he went across the gangplank to his bike, unwrapped it and roared off, leaving Moon's battered red car and Kirsten's shiny cream one on the pier.

I took a deep breath and looked PC Macdonald straight in the eye. 'I think I should tell you this. It's to do with our passengers. I saw Moon, the woman who died, I saw her walking along the road with Kirsten, her sister, and then I saw her red jacket climbing upwards. The sister, Kirsten, she was wearing green, and I didn't see her, but I'm not sure whether I would have. Then, at the top, as I was coming back, there were two people there.'

Magnie's eyes jerked towards me. PC Macdonald's pencil stopped moving for a moment. 'You saw two people at the top of the hill?'

I nodded. 'I presumed it was Moon and Kirsten, but Kirsten said she didn't go up, and actually I couldn't see who it was. The sun was behind them. They were just silhouettes.'

There was silence while he wrote it down. He hesitated as if he wanted to ask more, then, reluctantly, closed his notebook. 'I'll let DS Peterson ken. She's on Papa right now, and she'll be going back there the morn, so it may be this evening, or more likely Tuesday. She'll be investigating this case too.'

I managed to keep a bland face at the mention of DS Peterson. As fellow strong women we should have got on like a house on fire, but sometimes people just rub each other up the wrong way. She'd be after me soon enough, I had no doubt. Even if they sent Gavin up to begin his Shetland career three weeks early, he wouldn't be allowed to interview me. I'd save the conversation I'd overheard on Vementry for her. Kirsten wouldn't volunteer it.

As soon as PC Macdonald turned away, I wished Magnie a good night aboard and a safe trip tomorrow to Scalloway, *Swan*'s winter quarters, and headed up onto the pier. Dad's car was stiflingly warm after the cool evening air. I opened a window.

'Cassandre!' Maman protested.

'Sorry.' I wound it back up, leaving just a crack. The sky was still dimly lit, though the sun had gone below the horizon now, and the wind had fallen to stillness.

Maman gave me a sideways glance. 'You are not going to tell me about it, then? Your passenger who died?'

'She fell from the highest hill.' I grimaced. 'Her mother and sister went back with her body, on the lifeboat. The motorbike man, he was her uncle.'

'An accident?'

I shrugged. She could see I didn't want to talk about it. 'But what is this of a dead man on Papa Stour?'

I shook my head. 'I really don't know anything about that.

He was only found after we'd left the island. He's the brother-in-law of Geordie, the engineer on this voyage, the one who rushed off in the car.' I felt a wave of pity for Jen sweep over me, and was glad I was going to help her. 'He and his wife were expecting a baby, a late baby, when they'd given up.'

Maman's dark lashes swept down and up again. 'Yes, that is sad. And did he have any connection with the woman who fell from the hill, on Foula?'

Geordie was younger than Jen. He'd been in bed, asleep, while they'd been dancing for Stevie's video camera. 'No,' I said slowly. 'I don't think so.'

We reached Bixter, and turned up the Aith road.

'There is rabbit with olives, simmering in the oven,' Maman said, putting her foot on the accelerator for the mile of double track. 'And you must show me the turn-off to where you are going to live, as we pass it.'

There was a wistful note in her voice, and I realised that she wanted to see our cottage. Of course she did; I was her daughter, about to move in with the man she thoroughly approved of. She'd want to know what our house was like.

'How about stopping for a look?' I asked impulsively. 'It's only a mile off the road, we wouldn't be more than, oh, twenty minutes later, if Dad can wait for his dinner.'

'I will tell him to have an extra whisky while he waits.' She had a hands-free worked from the steering wheel, but talking still distracted her, and I tried not to think about how close the wheels moved to the car-swallowing ditch on each side as we passed Michaelswood and negotiated the Z-bend into Aith. Now we were looking straight up the stretch of water between Aith and Brae. From here, Brae was a string of neon orange lights; from Brae, Aith was known as the 'white city' because of the way the sun caught the houses. We'd be halfway between at the Ladie, with headlands shielding our house from both sets of streetlights.

The dark was thickening around us now. We came past East Burrafirth, and on into moorland, where the headlights lit up only road, passing places, the grass verge with tufts of heather. 'The turn-off's in two hundred metres – a hundred – on the left.'

Maman skidded Dad's 4x4 around, and set it at the track between the South Voxter houses, and on upwards.

'There's a gate soon.' I unbuckled my seat belt and leapt out to open it, then closed it behind her. 'Nearly there now – just up and over the hill. You don't need to go right down to the water, there's a parking place level with the house.'

She rattled over the gravel track, and stopped opposite the cottage. The whitewash gleamed in the dark, but it looked very small and old-fashioned, with the roof coming down low, and the porch jutting out behind. I suddenly felt a squirm in the pit of my stomach, and hurried into explanations. 'It belonged to the old lady with the broken leg that I helped out for a bit. Tamar. She was a great character.' A pang of loss shot through me. 'I wish you could have met her. She'd been a wildlife photographer, then she retired to the family home and watched otters from her window. You can't see it now, but the view is great – out over the sound, and from the bedroom you can see right out into the Atlantic.'

She put an arm around my shoulders and gave me a little shake. I could hear the laughter in her voice. 'I grew up on a farm, remember. You can't surprise me with a Rayburn and an old-fashioned couch. Nor your Gavin either.'

I thought of Papy and Mamy's house, that we used to visit for Easter and the October holidays, facing onto the farm courtyard with sheds all round, and hens coming into the house if you forgot to shut the door, and the great square stove that heated the whole house, and grinned. 'No hens in the house here – yet.'

I was just opening the gate when a whinny came out of the blackness, followed by a galloping of hooves. I remembered that Tamar's niece had installed a pair of Shetland ponies on the croft, in the park just by the house. They came charging up, manes flying, and shoved their noses over the fence. One was what horsey folk would no doubt call skewbald, that was red and white in Shetland, with enough blond mane to do for a dozen Hollywood starlets, and the other was smaller, black and white and muddy. They were both obviously expecting a car to mean food.

'Sorry, guys,' I said. 'Once we live here.'

They watched in unimpressed silence as we made our way along the path. I found the key hung in the inside of the shed door, unlocked the kitchen door, and led Maman in.

I hadn't seen it since Tamar's family had cleared it for letting. It felt cold, and there was a lingering smell of paint. The living room was shining white now. The layout was the same, with the Rayburn taking pride of place, but all Tamar's table clutter had gone, and the shelf was cleared of books. There was a new couch in the sit-ootery, covered with a flowered throw, and an armchair. Her desk had gone from her old-fashioned sitting room, and there was another flowered throw on the rarely-used sofa.

'Well,' Maman said, looking round at the cleared emptiness, 'it has been done up for visitors, of course.'

'It was much nicer before,' I said sadly, 'with all Tamar's clutter.'

'But then you might feel you were living with her ghost.'

The thought of a ghostly Tamar's sardonic eye on us as Gavin and I settled in together made me glad of the new paint and refurbishing. 'Heaven forbid! Are you okay on the stairs?'

Maman gave me a withering look. 'I'm not an old lady yet, Cassandre.'

I shrugged, and waved her ahead of me up the crofthouse stairs, upright as a ladder, with only a rope handrail on one side and a wooden bannister on the other, accepted by Tamar as a concession when she turned ninety. 'The bathroom's at the top, straight ahead, and a bedroom on each side. I haven't decided which will be ours.'

'The one which was Tamar's,' Maman said briskly. 'Otherwise it will still be her room, and you will be visitors.'

I thought about it as I climbed the stairs and realised that she was right. It was by far the nicer of the two rooms as well, with a windowseat beneath the dormer window that looked out over Papa Little, and a little stove, and bookshelves fitted into the straight bit of the wall. Besides, when we went into it, it wasn't Tamar's room any more. All the books had gone, and her pictures. Only the sketch of a horse over the mantelpiece and the little black stove were left to remind me of how it had looked. The sloped walls had been repainted cream, and the single bed and chest of drawers replaced by a double bed with drawers underneath. Yes, Gavin and I would be fine here, and we could use the spare bedroom as overflow space.

A sudden spasm of panic gripped me. 'Oh, Maman, it is going to be okay, isn't it? We're both used to living alone, organising ourselves. Aren't we going to be constantly clashing?'

'Not with goodwill on both sides.' Maman smiled. 'Here is the advice I wish my mother had given me when I married your father: don't even bother to argue about the things that don't matter to you, if they do matter to him, and be sure you have good reasons for standing firm on the things that matter to you.'

I thought about that for a moment. 'And if we both have good reasons for standing firm on different sides of something?'

'Then decide if it is worth disagreeing over, or agree to differ.' She gave me a sideways glance. 'But he is sensible, your Gavin, and you have the same values. That's what matters. It will be fine. You'll see.' She smiled and linked her arm through mine. 'Now, are you hungry?'

★

The rabbit with olives was just as good as I'd expected. Dad radiated smugness that we'd gone to look at my first house ashore, but managed to save the questions for when he and Maman were alone. Cat greeted me with the disdain of one who wasn't going to forgive being left in a hurry; Kitten copied him, turning her back on me with the hauteur of an eighteenth-century marquise confronted by a revolutionary. Neither of them was pleased to be bundled into a basket again for the journey home to *Khalida*.

We were there now. Cat was off exploring the further reaches of the shore; Kitten had remained on board, and was washing her white paws on the berth cushions. The bollards of the marina gave a silvery gleam through the cabin windows, and *Khalida*'s lantern shone a gold glow across her white ceiling and wooden walls. The oil-filled radiator made it beautifully warm inside. There'd been no word from Gavin, but the signal was lousy out in the marina here. I picked up my washing gear and headed up onto the pontoon.

The phone pinged as soon as I'd reached the shore road. I got into the shelter of the changing rooms (blessed with a shower and underfloor heating) and sat down on a bench to look. Two texts. One was from Gavin: *Now what? Speak to you when you get back to Brae.* The other was that I had two voice-mails. I dialled 121 and waited. The first was DS Peterson, crisply efficient: 'Hello, Cass, this is DS Peterson. Please give me a call to let me know when you'll be back in Brae, so that I can come and interview you.'

The second was from Jen, sounding breathlessly nervous. 'Cass? It's Jen here, Geordie's sister, we met on Papa Stour yesterday. Geordie said he'd asked you to come and keep me company. I don't want to put you out, I'm sure you have a dozen things to be doing. I . . . em, I'll try you again later.'

I sat in the warm changing room and thought about that. I wasn't sure whether she genuinely didn't want me, or just didn't want to be a nuisance. I listened to the message again, and still wasn't sure, then dialled the number. 'Jen? It's Cass.'

She made a soft 'Oh' sound, then rushed into speech. 'Oh, Cass, thanks for getting back to me. I hope you didn't think Geordie was taking a right liberty, but he's saying you're not doing anything, and I admit it would be fine to have company for this couple of days, if it's no' a nuisance to you.'

'It's no bother at all,' I assured her. 'You're giving me a last good sail before my mast has to come down. I'll be with you tomorrow morning.' Light southerly winds, the forecast had said. I could rig my striped geneker, and skim to Papa in a couple of hours. 'Which is your house?'

'The grey one on the upper side o' the road, by the Stofa. I'll keep an eye out, and come and take your lines.'

'Then I'll see you tomorrow.'

Gavin next. He'd be at home now, in his Inverness flat. He answered on the second ring, as if he'd been waiting for me to call, and his voice was teasing. 'Now what have you been up to?'

'Nothing to do with me,' I said. 'Are they going to send you up?'

'It's no' decided yet. I've got to finish several cases off here, and Freya's perfectly able to handle it on her own, so I'm being backup.'

I made a face at the white wall opposite me. 'Geordie asked me to go and keep the dead man's wife company, just these two days till he can get back. I said I would.'

I could hear he didn't like it, in the silence before he answered. 'You'll remember it's Freya's ship?'

'I'll remember. I'm not investigating anything, just being sociable for Jen.'

I could feel his scepticism in waves down the phone line, so I quickly diverted him to an account of how well Kitten and Maman had taken to each other. 'There's an iron paw in each of those tiny white mittens. She even sat on the table while we were eating.'

'Tell her not to get used to it.'

I smiled. 'Oh, she makes it very clear she's not on the table, as such, and definitely not cadging anything, just happening to be sitting on a tiny corner of this horizontal surface, to keep us company. Then you see the little nose quiver, and she starts oozing closer, and before I could object, Maman was giving her bits of rabbit from her plate. Maman! I was never allowed pets when I was small.'

'Your mother's a natural cat lover. Elegant, autocratic, used to the best . . .'

I laughed and agreed. 'We stopped at the cottage too. It's all ready for us – repainted, and cleared, and a double bed in the bedroom. We just need to get our stuff there. I rather like the idea of having a bookshelf. One where I can keep any books I want, I mean, instead of having to pass them on as soon as they're read. Anyway, I won't be able to go there for a day or two.'

'More like a week, if you're having fun getting under Freya's feet. That's okay. We can set everything up together, and raid the charity shops for old-fashioned china and glasses, if they've gone for rented-house plain white crockery. You could start collecting ornaments too.'

I snorted at that. 'They have to be dusted.'

'So they do. So I can't bring up my shinty trophies?'

'Do you have any?'

'No. I won a little cup for shooting once, but you wouldn't consider that anything to be proud of.'

'You won't have to keep a gun in the house, will you?' My stomach tightened at the thought.

He laughed. 'Cass, *mo chridhe*, you have no idea of the paper-work it takes for a policeman to get his hands on a gun. Definitely not.'

We chatted for a few minutes longer, and counted the days till we'd be together, then I put the phone away and had my shower with a light heart. I even found myself whistling as I made my way back along the pontoon. I gave the metal pulpit of *Khalida*'s bow a pat as I passed. 'Sailing tomorrow, lass,' I told her, and pottered happily for half an hour, rigging the geneker sheets in the silvery light, with help from Kitten pouncing on them, and hauling the sail in its bag up onto the deck. Cat returned while I was doing that and sat on the cabin roof to watch approvingly. He knew what preparing sails meant. While I was at it I rigged fenders and a fender board ready to put down, and then went below into the warm cabin. Pyjamas; into my berth. It was a bit of a wriggle and shuffle to get into my narrow quarter-berth, after I'd got used to the spacious open bunk of *Sørlandet*, but it felt secure, safe, familiar. Cat came to curl up in the crook of my neck and after a minute Kitten followed him, nosing his paws into a comfortable position for her to snuggle into his stomach. Their double purr had me asleep within seconds.

Chapter Twelve

Monday 21st October

Tide times Aith
HW 02.25 (1.8m); LW 08.25 (1.1m);
HW 14.48 (1.8m); LW 21.27 (1.0m)

Sunrise 07.58, moonset 16.07; sunset 17.39, moonrise 21.23.

Crescent moon

I'd set my mental alarm clock to wake me at seven. I wouldn't be going through Papa Sound, where the strong tides were, but I might as well go at a time which had the tide sweeping round St Magnus Bay with me rather than against me. I had plenty of leeway, according to my battered Tidal Atlas; it turned to go with me at four hours before HW Dover, and turned against me at four hours after. The westside tides were two hours earlier; that made it from low water here until two hours after high tide, and since low water was at half past eight, that gave me all morning to get there.

The forecast came on at 07.10. There was a gale far out in the Atlantic, but the fine weather would continue till midweek. My barometer had shifted another point downwards; a slow, steady drop, not the sudden plummet that meant you had to scurry for shelter. No change immediately, but poor weather on the way.

We left the berth at 08.00. Ah, it was good to be out in my

own boat again, where every sound, every movement, was familiar as my own heartbeat. Cat had his life-vest on, and was crouched in his usual place by the bulkhead, eyes bright; I'd put the lower cabin washboard in place, with the cat-flap closed, to keep Kitten below. She squawked for a bit, and jumped up onto the fiddled shelf to look at the water going past, bracing her little legs against the tilt of the ship, then jumped down again and curled up in my berth, apricot tail-tip flicking indignantly from time to time.

We motored directly into the wind for the length of the voe, and paused off Papa Little to hoist the sails, then turned into the Røna. Now the wind caught *Khalida*, swelling her red, white and blue geneker into a beautiful curve, and filling her mainsail. She surged forwards, and I sat back, one hand lightly on the tiller, enjoying the day. The cold in the air sharpened the colours, made everything closer: the cliffs of Muckle Roe, shining red in the morning sun, with every cleft given a sharp-edged outline by its shadow, the houses at Weathersta lit by a shaft of sunlight so that the nearest wall shone bleached-white. As the sun went behind the mottled clouds, the patches of light moved, turning the dark-chocolate heather to the dusky mauve of black grapes. The Atlantic swell took us as we came closer to Vementry, but it wasn't strong enough to knock the wind from *Khalida*'s sails; she went smoothly up over each crest and glided down its back.

We came between the guns of Vementry and the Roe light, and out into the ocean, just as I'd done in the *Swan* on Saturday. A distant throb of an engine, a white wash on the water, would be Geordie crossing back to West Burrafirth. A kittiwake hovered over us for a moment, then soared away, back to its cliffs. I set my course for Housa Voe, put the autopilot on and headed below to make a cup of drinking chocolate, fielding Kitten on the way. She gave a growl as I put her back below. 'You can come out when we get to Papa,' I promised her, and managed to get back out into the cockpit without her escaping.

The steam from my mug was warm on my face. I felt I was suffering from too many deaths on too many different islands: Moon on Foula and Kenny on Papa. No, it was the other way round. Kenny had died before Moon. If his body really had been the dark shape I'd seen, he'd been killed before seven, when I'd gone up on deck. I wondered what he'd done after he'd seen me back to the *Swan*, whether he'd gone home, or gone back to the West Voe to wait for the men in the motorboat to return. Jen would know if he'd gone home. That would help the police narrow down the time of death. The metereologists would know what time the frost had come down, so whether the ground under his body was frosted or not would be significant. I had a cold feeling in the pit of my stomach. I might have been the last person to see him – apart from his killer.

Then there was Moon, and the two figures I'd seen up on the Sneug.

Thinking about that reminded me of DS Peterson's call, which I still hadn't answered. I checked my mobile and was surprised to find a good signal. That gave me no excuse. I sighed and found her number.

She answered straight away, brisk and clear as if she was in the next room, but with a background rumble, as if she was in a car. 'Now, then, Cass. Thanks for getting back to me.'

'How can I help?'

'I need to get a statement from you about Saturday on Papa Stour. I know the *Swan* had sailed by the time the body was found, but given that he died during the night, any of your passengers could be involved, and of course this second death, if it wasn't just an accident, makes that even more likely.'

'I don't think it was an accident,' I said. 'There was somebody else on the hill with her.'

'Yes, PC Macdonald told me you'd seen someone. Can you give any description at all?'

'Not even male or female. The sun was going down behind them, so all I could see were the two silhouettes.'

'Okay, well, don't think about it just now. When I see you I'll try and jog your memory. When can we meet up? Are you in Brae now?'

'On my way to Papa.'

There was a short, ominous silence, which I didn't rush to fill. 'For any particular reason?'

'Geordie asked me to come and keep Jen company until he can get home on Wednesday.'

'Then I'll see you there later today. A charter boat is bringing us out. What time do you expect to arrive?'

'I should be moored up by eleven.' I hoped the charter boat wouldn't take up too much of the ferry pier. I could easily go to the old pier, but *Khalida* was much lower than *Swan*, so it would be a bit of a climb for getting on and off, maybe dangerous for Kitten. A gangplank to a good concrete pier would be far better.

'We'll be there at ten. I'll come along when I see you come in. How long are you staying?'

'Undecided.'

'Very well. I'll see you on Papa around eleven.' She rang off. I made a face at the phone and stowed it away again.

There was a lit-up grey shape on the horizon. I reached into the cabin for my spyglasses. Yes, it was the Coastguard tug at the Ve Skerries, keeping an eye on *Dorabella* until it was time to have another shot at getting her off the rocks. High water would be mid-afternoon. No doubt the lifeboat would bring her crew out and stand by.

I sailed onwards, enjoying the morning. I was just passing West Burrafirth when a bright yellow motorboat came charging past me: DS Peterson's charter boat. It went into Housa

Voe, and I followed. From here, the police presence on the isle was visible: a flimsy-looking white tent with two officers guarding it shoreward of the phone box cottage and a swarm of white-clad officers around it, one police car at the pier and another along at the school where we'd eaten after the concert. Presumably that was their Papa HQ. The motorboat was casting its lines off again, engines churning. I set the engine to idle, waiting for it to go out. It backed off with a roar and headed at speed for the voe entrance, then turned right. A minute later and I saw it between the stacks, heading for Foula.

I went forrard and got my fenders arranged, then putted gently in forwards of where it had been. I was just reversing *Khalida* to stop when Jen came walking briskly down the road, come to take my lines, as she'd promised. Behind her was a tall woman with a black suit and shining blond hair. DS Peterson. Freya. By the time they got to the pier, *Khalida* was lying alongside, and I passed Jen up the bowrope. 'Just make it fast, any old how. I'll do them properly in a minute.'

She wound it around the cleats, and I climbed ashore to bring the stern rope. I left it with enough slack to allow for the tide, and found a plank to use as a Cat and Kitten gangway. Cat came out to investigate it, sniffing with interest at this new place, Kitten at his heels. I turned to look at Jen properly.

'Thanks.'

She waved a hand to disclaim. The serene joy had gone from her face, leaving it troubled and vulnerable. 'Thanks for coming.' She glanced over her shoulder at DS Peterson, waiting ten metres away. 'DS Peterson was saying she wanted to talk to you, but you likely had an early start. I've soup and bannocks up at the house.'

'I'll get the interview over first.' I looked over her shoulder at DS Peterson. 'Aye aye.'

'Hello, Ms Lynch.'

'Go aboard.' I motioned her towards *Khalida*, and added to

Jen, 'I'll be over as soon as I can, if that's okay. You go ahead and eat.'

She shook her head. 'I don't have much appetite right now. I'll wait for you.' She gave a sudden sideways smile. 'It'll give you an excuse to keep it short.'

I smiled back, added 'See you later' and followed DS Peterson on board. She managed the drop neatly enough but I was pleased to notice she sat down on the damp place where I'd hauled in the extra length of one mooring line. She didn't comment. 'Would you prefer up here on deck or below?' I asked.

'Oh, up here's fine. It's a bonny day.'

'It is indeed,' I agreed.

She had a funny knack, DS Peterson, of turning wherever she was into her personal office. Even against the summer-faded woodwork and white fibreglass of *Khalida*'s cockpit seats she looked as if she just had to snap her fingers and a uniformed officer would appear with a computer. She was taller than me, Gavin's height, with straight, fair hair held at the nape of her neck by a clasp, and eyes the green of shallow sea in sunlight. Mermaid's eyes, I'd always thought, indifferent to human wants and failings. Every so often she tried to be chatty about furniture or flats, but I didn't believe it; she lived in a cavern under water, hidden behind waving kelp, and when she walked on land each step was a knife stab.

There was a short pause while she got out her laptop, then she raised her head and looked at me enquiringly.

'I think I have three things to tell you,' I said. 'First of all, Moon had an argument with her sister on Vementry.' I went back to Saturday morning, and did my best to recall the exact words of the quarrel by the guns.

'So,' DS Peterson said, 'to sum up: Moon was accusing her uncle, Stevie, of taking videos of them naked when they were children, and Kirsten was denying it all. Did you get the

124

impression Moon had taken it as far as making a statement to the police, or to a lawyer?'

I nodded. 'She said she'd gone as far as going to a lawyer about it, and then wasn't sure enough to go on.'

'Wasn't sure she wanted to go to court over it?'

'Wasn't sure enough it had happened against Kirsten saying it hadn't. She was a strange kind of crater. There was something childish about her.'

'She didn't say which solicitor?'

I began to shake my head, then remembered Isla's awkwardness in the school on Saturday evening. 'Geordie's wife, Isla, she works to a solicitor in town, and it was obvious she'd recognised Moon, and wanted to avoid her.'

'I'll find out who she works for. Perhaps Moon told him what it was about before she backed out. And then Moon remembered the other girl, Jen.' I nodded. 'And met her again here on Papa.'

'Yes.'

'Did Jen recognise Moon?'

'She remembered her name, and that her big sister – Sky, Kirsten was called then – used to babysit her.'

A spasm of distaste crossed DS Peterson's face. For a moment she was human after all. 'Skywalker, I ask you, and Moondancer.' Her green eyes flicked up to mine. 'Their mother, Amitola, she was christened Agnes.' She shook her head and glanced back at her laptop. 'What impression did you get of how Jen reacted to Moon bringing up their childhood? I understand it is just an impression.'

I didn't like discussing Jen with DS Peterson. 'She was troubled by it, just for a moment. She said it had been a bad time for them. But then she took a deep breath and her face smoothed out again. She'd put it behind her.'

'Jen's mother took the father to court for assault. Thirty years ago. He got off without a prison sentence, but there was a lot of local feeling about it.' She went into dialect. '"It's one thing to gie the wife a slap when she's out o' line, but to burn her wi' a cigarette, na."'

I stared at her. She shrugged. 'My mam's that age, and from Lerwick. She remembered it all. She said Renwick said his wife was mad, always forgetting things and arguing. He insisted that she'd done the burns herself, just to spite him, to get him into trouble. Naturally nobody believed him. It was a line of burns right down her arm. He moved away from Shetland, and nobody heard more of him. It seems he changed his name from Paul Renwick to Paul Roberts, and took up a teaching post in Leeds. I'll re-check the trial records but I'm pretty sure there was no mention of child abuse.' She sighed. 'But then, thirty years ago, nobody had heard of child abuse.' She paused for a moment, thinking, then looked back at me. 'Second thing.'

'Has anyone mentioned Moon's accident in the caves?'

Her blond head jerked upwards. 'No.' Her fingers returned to the keyboard and rattled furiously as I described how Moon had fallen out of the RIB. 'She was between Stevie and Kirsten, with Amitola opposite her. It was black dark in the boat. I thought I felt a movement, but I didn't see anything.'

'But Kirsten and Stevie were the ones with the best opportunity.'

I nodded. 'And Kirsten said something about it being a warning. It sounded flippant, but it might have been meant more seriously.'

'Moon herself didn't give any clues as to who?'

'No. Once the shock was over, she didn't seem bothered. She just said she hadn't been holding on properly.'

'Who's your guess?'

I spread my hands. 'Amitola's least likely. Impossible, even. She and I were in the bows, shining the torches forward. I wasn't looking at her, I was focused on where we were going, but I don't think she could have wedged the torch and turned around in the boat to push Moon without me seeing her, or feeling the movement. Kirsten and Stevie are both possibles. Stevie was beside her, and Kirsten opposite.'

'And your money's on . . . ?'

'Kirsten,' I said positively. 'She just had to lean over fast and shove with both hands on Moon's chest, or lift one foot and tip her backwards. Stevie would have had to turn almost right around to grab her and push her off from an awkwkard angle.' I spread my hands. 'But I don't have anything like evidence either way.'

'Understood. So. Third thing. This second person on the hill with Moon on Foula. Imagine yourself back there, start by telling me where you were, and what you were doing, and then we'll move on to what you actually saw.'

It was a method she'd used on me before, and I did my best, but at the end of fifteen minutes we were still no wiser. I'd seen two dark figures backlit by the sun, both wearing jackets and trousers, too far to see length of hair or details of walk. I only knew that there had been another person.

'You're certain? Not a trick of the light? The sun was in your eyes. A brief double vision?'

I shook my head. 'No, I'm certain. There was somebody else up there with her.'

'That's very interesting,' DS Peterson said, closing her laptop. Her green eyes met mine. 'Because we took statements from the three other passengers yesterday evening. Amitola's least likely to be the person you saw. She went along southwards, away from the Sneug, and sat on the shore, thinking, she said. She was worried about Moon. Moon had been acting oddly recently, she said, but when I pressed her for details she got too upset and I had to stop.'

'She was blaming herself for not having listened to her about Stevie, or for having let Kirsten persuade her it was all nonsense.'

'Do you have any evidence that she knew about it?'

I shook my head. 'But after Moon went in the water, she fussed as if Moon was a child, and then when she didn't come back, on Foula, she was more worried than Kirsten or Stevie. And she said to Kirsten, after the body was found, that they should have listened to her.'

'But she didn't actually mention the alleged child abuse to you?'

'No,' I conceded. 'She just said something about her being imaginative, and easily influenced.'

'A woman in one of the houses saw Amitola go down the beach and sit down, but didn't particularly notice her after that.' She went into dialect again. '"She couldna been there, she coulda no' been." Magnie, your skipper, saw her coming back along the road ahead of him, so she'd have had to move very fast to get up the Sneug from there and down again before him, and she'd have been lucky not to have been seen coming down. Kirsten said she wanted to climb the Sneug but changed her mind when she saw how steep it was, and how wet the grass was – slippery. That was why Moon went up alone.'

'Yes,' I agreed, 'it was Kirsten who said she wanted to climb. She'd remember that we heard her. I walked along the road behind them, and there was a prickly feeling. I wonder if Moon took the chance to start hassling her about supporting her statement again, and that's why Kirsten chickened out of climbing. She'd already seen how steep and high it was from the sea. Maybe even she'd suggested climbing it to get away from Moon, thinking that Moon wouldn't.'

'Maybe – though that's all more conjecture.'

'I don't remember the grass being that wet, but it was a misty morning. I'd have thought it would be dry by then.'

DS Peterson shrugged. 'That's what Kirsten said. She most certainly didn't mention videos, or regression therapy or recovered memories. Or Moon falling into the water in a cave.

She insisted that Moon was fine as they walked along, not at all upset. According to her everything was all perfectly normal. The grass was wet and Moon must have slipped.'

She paused and glanced at her notes. 'Stevie said he'd climbed the Noup. A man from the house at Mornington which looks along the "burn o da Daal" saw a black-headed body going along the valley between the Noup and the Sneug – a man, he thought, but he couldn't swear to that, with aabody dressing alike these days – he didn't see him on the Noup, but he wasn't looking. Times? No idea.'

'They don't do time on Foula. So any of the three of them could have done it,' I said, thinking it through. 'Kirsten said she didn't go up, but she could have, after all. If Moon was wanting to hassle her, it's not likely she'd have gone off up the Sneug while Kirsten stayed behind. Either Stevie or Amitola could have gone along the valley between the Noup and the Sneug and climbed up the back of it. Except that they both thought she was with Kirsten. They wouldn't have expected to get her alone. So Kirsten's the most likely one.'

'For both incidents.' She raised her head from the laptop. 'Any idea of motive?'

'She's ambitious. She wants to lead the council, and a scandal would stop her doing it. But whether that's sufficient motive to actually kill her sister . . .'

DS Peterson nodded in the direction of Foula. 'We'll see what my officers can bring back by way of footprints.' She tapped a last few notes into her laptop, then closed it and looked across at me. 'Don't forget why I'm here. Do we have one case or two? All you've told me about Moon's case against Stevie, that brings Jen into it. Now what I need to figure out is whether that links up with Kenny Wishart's death.'

She rose. 'Jen's waiting for you, and I still have a couple of houses to go to. I'll talk to you about that later.'

IV
A Warm Night

Chapter Thirteen

It was only a short walk to Jen's house. I hadn't seen it properly in the dark on Saturday evening, but I remembered which one it was, the one above the road whose lit windows had been masked by branches. This garden hadn't yet abandoned summer. The rugosa leaves were variegated with cadmium yellow, and waxy orange-red hips shone out as if they'd been polished, but within their shelter were the last white marguerites, and bedding plants still unspoiled by the frost: rose snapdragons, velvety purple pansies, dahlias flaunting spiked yellow heads. In one corner, a great clump of Shetland delphinium shone gentian-blue above shiny green leaves that were just starting to turn mahogany red at the tips.

'You're a gardener,' I said.

Jen nodded. 'Yea, I aye spend time outside. I just like seeing things grow.' She spoke with an effort, as if her cherished garden had lost all importance with this sudden blow. She had to rally, for the baby's sake.

'My friend Inga told me that it was the only thing she could do outside while her bairns were peerie. Once they were in bed she had to be within earshot of the house.'

Her eyes brightened. Her hand curved around her stomach, as it had done on Saturday evening. 'Of course. And by next summer he'll be big enough to sit in a playpen outdoors on bonny days.'

'The summer after that he'll be a holy terror, like my pal Inga's Peerie Charlie. I babysit him. Filled with energy, and remembering every word I ever said to his advantage.'

She smiled properly at that. 'You don't have children yourself yet?'

'Gavin and I are only just moving in together.'

We'd reached the front door. The house had been a traditional two-storey crofthouse with upstairs dormer windows, and the porch extended out to make a bathroom and lobby, like the Ladie, but this one had also been lengthened to the side, with an extra door in the middle of the new piece, and it was this door that Jen opened. 'Come in, take a seat.'

It was a light, bright room, a cross between indoors and conservatory, with bamboo chairs with flowered cushions. The house wall had been opened to make the kitchen part of the space; the door and front windows looked out over Housa Voe to the stacks beyond, with Sandness misty in the distance. A quick glance showed my *Khalida* still in her place. I could just make out the grey blob of Cat still sitting on the pier. The side windows faced down towards the kirk, over a shed and an enclosure made of tarred logs, with one end open.

'What's that?' I asked.

'That's the Stofa,' Jen said. 'Did you get a look at it on Saturday?'

'No, but Geordie told us the story as we passed.'

Jen smiled. 'Did he tell you that Ragnhild spat in Thorvald's face, and called him a Judas?'

I shook my head. 'He was over polite to mention spitting in front of paying passengers. Good for her!'

'They weren't afraid, those Viking women. Like the suffragists back a century ago, the graduates who took the University to court.' She looked up at me and smiled, that half shamefaced smile of a woman who's spending good housework time on studying. 'I'm doing an OU degree on the fight for the vote. Studying at home, like women did before they were admitted to University. That wasn't until 1889 in Scotland. Before that, well, St Andrews University ran a degree course for women, the LLA – Ladies Literate in Arts. They sat the same papers as men, and here in Shetland it was mostly done by primary school teachers, to qualify them for secondary teaching.' She paused, out of breath, and waved the digression away. 'This court case, it was 1906. See, there were two Scottish University MPs, elected by "persons" who had graduated, that was what the rules said, "persons", so Elsie Inglis and Chrystal Macmillan asked for their voting papers.' She saw on my face that I'd never heard of either of them, and smiled. 'Elsie Inglis, Dr Inglis, she was one of the first women doctors in Scotland, and ran her own hospital in Edinburgh. Have you never come across her? When World War I began, she offered the war office a fully-staffed front-line hospital, with doctors, nurses, orderlies and ambulances. Their representative said, "My good lady, go home and be still." So she went to the women's suffrage society instead, and founded the Scottish Women's Hospital. She went to Serbia and Romania, and she and her unit were the last across the Danube when the Germans marched in.'

'Wow!' I said. 'And the other one, what did you call her, Macmillan?'

'Macmillan had a first-class Honours in Maths and Philosophy. When the University said no, they took them to the Court of Sessions, and then to the House of Lords. Chrystal Macmillan pleaded their case there. The newspapers nicknamed her "the modern Portia". It was mad!' Jen made a face, laughing now. 'Macmillan was considered fit to conduct a case in front of the highest court in the land, but not fit to vote.' She nodded across at a tall open desk, like an overbed trolley. It was covered with papers. 'I'm reading the transcript right now.'

'I take it she didn't win.'

'The Lords ruled that in the context of the vote, "person" meant male, only. Christina Jamieson – she was our leading suffrage campaigner here in Shetland, she grew up over in Sandness.' Jen nodded towards the window. 'That house just below the school. Cruister. Her father was the teacher there. Well, she had a good comment about it – "If you call a woman a person, you use unparliamentary language."' She cut herself short. 'Don't let me bore you about it! Do give me your coat, and sit down.'

She took my jacket away into the house. I sat down at the table and looked around. There was an armchair with an extending footrest by the window, and a tapestry frame on a stand beside it, a pattern in swirls of blues and greens. The desk she'd indicated had an open A4 file on it, with narrow-lined paper filled with slanted writing. There were a couple of academic-looking tomes beside it. The one on top was *A Guid Cause: the women's suffrage movement in Scotland*, with an old photograph of a little girl bagpiper wearing a 'Votes for Women' sash.

A clutch of framed photos were hung on the wall: Jen and Kenny's wedding in the centre, and Geordie and Isla's, then Geordie's children at various ages clustered around them. The sun glinted rainbows off a collection of cut-glass animals on a corner shelf. I was glad I'd left Cat and Kitten at the boat; Kitten, I'd discovered, took any small object on a table as a personal challenge, working it forward with one delicate paw, hooking it over the fiddle, and watching with interest as it plummeted floorwards.

'There,' Jen said, coming back with a loaded bread plate in each hand. 'Now, my visitors polished off a good bit of it, but I still have a few bannocks and fancies left over from Saturday night's do.' She set them down on the table in front of me. 'The soup's lentil, is that fine for you?'

'Grand,' I said.

She said a formal grace, thanking the Lord for the food, and thanking me for coming. The soup smelt very good, and the bannocks looked excellent. I put a slice of cheese on one and tucked in.

Opposite me, Jen took a couple of spoonfuls of soup with an effort, then laid her spoon down. 'You need to eat,' I said gently. I put a slice of cheese on the other half of my bannock, cut it in halves again and passed it to her. 'Your baby needs that protein. Go on. Shall I make a cup of tea to help wash it down?'

She half rose. 'I'll get it.'

'You sit and eat.' I remembered that women could be very territorial about their kitchens. 'If you don't mind me ferreting about.'

She shook her head. 'No, go on. Peppermint tea for me, please. It's all by the kettle, and the milk's in the fridge.'

She began eating the bannock with more determination than enthusiasm, and I made the tea and brought her mug over to her. 'So,' I said, 'tell me about this woman who called her landlord a Judas. What happened to her?'

'Ah, well, we dinna ken that. Why would they record the history of a woman? We ken about him, though. The other male landlords rallied round to support him.' She made a face. 'Naturally. So the Ting, the Parliament, found for him.'

'Not a surprise.' I wondered briefly how Moon's court case might have fared in these times; if justice was more even-handed, or if her hippy name and colourful dress against Stevie's insurance man's suit would still have told against her.

Now Jen had got interested in the story, she was eating without thinking about it. 'He got granted Papa Stour by King Haakon, and married one of his relatives. He had a son, he was a Tirval too, and it was him that marooned his daughter on the Maiden Stack to stop her running away with her lover.'

'I hope she climbed down and escaped.'

'She did — well, the tradition is that he climbed up and

rescued her, but she'd still have had to have got down somehow. Tirval went after them and brought the man back to Papa Stour. He convened a holmgang, a fight to the death, and killed him. That was in the circle of stones up on the hill there. He wanted more vengeance though, so he set sail with all his sons to the place they'd been given refuge, the girl and her lover, to punish the folk there, and their ship was wrecked on a skerry just south of Egilsay. The rocks are still known as Turvald's Head.' She smiled. 'And so Sir Tirval's daughter Herdis inherited the island. The Vikings had no problems with women inheriting.'

'Good,' I said. 'Nor with them fighting, apparently.'

She raised her head. 'Oh?'

'It was an article I read. Apparently even as late as the seventies, when they were excavating, the rule was weapons equalled male grave, spindle wheels equalled female, even when the archaeologists said the bones with the weapons looked female – but of course they couldn't possibly be. Everyone knew women didn't fight.'

'Apart from the Amazons,' Jen said. 'And the women who dressed as men to go with their men into battle. The Russian army had women serving in World War I.'

'Really?'

'Oh, yes, and there was Flora Sandes, in the Serbian army. I've been reading about her too. She was one of the many women who formed units to go as nurses, then when the Germans advanced, they didn't have the hospitals any more, and she enlisted in the army. She ended up a captain.' She held up her hand. 'I'm off again. I'm sorry. I've just got so absorbed in it all. So what about the women warrior Vikings?'

'Oh, well, someone decided to test the bones properly. Surprise, the ones that looked female actually were. Women warriors.'

'The idea of the Valkyries had to come from somewhere.'

She'd eaten all of that bannock now, and most of the soup, and she was well through her cup of tea. Her cheeks were regaining some colour, and her eyes were brighter. Then a tall shadow crossed the light window, and there was a knock on the door. Jen and I looked at each other in startled surmise, and I rose, just as Jen was struggling to her feet.

The door opened before I could get to it, and Paul Roberts walked in.

Roberts looked every inch the retired teacher in a dark suit and ironed white shirt. He'd obviously stopped to comb his hair before he came in, for it was neatly parted to give the fringe an upside down V immediately above his nose. He called the traditional greeting as he came through the door, 'Aye aye, anybody home?' and came forward to Jen, one hand out. He was smiling that smooth smile with no teeth showing, a headmaster ready to placate an anxious parent.

'I saw your brother go off in the motorboat this morning, so I thought I'd come up to see how you're managing, and if there was anything I could do to help.'

Jen shook his hand, then waved him to a chair. 'That's awful good o' you. Sit you down.' She paused a moment, looking at him uncertainly. 'You're Paul Roberts, aren't you, Tammie's tenant that arrived on Saturday? Can I make you a cup of tea? Do you ken Cass?'

'We met on Saturday,' I said. 'Bide still, Jen, I'll make the tea.' I looked across at Paul. 'Milk, sugar?'

'Just milk.' He dropped into the seat I'd left without a by-your-leave. 'I came to offer my condolences, and to see if there was anything I can do.'

Jen shook her head. 'You're very kind, thanks to you, but I have Cass here wi' me eenoo, and me brother Geordie'll be home on Wednesday morning, and Mam.'

Out of the corner of my eye I saw him lean forward. 'Jen,

you don't ken who I am, do you?' There was a touch of offence in his voice. 'Do you really no' recognise me?'

I came out of the kitchen like a shot at that, eyes fixed anxiously on Jen. Her face had gone white. 'Paul Roberts?' She shook her head blankly at the name, but one hand went up to her breast, as if her heart was thumping. Her voice sounded as if she was struggling for breath. 'I dinna ken a Paul Roberts. I've never heard that name.'

'Paul Renwick. You ken you do ken me, really.'

I could see the pulse in her neck racing. Red flushed up into her face. 'You're never my father?'

He nodded, and reached across the table to lay his hand on hers. 'Come home to get to know you again – to help you through this.'

She drew her hand back as if his touch had burnt her. 'You're really my father?'

He nodded and leaned back again, confident now. 'I'm surprised you don't ken me. I'm no' changed that much.'

The hand at Jen's breast tightened. She was silent for a moment, then spoke in a harsh voice. 'I'm no' laid eyes upon you since I was eight. Why would you expect me to remember you?'

He hadn't expected that. His voice was smooth as pouring cream. 'Why, we were great pals, you and I. I'd never have expected you to have forgotten your daddy.'

Jen rose abruptly and staggered as if she'd turned giddy. I caught hold of her arm and steadied her. 'I need to talk to my mother about this. About you turning up out of the blue like this. I need to ask her – ' Her voice trailed off. I put my arm around her waist and looked Paul Roberts straight in the eyes.

'Paul, this has been a shock for Jen. I think she needs to lie down.'

He was still smiling that smooth smile. 'A surprise, I hope, rather than a shock. You help her to bed, and I'll make a cup of tea and bring it to her.'

I felt Jen recoil. Her 'no' was barely audible. I drew myself up to my unimpressive five foot two, thought of myself as *Sørlandet*'s second mate, and spoke with all the authority I could muster. 'I think you should leave now. Jen will invite you back when she's had a chance to talk to her family.'

Now he really was black-affronted. The colour rose in his cheeks, and he opened his mouth. I tilted my chin towards the door, and kept my eyes locked on his. 'If you don't mind.'

He minded a lot, but he gave another smile and tried to make it his own choice. 'Well, I'll leave you now, Jen, since you're in the capable hands of your friend, but I'll be back to see how you are soon.' Jen pressed back against me as he came over to us, and gave her a kiss on the cheek. 'I'm very glad to see you again, little princess.'

The door closed behind him. Jen let go of my arm and ran across to turn the key in the lock. Then she turned back to me, and rubbed her cheek angrily.

'I think you should have that lie down,' I said. 'I'll make another cup of tea. Do you have camomile?'

She nodded. Suddenly she collapsed into her chair, as if all her strength was gone. She was shuddering as if she was cold. A hot water bottle too, I thought, and a spoonful or two of honey in her tea. I helped her stand again, and got her through to the bedroom. Someone had tidied up since yesterday, Ruby maybe, for there was no sign of Kenny's presence there, no pyjamas or slippers ready to put on, no half-read copies of *Sea Angling* or *Farmers' Weekly* at what had been his side of the bed, and only one set of pillows in the middle.

Jen stopped dead in the doorway. 'No, I can't lie down. I don't feel safe here. He said he'd come back. Let's go somewhere else, somewhere he won't expect. Let's go to Uncle's.'

'Well, if you want ... Who is Uncle, and where does he live?'

'The cottage above the pier, right there. Your cats could

141

come too, he likes animals. He has a cat of his own, a stripey that follows him everywhere, and three goats.'

Her mother had come from Papa. 'Your mother's brother?'

She shook her head, impatient to get away. 'Oh, no, he's everyone's uncle. He'll be yours too, once you see him. Let's, do let's.'

I didn't want to argue against her sudden determination. She gestured down towards the pier. 'It's the white cottage on the headland there.'

'Okay,' I said.

Jen collected her handbag, and locked up the house, and we walked slowly back along the road. She was still white with shock, and I felt uneasy. There was no reason why Paul Roberts should interfere with my *Khalida*, but I wished I'd locked her up. Besides, much as I'd taken against him, unless we had two murderers, which was surely unlikely, he wasn't responsible for Kenny's death, for he couldn't have been on Foula to kill Moon.

I felt a jolt run through me at the thought. Who said he couldn't have been? Goodness sake, Cass, I scolded myself, you're thinking like a landsman already. Paul Roberts had grown up in Shetland. I had no doubt he'd be able to handle a boat. He could well have one. We'd spent time going around the back of the cliffs of Foula. If he'd come directly from Papa in a fast RIB he could easily have come into the pier before us. Using DS Peterson's technique, I tried to remember what boats I'd seen there. I'd been on rope and fender duty as Magnie had edged her in. I imagined the feel of the rope in my hands. I'd been standing just forward of the capstan. I saw the pier coming closer, remembered myself judging the distance ready to jump. Yes, there had been a boat there, tucked into the shore, a black RIB with an orange steering column, tied well forward to leave the pier free for larger boats – or to be less noticeable. It had left just before I'd got back to the *Swan* – because the owner had finished his business on Foula, or because he didn't want to be seen?

We'd come to the pier now. Jen went on ahead to prepare Uncle while I ran down to lock up my cabin hatch. Cat and Kitten were dozing in the cockpit, Kitten a small gingery lump snuggled into Cat's creamy belly. They lifted their heads as I came on board, then Cat rose and stretched. 'We're invited to tea, guys,' I said. 'Come on.' I locked up the cabin hatch and stood for a moment, looking around.

Yes, there was a black RIB with an orange steering column floating gently at the small jetty. There were plenty of them about, of course, though they weren't quite as common as grey ones, but it could be the one I'd seen on Foula.

I'd just reached the pierhead, Cat at my heels and Kitten in my arms, purring loudly at being carried, when my phone pinged in my pocket. It was a text from Gavin. *Moon's death not accidental. Sending me up tomorrow. Is there handy key for cottage? xxx*

My heart gave a leap. I wouldn't see him today, but maybe tomorrow. I texted back, *Wonderful news. On hook on back of door in garden shed xxx* and went on with a springier step.

Chapter Fourteen

There was a wonderful smell of fresh baking wafting from Uncle's open door. He had a traditional cottage with a stone-walled area in front that held the afternoon warmth. It was jumbled with flowers spilling out of every sort of container: a rusty kettle, a cracked china tureen, a catering-size tin. There was a shed made from a black-tarred upturned boat, and the last orange montbretia curved over smooth white stones from the beach. Beyond the stone wall, three goats raised white-blazed noses to stare at me with yellow eyes, and beyond them the bay was spread open, with the sun just starting to catch the stacks on the other side and light the hills of Sandness and West Burrafirth beyond.

Kitten squeaked and wriggled to be set down. I deposited her, and called out 'Hello!' as I came in through the porch and into the kitchen.

Jen was setting the table, and Uncle turned from the Rayburn and came over to meet me. I recognised him straight away: the old man who'd been watching Paul Roberts as if he was trying to remember where he knew him from. I saw at once why Jen knew she would be safe here. He radiated safety and security, like a friendly magician in a fairy tale, with twinkly dark eyes and rosy cheeks. He was still wearing the black skull-cap I'd noticed in the school after the concert, along with a chef's striped apron. He held out his hand, formally. 'I'm Uncle. Cass, I'm pleased to meet you.'

His English was perfect, but there was no doubt about his nationality, German or Austrian. He was old enough to have been a child refugee from World War II.

He gave me a quick look. 'You are wondering how I came to be on Papa, and what I am doing here. All in good time. A cup of coffee first. Come into the snug.'

The snug was the other downstairs room, glowing with red textiles: a woven wall hanging, an embroidered rug on one couch and a crocheted one on the other, a red Persian carpet, cushions in red and gold sari material. The little black stove was already lit. I felt my face flushing with the warmth. Cat strolled straight to pole position in front of the fire; Kitten followed him, sneezing at the heat.

Uncle came through with coffee cups and the pot on a tray, and dealt out little black French café coffees all round, then sat down on the couch opposite us. He nodded at me. 'Jen has explained me, no?'

'No.'

'Then I will explain myself.' The *w* came out slightly emphatic, as if he had been carefully taught not to let it sound like a Germanic *v*. I leaned back on the couch, eyes half-closed, staring at the flickering orange in the fire and listening. 'I am Uncle. My whole name, oh, I have not used it for many years, since I retired here to keep goats and watch birds. Before that, I was a doctor in Leeds, and before that I came from Bonn with the *kindertransport* in the early years of the war. I was out playing in our garden one day. I was not yet at school even. I heard shouting, and the noise of things being broken. I was frightened, and I hid. When I came out my parents were gone and our house ransacked. They had been sent as slave labour in the east. A neighbour took me in and smuggled me out of the country. It probably took all the savings he had. You see, I have experienced the worst and the best together, early in life. That is the key to my character, if you need one. Nothing now surprises me. That is why they came here to talk.'

My eyes flew up to his face. He nodded. 'The people of the island. Betty, and Geordie, and Tammie, and Kenny. This was on Saturday night. They wanted to talk, you see, but not in front of visitors, about what could be done about this man who had come to disturb our peace. I have already told this to the police officer but I will tell it again to you.'

He had a vivid way of speaking which recreated the scene for me. They'd arrived at Uncle's well after ten. They'd met here because Kenny was adamant that Jen shouldn't be told unless it was impossible to make Roberts leave again, and Geordie felt the same about his children. This was a grandparent they'd never known and didn't need. He wasn't coming back into their lives.

They'd sat in this room: Geordie and Betty on the couch Jen and I were sitting on, Kenny and Tammie opposite, and Uncle on the wooden rocking chair in the corner.

'We have to get rid o' him,' Betty had insisted. 'Leopards dinna change their spots. He's a violent man, a dangerous man, and he's no' coming back into our family.'

'Can you give him notice to quit?' Kenny asked Tammie.

Tammie shook his head gloomily. 'There're laws about that. I looked them up before I came. If someen's paying their rent you can only get them out if you're planning to sell the property or do major repairs, or if you or a relative o' yours is planning to bide in it. He's paid me six months' rent, and the law says he's entitled to stay.'

'You don't have someen, a niece or nephew who could say they wanted to spend the winter on Papa?'

'No' convincingly,' Tammie said. 'I tried to think o' someen, but nobody that would come in the winter. If it had been summer, now . . .'

'Summer's too late,' Betty said. 'We want him gone now.'

'It has to pass a court if need be,' Tammie said apologetically. 'I wish I'd kent . . . but, well, his letter seemed fine, and his references from the bank manager and the minister checked out.' His

146

face darkened. 'If I'd kent who he was he'd never have come across the briggistane.'

'A false name!' Kenny said. 'Does that no' show malicious intent?'

Tammie shook his head. 'We canna just assume he's up to no good.'

Silence fell on the room then, except for the crackling of driftwood in the stove. Then Geordie swore, and thumped his fist on the arm of the sofa. 'No way o' getting him out!'

'He would fight too,' Betty'd said. 'He aye enjoyed a lawsuit. It gave him his chance to look important in front o' the Sheriff. He only took on ones he was sure he'd win.'

Tammie shook his head. 'The only possible might be if he "acts in an antisocial manner." The book o' rules said that was anything which caused another person alarm or distress or was a nuisance or harrassment. I could go to the police to have him evicted then.'

'But to do that,' Kenny said, 'he has to have caused the nuisance first.'

'Can we no' go to the police now,' Betty said, 'and explain the situation? He's planning to cause us harm. He's come here deliberately, now, under a false name so we wouldna ken it was him, when we were all free o' him, and when Jen was having her bairn. It'll cause her distress. Can we no' take out an order against him to stop him doing it?'

'It would be worth a try,' Kenny said. 'Can you ask Isla about that, Geordie? She might ken, from working in a lawyer's office an aa.'

'I'll get her to ask her boss,' Geordie said.

'I don't suppose,' Tammie said, 'that it might do any good for you just to geng to him and say you dinna want him here? I'll gladly return him his rent if he wants to leave.'

Betty had snorted at that. 'No' he. He's laid all his plans cleverly, coming back like that without any o' us kenning who he was. He's no' just going to give up for the asking. And he has a right to see his grandchildren. There was a case about it in the courts. I mind it. The mother wouldn't let her parents see them, and they got a judgement saying she had to. He'll ken aa aboot that, trust him. I can see him going down that route if he was thwarted.'

Geordie's jaw set. 'He's no' coming near my bairns. I'll fight any court in the land for that.'

'He's no' coming near Jen,' Kenny said.

They discussed it all for a bit more, Uncle said, but they could all see there was nothing to be done. Paul Roberts was here legitimately, he couldn't be evicted and he wasn't likely to take a request to leave peaceably. The meeting broke up gloomily about midnight. Tammie, Geordie and Betty went off together along the grassy path to Betty's house, and Kenny set off up on the road.

'So that explains how he came to see the torches,' I said. 'He must have seen Paul Roberts and the other one moving on the road, and wondered what they were up to. He went up the hill above the cottage here to watch them, and then I arrived too.' I remembered, as I explained that night to Uncle and Jen, that I hadn't yet told DS Peterson about it. I would need to do that. 'I met Kenny up on the hill,' I finished, 'and he saw me back to the *Swan*. I don't know what he did then.'

Uncle was silent for a moment, considering this. 'So Kenny might have followed the Roberts man back to his house? That explains what he was doing there.'

I looked at Jen. 'Tell me about how your mother came to find his body,' I suggested.

Jen set her cup down. Her face was pale but determined. 'Yes,' she said, 'I'll tell you.'

She'd slept heavily, she said, and not woken till nine. She wasn't surprised that Kenny wasn't there, because he would leave her to sleep, these days, go out and feed the dogs, have a general check around, and then come back and bring her a cup of tea in bed. She'd had a late night too, chatting with the friends who'd come over for the music evening, so she thought he'd just left her to a lie-in. When she got up she'd seen us through the gap between the Maiden Stack and the far side of Housa Voe, steaming off towards Foula, a bonny sight with the brown mainsail up. There was no sign of life from her friends, so she had a shower, but once that was done and Kenny still hadn't come back, she began to be – not anxious, exactly, but wondering if he'd found a ewe in trouble, stuck on its back in a ditch, and was having difficulty freeing it. When she was dressed she went out to look around, but there was no sign of him, and all was quiet down below the house: the kitchen light was on in Geordie's, and she could see Isla moving about inside; there was a trickle of blue smoke from Betty's chimney, and from Tammie and Ruby's at Hurdiback; their back door was open, with Tammie on the briggistane, smoking his pipe. There was no sign of life in the phone box house next door to them.

Then she saw Betty, pinny, rubber boots and headscarf on, coming out of her door and heading towards the phone box house. There was something odd enough about the way she was moving that drew Jen's attention: something furtive in the way she was glancing around her, as if she didn't want to be seen, yet a determination about the way she was walking. She moved like that almost all the way to Hurdiback, and then disappeared behind the sheds, appeared again briefly in the gap between sheds and house and disappeared again. Jen hesitated, wondering. What was she doing, that she should be so uneasy about it? She had a cold feeling inside about that, and she wished Kenny was here. She went along the front of the house and stood at the north gable, the highest point, where she could see over the roofs. Betty hadn't gone into Hurdiback, but turned seawards, and was making for a lying-down moorit sheep. She'd almost reached it when she gave a cry that reached Jen as a thin wail borne on the wind, and dropped like a stone. In his back door, Tammie lifted his head, but the house masked what was happening below it. He kept listening for a moment, then knocked out his pipe and went back indoors.

Jen woke out of her trance then. She leapt for the car and turned the key with shaking fingers. In less than two minutes she was at Isla's, bursting in the door. 'I think Mam's had some kind of attack, down below Hurdiback.'

Isla left her breakfast half-eaten on the table, and shouted to the children that she was just going out. They drove together along the half–mile of road to the turn-off, too worried to talk, and jolted down to Hurdiback, where they found Tammie and Ruby already coming out of their door. Jen and Isla burst together out of the car and ran to the two still figures on the grass. It was only once she'd reached Betty that Jen realised the other shape was Kenny, lying there in last night's clothes with the sun reddening his face. She gave a howl like an animal and dived to him, calling his name. She knew the moment she touched him that he was dead.

'His face was stiff, his jaw, and cold, so cold. I didn't know what to do then. I think I just kept calling his name, and crying, and shaking his shoulder, as if that would do any good. Isla kept her head though, she called me to help her with Mam.'

Betty was alive. Her face was an awful blue colour and her heartbeat was all over the place, but she was still breathing. Isla stayed with her while Ruby hurried into the house to grab a blanket from the bed. The Roberts man had come out by now to see what was wrong, and Tammie ordered him away roughly: 'We're no' needing you here.'

'I thought it was anxiety over Mam,' Jen said, 'that made him sound so rude.' She nodded to herself. 'I understand now.'

Betty came around then, and Isla and Tammie made a chair

of their hands and carried her to her house, with Jen following. They supported her over the briggistane and into her bedroom. 'Kenny!' she said, and Isla hushed her straight off.

'Don't even think about it. Just concentrate on breathing steadily. Let's get you lying down.'

Isla helped Betty into bed while Jen got tea and a hot water bottle, then Isla dialled 999 and asked for the coastguard.

'We were lucky. The lifeboat was all set to come out to the trawler for high water, to stand by while the tug tried to get it off, and when I got through to NHS 24 they told us they'd send a doctor straight to Aith, to come out with it. I was that relieved that help was coming as soon as could be that it was only after she'd put the phone down that we realised she'd never mentioned Kenny.'

She'd broken down then. 'Hysterics,' she said briefly, her face reddening. 'Once Mam was safe, then Kenny, lying there, it just rushed over me in a flood. I couldn't bear it.'

His body was to go home, she'd insisted. Isla had been dubious, but Tammie had seen it as right and proper that the man should be brought home to his own house, and laid out decently, and he'd called one of Isla's visitors to help him. They'd told her she was to bide there with her Mam and keep her calm, focus on the living. Ruby would explain to her visitors, and lay her man out.

She felt too weak to argue, but she'd watched from the window as they went back and fetched Kenny from where he'd been lying. Uncle was there too now, but even with the three of them Kenny had been too heavy to lift; they'd had to hump him into a wheelbarrow and trundle him to Tammie's Land Rover. She'd begun crying again at that, but more quietly, and her Mam lay and watched her with a look of horror on her face.

They'd heard the roar of the lifeboat's engines long before they'd seen it. Isla had gone down to the pier to meet it and bring the doctor back. Once she'd looked to Betty, Isla told

151

her about Kenny. The doctor ticked her off good and proper for not having told the emergency services. 'You shouldn't have moved him. What did he die of?'

'I didn't look,' Isla said. 'We were too worried about Betty.'

The doctor gave her a disbelieving look, and Isla blushed. 'I didn't think o' it,' she said defensively. 'He was dead, I could see that, and she wasn't. She needed to be cared for straight away.'

'It was my fault,' Jen said. 'I couldn't bear the thought of him lying there.' Her voice began to catch in her throat again. She took a deep breath to steady it. 'They've laid him out in the house. Ruby said she'd look to him. He's there now.'

The doctor shook her head, and gave it up as a bad job. Betty was out of immediate danger, she said, but she wanted her in the hospital as soon as possible. Who would go with her? She was looking at Jen as she spoke, but Jen shook her head. 'I need to bide here,' she'd insisted, and after she'd given the gut reaction she began to think of reasons for it. 'Isla, you'll need to be at your work tomorrow, and the animals will need to be fed. I'll bide here and do that. I have my friends till the ferry leaves today, and if I'm lonely tomorrow I'm sure Ruby'll come up and sit wi' me.'

They could see she was determined, so they let her be then. The doctor busied herself about Betty and got her comfortable in the stretcher for the lifeboat, and then supervised her being got on board. Then she went up the Biggins to look at Kenny.

'That was when I learned that someen'd killed him,' Jen said. Her voice remained steady, though her eyes were bright with tears. 'Ruby had washed him, and dressed him in his dark suit, the one he'd worn for our wedding, and he looked that peaceful you'd think he was just sleeping. The doctor said we shouldna' a done that, but I'm glad I remember him that way. She examined him, and said he'd been hit on the head with something heavy, and that the police would need to be notified. She did that, and then she went off in the lifeboat, and Isla took the bairns too.'

Her friends had wanted to stay with her, awkward in their shock and clumsy comfort, but she chased them out to explore the island, and sat there alone with her man all that lunchtime and through the afternoon. She hadn't cried then, she said, just sat by him, holding his cold hand and talking to him. It was only at four, when her friends came back, that she'd been coaxed away from him and into her chair in the sunroom, answering when she was spoken to and just looking out of the window. 'I wasn't even thinking. I just sat there. Then the ferry came in. There were two police officers on board, and a white van, just like an ordinary white workers' van, and that drove straight up to the house, and the men in it took Kenny away. My friends went too. Maria wanted to stay, but I kent she had her work the next day – ' Suddenly her face was stricken. 'Today. Is it really only yesterday it all happened? It feels like a long time ago.'

The van had driven straight back to the ferry, but the police officers had stayed on Papa. They'd asked permission to use the school as a headquarters, and put up a funny, flimsy white tent around that piece of ground where Kenny had lain. Then they'd come up to Jen. There'd been a middle-aged man with a reassuring manner, and a young lass – Shona, he called her. She was kindly too. 'They had to stay on the island overnight, to secure the site. They said Isla had said they were to bide at hers and just help themselves to anything they needed.' Her mouth twisted. 'But Kenny had to go to Lerwick on the evening ferry, the one everyone was going back on. They said he had to.'

By now I was feeling as incredulous as DS Peterson would have when she heard this account. I knew Jen had lived on Papa since she was a child. Here, living close to nature, away from the busy world, she would have simpler values, just as I did at sea, but surely, surely, she must have read the occasional detective story, or watched one on TV. She seemed to read my thoughts and made a brushing-away gesture. 'I ken, I ken. We shouldna a moved him like that. Yon blond policewoman that you spoke to this morning, she wasna pleased wi' me about it. But I couldna bear him lying there like that. Anyway, Geordie came off the ferry, and the WPC, Shona, she stayed with me that night too. She brought me cups of tea, and the other man, Alex, he came up later, and then the blond wife. She asked me about what had happened, but I couldn't tell her anything. I hadna even kent he wasna hame. These nights, I'm that tired I sleep like the – ' She caught the word in her throat. Her eyes filled with tears. 'I didna ken that he'd been out watching that man – I didn't ken he was here. They asked all sorts of questions about whether Kenny had any quarrels wi' anyone, but I told them no. Kenny wasna on bad terms with anyone. There's barely anyone here to be on bad terms wi'. And they wanted to ken what he was doing down there in the middle of the night, or the early morning, and I couldn't tell them that either.' Her voice rose slightly. 'I didn't even ken he was out until the morning, when I got up and he wasn't there.' She took a deep breath. 'I understand now, now I ken about him, that man, having come here, and Kenny following him in the night. I ken now that he didn't come home that night. Na, he went back. Don't you see? He was angry, so angry he was boiling with it, and he went along to the cottage *he* was biding in, all set to confront him. He was going to threaten him, tell him he was to leave or else. He aye had a temper, Kenny, and this would have had him neither to hold nor bind.'

'Yes,' Uncle said. 'Yes, this could have been so.'

They knew Kenny. If it sounded plausible to them, then it was. 'Threaten him physically, you mean?'

Jen nodded. 'If he was angry enough. He's not very good

with words, Kenny. He's older now, of course, but when he was a teenager he'd get into fights, just because he couldn't manage a clever answer.' Her face went suddenly bleak as it hit her again that he was gone. 'And that man killed Kenny. I know he did.'

I tried to imagine myself in Kenny's place. He'd left the meeting at Uncle's and headed up the road alone; Geordie had gone with his mam to her house, and Tammie and Ruby had gone that way too. He was seething with anger. He and Jen had just achieved what they'd always wanted, a baby, and she was serenely joyful, and now this. The father who'd made her childhood miserable was back, squatting like a toad in the middle of their island, and there was nothing legal to be done about it, he couldn't be turned out.

As he was striding along the road and fuming, he saw the torches in the distance, men messing about with a boat. Trouble already! He'd gone up the hill to see what was happening, and found that nosy lass from the *Swan* up there too, watching. He'd got rid of her and . . . what? Seeing Roberts up to something would have stoked that pent-up anger I'd sensed coming from him. He'd have waited in the dark for the RIB to return, and then he'd followed him back to the cottage – no, that would have lost him the element of surprise. Much better to wait for Roberts at the cottage, to tell him he had to leave the island. He might well have picked up a handy chunk of fence post to use as a threat or a weapon. No, it would need to have been Roberts, aware of someone waiting for him, a dark shadow by the cottage that shouldn't have been there, who'd picked it up and kept it ready in his hand. Roberts had struck out, either meaning murder or harder than he'd meant. Now he had a dead body on his hands. Easiest to throw the fence post away, go to bed and deny all knowledge. There was nothing to connect him with the body, except for where it was, and as I had no doubt he'd said to DS Peterson, smiling that polished smile, murdering your son-in-law is hardly a good way to renew your relationship with your long-lost daughter.

He wasn't a stupid man, I thought. If that had been the way it had been, he could have come forward and said Kenny'd attacked him. Self-defence, a fight in the dark, no witnesses. Unless Forensics came up with something to suggest otherwise, he'd walk away uncharged.

Much as I hadn't taken to him, I didn't share Jen's certainty that Paul Roberts was the murderer.

Chapter Fifteen

It was just after four now. The shadows were beginning to lengthen, the light turn to gold, but the air was still warm, intensified by the coming front. There was activity on the yellow charter boat: DS Peterson climbing aboard, followed by several of the ones I'd taken to be her Forensics team, then there was a gush of blue smoke from the rear of the boat and off she set. Now, as the ghost said in the story, we were all locked in for the night.

We thanked Uncle and set out back towards Jen's house. I wasn't sure what to do next. DS Peterson would probably have left officers on duty at the school, but that was on the other side of Jen's house from Roberts's cottage. I could leave her for ten minutes while I walked over to ask if they'd post someone at her door, and hope that he didn't return while I was out. I wouldn't put it past him to be watching us.

I didn't want to leave Jen alone ashore this night, but I didn't want to leave *Khalida* unguarded either. I supposed I could leave her if need be, well locked up and tied to the pier with fiendish knots (though a knot was only as strong as the knife that cut the rope), and bring Cat and Kitten up for a night ashore, so long as I kept Kitten well away from Jen's collection of glass animals. I wrinkled my nose and looked across at Jen. 'Shall I stay the night with you? Onshore, I mean, at your house?'

'He'll come back,' she said. Her face was bleak. 'You startled him once, but he wouldn't be afraid of you. He won't stay away on your account.' She looked towards the phone box cottage and shuddered. 'I wish Mam was here. I wish they all were. Geordie said on the phone this morning they'd let her out tomorrow, but of course there's no ferry till Wednesday and he didn't want to bring her across in his own boat. It would be too cold a journey for her.'

I glanced at the shining water. 'I could take you over to the mainland, if you wanted. If there'd be room for you to stay with them. I could easy take you to West Burrafirth, or Aith, if Geordie or Isla could come and pick you up from there.'

Her face brightened for a moment, then she shook her head. 'I canna. I hae the hens to feed, and the dogs, in the shed, Kenny's working dogs.' She bit her lip. 'And Mam's cow to milk.' She turned to look back at me. 'She does the milk and I do the eggs. How are you with kye?'

'I have milked a cow,' I said, 'but she was a Highland, and a very peaceable beast. I can give it a go. I was no use at the last bit, what do they call it, the stripping. You'd have to do that.'

'Kokka's peaceable.' Her face brightened suddenly. 'I ken! We could stay aboard your boat. Not at the pier, we could anchor out in the middle of the voe. He couldn't get at us there.'

'But,' I protested, 'my *Khalida*'s not at all what you're used to.' I thought of her comfortable house. 'Really, she isn't.'

Her jaw set. 'I'm no' waiting indoors for him to come back. I'm no'. And you ken what it's like here in Shetland, and worse on the islands like this, I could key the door but a good kick would knock it in, and then where would we be? No, let's put ourselves out o' his reach for today and tomorrow, or until – ' She broke off there.

'Until?' I finished for her.

Her eyes were hard. 'Until they arrest him for Kenny's death. He did it, Cass, I ken he did. Mam would say the same. He's a violent man. Dinna be taken in by the way he smiles, as if butter wouldn't melt. I spent me childhood in fear o' him, until we escaped to Papa here, and Mam told us he'd no' hurt us any more.' She shook her head in exasperation. 'And that's thirty year ago, and you'd think I could just tell him to get out, but my belly feels sick just looking at him. When he cam' in, I didn't ken who he was, but my gut knew.' Her eyes filled with tears. 'Cass, I just don't want to have anything to do with him. I don't want to wait in the house for him to come back. And I'm not going to Tammie and Ruby, or Mam's house, that would be nearer him, and I'm not having him bothering Uncle in the middle of the night, with the police officers all down at the schoolhouse or sleeping at Geordie's.' Now she was crying in earnest. 'If Kenny had been here . . . if Kenny had been here, he'd never have dared . . .'

There was nothing I could say. 'Okay, then. A night aboard. How about you bring some of those eggs and we can have an omelette aboard *Khalida* after we've meated everything?'

'An omelette would be lovely.'

I gave the worktops a quick wipe while Jen packed a bag for the night. Hens first; she scattered the grain for them and we left them pecking contentedly in their run in the adjoining field. I suspected Gavin might want hens too; he was used to the freshest of eggs at the family farm. 'No polecats?' I asked.

'No' on Papa.' She took several tins of dogfood to the shed, where she was greeted by a storm of barking. We left the car by the house, keyed all the doors and walked down to Betty's cottage, where Jen milked the cow and turned it and the calf back into the field. 'Shall I bring some milk too? It's no' pasturised, mind.'

'Real milk, lovely.' I took the can from her, then she locked Betty's door too, and called in quickly to tell Ruby next door that she was trying a night on board my yacht. She didn't go further than the doorstep, feet poised for flight, eyes flicking constantly to the closed door by the phone box. I heard cluckings of concern which Jen waved away. We walked to the pier together. I paused at the waiting room. 'Last chance toilet – well, no, I do have one, a pump-action.'

'I'm afraid I'm getting up a lot in the night right now.' She patted the bump. 'He's sitting right on my bladder. One of the joys of pregnancy, along with swollen ankles.'

'Are you really sure you should be spending the night aboard a small, old-fashioned boat?'

She looked down from the pier. 'She doesn't look that small to me. She's a lot longer than *Selkie*.' Her face twisted. 'Kenny's boat. We've spent a few nights aboard her. She's a motorboat. I've never sailed.'

'Trust me,' I said. '*Khalida*'s the baby of the fleet, with no mod cons whatsoever.'

'And you love her like that.'

'She's my home.' I felt a pang, and pushed away the thought of her sitting emptied in her marina berth while I lived ashore. I put the eggs down on the edge of the pier, where I could reach them from the boat, and slung Jen's bag into the cockpit. 'Come aboard – oh, I forgot to ask, are you okay with cats?'

'You have a cat on board? What does he do when you're at sea?'

'Mostly as he likes, but the kitten gets shut below.' I helped her down the gap between the last rung of the ladder and the boat, retrieved the eggs and stood back to let her go first into the cabin.

'Oh, but this is lovely! It's like a play house.' She sat down on the faded navy cushions of the settee berth and looked around her at the wooden walls, my berth tucked back under the cockpit seating, the chart table, the cooker, the toilet behind its wooden bulkhead. 'And you have a table, and a cooker . . . a fridge?'

'No mod cons,' I reminded her. 'If it needs to stay cool it's under that cushion there, below the waterline.'

'Where will I sleep?'

'In the forepeak, that triangular berth up in the front end. It's the widest. Handy for the heads too – the toilet.' I stretched past her to sling her kitbag forward. 'Make yourself at home. I'll just get us ready to leave. Better to anchor out while we can still see what we're doing.' I gave her a doubtful glance. 'Are you really sure about this?'

Her jaw set. 'I'm certain.'

I took off a couple of the ropes, and set the rest so that they could be undone in seconds from on the boat, then I flaked the anchor chain in long lines along one side of her. Cat appeared from on shore, with Kitten behind him, and jumped lightly onboard. He knew all about getting ready for sea. Kitten hesitated over the drop, then made a leap for it, ignoring her gangplank, and landed with a thump on the wooden cockpit seats. I eased *Khalida* away from the pier and putted gently out into the bay, then dropped the anchor and motored backwards to set it. Cat watched with interest and a touch of surprise; he knew about anchors, but usually we went further. Kitten, seeing we'd stopped, did a patrol round the decks and peered down at the water. It was the first time I'd anchored with her aboard, but so far she'd never fallen off in the marina, however precariously she balanced on the gunwale. I hoped she wouldn't fall in now. I waited for several minutes up in the cockpit, in the last golden sun rays, watching the anchor buoy lined up with the square white light box. The transit stayed the same. Satisfied, I nodded to myself and headed back below.

Jen had put a fresh downie cover and pillow slips on the forrard berth, and found the frying pan in the locker below the cooker. I hoped it didn't all look too grubby to someone accustomed to a pristine house with dishwasher. 'I was going to start on the omelette, but I couldn't get the gas to work, and I thought you must have a switch-off somewhere, but I didn't want to disturb you while you were anchoring.'

'Oh, it's up in the cockpit.' I went back up to switch it on, and then lit the oil lamp so that the woodwork shone gold. It was strange having another woman aboard. I'd been used to my engineer friend Anders and his pet Rat, and of course Gavin had had several nights aboard, but I'd never had a female crew. It felt surprisingly companionable. Cat and Kitten came below as dusk fell and I fed them, then Cat came graciously to be admired; Kitten perched on the upright fiddle that held the books in their place when the boat was tipped over to window-washing angle, and sat peering down at Jen like a little owl.

'She's so pretty!' Jen said. 'Tiny too. Is the grey one the mother?'

I shook my head. 'Adopted father and boyfriend combined. She was a semi-feral cat on shore, but she nearly drowned when we tried to sail off and leave her behind.' The delay in fishing her out had saved me from being sunk in deep water by a maniac with a speedboat, so I reckoned she'd earned her berth aboard. 'I think she's about four months old now. She's just going to be small.'

Kitten gave me a glance which made it clear she knew she was being talked about, and balanced on three paws to wash her whiskers.

'She's getting spoiled,' I added. 'She's very clever, she runs rings round Cat.'

We ate our omelette with cheese as the last light slanted through the cabin, and then I fished out a tin of rice pudding and another of peaches. Jen looked at them and suddenly laughed. 'It's like we're camping.'

She made a better meal away from the house where everything reminded her of Kenny, who was never going to return for his tea. I was just thinking that when she said, 'It's like being out of the world, on a boat. All the things I should be thinking of and worrying about, I'll deal with them tomorrow.

For today I'll just enjoy the sound of the water, and this soft light.' Her eyes went bleak. 'I might even sleep. You don't think it's wrong of me to be glad not to think about anything for right now?'

'I think it'll do you good,' I said. I paused for a moment, trying to think what would be most helpful to say. 'It's all going to be hard, I know, but the most important thing is that you protect your baby. That's what matters right now, isn't it? He, she's what you have left of Kenny. He needs to stay in there safe and sheltered until it's time to come out, not be jolted out by anxiety.' I added, more softly, 'You'll have time enough to grieve, later, once all this is cleared up. For now you need strength.'

Her hand curved round her belly again. 'Yes. I'll be strong.' She looked around the cabin. 'What do you do in the evenings when you're at anchor like this?'

'Oh, it depends. If I'm on my own I read or do maintenance – there's always something to be done on board a boat. If I have company, well, that depends too. Do you play Scrabble, or Hnafatafl?'

'We used to play Scrabble as children, Geordie and I. Is Hnafatafl the Viking game, with the little warriors?'

I nodded. 'I'm not very good at it. I'm not chess-minded. Gavin, my partner, he took to it.'

'I don't think I'm chess-minded either. Let's try that.'

I set out the board in the gold light of the oil lamp, and we began moving the pieces, but neither of our hearts was in it. In the end, Jen sighed and laid her hands on the bump. 'I can't concentrate. All I can think of is Kenny.' She paused, and added, in a hard voice, 'And my father, turning up like that. Kenny would have protected me from him, that's why he killed him.'

I wondered what she'd told Kenny about her childhood; if she'd given him a strong motive to attack Roberts.

163

'Jen,' I said, 'you know you were saying, the music evening, you were talking to Moon, that you remembered her big sister?'

Jen nodded. 'Skywalker. Sky. Dad was pals wi' her uncle Stevie, so I think that's why she used to babysit us. I'd only just started school then.'

'Yes.' I took a moment to think, trying to get the right words. 'Moon was arguing on Vementry with Sky, Kirsten, her sister, about their childhood. She was remembering their uncle Stevie taking videos of them.'

Jen's eyes shot to mine. 'Videos?' Her mouth twisted in disgust. 'You mean dodgy videos? Child porn?'

I nodded. 'Soft porn, I suppose you'd call it. She was talking about them dancing after their bath with no clothes on. That seemed to be all, nothing worse.'

Jen shuddered. The oil lamp didn't give enough light for me to see the expression in her eyes, but the silence between us lengthened and lengthened. The ripple of waves against the hull sounded loud in the darkness.

'I don't remember anything like that,' Jen said at last. 'Does Moon say I did?'

I tried to break it gently. 'I'm afraid Moon had an accident on Foula. She slipped while she was climbing the Sneug, and fell.'

Jen's hands tightened on her bump. 'Moon's dead?'

I nodded.

Jen's voice was sharp. 'But Sky, Kirsten, she remembers this too?'

I shook my head. 'She told Moon she didn't remember anything about it.'

'Nor do I.' Jen's face was set. 'I don't remember anything from that time. Not anything. I don't want to remember.' A shadow of Saturday's joy passed over her face. Her hands caressed the bump. 'I've made my peace with my childhood now. I'm looking forward, not back. I don't want to dredge anything up, and I don't want my father back in my life. If need be I'll pay Tammie and Ruby his rent for whatever their rent-period is, so that they can evict him without losing by it.' She began picking up the little figures with steady hands, then paused. 'Poor Moon. She was only four years older as me, forty six. That's too young to die. Did she just slip on wet grass?'

I couldn't bear to say any more. 'They don't know what happened. The police'll report what they find to the Procurator Fiscal.'

Her mouth fell open. 'But it was an accident? Not – ' Her lips began to frame an *m* and then changed. 'Not what happened to Kenny?'

I was going to have to tell her the truth. 'It may not have been an accident.' I made a gesture with my hands, trying to find the words. 'I saw two people up on the hill, but nobody on the boat admitted to having been up there with her.'

She was silent for another long moment, and then she sighed. 'I think I need to go to bed now. It's been too long a day. But we will be safe out here, won't we?'

'Yes.'

'If anybody tried to come out to us, we'd hear them.'

'Yes, we'd hear them.' I didn't add that I intended to sit up in the cockpit all night, with the handheld radio and my best flashlight beside me. Nobody would sneak up on us on my watch.

I made us a mug of drinking chocolate each, and then went up into the cockpit while Jen got ready for bed. The tide was moving towards its lowest, with the beach sloping down under rocks festooned with seaweed to the calm sea; the sky was clear, with a silvery glow to the nor'nor east where the crescent moon would soon rise. The water around us was softly fretted in the light breeze, and *Khalida*'s anchor light spotlit us in a

165

circle of white. I wondered for a moment about turning it off, to make us less visible; after all, it wasn't likely another yacht would be coming into Papa in the middle of the night at this season. No, I'd leave it as it was. Paul Roberts would see us, but equally if he came up close we'd see him by its light. I fished out my mobile. The signal was wavering between one and two bars, which might get me through. I called Gavin before it disappeared altogether. He sounded harassed.

'They're not keen on sending me up early, I've got too much to finish up here, and Freya's perfectly capable of dealing with it.'

'I'll be glad when you get here,' I said. 'I'll tell you all about it later, but Jen and I are moored up in the middle of Housa Voe, ready to repel boarders.'

He was quick. 'Her father?'

'Mmmm.' The signal cut out at that point, and I redialled. I'd wanted to tell him about Jen's memories of Moon, and her denial of Moon's story of Stevie's videos, but it was all too complicated to explain on a line that cut out every thirty seconds. 'Sorry, this is going to keep happening. I've taken all precautions for our safety.'

I could hear he was smiling. 'Handheld in hand, heavy wrench to smash knuckles in the other?'

'Flashlight,' I retorted virtuously. 'Smashing people's knuckles counts as assault. My policeman boyfriend wouldn't approve.'

'He'd approve even less of you getting attacked.'

'The wrench is on the cockpit seat,' I conceded.

'Use it if you have to.' He was perfectly serious. 'I mean it, Cass. If anyone comes out to *Khalida* they're not selling fresh fruit. Don't hesitate to whack hard.'

I smiled to myself, thinking of the seaports I'd been in where fast reactions were a necessity for an unaccompanied woman. 'Don't worry. I'm protecting –' The phone went dead as I finished the sentence. '– Jen and the cats as well.' I redialled.

'This is hopeless. I'll say goodnight now, and speak in the morning.'

We managed good night and then I went back below to dress in warmer gear, my fleece suit and sailing boots with extra socks. Jen was lying in her bunk with Kitten purring beside her, having her belly stroked; Cat came back up into the cockpit with me. 'We're on watch, boy,' I told him. He gave his soundless miaow and settled down in the cockpit, elbows tucked under. He knew all about night watches.

It was a bonny night. The light breeze had turned cold, but the moon shone now on the bay, turning the water to silver, and making sinister shadows of the stacks to the south. The sky was clear. I tilted my head back to look at the familiar northern stars: the Plough was just visible out of the moon's glow, with the sickle of Leo's head and the long triangle of his flanks behind it. Casseiopea, the Square of Pegasus. The Milky Way was a broad dusty ribbon across the heavens. A plane moved across, red and green lights flashing, people on their way to America. I thought of them up there in the sky being fed decorative meals on trays, and wondered at the contrasts of the world. I wouldn't swap, that was for sure; this shabby cockpit, this starlit bay, the simple lifestyle I'd chosen, were all I wanted.

It was Cat who spotted movement first. I was near to dozing off when I felt him stiffen beside me, and sit up tall, looking intently in the direction of the pier. The launching strip was shadowed by the taller pier beyond, but I thought I saw a dark head move for a moment against the lighter surface of the ferry pier. I lifted my ear flaps up and listened intently, closing my eyes for a moment. The soft rattle of waves on *Khalida*'s hull; the waves washing up the shore and rolling reluctantly back seawards, as if unwilling to give up the land they'd just taken. The creak of my anchor rope, and then another creak, from further away. I opened my eyes again. I hadn't really believed we'd be disturbed, but here he was. Something white was detaching itself from the pier, the skiff I'd noticed earlier. As it came out into the silvery moonlight I could see a dark shape silhouetted against the water.

I slumped down so that I was hunched into the shadow of the cockpit bulkhead, my head below the cabin roof, and waited. The dinghy crept slowly towards us in almost complete silence. If I hadn't been listening for it I would never have heard the soft rattle of water on fibreglass, the creak as the oarsman leaned back. Only watching the oars move let me hear them dip into the water. He was being careful. The rower paused a hundred metres off, and gave *Khalida* a long scrutiny. No cabin lights showing. No obvious person on board. Beside me, Cat crouched down again, whiskers bristling. A low growl rumbled in his throat, and I put a hand on his back to calm him.

Satisfied, the rower dipped his oars into the water once more. He slid alongside, quiet as a shadow. I waited until he shipped his oars, then leapt to my feet, switching the torch on, and shining it straight in his eyes. Dark toorie-cap pulled well down, dark scarf pulled up over nose, dark jacket. Nothing I could recognise, except that the bulkiness looked male. The eyes sparked in the sudden bright light. The dipping oars froze.

'Hey!' It was Roberts's voice.

I kept the flashlight glaring on him, and spoke loudly into the handheld. 'Shetland Coastguard, Shetland Coastguard, this is yacht *Khalida*, anchored in Housa Voe on Papa Stour. We are being accosted by a white fibreglass skiff with one person in it. He hasn't identified himself, but he came from the Papa landing stage. Over.'

The Coastguard came back straight away, loud and clear in the still night. 'Yacht *Khalida*, this is Shetland Coastguard. Please go to channel 67.'

'It's Jen's father,' Roberts said. 'I'm just come to check that you're all right out here on your own.'

'Yes,' I said clearly, 'we are.' I lifted the handheld and began tuning the channel upwards. 'Channel 67.'

That decided him. The skiff turned in a backwash of water and the rower pulled strongly for the pier. I kept the light trained on him as I explained to the Coastguard that our potential attacker seemed to have backed off. 'Thanks, though. It was knowing you were on the other end of the line that cleared him. I don't think he'll try it again, now he knows I'm on the watch.'

He had gone out of the light of my torch now. I switched it off and watched him go into the shadow of the pier. I heard the bump of fibreglass on concrete, the skiff being pulled up. I kept staring at the dark hump of land, and thought I could make out a figure walking across the grass. Round one to us.

The speaking had woken Jen. I heard a sleepy voice call in alarm from below, and went down to reassure her. 'Your father came out in a skiff, but I cleared him. I don't think he'll try again this night, but I'll take my downie up into the cockpit.'

Her face was white in my torchlight, her eyes wide and startled. 'Shall I help you keep watch?'

'No. You get a good night's sleep, and you can keep watch during the day.' I gave her what I hoped was a reassuring smile. 'I really don't think he'll come back. I called the Coastguard, and he scarpered when he heard him answer.'

'Okay.' Her voice was tense. 'What do you think he was doing here?'

'Trying to intimidate me. Listen, go back to sleep. Your baby needs your rest. We'll worry about him in the morning.'

I spent the rest of the night awake, huddled under my sleeping bag, but Paul Roberts didn't return.

Chapter Sixteen

Tuesday 22nd October

Tide times Aith
HW 03.47 (1.8m); LW 10.02 (1.2m);
HW 16.11 (1.8m); LW 23.01 (0.9m)

Moonrise 22.37, sunrise 08.00; sunset 17.36, moonset 16.37.

Waning crescent moon

Uncle had invited us for breakfast, promising a glowing Rayburn and cinnamon rolls. We dressed and washed our faces on deck, then hauled the anchor up, Jen sloshing the kelp off with a bucket of water as I raised it. We headed in gently and moored at the pier again. I locked up *Khalida* and called the cats, and we strolled up the hill to Uncle's cottage. He had watched us coming in, and the cinnamon rolls were steaming gently on a plate in the middle of the table, the best *shillingboller* like you'd find in Bergen. There was dark rye bread, and slices of ham and cheese, and a coffeepot. I took off my outer jumper, slid in behind the table and tucked in.

'Now,' Uncle said, when the story of the night's alarm had been told, the serving plates had been half-cleared, and neither Jen nor I could eat another scrap, 'now we will sit in the snug, and plan our campaign of action. You cannot live anchored in the middle of the voe for the rest of your lives. No, Jen, leave these. I will clear later.'

'We need to prove he murdered Kenny,' Jen said. 'Then the police will arrest him and take him away.'

'I think there might be something you could do about getting him out of Tammie's house,' I said. 'You can use any name you like in Scotland so long as you're not trying to gain an advantage by it. Well, that's what Roberts was doing – using another name to get the house. If he'd used his own name you or Geordie or your mother would have recognised it the moment Tammie told you about him. Ergo, he was trying to take advantage of something he wouldn't have got with his own name. Didn't you say Geordie was going to get Isla to check that out?'

'You should write an account of his visit to you last night,' Uncle said. 'And yesterday afternoon too. Tammie said he could be asked to leave if his behaviour was unacceptable.'

I thought about that. 'He didn't say or do anything unacceptable yesterday. The objectionable thing was him being there at all. And out in the voe there was no sign of him trying to cut us loose or anything like that. He knew Jen was on board. He wouldn't want to harm her.' I paused to yawn. The long night was catching up with me. 'I think he just wanted to give us a fright, under the guise of checking we were okay.'

'He killed Kenny,' Jen repeated. 'Kenny tackled him, told him to go, and he killed him.'

'I haven't talked to DS Peterson about Saturday night yet,' I said. 'About Kenny being out on the hill. Does she know about the meeting here?'

'I have not yet told her,' Uncle said. 'Maybe Tammie has told her, or Geordie.'

'I think you should tell her,' I said. Jen made a dismayed sound, and I looked across at her. 'I know I would say that, but they're the ones who're trying to piece the puzzle together. They can't do it if they only have half the pieces.'

Jen nodded, reluctantly.

'I will tell her,' Uncle said.

'Uncle,' I said, abruptly. 'In the schoolroom, after the concert, you were looking at Paul Roberts as if you were trying to re-member where you'd seen him before. Did you recognise him?'

His dark eyes looked at me thoughtfully. 'Doctors take con-fidentiality seriously. I might be able to help, yes.' His mouth closed firmly on the words, and I knew that was all he would say. 'Now, Cass, you are in no shape to plan action. You were on watch all night.' He picked up a scarlet and orange throw from the basket chair and handed it to me. 'Lie down on the couch and catch up on your sleep. I will walk back with Jen to her house while you rest.'

'Oh, yes, please,' Jen said. 'I must feed the animals, and have a shower, and put fresh clothes on.'

'There, you see,' Uncle said. 'I will watch Jen and your boat for you.'

I had no doubts at all that he would. 'Thank you.'

I woke refreshed an hour later, and was just making myself a cup of coffee when a shadow crossed the window, and there was a knock at the door. Cat sat upright on the sofa; Kitten growled and vanished under it. I opened the door and found myself confronting Paul Roberts on the doorstep, a dark shadow against the sunny bay.

'Hi,' he said. 'You weren't at your boat, so I thought you might be here, since you weren't at Jen's. I wanted to talk to you.' He was using that polished smile. His eyes flicked to the kitchen behind me; I leaned against the door jamb, making it clear I wasn't going to invite him in, and waited.

The smile stayed pinned on. 'A cup of coffee would go down well.'

'It's not my house,' I said curtly. 'Now, you were wanting to ask . . . ?'

If my rudeness threw him, he gave no sign of it. He spread

one hand in an explaining gesture. 'I was just up at Jen's, and she had this ridiculous idea – of course in her condition women are prone to fancies.' His eyes fastened on mine almost as if he was trying to hypnotise me. 'She'd got this idea I'd tried to attack you on your boat last night.'

'Really?'

'She said that I'd come out in the dark. Well, of course you know better than that.' His voice was caressing, luring me into a conspiracy with him against fanciful pregnant women. 'I did come out, of course, to see if you were okay, anchored up. I was concerned about you, two lasses on your own like that, and with this murder and all. I wanted to make sure you were all right, and if I could help with anything.'

He paused there, looking at me.

'That was good of you,' I said civilly.

'I don't know how Jen got the idea that it was the middle of the night. I suppose she'd dozed off, the way pregnant women do, and woke with no idea of the time.' His smile felt like it was pinning me to the door jamb. 'But you have more sense. You ken it was nothing like that. The sun had barely gone down, and there was plenty of light. You had no difficulty seeing me coming over, now, did you?'

If I hadn't seen Jen's fear and heard Betty's story I'd have thought what a nice, reasonable bloke he was. As it was, I waited in silence to give him as much rope as he wanted. The smile and stare intensified. 'And you definitely weren't in bed yet – you were chatting on the phone when I came up to the boat. Well, you wouldn't be doing that in the middle of the night, would you? As for attacking you, well, that's just nonsense. You can bear me out that I didn't lay a hand on your boat.'

'Yes,' I agreed. 'You didn't touch her. But nor did you do any of the normal things, like hailing her before you came up close.'

'I was waiting to see if you were awake. I didn't want to

173

startle you.' I opened my mouth to point out that if he thought we were asleep it couldn't have been that early, and he quickly changed tack. His voice hardened. 'Then you shone that torch straight in my eyes. It dazzled me, and I saw you were managing fine, so I just left you to it. I had things to be doing ashore.' He finished contemptuously, 'Better things than running about after a couple of self-willed girls.'

'Women,' I said. He stared at me. 'At our age, we're women. As to the time, it was the Coastguard I was calling, and the call will have been logged.'

Anger flared in his eyes. 'You could have called the Coastguard at any time, pretending I was there. I say it was just after sundown.' He was leaning in towards me, shutting out the sun. His mouth hardened and his voice changed to a snarl. I felt a twist of fear in my belly. 'I know all about you, a hand-to-mouth sailor who killed her boyfriend. Nice company for my daughter!'

'If it comes to the police we'll see who they believe,' I said. His fist clenched, and I wondered if I'd gone too far. I took a deep breath and twisted his tail. 'I thought when I saw you appear that you were maybe visiting an old friend.'

He gave Uncle's flower-filled tins a contemptuous look. 'Who would I know here?'

'Uncle used to be a doctor,' I said clearly. 'In Leeds.'

His eyes blackened with anger, his brows twisted down. He took a half-step towards me.

I kept my voice level. 'And now I'd like you to leave, please.'

He didn't move but stood there glaring at me. The seconds ticked by. I wanted to back into the house and slam the door behind me but he was too close; he'd have it open, and then I'd be in the house with him, and I didn't like that idea. I felt safer out here in the open. I tilted my chin and looked as determined as I knew how. His eyes narrowed to dark slits. 'I'll hear if you've been telling lies about me,' he said. 'I'll have you in court faster than blinking.' He slammed round on his heel, then turned back. 'And you stay away from my daughter.' His voice was filled with menace. 'Or else you'll regret it.' His eyes flicked towards the pier. 'You and your little boat.'

His steps scraped on the path and the gate banged behind him. I leaned against the doorpost, knees shaking. I'd come across some awkward customers in my time, but not many in whom violence simmered so close to the surface, like a shark in shallow water.

I closed the door behind him, and shot the bolt across, then went out to the back door to make sure he really had gone.

He'd got as far as halfway to the pier, the place where I'd received Gavin's texts last night. He was speaking on the phone, shoulders tensed up with anger. I couldn't catch the words, but the tone was clear; he was complaining about someone's behaviour, and it was a fair guess it was mine. Good. He half-turned and I ducked back hastily, just catching the words 'on board her boat.' I didn't know if he'd seen me, but I retreated into the house anyway, and locked that door behind me too.

On board her boat. I wondered who he was sounding off to.

My hands were trembling as I went to re-boil the kettle. I'd just poured the water into the cup when the window darkened again. I grabbed the poker from by the Rayburn, and went back to the door, teeth gritted. 'Who is it?'

'Police – DS Peterson.'

I unbolted the door and opened it. We stared at each other for a moment, then her eyes dropped to the poker in my hand. Her fair brows rose. 'I take it you've had a visit from Mr Roberts this morning.'

I looked at the poker in a surprised way, as if I wasn't sure how it got into my hand. I wasn't going to demean myself by lying to her.

DS Peterson smirked, as if she was awarding herself a point.

'Always a bad idea to give a man like that the excuse that you threatened him with a weapon,' she said sweetly. Her green eyes looked straight over my head. 'Especially when you're so much smaller than him.'

I took a deep breath then stepped back from the door and motioned her in. There was a younger officer following her, notebook in hand.

'This is PC Shona Jarmeson.' DS Peterson seemed to decide to begin again. 'Good afternoon, Cass.'

I looked up at the clock and realised with a shock of surprise that it was indeed afternoon. 'Hi.' I dropped the poker back into the peat bucket and indicated the kettle. 'Tea, coffee?'

'Go for it.' DS Peterson unwound the scarf from her neck and looked more human. 'Black, please, for both of us.'

'Like on a boat?' I hazarded a guess. 'You're making drinks all over the place and can't rely on a source of fresh milk?'

'Bang on.' DS Peterson accepted the mug I held out. 'Jen Wishart and Mr Kratter told me you'd be here. They said you had more information for me.' *Holding out on me again*, her expression said, but I wasn't going to let her wrong-foot me.

'About Saturday night?' I said. 'And did they tell you about last night?'

She nodded. 'Yes, to both. Shall we sit down?' She gestured towards the snug. 'Get your visit from Roberts off your chest first. I can see you're still seething with it.'

'A nasty piece of work,' I said. 'He came to try and get me to endorse his version of his visit to us at anchor last night.'

'Which was?'

'It was simply a neighbourly call to check we were okay, two "girls" on our own, and one of them pregnant and prone to all sorts of fancies. It wasn't night at all, but just after sundown, and when I shone a torch on him he saw we were fine and rowed away again.'

'I've had Jen's version. Let's have yours.'

'It was certainly night, though the moon made it light. I called the Coastguard as he approached, and they'll have logged the time. He came out very stealthily, heading for the cockpit of the boat. His face was muffled up.' I grinned. 'But he doesn't deny it was him. He'd have been better saying he'd been in his bed throughout.'

'But he didn't, in fact, damage your boat.'

'No.'

'And just now, did he do anything that could be construed as a threat?'

'No.'

'Or say anything threatening?'

I ran the conversation over in my mind. '"Keep away from my daughter or else you'll regret it. You and your little boat."'

DS Peterson raised her brows. 'Who does he think he is, the witch in *The Wizard of Oz*? Well. Unpleasant but not actionable.'

'Can't you take out an order against him if he keeps trying to visit Jen?'

DS Peterson put on a man-to-man voice. '"My ex-wife turned our daughter against me, m'Lud. I just want the chance to get to know her again, and be a grandfather to her child, especially now she's lost her man."'

'No fellow-male Sheriff will stop him being a comfort to his daughter in her hour of need?'

'Doubt it.' She brooded on that for a moment, then changed subject. 'Saturday night. Let me fill you in on what we know about the earlier evening, then you can tell me your part of it.'

She launched into an account. They'd chartered a motor-boat as soon as they heard from the doctor. 'Isla Ratter, your *Swan* engineer's wife, she offered the use of her house for accommodation, and we set up our incident room in the school. We did a house-to-house round the island.' She paused, and clocked me thinking that that wouldn't have taken long with only eight inhabitants.

'Including weekenders,' she pointed out tartly, 'and every one of them with visitors over for the music weekend. They'd a concert planned for the Sunday afternoon, but they didn't hold that, though they did have a service in the kirk instead. The ones who'd come in their own boats went during the day, but most of the visitors cleared on the evening ferry. There're still a few to be interviewed on the mainland, but my officers had managed to talk to most of them between church and leaving on the ferry, and almost all of them could vouch for each other.'

She paused and took a drink of her coffee. 'You know what it's like. They were friends who'd come over, and once the supper in the school and the sword dance were over, well, every house had a living room of folk with someone playing a fiddle in a corner, and someone else joining in on a guitar, and everyone else chatting nineteen to the dozen half the night, or packed so tight into spare bedrooms and sofas that anyone going out would have been noticed. Jen was with her friends at the start of the evening, and they're all agreed Kenny wasn't there, but there were parties all over, so they just assumed he was in someone else's house. Her friends sat up a bit longer, then went to bed too. None of them heard Kenny coming in – nor Jen going out, if she did. Isla said Geordie was with her, but not Kenny. However her friends say Geordie was there for a bit, then went out of the room for quite a while – they weren't surprised, he's not as sociable as she is. Betty, his mother, she was there, a bit agitated and absent, "upset looking". Geordie walked her home, that was about ten, someone thought, and he was gone a good while. Someone else said that when he came back from that he was a bit grim and thoughtful looking; he didn't come in, just put his head round the door, and said he was tired, he'd been out on the *Swan* all day, and he went off. He could have

178

gone back to Roberts's house. Roberts just said shortly that he wasn't a party person. He'd gone straight home after the sword dance and watched TV.'

'Did Roberts tell you that he's Jen and Geordie's father?'

'He did,' DS Peterson said. 'He said we'd find out about it soon enough. His ex-wife was bitter against him, and he'd come without her knowing because he reckoned he had a right to get to know his children and grandchildren. I can't see how that's relevant to Kenny's murder – at least, it gives Kenny a motive to attack him, but not the other way round.'

She glanced at her notes. 'Tammie and Ruby Williamson, the old couple who rented him the house, well, they went across the bay to another full-time inhabited house, and sat there speaking for a bit. Then they went home and to bed. They noticed Roberts's light was on, and heard the TV going, but naturally didn't look in to see if he was there. Is that all of them? Oh, the old man who lives above the ferry terminal.' She checked her notes. 'Mr Kratter. Yes, he was at Geordie's too, the nearest party, I suppose. His first story was that when Betty got tired he walked her home and then went home himself, and stayed there, he said. He was the only one who didn't have guests over, he said at first – he struck me as a bit of a solitary character. I got a new version when I talked to him and Jen this morning.'

I opened my mouth, and she spoke smoothly over me. 'Then there were the outsiders, on the *Swan*. Magnie, you and Kirsten left the school together, not long after the sword dance finished, and went back to the *Swan*, where you all turned in, according to Kirsten. The other three stayed on. Stevie was chatting to Tammie and Ruby, and when they left to go over to their friends, he said goodnight and headed back along the road towards the *Swan*. Moon and Amitola stayed for the jamming session in the school, then left when the party broke up. We don't have Moon's version, of course, but Amitola said they came straight back to the boat and to bed. Kirsten can't confirm that; she's one of these people who sleeps plugged into music.'

'I was conscious of people moving about on deck,' I said, 'but I couldn't tell you who, or when, and I didn't go into the main cabin until morning. But I was up in the night. I need to tell you about that. I think I might have been the last person to see Kenny.'

V

Building Clouds

Chapter Seventeen

I did my best to describe what I'd seen: the torches, the RIB waiting, the departure towards the Ve Skerries, Kenny startling me and walking me back to *Swan*. DS Peterson was silent for a moment, thinking about it. 'So, you just woke? Or did something disturb you?'

I spread my hands. 'I really can't tell. I was expecting people coming back, so someone going off might have roused me; or maybe my subconscious had noted that everyone was on, so there shouldn't have been anyone moving about.'

Shona noted it. 'Time?'

'Between midnight and one, I reckon, but I didn't look at a watch. The tide was high.'

'And Kenny Wishart,' DS Peterson said. 'It seems possible that on his way home from their meeting here he spotted the torches, and decided to investigate. Did he follow them, do you think, or did he go straight up the hill to keep them in a wider view? I understand it's only an impression.'

'Up the hill, I think. I wasn't aware of anyone else following them.' I remembered the feeling that I was being watched. 'But that may not be right. He could have been behind me. And he knew the ground, remember, so he could've been very stealthy.' I looked straight at her. 'Have you asked Paul Roberts about whether he saw Kenny that night?'

'He says that he didn't. He watched the TV, he went to bed,

he slept. He didn't hear any noise in the night, and he definitely didn't mention any midnight excursion. How sure are you that it was him?'

'Not at all sure. The cottage door certainly opened, and then the torch went off up the road and over the hill. The best look I got at them was in the West Voe, in the light from the RIB, but they were silhouettes against it. I'm sure there were three of them, one burly one, one medium and one tall one that I took to be Roberts.'

'Definitely all male?'

'I had that impression, but I couldn't swear to that either.'

'And they all went off together in the RIB?'

I tried to re-visualise the scene. 'I just don't know. I thought they did, but it was dark, and the lights were shifting about, then they put the torches out and snicked on the boat's own steaming light, and that was all I saw after that.'

'What I'm trying to get at, without putting ideas into your head, or words into your mouth,' DS Peterson said, 'was this: could Kenny Wishart have been one of them?'

'That occurred to me at the time. He might have been the medium-sized one. He came up from behind me on the hill, but it was dark enough for him to have gone around in a circle without me seeing him.'

'So, to sum up, Kenny was either involved in a clandestine visit to the *Dorabella*, or he was watching those who were. Either he and two other men, or three other men, were involved, one burly, one medium, one tall. Dress?'

'Sensible. Toories and jackets with light-reflecting tape on them. Not hi-vis jackets or any kind of uniform, like ferry or roadyman issue. Just navy or black. But you know, it might not have been as clandestine as it looked. If the RIB came from the other boat, which I think it must have, because I'd definitely have heard it if it had come round from the pier, then the West Voe was the nearest place to get people from Papa. It saved the RIB from going halfway round the island in the dark. And if they were trying to get her off, well, in the dark was when high tide was.'

'So you think it could have been a legitimate attempt to tow the *Dorabella* off. Was the other boat perhaps the Coastguard tug?' She turned her head to Shona. 'Check up on that, Shona. Thanks.'

Shona nodded, and went out.

'It wasn't showing tug lights,' I said. 'It was a motor vessel over fifty metres, with two masthead lights. The Coastguard tug is over fifty metres too, but it would have three white lights, one masthead, then two on the other mast if it had been towing. Also, I asked Stevie, Stevie Shearer, one of the folk on board the *Swan*. His firm insures her, so he'd have a legitimate excuse to be present at any salvage attempts. I asked him about floating her off, and he only said that they were going to try and get the hold emptied. He didn't say anything about trying to shift her during the night, which you'd have thought he would, if it had been a legitimate attempt. The opposite in fact: he said very definitely that they were waiting for daylight to try again.'

'Did you believe him?'

I shrugged. 'Hard to say. He's a funny one. He's serious for a few seconds, then he cracks an awful joke that makes you feel you can't take anything he says seriously. Yes, I think I did. My thought was that there were more fish in the hold than there should have been, and they were transferring the extra. They wouldn't want an insurance man watching that.'

'That of course is slander, and I couldn't possibly agree with it.'

Our eyes met, in perfect agreement for once. 'No evidence,' I said.

'None. But that's not my case. So it looks as if there were two people on Papa that night who were connected with the

Dorabella. We need to find out who owns it.' She tapped a note into her phone. 'Black fish. That gives us a possible motive for murder, if someone thought Kenny Wishart had seen them offloading illegal catch.'

Shona came back in. 'It wasn't a Coastguard attempt at getting the *Dorabella* off, and they weren't informed that any such attempt was to be made. He didn't sound best pleased about it. Furthermore, there were no vessels on the AIS at the Ve Skerries that night, meaning that the vessel you saw, Cass, had switched its AIS off.'

'Sinister,' I agreed.

'Right,' DS Peterson said. 'We need to get going on this one. Ownership of the *Dorabella*. Ships' papers. Tug the grapevine for any fishing boat that might have been gone from its berth during Saturday night, and any fish landed on the quiet. Any word of fish sales. See who's on duty in Lerwick, and put them on that. After that, send Forensics over to the West Voe to see what they can find by way of footprints. Probably too many, given the number of people who say they went for a bit of a walk after breakfast, to blow the clouds away.'

'Clear the hangovers, more like.'

'Far more like. But they might be lucky.'

'The *Dorabella* doesn't help with why someone killed Moon,' I said. 'She didn't see the RIB, nor Kenny, I don't think, not to recognise. She just saw that I'd been brought home by someone.'

'She stayed on deck after you went to bed?'

I nodded. 'And she was, oh, pleased with herself in the morning. Scoring Stevie off. She'd found Jen. If there was any truth in her accusations, and she believed there was, then she'd got her backup.'

'But from what you said, she didn't have backup. Jen didn't remember.'

It was true. I frowned. 'Nor she did. But Moon was talking

186

about Kirsten babysitting, and that she'd met Jen, as if she'd got the witness she wanted. Odd.'

'How did Stevie react to that?'

'Unconcerned. He just kept cracking jokes.' I hesitated. 'How and when was Kenny killed? Do you know yet?'

'Not officially. The bodies only went down on the boat yesterday evening. When, well, you saw him about one, you think, and he was found about ten.'

'There was something I took to be a black ram lying down,' I said. 'First thing. Half seven. And Jen said, she maybe said it to you as well, that his face was stiff.'

'Rigor. Sometime between when you last saw him and the early hours, and not first thing in the morning, is as good as we'll get. As for the weapon, well, it looked like a blow on the head with a handy piece of wood – something like a chunk of fence post. There just happened to be such a chunk lying a strong throw down the field. We sent that down in the white van too.'

'No sign of where it came from?'

'Lying by the fence running from Betty Tammason's house down to the beach, just ten metres from the house. The bald patch in the grass fitted perfectly.'

'Pick up something handy and hit out with it. Not premeditated then?'

'Possibly a weapon grabbed as you saw a stranger hanging around outside your house. I saw no sign of a fight on Kenny's body, and it was a blow from behind.'

I was silent a moment, digesting that. If Roberts had seen Kenny outside his house he might well have gone out, picked up a weapon and gone straight into attack mode – except that Kenny would have seen him coming out. He wouldn't have turned his back on him. Also, the fence from Geordie's mother's house to the beach was well pierwards of even the road to his cottage, so he couldn't have just picked it up. He'd

187

have had to have been outside Betty's cottage when he saw Kenny skulking around – and why would he have been there?

'And,' DS Peterson added, with more than a touch of exasperation in her voice, 'there was no point whatsoever in looking for significant footprints or DNA after the circus that went on when they found the body. Forensics will look, of course. It's amazing what they can find.'

'Yes,' I agreed. 'I wondered about that. You'd think everyone knows by now not to touch a body or interfere with a crime scene.'

'You'd think,' she agreed, with heavy sarcasm.

'You didn't get any idea of who it was suggested moving the body?'

She gave me a sharp look, as if she'd been thinking along those lines too. 'Definitely Jen. They were all agreed on that. She had a fit of hysterics at the idea of leaving him there. It didn't seem that anyone tried too hard to dissuade her though. By the time we got there he'd been laid out too, washed and reclothed, and the clothes he died in burned in the Rayburn.'

'So we have footprints from Jen, Isla, Tammie and Ruby and Paul Roberts all over the scene, and no chance of anything from the body. Forensics isn't happy. Good grief, even watching *Midsomer Murders* would teach you better.'

'Jen didn't kill Kenny,' I said. 'She's shattered.'

'Agreed. But did anyone expect Kenny at Roberts's house?'

I hadn't thought of that. 'You think she thought it was Roberts she was hitting?' I thought about it for a moment, trying to articulate my instinctive 'no', then shook my head. 'It was a bright, bright night, with the moon up. She'd have known her own husband. It's not just a matter of seeing his face. There's the shape of him, and the way he moves. And then . . . I was there when Roberts came to her house, yesterday. She didn't know him. I mean, she didn't know he was her father. I'm sure she didn't. So she'd have no motive for killing him.'

'The spouse is always the first suspect.'

'Whose spouse?' I asked.

Her eyes met mine. 'Wouldn't your comments about knowing Kenny apply to his mother-in-law as well?'

'I suppose so. But they'd had this meeting, and they'd seen there was nothing to do about him. Suppose Betty decided to take matters into her own hands.' I tried to put myself into the place of an embittered woman. He'd ruined her life but she wasn't having him coming back to put pressure on her children and grandchildren. She'd kill him rather, but he was tall and strong, so her only chance would be if she caught him from behind with something like a hefty chunk of wood. She was awake thinking about it all, when she saw the torch moving at his door . . . At that point my imagination gave out. 'She could have seen the torch moving, but would she really have gone out, and got the weapon and then waited there all those hours for him to come home again? And even in the shadow of the house she'd have known Kenny . . . it doesn't make sense.'

'So the people who most wanted to kill Roberts wouldn't have killed Kenny by mistake.'

'I don't think so. So, if it was Kenny they meant to kill, who had a motive? Roberts, if he was going to keep him away from Jen.'

DS Peterson didn't comment on that one. 'Well, thanks, Cass.' She rose, and I put out a hand to detain her.

'I did have another idea,' I said. 'If the two deaths are connected, well, Roberts should be out of it for Moon, but there's a black RIB parked at the pier, and I'm certain I saw one very similar at the Foula pier when we arrived there.'

Her green eyes sharpened, like Cat spotting a bird in a bush. 'Timings?'

'We went round the island first,' I said, 'and arrived at the pier just before half past twelve. Jen said they found Kenny

189

about half past nine, so there was plenty of time for a RIB to get to Foula. Roberts wasn't involved, once they'd got Kenny's body to the house. Everybody else was busy; Jen and Isla were dealing with Betty and Ruby was laying out Kenny. They couldn't have disappeared for, oh, three hours minimum. No, longer. It left while we were eating our soup and waiting for Moon. Two fifteen, maybe.'

'The lifeboat arrived just before eleven, and took Isla and Betty and the children away just about straight away.' She gave me a straight look. 'Jen was alone, insisted on being alone, until Ruby went up to her at four. How fast would this RIB go?'

'She was alone with Kenny. I don't believe it – good grief, she's still in shock.'

'If she'd left in the RIB at eleven thirty, could she have been at the pier before you?'

'Just,' I conceded. 'And if she'd left at 2.15, yes, she'd have had plenty of time to make it back for four. She'd have been seen though, and Paul Roberts too. Tammie and Ruby's windows look straight out onto the pier.'

'I'll ask them about that. Thanks, Cass. You've been a good help. Let me know if anything else comes to you.'

I made a vaguely agreeing sound, and watched them walk out into the sunshine. It wasn't as bonny a day as it had been; the sky above was still summer-blue, but at the far edge of the horizon there was a faint rim of cumulus cloud building. The front was on its way.

Chapter Eighteen

There was no sign of Jen and Uncle on the road. I checked my phone for texts, but there were none. Gavin would be on the 17.55 from Inverness, arriving at 19.40. He'd probably go straight to the police station in Lerwick, and be home for bed-time. I might manage to talk to him then, signal permitting.

It was just after two, well past lunchtime, but I was still full of Uncle's breakfast. A walk would do me good. I could put Cat and Kitten back to *Khalida* with the cat flap unlocked, and then set out across the island to meet Jen and Uncle returning. I felt restless, as if I should be doing something, asking ques-tions, looking for clues – but, I reminded myself, this was DS Peterson's ship.

I'd only got as far as the ferry waiting room when a woman came out of it, white-haired, but trim and fit and upright. She was wearing a cleaning overall and carrying a bucket with a red-topped bleach bottle in it. She paused with one hand on the gate, gave me a swift look-over and smiled. 'Aye aye. You'll be Cass, the sailor. It's good o' you to come and gie Jen a hand. I'm Ruby o' Hurdiback. It's a bonny day.'

'It is that,' I agreed. 'I'm just off along to Jen's.'

She fell into step beside me along the road, swinging along vigorously. Seeing her up close it was hard to tell what age she was. Her hair was smoothly white, but her tanned face and dark eyes suggested she'd been a 'black' Shetlander, with the coloring of men from a wrecked Spanish Armada ship passed down over four centuries. Dark folk went white early. I'd already spotted the first threads of grey in my hair, and I suspected Maman would be pepper-and-salt if she ever deigned to permit anything so frightful. The name Ruby tended to belong to older Shetland women, the great-grannies of children now at school, but this Ruby's wrinkle-free skin, her even teeth, her quick walk, made me think she was a generation younger than that. As a permanent resident she'd be one of the people who made things happen in the community.

'This is an awful thing,' she said. 'Kenny being killed like that. I can hardly believe it. Mind you – ' she gave me a sideways look, as if wondering how I'd take it, 'wir ghosts kent. They were awful restless that night.'

She said it in such a matter-of-fact way that for a moment I wondered if the normality of her appearance covered some small-island madness. 'Ghosts?' I managed.

We'd reached her turn-off. She nodded vigorously. 'Yea, yea, they aye ken when there's something afoot. Will you come down and take a cup o' tay?'

I hadn't wanted to go near Paul Roberts again but he'd not threaten me under Ruby's wing, and besides, I'd felt I should be investigating something. *Freya's ship*, I heard Gavin whisper in my head, and retorted defiantly that having a cup of tea hardly counted as interfering. Besides, I was intrigued by the restless ghosts who had known there was murder afoot. 'Wouldn't say no to a cup of tea,' I agreed, and turned down the drive to Hurdiback with her.

Their house had two stories, a substantial 'sit-ootery' porch and a side extension. The upper windows were as tall as the lower ones, tucked in under neat slate hats. All the windows were new, double-glazed in plastic frames, and the house gleamed with a this-summer's coat of whitewash. Tammie and Ruby didn't let things slide around them.

'Come you in,' Ruby said, motioning me through the sit-ootery into the front room. There was new wallpaper in a small–pink–lozenge pattern, but the furniture against it had been brought in when the house had been built: a solid mahogony dresser with a glassed upper section holding pink and white china, a bookcase with a marquetry-decorated top, and those upright armchairs with chintz covers and rounded arms, one on each side of the fireplace. The fire itself was a glass box, like Snow White's coffin; Ruby flicked a switch and flames instantly curled up lazily around the darkened logs. Only a closer look, once she'd gone to the kitchen, showed me that the flames were strips of thin white cloth, blown by a fan and lit orange from below. I was still gazing at it when she bustled back in with a tray, which she plonked down on the low table. 'Dip dee doon.'

The couch was a deep leather affair which was going to take serious leg muscles to get out of. I sat down, trying not to lean back. 'I was admiring your fire – I'm never seen one like it.'

'We got it fae the Lerwick Building Centre. It's electric, and you need to keep the water beneath it filled up, to make the steam, but it's right bonny to look at, and it fairly heats up the whole house once it gets going. This was the first year in all my life that I've no' had to work wi' peats.' She nodded at the filled peat basket beside the fire. 'Tammie insisted on that, just for show.'

She went back into the kitchen, and I realised, looking round, that the wall behind me was thick with framed photographs. A schoolgirl, a graduation photo, a wedding, a pair of toddlers, more school photos, and more – and then I realised that these were Geordie's children, and the wedding was Geordie and Isla. The schoolgirl, the graduate, were Isla. Tammie and Ruby were Isla's parents.

I should have thought of that before. Isla had said she'd grown up on the island, and that meant her parents were here.

I'd taken Tammie and Ruby as being out of the murder equation, but as Isla's parents, as Paul Roberts's fellow grandparents, they were deeply involved. They wouldn't want him coming into their grandchildren's lives, upsetting everything in their secure world; and they were right here on the doorstep, able to watch and wait to come out at the right time, pick up a handy piece of wood and strike with it – except I was getting confused again. Paul Roberts was so obviously the person who should have been murdered that I was assuming that he had been the intended victim. Tammie and Ruby would have had no motive for killing Kenny, and more to the point, as I'd said to DS Peterson, they'd have known him, even in that dim light.

I heard Ruby coming in and moved hastily to look at a big framed photograph on the far wall. It was an old one, maybe early last century, going by the long skirts, wide belts and white blouses of the women. Each of them had a bicycle, and they were gathered in front of a large tent with a dark flag flying from it.

Ruby came back in with the teapot. 'Now that's an interesting photo. The woman third from the left, that's me grandmother when she was a lass. It was taken in 1909, on the Sands o' Sound. "The bicycles were a great thing for lasses," she used to say. They used to go for runs out into the country. Before that she'd never seen further than the outskirts o' Lerwick.'

I peered closer. 'Did they go camping?'

'That was their day out on the Sands o' Sound.' Ruby laughed, and began to pour. 'Milk now, sugar?'

'Just milk, please.'

'It was the socialists organised that. It's the red flag flying. See, my grandmother told me, the women that were asking for the vote, they were involved in the Labour movement too. It was a new parliamentary party thenadays, o' course.'

194

'I thought the suffrage women were all middle class.'

'Na, lass, that's a myth. The middle-class ones got photographed, the working-class ones, like my grandmother, they got on with fighting. They wanted the same as the Labour men, she told me. They wanted decent wages, decent housing, better conditions. So they got together in the summer and had a spree, and talked about how they were going to make a better world. Ah, well . . .'

She sighed, and proffered me the bread plate. 'He's a fine baker, is Uncle, but that continental stuff just evaporates in your belly. You help yourself.'

She'd brought enough biscuits and cheese for lunch for three, along with a variety of generous slabs of cake. I calculated how little I could get away with eating without insulting her hospitality, took one of the water biscuits with cheese, and waved my hand towards the smaller photos. 'Your grandbairns performed awful well on Saturday evening.'

She nodded vigorously. 'Cathy, she's a right bonny singer. She has her own band at the school, well, you heard them all. They want to turn professional the minute they're old enough. Andy, he's into machinery. Tractors, you ken, and diggers, aa that kind o' thing. He'll be an engineer like his father, I've nae doot. And his grandfaither – Tammie aye had good hands for a machine.' She sighed. 'And now that man's come here upsetting us all. Tammie was that mad when it turned out to be him, but as Betty said, well, how could we ha' kent, wi' him giving a different name?'

'How did he come to ken about the cottage?'

'We never found that out, but Tammie'd said to various folk, you ken, just chatting, that he was doing the old house up for a summer let, and one o' them musta told this Roberts man, for we got a letter from him, saying he'd heard we had a house to let. He said he wanted to bide here over the winter. He'd retired from being a teacher in the city, and he wanted peace and quiet. He was an Elder o' the Kirk where he bade now, if we wanted references, no, no' an elder, but in the church council, I think he called it. It had to be at a reduced rent, o' course, out o' season, but we spoke about it and said, well, why not? It would keep the house warmed and ready for the summer, and give us a bit extra. Well, Tammie checked the references and they were all fine. His bank manager and the minister o' his church. How could we a thought of him living under a false name all these years? So Tammie wrote back and said he could come, and he arrived on Saturday.'

She paused for breath and another sip of tea. 'I kent him straight off. He'd changed a lock, of course, wi' the short hair and the respectable clothes, but I kent him.' She made an excusing gesture. 'Well, I was just a young lass, and they were kind o' fascinating to me, that "alternative" lifestyle.'

She was taking my breath away. 'Hang on,' I said. 'You mean Paul Roberts was one of the hippy colony folk here, back in the seventies?'

She nodded vigorously. 'Yea, yea, there were a whole hush o' them biding over in the Hoogan houses, across the headland there. Maybe, oh, a dozen of them.' She paused to think and count. 'They'd kind o' come and go, but I'd say the main colony was that, ten or twelve adults. All peace and love and alternative ideas, and they dressed in long skirts, the lasses, and the boys had those jeans with the flappy bottoms, loons did they call them? – and they aa had long hair with headbands. You'd hear them singing songs wi' the guitar, on a still night, and no doubt they were growing all sorts o' plants in the house, drugs, I mean. They tried to grow their own food, though I dinna ken how successful that was, and of course it was all homemade bread and yoghurt brewing on the windowsills. Me midder forbade me to go anywhere near them, though Granny just laughed, she was well through her eighties then, and said each generation dreamed o' making the world better.'

196

Amitola. She was the least likely for Moon, DS Peterson had said, and there hadn't seemed to be any link between her and Kenny's death, but now it seemed she'd known Roberts. They'd lived together in the commune which had ended badly for her. I leaned forward.

'There was a woman on the *Swan*,' I said. 'You know, the party that came to the concert. We sat upstairs in the kirk. The older woman with the long, dark, curly hair, held back with a scarf like a headband, and brightly coloured clothes. She was speaking about having lived here then. Do you remember her?'

Ruby thought for a moment, then shook her head doubtfully. 'Lass, I canna tell you that. I minded the Roberts man because I was a young lass, and he was that handsome, wi' those skinny jeans and his hair hanging down at the side o' his face, and a smile that made you feel you were the bonniest lass he'd ever seen. I had quite a crush on him. He wasna called Paul then, they all had other names. Indian, I think, what they call Native American now. They were all into being brothers with the earth, and worshipping the Great Spirit, that kind o' thing. He was Cheveyo. Spirit Warrior it meant, he told me. I never heard his surname. They didn't use their other names at all. If they had a leader, he was it. He was their shaman, they called it, their connection with the spirit world. He'd go into trances and send his spirit out to find out what was happening at a distance, and come back to advise the community.' She smiled suddenly. 'It was a strange kind o' ritual. I mind once sneaking out and creeping up to watch in the window. The air in the house was filled wi' that scented smoke, joss sticks, and he lay wi' a blanket over him, and all the others around in a circle holding hands, and chanting over him, and he was writhing and muttering in the midst o' them.' She shook her head. 'Daft nonsense. But as for the lass, well, I'm just no' sure. I did think on Saturday night that her face was familiar, but goodness, that's reaching back over forty years, and I never actually kent her.'

'Amitola,' I said. 'That was her name, Amitola. She was sitting over by the door in the school after the concert.'

She reached forward to refill both our teacups, then suddenly sat upright. 'My mercy, yes! Now how could I have come to forget that? I suppose you didn't see the women out as often as you saw the men. Yes, she was one of the mothers. Two, she had, two little girls. Her older lass was the first one to be born on the island – the first child to be born on the island since the big hospital opened in Lerwick, and they took mothers there for safety. It didna mean much to me then, of course, but I mind now my mother talking about it. There were several babies born here on Papa, maybe five or six, they insisted on having them at home.'

'They had them here?' I thought about the stretch of water between them and help, and the doctor and midwife on the wrong side of it. 'But – '

'Oh, yea, natural birth and aa that.' She shuddered, thinking about it. 'It seems crazy, doesn't it? Living in far frae sanitary conditions, and no medical help if it was needed. That was what broke the colony up in the end. There was one birth went wrong, and the baby died, and they only just saved the mother, she had to be taken off to the hospital by the lifeboat.' She shook her head. 'But I mind her now. Two peerie lasses wi' fair curls. Awful bonny, they were. She gave them daft names, but kind o' pretty too. Skywalker and Moondancer. Let me think now. I was just taking my eleven-plus when Sky was a toddler, and then Moon came along two years later. I was at the Lerwick school then, and only here at weekends, but I'd play with them on the beach, making sandcastles. Goodness, I'd forgotten all about that. I wonder what came o' them?'

'They were here on Saturday too,' I said. 'Sky, she's called Kirsten now, she was wearing a green jumper. She works to the council.' I didn't feel I could mention Moon.

Ruby shook her head. 'Well, well, little Sky and Moon. I

wish I'd kent. I'd a likit to see them again. I was working when they left. They just packed up and went, no' that they had much to pack up, it was a "found lifestyle", I think they'd say nowadays, with chairs and tables made from fishboxes they found apo the beach, all that. I came home for the weekend, and they seemed to be still here as normal, though I didn't see the peerie lasses out, then I wasn't back again till a month later, and they were gone.'

I was silent for a moment, thinking. If Roberts had been one of the hippy colony with Amitola, could he also be father of Sky-Kirsten, and Moon? I asked directly, 'Who was Sky and Moon's father?'

Ruby looked daunted for a moment. 'Lass, I dinna want to make assumptions. I ken the older folk, me mam, kind o' assumed they were into free love, and anybody went wi' anybody.' Her cheeks reddened. 'But I dinna ken. We didn't aften see them out all together, you never really got the chance to sort them into pairs. I couldna tell you. The times I'm minding playing wi' Sky and Moon, well, it was when they were big enough to go out on their own, though when I say big enough, well, Sky would maybe be five and Moon three, and the pair of them would go running down to the beach on their little legs at all hours, in bare feet if it was summer, and rubber boots in the winter. We bade over at the house by the kirk then, that's where I grew up, so I'd see them, and go down and, well, kind o' mind out for them, since nobody else seemed to be bothered. All the bairns ran wild. It'd never be allowed these days. Someone would fetch them back for meals, but it could be anyone. I don't mind it being Cheveyo very often.' She sighed. 'Ah, well, it was all a long time ago.'

'Did you mention all this to DS Peterson, the policewoman in charge?'

She shook her head. 'Lass, I didn't think o' it. She asked about how he came to take the house, and Tammie telt her, but I dinna ken if he recognised the Roberts man, Cheveyo, who'd been here then. He didna like them, even then. He'd just got his first job, and he'd sound off about he didn't see why he should be paying his taxes so that other men could hang around doing nothing. He had a particular dislike for Cheveyo, because I was kinda starry-eyed about him, so I kept quiet too. Do you think I should tell her?'

'I think you likely should.'

I was silent for a moment, thinking about it. Amitola had been here, one of the colony, along with Roberts, possibly her partner. The colony had broken up, and she'd gone to her mother in Lerwick, Granny's house that smelled so clean, with the magic bath. He'd gone off and trained to be a teacher, married Betty, had Jen and Geordie, and come back to teach at the Anderson. He'd been Kirsten's teacher, only she'd been Sky then. Skywalker. Of course he'd have recognised her name; but when he'd asked her to babysit, Amitola had put her foot down. What had Moon said on the boat, that last morning? Kirsten had babysat for Jen, and she'd only done it a few times, because Amitola wouldn't let her. I heard Moon's voice: *Mam said it had to be the last time, wasn't that right, Mam?* Amitola hadn't been listening properly, until Moon mentioned Roberts being Kirsten's teacher, then she'd said she didn't remember, and rose hastily to clear the plates.

Roberts's marriage had broken up after that, and he'd gone again.

Now, on this weekend, here he was. She'd been at peace; she'd gone with her girls to visit their old home and remember the happy times – and then, here he was. There'd been plenty of time during the concert for Amitola to look down into the body of the church and recognise Roberts as their leader. Cheveyo, their shaman. The one who'd run the colony in which a baby had died, and its mother had only just been saved.

After the evening in the school, she could have gone to talk to him – gone to confront him. DS Peterson could find out more, from Paul and Amitola. DNA would give Sky and Moon's father, if they weren't cooperating. *Freya's ship* . . .

I finished my refill of tea and set the cup down. 'You were saying something about ghosts.'

Ruby nodded vigorously. 'This house isn't haunted, you ken, no' inside. Naa, it's from outside you hear it, on a still night. People whispering.'

A cold feeling ran down my spine. 'Whispering?'

'Many's the night I've heard it. I canna mak out the language. I thought it might be German, but Tammie says that it's not, no' that he's heard them often, for he sleeps like the dead, or Norwegian, but our son, Ian, well, he speaks Norwegian, and he thought no, but it could be an ancient form of Norse for aa that. This might a been the spot where the girl, Herdis, Tirval's daughter, met her lover and planned their escape. You canna mak out actual words, but you can hear the stealthiness, and the desperation. Maybe it's folk from even further back, hiding from a Norse raiding party, monks who've heard how the Vikings have been killing people in the monasteries all along the coast.' She paused to finish her tea, and set the cup down. 'Papa Stour, you ken, it means "big island of the priests" but that doesn't mean they didn't kill them. They weren't Christian yet, the Vikings, when they first came here.'

'And Saturday night?'

'I woke, and they seemed to be speaking sharper than usual, though still in a whisper. You can never make out the words, just the sound of it, and this sounded, well, hissier, more angry than worried. As if two people were disagreeing about something.'

'You didn't get up and look?'

'Na, na, lass, what would be the point? Of course we aa kent about it, and many a time as bairns we sneakit over to listen and see if we'd hear them, or see anything, but you never did. You needed to be inside the house to hear them. I'm looked

201

many a time, when I first came here as a bride and heard it, but you never see anything. No' that I would go out to look, either! Naa. It's safe inside the house, you feel that. It's still now in the house, you see. The danger's outside where they are, whatever time they're back in.'

Maybe; maybe not. 'You didn't tell DS Peterson about them?'

'Na, na. She's een o' those modern kinds. She'd never have believed in ghosts. Na, na, I keepit that to myself.'

Another thing I'd have to pass on. I rose. 'Well, thanks to you for the tea. I'll get on wi' my walk now.' I hesitated. 'Their hippy colony was just near the kirk, wasn't it? Is there anybody living there now?'

'Na, lass, they left the houses in no condition for anyone to bide in. It was two houses they had, and they're both pretty well in ruins now.' She came to the doorstep with me, and indicated with an arm. 'No' the white house, that's East Biggins, but down past it. It's the old houses just below the kirk there, no' the one right opposite it, that was wirs, but the ones above the sandy beach. You can go back up onto the road and along, or it's just ten minutes walk over the headland.'

I strode off, passing the phone box cottage wide. The sun was warm on my face as I crossed the soft turf and headed over the back of the headland. I could see clear to the horizon, with its rim of grey cloud. From here, Sandness on the mainland was spread along across the shore: the long sand beach at Norby, the central cluster of Sandness with the hall, school and kirk, the knitting factory and council houses, and then, coming out towards me, Melby beach and Haa, with its little pier, and then, above the Haa, the old kirk and graveyard where the two swimmers of the *Ben Doran* men were buried. *Greater love hath no man.* There were aye flowers on the graves, Magnie'd told me. Fishermen didn't forget their own.

Below me was another bonny beach, the Kirk Sand, in a

little shallow bay open to the south, and edged with rocks except for this broad sweep of sand. This was the beach where Ruby had played with little Sky and Moon. The kirk stood sentinel above it, square in its graveyard, and the two ruined houses were to the right of the kirk, just below the road and only twenty metres above the beach. I could see straight off that they weren't inhabited now; one had gaping holes in its black tarred roof, and there were dark patches of stinging nettles growing right up to the walls at the back. The fields where the commune had grown their crops were still visible, with richer grass and a fine harvest of dockens enclosed by tumbled-down stone walls.

I walked down, thinking about it all. I could understand the impulse that had driven them out here to form their own community, away from the noise of the world and what they saw as its false values; that was in part what drove me to sea. Their worship, well, that sounded like all I'd ever heard about the hippy era, with the belief in everything being one, and the spiritual nature of the earth, and though I wouldn't quite go about it as they had, with shamanic rituals, there was a touch of that in modern belief too.

When I came around the front of the houses, the door of one was still closed, but the other's was leaning over at an angle, with plenty of room for sheep to make their way inside. I came up to the dirty window by the slanted door and imagined a teenage lass peering in at the strangers. There was nothing there now, just a jumble of fish-box planks under sheep sharn on the floor and a tangle of matted wool in one corner that I didn't want to look at too closely. If they'd had wallpaper or paint there was no sign of it now, just darkened whitewash on the walls.

I dodged the nettles and crossed the briggistanes to the other house. This had been in better repair originally, for the roof was mostly whole, though the wooden lathes showed through gashes in the black felt. The door had remained closed through forty Shetland winters, and when I tried it I realised why: it was a stout door, and locked. Someone had meant to return. I went to the side to peer through the windows. Yes, this was just as they'd left it, even with rotting fabric on one bed, an oilcloth on the table and a pile of dishes in the sink. A jug on the windowsill still had wisps of dried grasses in it. There was a Rayburn on the far gable, the old-fashioned cream-coloured sort, the cream spotted with rust. A pair of boots sprawled on the plate-rack above it, and a dishcloth still hung from its rail. The wall around it had had a mural of a rainbow on it, and the light dangling from the ceiling was swathed in a dust-greyed headscarf.

It was all melancholy, the abandoned remains of their ideal-istic, dangerous dreams. *There was one birth went wrong, and the baby died* . . . I thought of giving birth in this primitive place and shuddered. Even supposing I was just being prejudiced, supposing it had been kept clean enough to eat your food from the floor, and, yes, of course generations had given birth in such conditions – I paused to sort out my tangled thoughts. That had been then. The women who'd given birth in cramped crofthouses in past centuries had been surrounded by women who'd gone through this already. There would have been the local *howdie* in attendance, the midwife and healer, who'd supervised many a birth from a child helping her mother, who embodied the handed-down wisdom of generations. Even then, one woman in three died in childbirth. To risk giving birth here without even that informed helper there, just your fellow hippies whose mothers, if they had brothers and sisters at all, had gone into hospital and come out a week later with a clean, pink baby – it had been madness.

And Roberts had been their leader. Cheveyo.

I stepped back from the house and walked slowly down the yaird. They'd hauled seaweed up here to help grow their vegetables. The rich grass was cropped short by sheep, and the nettles trampled, as if it was a favourite sheepie place to shelter in a cold northerly. Over in one corner was a little patch of dark earth, where the grass had been torn up by the roots. Something pink shining against the black. I stopped, and stared, then went slowly over, treading carefully among the tussocked grass.

The grass had been pulled up recently it was still green, and there was darker earth at the heart of the roots. The space that had been uncovered was the size of a shoebox lid. At one end of it, thrust in to stand upright, was a cross of docken stems, roughly fastened with a twist of grass. Three stems of neon-pink campion lay below the cross.

I had found the baby's grave.

Chapter Nineteen

I turned my back and headed towards the kirk, pausing at the door to look across at the beach and ruined houses. How had the kirk folk felt about these aliens on their doorstep? Somehow, in Shetland, I didn't see them drawing fastidious Levite skirts aside as they passed. Oh, yes, there would be plenty of comment on what they were up to, but I betted young Sky and Moon and the other children of the colony would have found welcome, warmth, food and hand-me-down clothes in every inhabited house on the island, even if the adults kept themselves to themselves.

There was nobody inside. I drew the door to behind me, and went up to the gallery, where I'd sat on Saturday night. It seemed an age ago. The afternoon sun glowed through the window above the altar: Christ standing in a little clinker-built boat, with a lantern dangling from its bow, and the disciples crouched below him, faces turned up to him as he rebuked the storm with outstretched arms. The writing below began with a flourishing T: To the Glory of God. There was a list of names below, the men of Papa who'd died in the Great War. I said a prayer for them, and for Kenny and Moon, for the baby in that tended grave, and then leaned forward with my chin on my folded arms, letting the peace of the place enfold me and give me space to think.

The baby's grave. Somebody had cleared it in the last few

days. A memory flashed back, of Amitola trying to stride out ahead of the others as soon as *Swan* had docked, as if she had a private errand, and Moon catching her back. It could have been her baby. If it had been her baby, that made sense of her attitude to returning, the tension in remembering their idealist lifestyle which had ended in tragedy; except that unless she'd told them about the lost baby, she couldn't have tended the grave, because Moon and Kirsten had gone with her to see 'where they'd been born.' I thought it was the kind of act you'd want to do in private. There was Roberts; he'd been here, he was newly arrived and thinking of his children. Perhaps he'd remembered the one who hadn't lived.

The restless ghosts. I needed to think about them too. It could be, of course, that the ghosts Ruby said were a well-known feature of the house really had been restless, disturbed by the murder, but I didn't believe in interactive ghosts like that. The dead had already moved on to God's eternal time. To my mind, the ghosts people saw were some kind of replay, a DVD imprinted into the walls of a building that had held extreme anguish of mind, visible to people with the right 'tuning', just as children could hear bats squeaking. Whatever long-ago event had imprinted itself into Tammie and Ruby's house, those people weren't concerned with the present. No, the people who were disturbed by the present were us. There had been some kind of argument outside, held in fierce whispers for fear of waking Tammie and Ruby in the house.

Now, where did that get me? The obvious answer was an argument between Paul Roberts and Kenny. Roberts wasn't going to let him in to argue; Kenny wasn't going to go away. The argument ended in Kenny's death.

I shook my head, dissatisfied, and was just about to get up and go when the door creaked open below me, and Paul Roberts came confidently into the church. My heart plummeted. An encounter with him was the last thing I wanted. I wasn't going to let myself be afraid of him, but I didn't want another charged meeting in this lonely building. I hoped he hadn't seen me coming in here. I sat still as a mouse and waited, listening.

His footsteps echoed on the wooden floor below. He went up to the altar, and I heard the pages of the great Bible flick over. There was another silence, then the sound of a lid being opened, a wheezing noise from the harmonuim in the corner, the creak of bellows being pumped, followed by a quick riff of lighthearted jazz chords. Now might be my chance to get out of there, except that the moment I moved on these creaky floors he'd hear me, and I had the winding stairs to negotiate while he had only the straight aisle. If there wasn't an undignified struggle at the kirk door, he'd be on me by the gate.

I was just tensing myself to make a move when the chords stopped as abruptly as they'd started. The latch of the outer door snapped and a voice I hadn't yet heard said, 'I saw you come in here.'

It was a male voice, Shetland, older; it had to be Tammie. I relaxed cautiously as their footsteps came into the kirk proper.

'I'm wanting to have a word wi' you,' Tammie said. I risked a peek over the balcony. They were facing each other in the aisle, Roberts with his back to me. Tammie was a burly-build crofter type in traditional dress of blue boiler suit and yellow rubber boots, and with a toorie cap. He took that off now, in deference to the kirk, revealing tousled fair hair. He had a round face and ruddy cheeks, and a seamanlike look about him; I'd have betted he'd been on the fishing boats, or in the Merchant Service. His face was set in determined lines, mouth hard, brows drawn down. 'You're no' wanted here. I'll gie you back the rent money you paid me, in full, and you can leave.'

Roberts gave a contemptuous laugh. 'I'm no leaving. The law's on my side. You canna make me go.'

'Yea, I can,' Tammie said. His voice was like tempered steel.

I thought he'd move closer, but instead he took a step back, his eyes still hard on Roberts's face. 'I can talk to the police. Saturday night, I coulda slept badly. I coulda lookit out o' the window. It was clear moonlight, I'd a seen anything there was to see.' His voice diminished in volume, but sharpened in quality. 'I coulda seen you lying in wait for Kenny and hitting him wi' that piece o' fence post.'

Roberts's voice flashed back, like a snapped rope lashing out. 'You didna see that, because it didn't happen.'

Tammie ignored him. 'The policewoman's no' interviewed me yet. I was out on the hill when she came round. She talked to Ruby, but she's no' talked to me. It's no' like I'd be changing my story. I just need to tell her I saw you.'

There was a long pause.

'So that's it,' Roberts said at last. 'I leave or you frame me wi' a murder I didn't commit.'

'I ken what I saw,' Tammie said.

Roberts glanced at the hat in his hand. 'You're a godfearing man that takes his toorie off in the kirk. You're prepared to swear to a lie in court, on oath?'

Tammie ignored this. 'And I ken you.' The last word came out in a hiss, vehement. 'I kent you the minute you stepped off the ferry – Cheveyo.'

Roberts's head jerked up. There was a long silence. Then he came towards Tammie, who stood his ground, watching him warily, shoulders tensed to withstand an attack. Roberts didn't attack; he went past him and sat down in one of the pews. He made himself comfortable, one leg crossed over the other, hands elegant on the shelf in front of him, not looking at Tammie, and spoke smoothly as poured cream. 'There's no shame in once having been part o' a group that believed in ideals. Getting back to the land, having everything in common. I mind you now too. I remember you taking an interest in our colony. You watched us; you'd find a reason to be checking the sheep down near us. A peeping Tom, it was called then-a-days. There might be a nastier word for it now, with all this feminism and "Me too" nonsense. How would your wife like to ken about how keen you were on our lasses?' He gave him a long look. 'On one of our lasses.'

Tammie reddened, but he stood his ground, head slightly lowered, like a bull about to charge. 'There was a lass who nearly died out here, having a bairn wi' no doctor to help her. The baby that was buried on the croft, its death was on your head.' He let the accusation hang, then lifted his head up and stared Roberts in the face. 'I'll feel it no sin to bring you to book for murder. I've put your rent in an envelope in your porch. There'll be a ferry the morn. You can leave on that.'

His boots clattered out, and the door slammed behind him.

Roberts gave a low whistle. He stood, humming to himself, for a moment, and then he too strode to the door. There was a brief snatch of birdsong from outside before it closed behind him.

I sat there a moment, trying to decide what to make of that outburst of threat and counter-threat. *I'll feel it no sin to bring you to book for murder . . .* the baby whose grave had been cleared. *Its death was on your head.*

There was no sign of either man when I came out. I'd almost reached Jen's when I had that back-neck prickling being-watched feel. I turned and looked back.

Tammie hadn't gone far. He was standing by the ruined cottages, watching me, and now I saw him at a distance there was something familiar about his build. He could have been the burly man I'd seen at the RIB in the dark on Saturday night. He'd been a fisherman, and could well have shares in the *Dorabella*. Furthermore, I realised now, his cottage and Roberts's were side by side. I might have been wrong about Roberts being on the hill that night. It could have been Tammie's door which had opened and closed again.

★

210

I met Jen and Uncle at Jen's gate, on their way back to Uncle's cottage.

'DS Peterson's promised me a police officer,' Jen said. 'Well, two; the woman, Shona, to keep me company inside, and the other one to be on patrol during the night. You'd be welcome to come too, if you don't feel safe on your boat.'

'I don't,' I said frankly, 'but I'm not leaving her unguarded at night. I'll anchor off again.'

'But you will have supper with us,' Uncle said.

'I'll certainly do that.'

I picked up Cat and Kitten on the way, and we all strolled up together to Uncle's house. We were barely halfway there when there was an engine-sound from behind the stacks, getting louder as the boat neared. The yellow motorboat swept into the bay and I stopped to watch as it moored, ready to race down and help if it went near *Khalida*. It came alongside gently, with barely any wash, and the assorted police officers on the pier piled aboard, DS Peterson's blond head last. She raised a hand towards us, then stepped aboard, and the boat roared off. I kept watching until *Khalida* had stopped rocking to its wash, then went after Jen and Uncle.

It was a peaceful evening. Jen lit the stove and I chopped vegetables straight from Uncle's garden: the first carrots, mangetout, new potatoes. I could grow these, I thought, and began picking their combined brains about what I could plant now for spring. All sorts of things, it seemed: I scribbled down a list as they talked.

'I remember Tamar,' Uncle said. 'She was an interesting woman, who'd travelled widely. I'm glad you are going to keep her cottage inhabited, and her garden tended.'

'I'll try. I'm not a gardener.'

'You'll learn,' Jen said. 'It grips you. Your first crumble from your own rhubarb, your first pot of jam from your own black-berries, and you're hooked.'

211

A plate of fish appeared for the cats, and supper turned out to be a wonderful tomato-rich stew of smoked sausage along with the veg I'd chopped, lightly steamed. After it, we all relaxed on the couches in the red-draped snug, with the fire flickering between us.

'Now,' Uncle said. 'Now we have eaten and we are comfortable, we must make a plan. Jen, you will sleep well at home tonight, with your police officers to guard you, and Cass, you will be in the middle of the bay. Then in the morning I hope Geordie will come back, and Betty, and the children. You will not be alone any more.'

'I'm not alone now.' Jen turned her head to smile at me. 'Thanks, Cass, for coming.'

I made a disclaiming gesture.

'But we still have this man among us, making Betty unhappy, and disturbing you. Geordie and the children will have to go back to the mainland when school begins again a week on Monday. We need to get rid of him before then.' He sighed and rose. 'I will talk to the policewoman again. Perhaps she could lean on him to leave. Or it will be unpleasant, but if you log the times he tries to visit you – I am sure that he will try – then perhaps the police will take an interest.'

'He did it,' Jen said stubbornly. She rose and stretched. Her voice was hard. 'He killed Kenny. I know he did. I want him arrested and tried and convicted.' Then she yawned. 'Oh, it's my bedtime.' She cuddled her bump and the joy came back in her face. 'Little Kenny needs his sleep.'

I rose too, and headed for the door. 'Thank you, Uncle, for a lovely tea.'

'We expect you for breakfast,' he said. 'There will be cinnamon rolls for all when the ferry comes in.'

I glanced involuntarily at the pier, and the look reminded me. 'Uncle, who owns the black RIB at the pier there? Roberts?'

He gave me a sideways look, but answered calmly. 'No, Cass, it belongs to Tammie and Ruby.'

I thought about that all the way down to the pier, with Kitten on my shoulder and Cat trotting ahead. Ruby had been laying Kenny out, but Tammie had been a free agent, able to bring the black RIB over to Foula, to climb the hill and kill Moon – but I didn't see why he should have. He had no reason to kill Kenny, and Moon was no threat to him. Unless . . . I suddenly remembered Moon sitting up on deck that night. Unless it was that old chestnut, that she'd seen something. He and Ruby were the children's grandparents. He had every reason to want to get rid of Roberts. Suppose he'd killed Kenny by mistake, and Moon had seen him? And the argument that Tammie would have seen Roberts or Jen taking the RIB didn't apply to Tammie. It was his boat; why shouldn't he take it out?

My thoughts were going in circles again. I shoved them away, organised myself on board, chugged out into the middle of the voe and anchored. I should be safe enough, of course, but I'd sleep on deck just the same. The night was warm. I'd just gathered up my sleeping bag, our double downie and a waterproof sheet when my phone rang. I leapt for it.

'*Halo leat*,' Gavin said. The signal seemed slightly better than it had been last night. 'Just pausing between reading Freya's interviews. How are you doing, and where are you?'

'I'm anchored up in Housa Voe again. I'm doing fine. Are you at the cottage?'

'No, I'm still in Lerwick.' The signal cut out, crackled, and then let me hear his last word: 'tomorrow.'

'You went. What tomorrow?'

I managed to make out 'Papa' between crackles. Of course, there was a shorter-day Wednesday ferry, taking Papa folk over to the mainland first thing, and bringing them back again at afternoon tea-time, a hangover from the days when the whole of Lerwick closed for Wednesday afternoon. My heart leapt. 'You're coming to Papa, tomorrow?'

'. . . early ferry . . . see the terrain for . . . self . . .'

'You're going again,' I said. 'I'll meet you off –' My phone went dead before I could finish. I gave it up as a bad job, and settled myself along the port cockpit bench, smiling. He was coming. I'd see him tomorrow. Kitten wriggled her way into the warmth of my downie, with a look that said quite clearly that this wasn't usual practice, and she didn't approve; Cat sat on guard by my cheek, until it became obvious to us both that nothing was going to happen tonight. We slept.

Chapter Twenty

I was roused by the noise of an engine, distant, coming closer, and then cutting out. I was alert on the instant. I sat up and looked around me.

It was a bonny, starry night, with the moon playing hide-and-seek with the clouds. I took a long, slow sweep of the bay, starting at the pier and going around the bay to the Maiden Stack. There was nothing moving, just the waves lapping half-way up the shore. Low water had been just after eleven, so it had to be about two. I pushed my duvet aside and knelt on the cockpit seat to see over the cabin roof. The pier, the dark outline of the reef just off the shore beyond, the open sea, the reef on the south side of the entrance, the stacks. The water darkened as the moon went behind the clouds, and I had to wait, listening intently, and making out only the dim shapes of the stacks against the water, until it came out and flooded the bay with light again. There! Tucked in beside the stacks, where its outline against the silvery water wouldn't betray it, was a shadow of something paler against the darkness. I strained my eyes trying to make out its outline. It could be a boat. The noise I'd heard had been coming this way from out in St Magnus Bay.

There was nothing more. I watched, and listened, but there was no sound of anyone messing about in a boat, no chink of anchor chain or clunk of waves against a fibreglass hull, no wash that rocked *Khalida*, nothing to tell me that there was somebody out there in the shadow of the stacks, yet my spine prickled with uneasiness. I ducked down again and pulled the duvet back up, reaching out with all my senses for anything unusual. Nothing. Nothing. However quiet they were, if they tried to approach me in a dinghy, I'd hear them. I'd heard them last night; they wouldn't try that trick again.

If I hadn't been awake, I'd never have realised *Khalida* was swinging gently, imperceptibly round on her anchor. Only my view changed, from the curve of bay to the pier and the rocks. The wind must have veered to the west – and then I realised with a shock that we were moving. I lined up *Khalida*'s flagpost with the pale rectangle of Betty's house on shore and watched them separate, and a few moments after that my anchor buoy drifted past us. In the shadow of the stack, something moved. As our position changed, I saw it more clearly against the silver: a white, high-bowed motorboat with one person in it, head turned towards me.

The wind was pushing us towards the headland and the Hellirocks behind it. The person on board that boat was waiting to make sure we came to harm. Even as I watched, I heard an engine being started in idle, and then a very gentle throb of forward gear. The motorboat began to nose outwards, avoiding the dark shape of the south reef, and ended up in the middle of the channel. If I showed signs of life it would come in.

I looked around me. A hundred metres still to go from the shore. With the speed we were drifting at, and if I could unroll even a couple of feet of her jib unseen, *Khalida* would respond to her helm. The dark edge of her jib was towards the motorboat, so there would be only a tiny triangle of white to betray me to them. At this distance I hoped the watcher wouldn't see it. I undid the furler rope and pulled the starboard sheet in, quietly, quietly, so that there was no betraying noise from the blocks, and without using the rattling winch. Broadside on to the wind like this it wouldn't take much. I eased it out until there was a little triangle of white within the half-metre navy border, secured furler and sheet, and waited until I felt the wind begin to move her, then inched the tiller over. It felt like a long time I crouched there, heart thumping in my mouth, before at last I felt her nose begin to turn, so that she was going parallel to the headland instead of straight for it.

Now what? I glanced again at the motorboat, waiting in the centre of the channel for me to go on the rocks. There was only one way to evade it, and it was a risky one: to go between the stacks and out into the open sea, where I could lose it. I knew how quickly *Khalida* would diminish into the distance, even with her sails up, if I showed no lights to guide them to me.

I stared at the stacks in the moonlight. There was the headland, then a good gap between it and the Maiden Stack, then another gap, smaller, and nearer to the rocks. The chart which showed Papa was too small to be of any use, but my pilot and OS map were still laid out on the table. I reached below for them and the magnifying glass, hoping the moon would give me enough light, and switched the instruments battery on, then took off the cover of the depth sounder. Four metres below my keel. The map had a horrible scattering of rocks and stacks underneath writing marking *18th Century Leper Settlement* but it looked possible to go through if I bore due east, and went to the north of Maiden Stack. The pilot book seemed to have a clear channel between the headland and the Maiden Stack, though maybe that was just because they reckoned nobody would be crazy enough to try it. The whole area was marked as only two metres deep. Two metres at the lowest possible tide, which this wasn't, so that would give me an extra, maybe twenty centimetres, at a conservative estimate, and then I had maybe half a metre of tide flowed in to add to it. Two metres seventy gave me a metre twenty clearance for underwater rocks. On the far side of the channel there was a rock on each side. I'd have to go straight through and keep going straight until I was in deep water.

It was a crazy thing to do. I edged the jib sheet out to turn her nose towards the Maiden Stack and tried to think of alternatives. If I was to turn the motor on and head for the pier, shouting for help all the way or blasting my foghorn, well, it might scare that silent watcher off, but if he, she, was really determined to harm me, the motorboat could be brought in at speed, ram us and be off before anyone could run down to the pier. I could swim, and Cat might make it, but Kitten wouldn't, and I'd lose my boat.

No. I'd trust to my own luck and to the sea to get us out of this. I breathed a prayer, then set my tough little boat at the gap between the headland and the Maiden Stack. The wind was blowing from behind me, straight between them, and the gap looked reassuringly wide as I came up to it, half a dozen times the width of *Khalida*. If there were no underwater rocks, we'd be through and away before the motorboat came up to see how much trouble we'd got into.

It was heartstopping all the same. I edged her into the gap, pointing her nose straight through it, and at that same moment the moon went behind the clouds again, and I was left in darkness. The cliffs smelt of seabirds, an acrid smell that caught at my throat. In the time it took my eyes to adjust, we travelled ten, twenty, metres, and I felt each one, waiting for the shuddering bang that told me I'd hit a rock underwater, or a scraping against *Khalida*'s side from those invisible cliffs. I hoped that we weren't going fast enough to do any serious damage; that her fenders would protect her, that we'd be able to reverse out under engine if we got stuck, or wait for the tide to rise enough to get us out forwards. Gradually, the sea's glimmer became visible again, darkened by the cliff on each side of us. I'd made it halfway through. I took a deep breath, wrinkling my nose against the smell, and kept sailing. *Khalida* inched forwards, between the rough cliff faces, past the water sucking on seaweed-covered rocks at their base. Now I could see the port-hand one of the two outer rocks, but not the other one. I edged closer to it and prayed again as it slipped past.

Suddenly the depth sounder jumped to twenty-three metres. We were through! I kept going for another ten metres, then turned *Khalida* head to wind. I leapt for the mainsail, unfastening its bungees by touch, shoving them into my belt, and hauling the sail up as fast as I could, then returned to the tiller before the noise of it flapping could alert the motorboat to our escape. Eastward, westward? I had a second to decide. I turned her nose for home. I could skulk along off the Sandness-West Burrafirth-Vementry coast, and if my luck held I could slip into Nordera Voe. We'd be less visible near the land than in the middle of St Magnus Bay, and I was still shaking from so close an encounter with the Maiden Stack. There was no need to run the gauntlet of the Sound of Papa, with its strong currents and rocks in the middle. I grabbed at the jib furler and let it run, pulling the jib out to its full extent with the sheet. *Khalida* heeled over, and the water began trickling under her forefoot.

I was almost across at the headland of Little Bousta before I was able to see back into Housa Voe. It was hard to tell, but I thought the motorboat had gone; then, faintly, I began to hear the noise of an engine. It was coming this way, and at speed. I needed a closer bolt-hole than Vementry. Even West Burrafirth would take too long, and they'd expect me to go in there, with the helpful sector light.

Suddenly a light flared in the darkness, a long thin cone of light across the shifting water. Even at this distance I saw it light up Forwick Holm and the water beyond. Whoever was in that boat had abandoned stealth. He, she, meant to find me. They were trying the Sound of Papa first, then, when they didn't find me there, they'd come back this way. They'd be on me before I reached safety.

Inspiration flared like the light, like an answer to a prayer. There was a bay Magnie had shown me when he'd run me over to the Sandness school to talk about life on a tall ship. We'd gone along a single-track road off the main village. I could visualise the bay we'd stopped at, fringed with rocks to seaward, with just a narrow opening to a round bay and a shingle beach where a dozen seals basked. I could hear his voice clear in my head: 'If ever you fancy a stop here, you can come in no bother, as close as you like to the rocks on the right-hand side there. Just keep clear o' the Bousta Skerries coming in from the Brae direction.'

I was almost there anyway, and it was the sort of place which only local knowledge would think of. If I could get in there I'd be safe till morning. I bit my lip, considering, and wishing I had a chart plotter. A quick flash of a shielded torch showed me that it wasn't in the CCC pilot, nor on the more detailed chart of harbours. The OS map showed it as a clean run in, but the OS wasn't thinking about people's keels. I'd have to rely on the small-scale chart and my memory to get myself in there. There had been a pontoon too, the inevitable piece of salmon walkway at the left-hand side of the beach. It was a privately-owned jetty, but I hoped the owners wouldn't mind.

If I was lucky, if the moon came out so that I could see, I'd get in.

I could hear the engine noise ebbing and fading. The light flashed and dimmed. Whoever it was was still searching further back, nearer Papa, the Kirk Sands bay and Hamna Voe; he, she, hadn't expected our smooth exit and *Khalida*'s turn of speed under sail. The chart marked the five-fathom line as being outside the rocks; I came back into the cockpit, took the tiller in hand and edged her closer, closer, hearing the waves breaking on the cliffs in a fringe of white foam and watching the depth sounder all the way. It plummeted suddenly from thirty to seven, and I turned parallel to the coast again.

The light dazzled in my direction again. The engine noise rose. Glory be, as I was just beginning to think that I'd have to give the whole idea up and risk the open sea, the moon slid smoothly out from behind the clouds. The water dazzled. Now I knew where I was. The headland with the little island called the Skerry of Stools was just behind me. The next headland, just off my starboard bow, was the turning I wanted, and the chart had looked as if I wanted to keep clear of it. I was happy to do that, and I could see it well now, the white foam outline edging the black rocks. *Keep to the right-hand edge*, Magnie had said, as we looked at the bay. To starboard, the moon showed the other side of the opening, with the water stretching silver between them to the curve of beach.

The wind was behind me for going in. I nipped forward and dropped the mainsail, bundling it hastily up with bungees, then came back to the cockpit and half-furled the jib. I began edging into the bay. There was water breaking white on rocks to starboard, the green scribble of the chart, but still over six metres under my keel – 5.8 – 5.5 – and then it began to shelve towards the beach. It was a motorboat that had lain at the pontoon, I remembered, drawing at most a foot of water. It might not be deep enough for me. I furled more of the jib and hauled the kedge anchor out of the aft locker. It would hold her in this sheltered bay, in this emergency, if it needed to, but I'd try the pontoon first. The tide was rising, so if I touched I'd wait, then reverse once I was floating again.

I didn't touch. I rolled the jib completely and went in on *Khalida*'s momentum. By the time I was within grabbing distance of the pontoon I must have had only a paddling depth of water between my keel and the sandy bottom, but I was still floating. I flung a rope around the black tube and secured *Khalida* at this end, then hurried forward to tie her bow too.

I'd been only just in time. Seconds after I'd tied up I heard the motorboat, closer than ever, and saw the bright light pass the mouth of the bay. I listened, hands tight on the guard rail as the engine noise dwindled into the darkness, then clambered onto the pontoon and ran ashore and up the dark hill, stumbling on the uneven ground. The white light moved swiftly away on the silver sea, turned, came back halfway, then turned again and roared into Snarraness, out again, into the West Burrafirth channel. I waited for ten minutes more, but it didn't reappear.

My hands were shaking and my legs weak under me as I made my way back down the hill.

VI
Rapid Wind Changes

Chapter Twenty-one

Wednesday 23rd October

Tide times Aith
HW 05.14 (1.8m); LW 11.35 (1.0m);
HW 17.33 (1.9m); LW 23.01 (0.9m)

Moonrise 00.05, sunrise 08.03; moonset 16.58, sunset 17.33.

Waning crescent moon

It was almost daylight when I woke, just before eight. I'd risked sleeping below and warming myself up with a hot water bottle, for I was shaking as if I'd got flu. Cat and Kitten had stayed with me at first, but they were gone now, no doubt exploring the beach. I hoped Cat wouldn't find Kitten a dead fish; he could take it, but it would upset her young innards.

It was a bonny morning. The sun slanted in across *Khalida*'s chart table and onto the couch, lightening the faded navy cushions, and sparking gold lights in the wooden fiddle that kept my books in place at sea. Best of all, I thought with a bounce of my heart, Gavin was coming on the ferry. It left West Burrafirth at 09.00, so he'd be on his way from the house now, and on Papa by quarter to ten.

I wriggled out of my berth and went up on deck, stretching. There was a light breeze from the west and the clouds around the horizon had darkened from white to pearl grey. A dozen seals were sunbathing on the beach, grey, brown, pale yellow, with the white-fluffed pups among them. They raised their heads to look at me with mournful eyes. Cat was sitting on the end of the pontoon, enjoying the sun, and Kitten was exploring the stones beside it, probing cracks between them with a white paw.

I'd been too tired to look properly at my anchor rope last night. I looked now. The figure-of-eights round the cleat were just as I'd left them, and the rope stretched down into the water. I hauled it up, and up, and up, and found what looked like the whole length of rope apart from the splice to the chain. The ends splayed clean, cut with a sharp knife. I coiled it all up and stowed it away, thinking. No wonder I hadn't heard a dinghy. Someone had dived down and cut it.

The water was halfway down the beach. It was time we were going. I called the cats aboard, set the engine going and turned *Khalida* in a tight circle. Now I could actually see the fringes of brown rocks I was overwhelmed by my luck in having got in unscathed. I wasn't going to risk being stranded as well.

I got straight out and into open water, then set *Khalida* for Papa on the autopilot while I fed the cats and made myself a cup of tea. Uncle had promised breakfast. If ever there was a woman who needed a cinnamon roll or several, I was that woman, and I was sure there'd be enough for Gavin as well, if his duties allowed.

I brooded on that cut anchor rope all the way over. It wasn't surprising that I hadn't heard anyone if they'd swum over, presumably from that motorboat. My anchor buoy would have been visible in the moonlight, and I'd been only two hundred metres out, in four metres of water. It would have been easy for an experienced swimmer in a wetsuit to follow the buoy's rope down to the anchor, then feel along the chain to the actual anchor rope and cut that. Once I was loose, all they had to do was return to their boat and wait for me to get into trouble.

Amitola was a diver; she and Stevie had gone exploring underwater from the *Swan*. Tammie had been a fisherman; a lot of them learned diving, just to be able to free a rope-wound prop. Either he or Roberts could have swum out from the beach – except that the motorboat had come from outwith Papa. That might be something Gavin could trace: a high-bowed white motorboat with a searchlight that had been towed by car to somewhere nearby, Sandness or Melby, and launched there at midnight. Somebody would have seen it, and maybe even noted the car registration.

I'd just got into Housa Voe when I heard the ferry approaching. I managed to beat it to the pier, and had secured my warps and fenders when it came in with a high-speed rush and wash of water which bounced *Khalida* up and down. A quick glance showed me Gavin, leaning his forearms on the ferry rail and smiling at me. There were a couple of uniforms behind him. I gave him a wave, re-checked my fenders and set out up the old pier and towards the new one, Kitten on my shoulder and Cat at my heels. The ferry tailgate was already down as I approached, and a Land Rover came off. A scrambler motorbike roared out from behind it, went off-road to pass it, and disappeared in a cloud of exhaust fumes. After it came the foot passengers: Betty, looking bitter as ever, and refusing help from Geordie's arm to come off the ferry, or Jen's to walk up the pier. Geordie and the two children followed her, the children dangling bright rucksack schoolbags, and Gavin came after them.

The sight of him filled me with a sudden rush of love. He was dressed down for this one, in his green kilt and leather sporran instead of scarlet and goatshair splendour. He had a white shirt, no tie, and the tweed jacket with the baggy pockets. His hair shone russet in the autumn sun. I came forward and hugged him, enjoying the muscled warmth of his back under my hands. Kitten squeaked in protest and clung on to my shoulder with all four sets of claws. I put up a hand to steady her. He smoothed my plait with one hand. '*Halo, mo chridhe.* Yes, hello, Kitten.' He turned round. 'Hello, Cat.'

Duty done, he turned back to me, smiling. 'It's good to see you early.' He made a face, corners of his long mouth turned down. 'Though how much I'll see of you until this is cleared up I don't know.'

I was beginning to learn the ways of a policeman's girl-friend. 'Not much, I suppose. Come and meet some of the people involved.'

'I met some of them last night. A couple of them are on the ferry. Your birthday man and his sister.'

'Really?' I turned my head to look at the last passengers coming off. 'What are they doing here?'

'Shearer said being here reminded him what fun scrambling can be, so he took advantage of the fine day to come back. Amitola didn't say, but she had a spade with her, sticking out of a bag.' He glanced along the road. 'They didn't come to-gether, and seemed surprised to see each other.'

'A spade?' I thought of the turned earth at the ruined cot-tages, and held him back for a moment.

He glanced down at me. 'Anything you want to tell me about before we go up there?'

'Yes. *Yes.*' All I'd learned yesterday came back in a rush. Quickly, eyes darting round me for anyone close enough to listen, I told him about Ruby's account of the hippy colony and the baby's grave. He nodded, eyes intent.

'I'll get Freya on to all that. A home birth, the baby dying and the lifeboat bringing off the woman. We should be able to find out whose baby it was.'

'Ruby didn't know.'

'Roberts will. I'll ask him.' He smiled at my surprise. 'Ask-ing is often the simplest way of finding things out. He should know, and if he doesn't want to tell us, well, that could be sig-nificant too.'

'Keep an eye out for diving equipment, while you're in his house. A wetsuit, a snorkel.'

'Oh?'

I nodded over at the anchor buoy, floating serenely in the middle of the voe. 'That's my anchor. The rope was cut down at the chain last night. I had to drift out through the stacks and hide. A motorboat was looking for me. White, high bows, with a searchlight bar. I was hoping you might find out who it was. It came from outside this voe. Launched from a trailer at Sandness, maybe. There's a pier at Melby.'

His eyes sharpened. 'Hang on.' He fished out his notebook. 'White, high bows, searchlight bar.'

'Of course,' I added with regret, 'that eliminates Roberts for that particular bit of skulduggery.'

Gavin smiled. 'I get the impression you haven't taken to Roberts. Freya said he'd tried to bully you.'

'He didn't succeed,' I said briskly. 'Will we go up? Uncle's cinnamon rolls are calling me.'

I led him up after Jen, Betty, Geordie and the children to where Uncle was standing in his gateway. 'May I bring in one more? My partner, Gavin.' He wouldn't want to sail under a false flag. 'DI Gavin Macrae of Police Scotland.'

Uncle held out his hand. 'Welcome, Gavin.' His gaze went past him to the two uniformed officers, standing irresolutely at the top of the pier. He raised an arm and gestured them towards us. 'Come up, come up.'

There were cinnamon rolls, and proper French coffee, and a blazing fire in the stove. The two uniformed officers stayed in the kitchen, but the rest of us all squashed onto the sofas and chairs of the snug. Cat stretched out in front of the stove; Kitten curled up in my lap, taking all compliments from Geordie's children as her due. They were like each other and like Geordie, dark-haired and blue-eyed, polite enough but eyeing Gavin and me up with subdued wariness. Betty gave an account of her time in the hospital, and the children told Uncle all their plans of what they were going to do with the friends who would arrive to stay on this afternoon's ferry. Jen ate and cradled her belly with that inner smile. It was a million miles away from crazy dodging of rocks with my heart pounding, and a white searchlight combing the shifting sea. Uncle had noticed I'd been out of the bay, I was sure, but he didn't mention it.

'Well,' Gavin said, when we'd all finished eating and had our third cup of coffee, 'I suppose I'd need to justify my presence here.' He turned to Jen. 'I know you've already been interviewed by DS Peterson, but I hope you won't mind me asking more questions. I don't yet feel I have a sense of the kind of person Kenny was, and you're the one to tell me.'

Geordie's children rose. 'We'd better see what Dad's up to,' Cathy said. 'He said not to bother you for too long.'

'You're never any bother,' Uncle said. 'Take him a couple of rolls.'

'Your house isn't far, is it?' Gavin said to Jen. He made it sound diffident, but I knew he'd have studied the map before coming, and knew exactly where everything was. 'Shall I get a car to run you?'

'Oh, no, it's just a step, and walking's good for me.'

'See you maybe lunchtime, Cass,' Gavin murmured to me, and he and Jen headed outwards, followed by Geordie's children.

'It's time I was home too,' Betty said. She rose, and fixed me with her sharp eyes. 'Come you wi' me, Cass. There's things I want to tell you.'

We walked in silence over to Betty's cottage, leaving the cats back at the boat. Her funny turn didn't seem to have done her any harm, for she strode out briskly over the grass, and flung her front door open with a bang. 'Now go you in and put the kettle on, while I see to the cow. I'll no' be long.'

She changed her town shoes for rubber boots, put on her

230

nylon pinny and headscarf and headed out. I went into the kitchen, riddled and lit the Rayburn, then filled the kettle and put it on. It was an old-fashioned kitchen which had been done up to the extent of stainless steel sinks below the window, and modern units all round, but the Rayburn still held pride of place in the chimney nook, with an armchair on each side of it. The teapot was sitting on it, all ready. I found mugs by the sink, and teabags, and a jug of milk in the fridge in the back porch. There was a breadmaker sitting there, a boon to people in out-of-the-way places; I'd noticed Uncle had one too. I resolved to get one for our cottage. By the time Betty's footsteps clumped on the briggistanes again, the kettle had boiled, and the tea was ready to pour. It was the last thing I needed, after Uncle's breakfast, but no serious talk could take place in Shetland without a cup of tea in hand.

'Now, sit you down,' Betty said, gesturing to one of the armchairs by the fire. She put a mug of tea into my hand and came straight to the point, without any nervous preambles.

'I'm right blyde you're been able to come here and help us out, and I'm truly grateful to you for doing it. You're been involved in investigations like this before, so I hope you'll be able to make sure justice's done in this one.' Her eyes blazed. 'That man was responsible for Kenny's death.' Her chin jerked towards Paul Roberts's cottage.

'Paul Roberts?' I said.

She nodded emphatically. 'Him and no other. He can say all he likes to the police about having no motive, but him that's awa' was found right at the door of his house. He's a man o' violence. I ken that – who should ken better? I lived with it for ten years.' She took a sip of tea and lifted her head to look me straight in the face. 'You're wondering, the way everyone does, why I put up wi' it for ten years. You ken you wouldn't do it. The first sign o' violence and you'd be off.' Her mouth was a hard line. 'A poor, weak thing I musta been to bide wi' him.'

She leaned forward. Her voice softened. 'See, it's no' like that. D'you ken anything about domestic violence?'

I shook my head.

'Two women die in Britain every week, at the hands o' their pairtners.'

My mouth fell open. For a moment I thought I'd misheard. 'Two every week?'

'And rising. The numbers have gone up this last years, as times get harder. Men take out their frustration on their women.' She sat up straight, and snorted. 'I've reason to be interested in how the world's going for women victims. Less money, fewer shelters and so the number of deaths rises. I tell you, men are dangerous. You can say that the world's changed for women, and so it has, but the men haven't changed, and they resent the women. Did you ever hear that Trump speak? That's what the men are still thinking inside.' She indicated Roberts's house. 'Him too. I'm telling you, he's violent. He killed Kenny.'

She leaned forward again. 'You're just moving in wi' your policeman, aren't you? D'you expect it to all be plain sailing, wi' no arguments, no surprises about him?'

I shook my head.

'O' course no'. You're a sensible cratur, and you ken you're only seen a part o' him in your courting, and maybe the best side o' him at that. You're expecting there'll be odd ways you'll hae to adapt to, am I right?'

'Yes,' I agreed. I'd been trying to think about that. I knew Gavin was more old-fashioned than I was, though I hoped not to find out he was a dyed-in-the-wool Conservative voter.

'So you take the first signs as one of those odd ways. You're newly married, and you want to make it work. You can't just go racing back to your mam because he lost his temper once, or disagreed wi' you over the way you remembered something you'd done thegither. Then slowly you find that you're no' allowed to have your own memories, because he gets that angry when you volunteer something that he says was different. It's easier just to say it was the way he says it was. And then you find you doubt your own memory because he's so positive you're wrong. You get blamed for little things first, and inside you go, oh' I don't think it was me filled the kettle too full, or whatever, and gradually you began to doubt that too, and think you're a clumsy wife who can't be trusted to do anything, just like he says.' Her sharp eyes bored into mine. 'All this without a hand laid on you, mind. What can you complain about? How can you leave him, just for having a better memory than you?'

I remembered one skipper I'd had, in the Caribbean, who'd never allowed anyone but himself to do anything right. Three days of him had reduced me to sullen obedience to direct orders, but never taking my own initiative, and I'd left the ship at the next port.

'And by now I had the bairns. Aabody said what a good father he was, when we were out in the town, and how lucky I was to have a good husband.' Her mouth twisted. 'What can you say? *He's no like that at home?* Him a teacher too, nobody would have believed it. I just had to keep a smiling face and do my best, and all the time I was being eroded away inside. I felt like a nothing. I couldn't remember anything any more, I didn't have the confidence, and I was always losing things. And then I took to keeping a diary. Oh, he'd have been that angry if he'd known, but I found a loose floorboard when I was dusting under the bed, and I hid it there. I wrote down what I'd done. I even started to write down what he'd done, and said. I just needed to keep some sense of myself, of who I was. I wasna a silly peerie lassie. I'd been a teacher too. I'd geen to the University, I'd taken my degree.'

She paused to look out of the window for a moment, then set her cup down on the Rayburn with a snap. 'And I found out that I wasn't losing my memory or my mind. I had the diary to check with now. Then one day I was talking to another women whose man was like that – oh, you ken each other! – and she said this to me.' She took a long breath and gave the words clearly, spacing them out. '"It's not that he's forgotten. He does it on purpose, to put you in the wrong. To keep the upper hand over you." And it was true. Oh, I wasn't wanting to leave him, because of the bairns, he was a good father to them so long as they didn't cross him. And what would I do? I'd got my degree, and done my probation, but that was six years before. So I gritted my teeth and tried no' to annoy him, and cherished my sense o' who I was in my head. And then – '

She looked down into the fire, and spoke softly. 'Times were different then. They were innocent days. Nobody woulda believed me, I hardly believed it myself.' She lifted her head and looked at me again, eyes hard. 'When she went to the school, Jen began to get uppity. You ken, she'd contradict him, with "Our teacher says", or think for herself when he gave an order. "But, Daddy, what if . . . ?" She'd been his little princess before that, but now she was always in trouble with him. She was escaping his control. Then I found the photos.'

There was a long silence. She looked at me, and nodded. 'Photos o' Jen wi' nae claes on. Photos he'd asked her to pose for, no' knowing what they meant.' Her mouth twisted. 'They were in his desk. I felt sick just looking at them. There were several packets o' them. Now I ken he musta been selling them, but we kent nothing about any o' this then. The Cleveland scandal, that was the first most of us had ever heard o' such a thing as adults sexually abusing children, and it wasn't till a couple of years later. Then I understood what he'd been doing, but at the time I just stood there with the photos in my hand feeling sick. I had to get us out of there.'

She paused, and glanced down at her arm again. 'I needed

evidence o' physical harm. I needed this.' Her lips thinned, set in a determined line. Abruptly, she thrust her arm out, and pulled back the sleeve. There was a line of puckers running from elbow to wrist along the inner arm. 'Cigarette burns.' Her eyes narrowed to slits of granite; her voice grated. 'These were what I took to the lawyer, for my divorce, to get the bairns and me free o' him. I talked to the friend who'd helped me. *He* didn't know her, nor anything about her. I took some of the bairns' clothes to her the next day, while he was at work, and the following day I took the bairns and left them with her while I filed for divorce, and then we all got on the ferry to Papa, where my dad and my uncle would protect me from him. They'd no' have believed about Jen, but they believed the burns.'

There was a long silence. Her head came up again. 'But I still lived in fear o' him until Saturday night. Until I saw him again. I'm no' afraid now. You'd a thought it would be the other way round, wouldn't you, that I'd ha stopped being afraid until the sight o' him brought it back?' She shook her head. 'Well, yea, it did bring it back, and for a moment I felt sick right in my belly, but after that suddenly I was just blazing mad. Him coming here, and behaving as if nothing had ever happened. Making it my fault he had to change his name and go elsewhere.' Her head was high, her eyes defiant. If I'd been Roberts I'd have backed away from her. 'I'm no' his wife any more, and there are laws to protect me if he lays a finger on me. And he's no' coming anywhere near my grandbairns.' Her face was set in determined lines, her voice harsh. 'I'd kill him first, and go to prison gladly for it.'

She meant it. I looked at the left hand that had indicated the burns, that had set out the cups and poured the tea, and at the puckered scars up her right arm, and wondered at the courage, the desperation, that would drive a women to injure herself like that to set herself free.

'You need to tell Gavin about this,' I said at last. 'Or DS Peterson, if you haven't told her already.'

Her mouth twisted. 'The police don't believe you. They didn't then and they still don't. Oh, I ken, they've had all this "awareness" and "sensitivity" training, but the men still stick together. You tell your Gavin to look up the court case. He'll maybe believe that.' Her mouth shut like a trap.

I let the silence hang for a bit, then asked one of the things I'd been wondering about. 'Did you know that your ex-husband lived here, before you married?'

She looked at me with astonishment. 'He bade here, apo Papa? But he was a Burra man, he had no connections wi' the isle.'

I nodded. 'He was one of the hippy colony, over the headland there.'

'The hippy colony?' She shook her head. 'It was, I'll no' say before my time, but I was just a peerie lass then. I canna mind anything about them other than they were there. Me mam telt me to keep well clear o' them, and I did. He was a good piece older as me, you ken, a mature student when I was straight from school. He never would say his age, but when I saw our marriage lines I realised. He was thirty-four to my twenty-two.' She was silent a moment, thinking about it. 'But I don't see what that has to do with anything. Kenny came between him and Jen, and he killed him for that.' I didn't reply, and she poked her head forward and peered at me with those small, sharp eyes. 'Are you just trying to make it clever? Why should it have anything to do with those hippies?'

'I don't see why it should, but I think it might, all the same.' I was about to add that the folk on the boat, Amitola and her daughters, had been connected with it too, but then realised I'd have to talk about Sun and Moon's father, that they might be her children's half-sisters. I wasn't going there. 'But now you're here, you and Geordie, you'll protect Jen from him bothering her.'

I was in the doorway when I remembered the question I hadn't asked. 'How did it come about that you found Kenny's body?' *Something furtive in the way she was glancing around her*, Jen had said, *as if she didn't want to be seen*.

'Find him? Lass, he was just below the briggistane there. I saw him from me doorway.'

I glanced down towards where he'd been lying, and was pretty sure I couldn't see the spot from here. 'You weren't on your way to visit Roberts and tell him to go?'

Her eyes glanced sharply at me and moved away again. The thin mouth pursed up. There was a long silence. I could see she wasn't going to tell me anything she didn't want to. 'I won't say I hadn't thought of it,' she said at last.

I looked at her standing there, with one of the puckered burns just showing below her sleeve, and knew it was all I was going to get out of her. 'Thanks for the tea,' I said, and headed back towards the pier.

Chapter Twenty-two

It was half past eleven now. I walked briskly to the pier and *Khalida*. I checked that her ropes were fine for the rising tide, and that Cat and Kitten were okay, peacefully curled up in my berth in their usual positions, Cat curled around Kitten with her head resting on his silvery belly. Kitten raised her head as I came in, and Cat opened one eye, then closed it again as he realised nothing interesting was happening. I locked the washboards again and left them to it. I'd catch up with Gavin, and say goodbye to Jen, then we'd be on our way.

It was still a bonny day, more like summer than autumn, with the grass still green on the verges and a last sprinkling of sea campion at the corner, magenta, blush-pink, white. The wind was shifting now, puffing from one direction, then another. The clouds were higher up the sky, long, dark skeins. The morning forecast gave me till the evening to get home.

I strode up the road, enjoying moving after a morning sitting about. The only sign of life in Geordie's house was a thump, thump, thump from somebody's music player, coming out of the window above the flat-roofed shed. The leaves of the yellow flag iris in the ditch below Jen's garden were pointed with rust-brown, like swords which had been left uncleaned.

I hesitated at Jen's gate, then went the half-dozen steps further. Since I was on Papa I might as well have a look at the Stofa. I came past the shed beyond Jen's house, and paused for a moment, something catching at my heart. It was the best type of Shetland man's shed, roofed with something corrugated which I hoped was iron, but was more likely asbestos, and with a big door in the middle for getting boats in and out. The front was harled, but the gables were still the old crofthouse's stone, and festooned with useful bruck that Kenny had kept, because you never knew when it might not be just the thing you needed to lay your hand on: a length of solid chain, a couple of lobster pot buoys, a necklace-ring of different coloured net floats, a red safety ring from a ship, all hung up on nails. There were the inevitable pallets propped against one wall, and a pile of breeze blocks, and a stack of metal fence-pieces for sheep-gathering time. It was all so very Shetland, and it conjured up Kenny as if he was standing in front of me. Now it would cut at Jen's heart every time she came out here, but later it would be a comfort.

The Stofa interpretation board was in front of the far gable. It had an account of the dispute between Ragnhild and Earl Thorvald, and a photograph of the document telling the story in tiny dense handwriting, with dangling ribbons and faded seals on its bottom edge. Beside the text was an artist's impression of what the Stofa had looked like then: a log cabin with one stone wall, a thatch roof, a door at this end, and a trickle of smoke issuing from a hole in the middle of the roof.

Below was a bit about the archaeology. The timbers, they reckoned, had rotted away – I took that with a pinch of salt, as I couldn't see Kenny's ancestors leaving good timber to rot. Converted to roofs or boats would have been my guess, or at worst used for firewood. The floor, however, had been left, and carbon-dated to between 1200 and 1400 – Ragnhild's time. It wouldn't have had quite such a *Little House on the Prairie* look either, for the board explained that it had stone walls all around the outside of the wooden house, to protect the timbers. And the inhabitants, I thought. I betted they stuffed the gap with sheepskins, and hunkered down snug as bugs in rugs around their fire.

I turned with interest to the Stofa itself. I'd been inside the replica house at Haraldswick, but it was made only of stone. This was quite different. The actual foundations were further over in the field, and the replica was just four courses of logs, to waist-height, and dark with creosote. Gravel was laid where the wooden floor and hearth would have been. To give you the idea of the protecting wall, they'd reconstructed two sides of it in local stone that glowed red in the afternoon sun. I went inside and tried to imagine it roofed over, with the flames flickering on the walls, and Ragnhild and her elderly father and a handful of children sitting on benches.

I was just about to come out when a swirl of colour caught my eye, a woman coming up the road. My first thought was that it was Jen, coming up from the kirk, but it was a springier walk with a lithe, long stride, and the patchwork skirt was familiar: Amitola. The striped bag was slung awkwardly over one shoulder and cradled under that arm, as if it held something fragile, and a spade swung in her other hand. There was something forced about the jauntiness of the movement.

I went back to looking at the Stofa again, so as not to stare at her coming towards me, but she'd spotted me. She called, 'Hi, Cass!' then waited till she got level with me to add, 'I wasn't expecting to see you here. I thought you'd be on the *Swan* going somewhere else.'

I shook my head. 'She's gone to her winter quarters. I brought my own boat over.'

'I came back on this morning's ferry. On a pilgrimage, you might say.'

Her saying that much suggested she wanted to talk about it. There were dark shadows under her eyes, and a paleness under the skin that turned her tan to a weathered fawn, but there was a peacefulness about her face too, overlaid by something else that I couldn't quite put my finger on, a sense of her not being quite there. She hadn't exactly stumbled on the word 'pilgrimage' but there'd been a hesitation, as if she'd wanted to make sure she pronounced it properly. She peered over the end wall into the log-framed space. 'Is that the Stofa?' She set her bag down carefully, propped the spade beside it, and came around into the house. 'This is interesting.'

'What was your pilgrimage?' seemed too direct a question. 'You used to live here, didn't you?'

She nodded towards the headland. 'Over there, in the two cottages above the kirk sands. It was, oh, getting on for fifty years ago now.' She paused, a startled look on her face. 'Is it really? Yes, it must be. Sky, Kirsten, she was born the second year we were here, and she was forty-eight last birthday, and Moon – ' She bit the words off short and stood for a moment, contemplating the water. 'Goodness. How time does go.'

Yes, there was something wrong about her voice, about her whole demeanour. That walk had looked a parody of her normal stride; her voice was slowed, with a suggestion of slurring on the longer words. For a moment I wondered if she was drunk, and then I realised it was more likely that she was tranquilised, not enough to stop her behaving almost normally, but enough to clamp the grief for Moon away until she was able to deal with it.

She turned and smiled at me, and I saw for a moment the pretty girl she had been, all those years ago. She spoke brightly. 'You won't even think of time passing now, but it just goes, like that, and suddenly you're forty, and then fifty, and sixty, and any moment now I'll be seventy, and when I was eighteen and rebellious I never expected even to grow that old. Old age was for other people. We thought we'd be immortal – oh, not seriously, but that's the way it feels when you're young.'

'What was it like, your colony?'

'Yes, the hippy colony, that's what they called us!' There was no sign of resentment in her voice. 'The folk of the island were kind, but they thought we were very strange. We had all these ideals, you know, peace, and love, and getting back to nature, getting away from the corruption of the city and modern life.' She stumbled over the word 'corruption' and then speeded up her speech, as if she wanted to say it all before she lost the ability to speak. 'There were twelve of us, six couples, and we just wanted to live in freedom, doing what we wanted to do, living off the land and what we could make. Stella, she made rag rugs out of old clothes, and I painted little watercolours and framed them, and Chenoa and Chilam, they were sisters, they knitted ganseys for the Peerie Shop. My boyfriend, Paytah, he was a painter too, but big canvases, seascapes. He had an exhibition the year Moon was born and sold several of them, and Cheveyo sold photographs. That kept us going for a while. We shared everything, money, food, and we all worked together to grow what we could.' Her face was bright, remembering. 'We built a greenhouse with old windows inside one of the planticrubs and it was amazing what we managed to grow there, salad greens right from February, and then in the yaird we had vegetables to keep us going all winter. We had hens and a couple of goats for milk, and sheep, we spun our own wool. We made our own bread too, even ground our beremeal for flour. We couldn't grow wheat, but I made fantastic beremeal scones in the Rayburn.'

'It sounds like hard work,' I said frankly. 'Didn't you ever envy the folk on the mainland with electricity and washing machines?'

'Washing!' She made a face. 'We washed our clothes in the burn.' She shook her head. 'No, we envied nobody. It was hard but it was satisfying too, and surprisingly healthy. We got used to the cold. Nobody had any allergies the way so many young folk do now. I don't even remember any bouts of flu or sickness. We weren't mixing with other folk much. Cheveyo was the one who used to go into Lerwick.'

Cheveyo, Ruby had said, *Spirit Warrior*. Roberts. Amitola's voice had sharpened as she spoke his name. 'He was our leader, no, not leader exactly, but he'd been our inspiration to come here. He was keen to go somewhere where we could lead our own lives, away from the values our parents inflicted on us, and then somebody he knew told him about these crofts on Papa that were empty, only recently left, and so we decided to give it a go.'

This felt all wrong. I didn't want to ask questions. She knew what she was saying, of course, but I didn't know whether she'd be saying any of it without the influence of whatever she'd taken. But she wanted to talk; she rattled on.

'We were here for six years. Sky was five when we left, and Moon was three.' Her face twisted. 'Moon. I still can't believe it.' She turned her face towards me, eyes bleak. 'They won't let me bury her, not yet. They have to keep her, because it wasn't an accident that she died.' Her face was incredulous, bewildered. 'The policeman who visited me yesterday evening.' Her face lightened. 'He wasn't from here. He wore a kilt. He was on the ferry this morning. A kind face, he had – good eyes. You'd trust a man like that.'

I thought of Gavin's sea-grey eyes. My heart warmed with pride in him.

'He said – he wouldn't let me say it was an accident. He said somebody killed her. I can't believe it. But it was that that made me want to come back – ' Her eyes were wet. She blinked the tears away. Her eyes blazed suddenly. 'Things went all wrong.'

She turned her head away, gazing out over the headland. You couldn't see the roofs of the croft houses from here, nor the kirk, just the green hill. 'It was really wonderful at first, all living together. We all got on well. Sky was the first child to be born here. It was late summer, and a beautiful day, and the sea was warm, so we women all lay in it during the contractions, and then they helped me back to the house, and she was born there. That was amazing, this new life emerging, so little and red and crumpled, though at the time I was terrified too, in case something went wrong. Cheveyo said nothing would go wrong.' There was that hardening of her voice again. 'He said that childbirth was the most natural process in the world, and if only women would listen to their bodies, it would be easy for them.'

'And you believed him?' I said, before I could stop myself.

'He was, well, our guru.' She looked at me and shook her head. 'Things were so different then. You're so young, you have no idea. Men were automatically more knowledgeable than women, yes, even in the seventies where we were talking about equality and fighting for equal pay. It was a bit of a con really. Free love meant the men got to sleep around and pressurise women who didn't want to, on the grounds that they were frigid or had bourgeois hang-ups. The women still stayed at home and ran the house and raised the children.'

'No equality of tasks.'

There was a flash of normality in her expression, a sardonic look. 'The men's work was important, you see, composing poetry, or painting, or thinking enlightened thoughts. They didn't do mundane things like cooking meals or caring for children.'

I'd always suspected that women did more than their fair share of the work in these idealistic back-to-nature colonies. 'The genius's wife syndrome – he has time to be a genius because he doesn't have to do anything else. No worry about putting the black bags out, or what to have for tea.'

'Exactly.'

'Was that what broke the colony up?'

She shook her head. 'We all took it for granted. No. It was the baby.' Her hand cupped her belly, as Jen's had done. 'I was having another baby. I was seven months on. I thought it would be easy, because Moon had been quicker than Sky, but I started having odd pains. I wanted to go to the doctor, but Cheveyo said I was making myself ill by thinking that I was, and he convinced Paytah. Betraying their ideals.'

She paused and moistened her lips, eyes still on the shore across the sound; the shore less than a mile away, further than the moon, where there were doctors and nurses and hospitals. 'I was desperate. I was all set to sneak away from them and get on the ferry, get the bus to Lerwick and present myself at the hospital, or there was this boy here, Tammie, who'd always spoken kindly to me. I thought he might put me over to Sandness in his boat, for the doctor's surgery. But I knew that if I did that they'd be furious with me. So I hesitated, and then one morning I felt a pain like a knife through me, and, well, it was all day, and then the baby was born. She was dead. We buried her in the croft, in the corner of the yaird. Then about a week later I began running a temperature. I was really ill, delirious, and the other women insisted I was to go to hospital. The baby's death had frightened them. Stella went to the box and phoned 999, and the lifeboat came and took me off. I took the girls with me, and my mother looked after them.'

'Not Paytah? Didn't he go too?'

She shook her head. 'He was going to, the baby's death had startled him too. But Cheveyo told us if we went we couldn't come back.' Her voice shuddered with the pain she'd felt. 'Paytah chose the colony over me. Some of the others stayed on for a bit after I left, not long, maybe another couple of months. Stella and I, we still keep in touch, and I sometimes see Chiloa around the town, but I never heard from any of the others again. Not even Paytah. Men then, they didn't reckon so much to girls. There wasn't this "daddy's little princess" thing. It was the boy who counted.'

She smiled suddenly, face softening. 'But Stevie was still home at Mam's. He was a teenager then, and he was absolutely

245

great. He was their father-substitute, just the right age to be something between a big brother and a hero. I remember them all shrieking with laughter together. He had a video-camera, he'd saved up all his paper-round money to buy it, and they'd dance along to Kylie Minogue hits, then watch themselves. They loved him.'

I wondered if she was trying to convince herself, or me. I let the silence hang. The waves shushed in the distance, and land birds chuckled in the bushes in Jen's garden. Amitola stood for a moment with her hands on the walls, eyes closed, breathing deeply. Then she turned away from me, and spoke towards the sea in Papa Sound.

'I failed Moon,' she said abruptly. 'She said there was something wrong about Stevie. When I talked to Sky, Kirsten, she said Moon was making it all up, no, not quite that, but that the therapy was planting false memories. She insisted there was nothing, and I don't remember anything wrong, and anyway, Stevie wouldn't.' She paused, then repeated vehemently, 'He wouldn't. He loved them. He'd never have done that – I don't believe it. But when Moon began speaking about it, I didn't want to think about it.' Her dark eyes glittered with tears. 'I wish now I'd tried to talk to her about it instead of denying it all.'

Her voice trailed away. She looked out across the blue water again, then turned back to me. 'And I came to give Star a proper burial. That's what she was going to be called. Stargazer.'

I remembered the little grave in the corner of the old yard. 'It was you who left the cross and the flowers.'

She nodded. 'On Saturday, by moonlight. I didn't come back to *Swan* with Moon, like I told the police. I said I was going for a walk, and went back to the croft. But coming here had brought it all back, and I thought about the baby all weekend. When the policeman with the kind eyes said I

246

couldn't have Moon back, I realised I couldn't bear it, leaving my other baby lying there all alone in that neglected place. I knew there wouldn't be much left of her, just bones. I came over on this morning's ferry.' She looked across at the striped bag, distended round some kind of box, double the size of a shoebox. 'I was so afraid, digging, that I'd damage her, but she was there. The wooden box we'd buried her in had protected her, and the woollen blanket. I didn't unwrap it, just lifted her up and put her in the box.'

Suddenly her dark eyes were looking at me as if my head was glass, seeing right into my thoughts. 'You understand that, don't you? Your baby was lost too.'

It felt like she'd punched me in the stomach. For a moment I couldn't breathe. She kept looking at me, and nodded. 'I'm right, amn't I? I saw it in your aura, when you welcomed us on board. Another life that had been cut short. She was a girl too.'

Only Gavin and I knew about the baby I'd miscarried so soon after I'd known it was there. Only us, and my friend Agnetha, and yet here Amitola was, speaking with such certainty. I stared at her, and could think of nothing to say.

'So I thought I'd ask,' she said. She gestured towards Jen's house, and spoke with the simplicity of desperation. 'She has a kind face, that wife, and she seems to be the one in charge of the kirk. I want her to let me bury my baby in the graveyard there. I don't want a fuss or a service or anything like that, just to have her lying where she'll be tended.'

Goodness knows what regulations were being broken; but I thought Jen would be sympathetic. 'Good luck,' I said.

I walked the few steps to Jen's door with her, and stopped at the gate. 'Amitola,' I said, as she opened it, 'did you know that Cheveyo was on the island?'

She stopped dead and drew her breath in with a harsh rattle. Her head was turned away from me so that I couldn't see her eyes. When she swung round to face me her face was set hard, hiding her thoughts. 'Here? Now?'

'He was at the concert on Saturday night, and in the school afterwards. You didn't see him?'

Her lips folded tight. She shook her head, and her grey curls writhed around her face. 'No. No. I didn't see him.' Her eyes flared. 'Nor would I want to. It's all over and done with.'

She turned away from me, and strode up the path to the house.

Chapter Twenty-three

Geordie came out of the house a couple of minutes after Amitola went in, brows drawn down. He saw me standing there, and managed a smile. 'Aye aye, Cass, what're you up to?'

'I was just wanting to say goodbye to Jen. I want to be home before dark.'

'Aye, there's a good breeze forecast. She's got that wife from the *Swan* in with her ee now, but they'll likely no' be long.'

'I saw her go in.'

'Yea. They're plotting about breaking all kinds o' regulations. Jen just told me to go off and check on my own house, so I wouldn't need to be a party to it.' He grimaced. 'Ah, well. Thanks to you, Cass, for coming and keeping her company. She said you were a great help.'

I shook my head. 'I didn't do much.'

Geordie raised his hand and stumped off. I paused, thinking. I didn't want to interrupt Amitola and Jen, and I'd been conscious all day of a snoring noise in the distance, on and off, like a tractor shifting bales of silage, or a quad roaring round the hills: maybe Geordie's boy enjoying being a country child. I'd leave the women to themselves, and walk the ten minutes further to the airstrip, see what he was up to. Any right-minded child would take a used-once-a-week airstrip as a heaven-sent place to practise wheelies, if you could wheelie a quad, and I suspected that with enough determination and teenage daredevilry you probably could.

I gave *Khalida* a quick look (all well, Cat now investigating the shore with Kitten behind him, shaking her paws fastidiously every second step) and turned towards the kirk, strode past the Manse and school, and up to the end of the road. There was a long drystane dyke, slightly tumbledown, but reinforced by a stout wire-and-post fence, and a car-width gate marked 'Airstrip – no unauthorised entry'. I clambered over and found myself practically on the airstrip itself, a long, straight stretch of the local red gravel. There was a little shed with a yellow grit bin beside it, not nearly large enough to even pretend to be a waiting room; an emergency toilet for the pilot, maybe, or firefighting equipment. It had been white-washed, but that had been a good few years ago, and the outer plaster was starting to crumble.

I took the few steps further onto the airstrip itself and had a good look around. It was simply a length of levelled gravel, maybe five hundred metres long and twenty wide, with an orange windsock at each end. You'd need to know what you were doing to park a plane on it. The delapidated state of the shed made me wonder if there still were regular flights, or if it was emergencies only. Past it, some thirty metres further, was Hamna Voe, with the rocks where the Dutch brig had been wrecked. The sun was in my eyes; I shaded them with one hand and looked towards the direction of the noise.

It wasn't a quad I'd been hearing, but the scrambler that had come off the ferry this morning: Stevie. The drystane dyke seemed to be the boundary between cultivated land and rough hill, for there was no other fence in sight, which gave him the whole hill to roam over, provided he avoided lochs, sudden cliffs and boggy places. Now he was well over towards the gap between two lochs, the one Geordie had called Dutch Loch, and another one west of the voe where Roberts and the other men had met their RIB to go out to the stricken fishing boat. He went snoring up the hill a way then came back down in a roaring swoop, curving around the other loch, jolting over several ruts and then back around in a wide sweep, heading towards me. On the brow of the hill he bounced onto a tarry road that ran parallel with the airstrip then continued up to a grey and white agricultural shed. The revving up of the engine echoed off the tin wall of the shed then turned to a roar as he came sweeping down the road towards me. He swerved his bike from the track to the airstrip as soon as he reached it, and kept coming straight down, accelerating as he approached.

He couldn't have failed to see me. If I tried to dodge now I could be hit by him swerving to avoid me. Macho show-off. I took a deep breath and stood my ground, watching him come closer, closer, until at the very last minute he swerved in a circle around me, tight enough to have gravel stinging against my trouser legs, and roared off upwards again. If he'd been a teenager he'd deserve his bike getting confiscated. He should have recognised me, but given the full-face helmet and the speed he'd been moving at, I gave him the benefit of the doubt. What he didn't know was that I'd recognised him. I'd still been walking up from *Khalida* when he'd come off the ferry. He thought I was just some nosey passer-by.

I turned and began walking back to the gate. I wasn't going to give him the satisfaction of running. This time he came on the landwards side of me, circled again, and then stopped beside me. He cut the roar to an idle, and took his helmet off. 'Cass! How are you doing? Recovered from the weekend?'

His cheery tone startled me. There was no suggestion of apology for his first run round me. 'Yes.' I nodded at his bike. 'I heard that was you, coming off this morning's ferry.'

'Work gave me a couple of days off.' He turned away from me slightly, face bleak, mouth working, then turned back. There were tears in his eyes. 'Moon. My peerie Moon. I still canna believe it. I was glad of yesterday being busy, it wasn't really a day off, we were having a last go at shifting the *Dorabella*. No good.' He pulled the corners of his mouth down. 'Not even with an empty hold. So we took the crew on board, with the lifeboat in attendance, of course, in case anything went wrong, and stripped her of everything that could be moved. Emptied the fuel tanks as best we could.'

'So you're leaving her to her fate.'

He nodded. 'You'll have listened to the forecast. There's a gale coming.' The corners of his mouth turned downwards again, then he shrugged. 'Nothing to be done. Salvage what you can, and cut your losses.' He left a pause, then summoned up the cheery face once more. 'Here's one I saved specially for the next time I met up with you, Cass: Why does the Norwegian navy have bar codes on the side of their ships?'

He gave a pause to let me look baffled.

'So that when the ships come back into port they can Scandinavian!'

'That's awful,' I said, with feeling. I could see another one trembling on his lips. 'Enjoy your scrambling,' I said hastily, and got out of there.

When I came around the curve of the main road again, Amitola was striding down the road towards the kirk, striped bag cradled under her arm, and Jen was at the gate, watching her go. I lifted a hand to Amitola, and stopped by Jen.

'You just missed your Gavin. He left, oh, half an hour ago.' She gave me a warm smile. 'He's lovely. I hope you'll be as happy together as Kenny and I were.'

'Thank you. I hope so too. I've just come to say goodbye,' I said. I glanced over my shoulder at Amitola. 'You let her, didn't you?'

Jen looked surprised for a moment, then nodded.

'She told me about it, in the Stofa,' I explained.

'I told her to put her baby with the unbaptised infants, in the far corner,' Jen said. 'They'll be company for the little thing.'

'But still in consecrated ground. I'm glad.'

Jen stepped back and gestured towards the house. 'Will you come in for a cup of tea?'

I shook my head. 'No, I'll keep going. The forecast is for it to blow up through the evening, so I want to be home before then. I just wanted to wish you good luck. Let me know when the baby's born.'

'Good luck with your move. Remember now, if ever you're passing Papa in your boat, call in on us, you'll aye be welcome.' Her eyes lit up. 'Come and see Kenny's son.'

'Do you know it's going to be a boy? I wouldn't want to ask, in case they got it wrong, and I was all prepared for the other sex.'

She nodded. 'It's a boy.' Her eyes flicked to Amitola, striding along the road towards the kirk. 'She knew it too, without me telling her.'

'She knows things,' I agreed, and took my leave, pondering. Amitola had seen my child in my aura, she said. If it hadn't been true, I'd have dismissed it as nonsense. Sixties spirituality, being in tune with the universe, all that. My baby had died long before it had lived; it wasn't hovering round me like a ghost. *She*, Amitola had called it. She would have been a girl. She was with God, I reminded myself. Some day I'd meet her. I gave my shoulders a shake, said goodbye again to Jen, and strode off down the road.

I was just stowing everything away below when I heard Gavin's voice above me: 'Ahoy, *Khalida*.'

I came out into the cockpit and smiled up at him. 'Do you have time for a cup of tea?'

'Not really. I'll have one with the others later. I just came to say hello before you set off.'

He swung himself down the ladder and stepped neatly aboard. 'Hello, Cat, hello, Kitten.' He sat down on the cockpit seat, smiled at me, and held out his hand to mine. I leaned forward to kiss his cheek, conscious that his officers would be watching from not far away, and sat down beside him.

'You're leaving soon?'

I nodded, and glanced across at the sky to the north, where there was the first sign of an anvil forming on the grey cumulus. 'I want to be home before that black cloud gets here.'

'The ferry's 3.45.' He glanced at his watch. 'An hour. I'll need to do a bit more in Lerwick before I can come back west, but I'll be home for dinner.'

He said it so casually, as if it was taken for granted that we'd be together tonight in our own house, instead of it being the first time. I tried for an equally casual approach. 'Yes, see you later.'

Gavin gave me a long look that I couldn't quite read. 'I'll be glad to get you off this island. I don't think you're safe here.'

'I'm fine,' I said.

'You were cut loose in the middle of the voe last night.'

I conceded that one. 'But it was a boat from outside.'

He gave me that long look again. 'I didn't want to tell you before we had breakfast with him, but Geordie Tammason owns a white motorboat with high bows and a searchlight bar. I saw him checking it this morning, at West Burrafirth. It's on a trailer there.'

'Geordie!' I said. 'Gavin, no! I don't believe it.'

'I know.' Gavin smiled, and put his arm round my shoulders. 'He's a fellow boat-person, and you take him for granted. I'm not saying he was responsible, but he fits it all very well. Listen. We're still trying to chase up the *Dorabella*'s owners, but let's suppose Geordie owned shares in her. He's an engineer, used to working on fishing boats; why shouldn't he? And Geordie didn't sleep on the *Swan* that Saturday night. There was you

254

and Magnie to take care of the passengers. He spent the night at his own house. Now, you said you'd mistaken Paul Roberts for Geordie before, the first time you saw him. It was dark. Could the person you thought might be Paul, be Geordie instead?'

I considered it and gave a reluctant nod.

'And the door that opened, are you sure it was Roberts's door, or might it have been Tammie's?'

I remembered I'd thought of that, up at the kirk. 'I suppose it might.'

'You see what we're thinking. Geordie and Tammie, two Papa residents, both fishermen. Why shouldn't they both have an interest in the same boat?'

'But Geordie wouldn't have killed Kenny!' I protested.

'He didn't have a motive for killing Kenny, or not that we know, but he certainly had a motive for killing Paul Roberts, who'd come back here determined to associate with his grandchildren, Geordie's children. He's strong enough to lift and swing a fence post.'

It was all horribly true. 'But I think he would have recognised Kenny, if he got a good look at him.'

'Maybe he didn't get a good look. Maybe he didn't see who it was who'd been snooping about on the hill when he and Tammie were dealing with a black fish landing that could have given him a heavy fine or a prison sentence. The person went towards Paul Roberts's house, and Geordie took it to be Roberts.'

I remembered his white, shocked face after he'd spoken to Isla, and found out that Kenny had been murdered. *Poor Jen*, he'd said. *I wish she coulda been spared all this.* I opened my mouth and closed it again.

'Moon was awake on deck, you said, when you got back to the *Swan* on Saturday night.' Gavin's voice was soft, but determined. He wasn't going to let me pull wool over my eyes. 'She

255

could have seen Kenny being murdered, and recognised Geordie.'

'He didn't go to explore Foula − he stayed on board the *Swan* making the soup.' Even as I protested, I realised it didn't have to be true. The soup had been finished before we docked. All it was doing was simmering; and Geordie hadn't been aboard when I'd returned.

Gavin watched me thinking it through. 'He could have been the dark man the crofter saw going along the valley.'

'But why would Geordie want to cut me loose?'

'Who knows that you saw another person on the top of the hill? Did you mention it on board the *Swan* after Stevie left?'

I bit my lip. 'Yes.' Then I brightened. 'But Geordie had gone by then, to catch the ferry. So he didn't know.' Then I remembered *Khalida*'s candlelit cabin, and Jen asking if Moon had been murdered too. My heart sank again. 'I told Jen.'

'Geordie's sister, who might well have told Geordie over the phone yesterday.'

'She did speak to him yesterday.' I felt sick. I'd liked Geordie.

'It's just speculation, but you can see how it hangs together. Get yourself out of here, *mo chridhe*. I'll see you at home.'

He was just gathering himself to rise when two bicycles swooped around the corner above the toilets and hurtled down to the pier. It was Geordie's children. They'd obviously just meant to drop their bikes and come aboard but spotting Gavin made them stay upright, one foot on the ground, one on a pedal, looking as wary as otter cubs.

Gavin raised a hand to the youngsters, and headed off up the pier. I shaded my hand with my eyes and called 'Hi!' up to them.

'Hi,' Cathy said. 'Can we come aboard? We need to speak to you.'

Geordie's children. I couldn't think of any way to get out of it; but surely they weren't going to tell me anything that would

256

incriminate their father. I made a 'be my guest' gesture. 'Sure, on you come.'

They clambered down the iron ladder like children well accustomed to scrambling about in boats, and sat down in the cockpit. Cat reappeared with a visible sigh, and decided to let himself be admired; Kitten shoved after him. Her party trick was rolling on her back and holding her white mittens under her chin, and it never failed to make people go 'aaaah!'

It worked now. Cathy tickled her belly, and I explained the anti-Kitten-overboard precautions. 'I keep the washboards up at sea, with her below, but she's so determined a climber that it's not going to work for much longer. Cat has a lifejacket at sea, though on a day like this it's just an extra precaution.' *We need to speak to you.* The wind wasn't going to hit till the evening, and it would take me only two hours to get to the shelter of the Røna; I had time. 'Come below, while I get the kettle on.'

They followed me down the engine-box steps.

'Cool,' Cathy said. 'It's like a proper house, much nicer than Uncle Kenny's, with all the wood, and the cloth cushions.'

'Not as modern though,' Andy said, and got a sisterly elbow in the ribs. 'There's nothing wrong with not being modern,' he added hastily. 'It's just different.'

'You shut up,' Cathy said. 'Just ignore him, Cass. Your boat's lovely.'

'But old-fashioned,' I agreed. 'In loads of ways.' I turned to Andy. 'Her keel for a start, it's a totally different shape from the keels on modern yachts, that thin, deep keel with a bulb on it, like you might see out of the water in Lerwick. And don't even mention her engine. It starts and it runs, and you can hear it coming from a mile away.' I opened up the engine-box lid to let him see. 'A Volvo Penta, 1980s vintage.'

He was in there immediately, undoing the hooks to tilt the steps forward, and putting a hand in to touch the filters and

257

test the tension of the belt. 'Nice and easy to service, these, no complicated parts to them. Definitely no computer needed. How often do you change the oil and filters?'

'As part of the winter lay-up, whether they need it or not. It doesn't get as much use as it would like. I prefer sailing.'

'Where's your grease handle?'

'That nipple in the centre there. I give her a couple of skooshes with a grease-gun every time the engine's been run.'

The kettle squealed. I left him with his head bent over, made three mugs of drinking chocolate and found the Kit Kats. 'Have a seat,' I said to Cathy, motioning her to the bulkhead corner. 'Biscuit?'

'Oh, chocolate ones! Yes, please. Mum never buys them, she says we just eat them.'

'That's what they're there for,' Andy said, withdrawing his head from the engine and coming to join us. I gave him the other seat by the prop leg table and sat on the engine-box cover, looking at them both.

They were obviously brother and sister, both dark, with the same fine, straight hair, oval face and almond-shaped light blue eyes. You could see Cathy was accustomed to taking the lead, with that country-child confidence which had no resemblance to a town street-wise child. Down south, I reckoned, her peers would have a hard time placing her, just as I had difficulty in guessing the age of bairns south. She was early teens, but there wasn't a scrap of make-up on her tanned face; her clothes were bright lycra, a sporty top and stretchy black leggings. They'd guess a mature primary school bairn, maybe, until they spotted the poise of her head, and the decisive way she spoke. She knew who she was and where she was going, and seeing her now I'd have betted she was the main mover behind their band. Andy was a couple of years younger, just gone to secondary, and although he was quieter, used to his forceful sister speaking first, he had that same air of maturity. You could see

258

this pair being involved in all the life of a croft: milking the cow, rounding up and clipping sheep, helping with the peats and the hay.

'So,' I said, once the drinking chocolate was half-drunk, 'what're you wanting to speak to me about?'

Their eyes met, and Cathy nodded. 'Granny said you were going to find out who did the murder.'

'The police will do that. But fire away, if you think you can help.'

They exchanged looks again, and Cathy launched in. 'I don't know if it's anything to do with the murder, actually, but we thought we should tell someone, and you already ken some o' it, we didn't want to waste the police's time.'

'I can pass it on, but if it's something that matters you'll need to tell them again yourselves.'

'With our folk there?'

'Probably, since you're under sixteen.' There was no way this open-faced pair were involved in a serious crime they didn't want their folk to hear about, but there were plenty of country opportunities to break parental rules, like taking boats out at night. I looked straight at them. 'But we're talking about your uncle's murder.'

'And the wife on Foula,' Cathy said. 'The one who fell from the Sneug.'

'Her too. If you can help catch the person who did it, you have to grit your teeth and take the punishment for whatever you were up to.'

'Civic duty,' Andy said. 'We're doing it in SS.'

Cathy grimaced, and began. 'It's about Saturday night. Well, we were late anyway, going home from the music evening, and high from performing, and nobody felt like sleeping. I had all the lasses in the band squished into my room, and Andy had the boys in his room, and some of their parents were in the spare room and on couches downstairs, and, well, there were extra folk biding in every house on the isle. It'd been a right good day. I hope they'll do it again next year. Well, we'd both been aware o' something not right, with Mam and Granny and Dad and Kenny all talking to each other in corners at the school, in the evening, and then later when we got back Dad got a phone call, and the other person talked, and he said, "Yea, we need to decide what we're going to do about him," and then, "Yea, yea, I'll be there," and he and Mam gave each other one of those looks and Mam started chasing us off to bed.'

She paused for breath, and Andy cut in. 'So we were suspicious, you see, and we were determined to find out what was going on. We're no' babies, to be kept out of important stuff.'

'Fair enough,' I agreed. 'So?'

Cathy took up the tale again. 'So when we went to bed, we decided we wouldn't sleep. We switched the lights off after Mam came in to say goodnight and flyte about not chatting all night, but then we just waited, and Andy and I kept messaging each other, and then we heard Uncle Kenny coming in, and him and Dad going out. There's this flat roof under my window.'

A girl after my own heart.

'So we put a roll of clothes into each of our beds, to look like we were sleeping, in case Mam checked up on us, though we didn't think she would, with the others all there, so long as they were sensible and didn't make a noise, and they promised they wouldn't. Andy came into my room and we both climbed out of the window and onto the roof and then down from there.'

'We're done it a few times,' Andy said. 'If it's a bonny summer night, we take tab-nabs and have a midnight picnic on the hill. But this time we were trying to find out what all the fuss was about. So we watched where they all went. Dad and Uncle Kenny, they went down and got Tammie and Granny, and they all went along to Uncle's house. We watched them go in,

260

and then we followed, but it was no good. We could see them, because the curtains were open, but we didn't dare go too close, for fear of them seeing us, and we couldn't hear a thing.'

'We could see they were angry, though,' Cathy said. 'Fizzing mad angry. But since we couldna hear what about, there was no point hanging around to get caught as they came out again, so we started back along the road. And then, just as we were coming to the bend in the road above the waiting room, we saw somebody moving on board your boat.' She made a gesture pierwards. 'Not this boat, aboard the *Swan*. He came onto the pier, and snicked on a torch, and set out towards us. There was something kinda stealthy way about him, and we didn't want to be caught, so we ducked back and hid behind the waiting room.'

He. Him. 'Could you see who it was?'

Both dark heads nodded. 'It was the motorbiker man, the one whose birthday it was.'

'I kent by the shoulders of him,' Andy added, 'and the way he walked, and the light kinda gleamed on his leather jacket. We couldna see his face, but we're sure it was him.' He jerked his chin towards the airstrip. 'Him, that's snoring around up there right now.'

My heart missed a beat. Stevie Shearer had been one of the men I'd followed; one of the men checking up on the *Dorabella*, except that he hadn't admitted to it.

'We oozed back into the shadows and tried no' to breathe. His torch went creeping down past Granny's house to Hurdiback, you ken, the one with the phone box outside it where the new man's just arrived to. The new man was looking out for him, we reckoned – there was a light on in the house, and when the motorbiker man came to the door he came out straight away, and he and the motorbike man geed off up the road together.'

Stevie Shearer and Paul Roberts.

'And then,' Andy said, 'we saw you coming out as well. We kent you by the black jacket, and your walk, striding out as if you were planning to go a hundred miles.' Cathy elbowed him again. 'Well, she does!' Andy protested.

'And then,' she cut in over him, 'we started to see signs of the meeting at Uncle's breaking up an' aa. Dad came out first, wi' Granny and Tammie, and they began heading back for Granny's, and Uncle Kenny began walking along the road towards his hoose. So we had to decide quick what to do.'

'Dad and them obviously didna see the torch and the twa men walking, the rise o' the hill would hide it, but as soon as Uncle Kenny came up, well, he saw the light. We saw him stiffen, and stare, and then he headed up the hill ahint Uncle's house. We thought he was going to keep an eye on what was going on from there, or maybe he was going to cut around and get closer to them that way. So we decided we'd follow you all.'

'It's mad,' I said. 'The whole boiling of us swarming around the hill, not knowing the others were there. You musta been pretty quiet – I had an edgy feeling as if I was being followed, but I neither heard nor saw you.'

'You were the one we were worried about,' Cathy said. 'You and Uncle Kenny. You had the sense to go wi'oot torches and let your eyes get good in the night. The men, they'd no see a thing for their ain lights. You were following the men too, and we were following you, but Uncle Kenny was up on the hill. We were faerd he mighta seen us moving on the road, but he was likely too busy watching the men and wondering what they were up to.'

'And it was getting late, and Uncle Kenny might be on to us any moment,' Andy said, 'so we geed back home, and climbed in, and whispered to the others what was going on. We aa thought the men might be something to do with the trawler on the Skerries, their boat went that way, and it was high water in the middle o' the night. And then when we got to sleep, the next we kent was Mam waking us in a hurry to take some cereal and then go on the lifeboat with Gran.' His face lit up. 'It was cool, or it woulda been if we hadn't been so worried about Gran.'

'Then, once we got to the hospital, Mam telt wis about Uncle Kenny.' Cathy's face sobered. 'And we thought maybe us having been out, and seen the men like that, that we maybe should say something. We kent you'd tell them about the men, at least we thought you likely would, but we didna ken if you'd seen Uncle Kenny to tell them he'd been there.'

'You ken,' I said, 'you do have to tell the police aa about this. I ken you dinna want to have a perfectly good midnight escape route ruined, and I'm with you on that one, but you're going to have to tell for all that. It's really important.' Stevie and Roberts. If the police believed the children – and there was no reason why they shouldn't – this evidence would clear Geordie. 'I saw the men, I told them that, but I didn't see who it was. You need to go and tell them now, before they leave on the ferry.'

They agreed, reluctantly, that they would, and set off up the road, shoulders slumped, to where Gavin and his officers were sharing a flask of coffee. There was a short conversation, then Gavin motioned them to lean against the ferry pier with him, and listened, head bent, as they talked.

Paul Roberts, with his contempt for women, and that simmering feel of violence. Stevie, with his cheery jokes making a barbed-wire fence around him. Paul and Stevie, both linked with taking photographs of children. Stevie, who'd lied about going out to *Dorabella* that night; Stevie, who was on his scrambler right now, patrolling the width of the island between the people here and the north side, where you'd get the best view of the *Dorabella*. I was keen to get going, but I'd take a last quick stroll up the headland from where I'd watched the RIB heading out on Saturday night. That would give me a good view across to the Ve Skerries.

I grabbed my spyglasses and headed off up the hill.

VII

The Storm Arrives

Chapter Twenty-four

It was an easy climb, but I took it at a good pace, and was out of breath by the time I'd come to the top of the first summit. After that the ground was level. There was a fence between me and Stevie, and though I could see him moving on the hill, I hoped my dark jacket would camouflage me. Ten minutes later I was at the North Ness, looking out across West Voe towards Virda Field. There was a handy cairn, so I crouched down in front of it and balanced my elbows on my knees to steady the spyglasses. They were only a lightweight pair, but their magnification was good and even three miles away the spyglasses brought them clear to me: the white tower on the Ormal, the dark brown rocks, the sun glinting on the white superstructure of the stranded *Dorabella*.

My breath stilled in my throat. There was something moving aboard.

It was just too far for me to see. For a moment, the sun caught a flash of vivid pink, the colour of a girl's jacket. I leaned forward, willing my eyes to distinguish more, but I couldn't. I only had the impression that there was movement aboard, and the more I strained my eyes to see, the more I thought I must be imagining it, except that I did think I was seeing the dark shapes of people moving behind the white metalwork.

It could be idiot sightseers, who'd gone for a look after they heard the boat had been abandoned. It could be scranners, hoping for a chart plotter or life raft that had been missed in the scramble to take everything off her. I'd look stupid if I called the Coastguard for curious locals. Yet there was a voice within me saying *hurry, hurry.* I needed to tell Gavin.

I was too late. I was still ten minutes from the pier when the ferry coughed out a cloud of blue smoke, reversed in a smooth curve and headed out of the voe.

I got back to *Khalida* in double-quick time and grabbed my phone. Voicemail. Well, then, I'd go and look myself. It wouldn't take me longer than an hour just to do that detour. I was all ready to go. I had plenty of fuel. The anvil cloud on the horizon was still there, blacker than it had been, but not yet closer. We left the pier in a wide curve, then I followed the leading lights out into the open sea, and set *Khalida*'s nose northwards. The wind was still light, coming from the south now, so I unrolled her genoa to help with speed, but kept the engine ticking over. Half an hour to get there.

I was around the north-east corner of Papa in less than ten minutes, and set a course that would take me south of the southernmost skerries. I'd lost sight of them again, of course, but ten minutes later they came into view, the Ormal light first, and then the rocks, low grey lumps on the horizon. I adjusted my course and reached for my spyglasses. There seemed to be nothing on the white wheelhouse and railed foredeck now, except for a dark blob that could be a door left open. I couldn't see anything that might have caused the pink flash I'd seen. Barbie pink. There was no sign of any other boats, but anyone visiting would be on the other side of the skerry *Dorabella* was lying against.

Then the dark blob moved. Other dark blobs joined it. They were higher than I was; they could see further. They'd seen me coming towards them. The pink jacket waved frantically, and a spark of light flashed twice in my eyes, as if someone was trying to do Morse code.

Khalida was already going as fast as she could. I grabbed the white fleece from below and waved it in answer. I was coming. I'd be with them soon.

I rolled the genoa away and put the engine into gear. It seemed a long, long time with the white wings of foam spurting from *Khalida*'s bow with each wave, Papa inching behind me and the dark blobs clustered around the bow of the *Dorabella*. I throttled back some two hundred metres short of the skerry, trying not to look at the tumbled white water and dark fangs of rock to the north of me. I wasn't going anywhere near there, where the men of the *Ben Doran* had died.

There were women and children on board: six adults and four children, maybe upper primary age. I wasn't close enough to see the faces. A wave of rage shook me. The owners had emptied the boat of fish and electronics and life rafts, but wherever these women had been hidden, they couldn't be brought out in full view of the Coastguard and lifeboat, so they'd been left there to die in the coming storm. Women. Expendable. If I'd had Stevie there I'd have killed him myself.

A sudden puff of wind from the west set the mainsail shaking, and concentrated my mind. The wind had changed; the storm was approaching. The black cloud on the horizon had swelled to take up a quarter of the sky, and I could see its skirts of rain below it. The lifeboat could get here in an hour, but by then the wind would have risen. These women, these children, might have to watch it coming towards them and be unable to reach them, as the men of the *Ben Doran* had had to watch their rescuers leaving them to die at last as the storm rose. I was here, now. I'd look, at least, and if I thought I could get them off fast I'd try it.

The photos I'd seen showed clear water to the west of *Dorabella*, once you'd gone around the reef she was on. I put the engine to idle and thought. I didn't need loose cats on this madness. Cat and Kitten were sleeping below; I grabbed Cat's basket, put Cat in it before he'd woken up enough to protest, and shoved Kitten in after him, squeaking indignantly. I rigged the fenders and fender board to port, then chugged forward again, keeping a good distance from the jagged rock stretching seawards, and a wary eye on the depth. Once I was around it, I could see the boat properly. We were just past half tide, and she was sitting on the bottom, upright still, with a metre of her red antifouling showing below her navy hull. The Atlantic swell rose up and down her sides.

The noise was horrid. She didn't seem to be moving, but there was a grating sound from her keel, and each wave that came up under her hit the curve of her hull with a hollow metallic boom. The closer I got the bigger she seemed, and if it hadn't been for those dark eyes watching me with such hope and that black cloud on the horizon I'd have called the lifeboat and stood by till they came; but those westerly puffs were getting more frequent, and stronger, and the waves were starting to show white crests. Westerly would lie me against her; the fun would be getting off undamaged.

The women were clustered on this side of her, watching me. I put the engine back to idle and fetched out the longest lengths of rope I had, then darted below for my bosun's chair, the simplest and cheapest sort of strapped seat for hoisting me up the mast. It would have to do. I attached it to the longest rope and set it ready, then tied the boom out of the way to get the cockpit clear.

I manoeuvred cautiously up, heart in my mouth, until *Khalida* was lying alongside. The top of the red antifouling was level with my topsides, and her navy hull towered above me, taller than a pier to scramble up. The wind held us there, and the fender board scraped against *Dorabella*'s sides as the swell lifted us up and down. Even when we were at our highest the superstructure was still above the top of my mast. As we went up we came within three metres of the deck level, then dropped to over five. I felt a jar as my keel touched bottom in the trough, and hoped it hadn't done any damage. The sooner I got us all out of here the better.

They were ready for me. The children had been cleared backwards, and as soon as I picked up the rope the tallest of the women came forward, hands outstretched. As we went down I lifted the bosun's chair. Between the distance and the clanging she wouldn't have heard a word I'd tried to say, so I mimed sitting in it, and she nodded. The next time we came upwards I flung the end of the rope, and she hauled it up. I pointed to the black cloud, and shouted, 'Hurry!' She nodded. By the time I came up again, one of the women was ready in the chair, being lowered over the rail. They got her right into the cockpit and she scrambled out and called up. The chair whisked upwards and we were left looking at each other. She was my height, Middle Eastern, slim and beautiful, with great dark eyes and dark hair tied back in a plait. Her face blazed with fear and relief.

'We'll get you off,' I said. 'We'll get you all off.'

I could see she understood the determination, if not the words. She nodded, and turned back towards the trawler. Already the first child was dangling in the chair. We caught her, freed her, and I indicated to her that she was to go below. She went down the first step tentatively, then turned back and hugged me. She was crying, and I found I was too. The people responsible would pay for this, I vowed, and brushed the tears away. Second child. Third, and fourth. They huddled together on the couch, watching the red and navy of the *Dorabella* rise and fall. I ducked below to give them what remained of the Kit Kats, and found the next woman on board by the time I was back up. Only four left to go. The one who'd caught the rope first was in charge now, sending the heaviest person next with a comment that made them laugh, the sort of laughter that's dangerously close to hysteria. Three, and all the time there was that hollow clanging filling the air, and the shifting wind was cold on my cheek. Two. She'd saved the lightest till last. When she hauled the chair back up she put the end of the rope back around a stanchion on *Dorabella* as a pulley and dropped it back to us. Instantly four sets of hands came out to catch the rope and ease the woman in the chair down. There was an ominous creak from the stanchion. Last one. The tall woman gave the staunchion a shake, shook her head and swung her legs over the rail, watching intently until *Khalida* rose to the next wave, and dropped lightly aboard, into the outstretched arms of the others. All aboard.

My heart filled with relief. I'd been afraid it would have taken a lot of time, but they'd all made it to *Khalida* in less than ten minutes. I looked at the leader and made an 'Is that everyone?' gesture. She nodded.

Quick hands hauled the bosun's chair and rope on board. As soon as I was sure there was no last piece of rope ready to foul the propellor, I mimed pushing, and they shoved against the *Dorabella*. I gunned the engine as the swell sucked backwards, and *Khalida* jolted forwards, sluggish with the weight of these extra people on board, but the hands were keeping us clear, and the tall one had lifted the fender board and was using it as a lever to shove her stern away from the trawler. We managed to turn into the wind and slowly, oh, so slowly, pull away, out from the wrecked boat, then south around the rock. We'd done it.

The silence was bliss, though my ears were ringing. I set our nose to the left of Vementry Isle and drew a deep breath, then looked around at my companions. Two had gone below to be with the children; the other four were squashed into my cockpit, standing as I was, looking with disbelief at the boat they'd left. The first woman aboard had been Middle Eastern, and so were two others, and the children; the other three were African. They were all dressed in lightweight clothes.

'You need something warmer,' I said. I put the autopilot on and ducked below. The children were still huddling together, with the littlest one crying, and two mothers trying to comfort them. Clothes, hot drinks, food. I hauled out the polythene containers with my stock of jerseys and breeks, and passed them out. 'You can lie down if you like,' I said to the children, and turned the downie back invitingly in my bunk. I had a couple of spare lifejackets, for people in the cockpit. I went back to turn on the gas, and showed the first woman aboard where the water, mugs and drinking chocolate were, and how to put the gas rings on. The rice in my flask should be done now. 'There's food too,' I said, 'here. Help yourselves.' I opened up the tins locker, and showed her the rice in the flask. It wasn't much between so many, but it would keep them going. 'Make yourselves at home.'

She understood the gesture, and nodded. I headed back up with my spare jackets and offered them around. Below, the children were being squeezed into my bunk. One had spotted Cat's basket and was fiddling with the catch. I dived back below again and waggled my hand in a 'no' gesture, smiling so that she wouldn't think she was being told off. 'I don't want them to fall overboard.' I miaowed, mimed diving and did a 'splash!' noise which had them laughing.

Right. We needed to get home, and with the sea darkening to the north of us, we wanted all the speed and security my tough little boat could manage. I didn't trust the engine in serious waves which would stir up the gunge at the bottom of even the most carefully-kept tank, and cause a blockage. I wanted sails. I glanced over at the black cloud. Half an hour, I reckoned.

'*Merde, alors!*' the tall one said, following my gaze.

I breathed a heartfelt thank-you. Communication was possible after all.

'You speak French? Fantastic!' I gestured forwards. 'I need

to get the sails up. We'll go faster, and the movement will be smoother. In a minute we're going to turn the boat right around for me to hoist them. You take the tiller while I organise.' I showed her how to waggle the boat's nose, and touched the lazyjacks. 'The sail will go up between these.'

I hoisted the mainsail just enough to let me see what I was doing, and tied it down at the second reef, giving me only half its usual area. I'd unroll as much genoa as I'd get away with and roll it back up as need be. This westerly wind would sweep us home, and the waves hadn't had time to build up properly, so we should be safely within the shelter of the Røna before the worst of it hit.

'Okay,' I called back to my helper. 'Turn her so she's facing the other way.'

I had only half the sail to haul up, and as soon as we came nose to wind I pulled it quickly, and winched it bar tight. I gave the woman a thumbs-up and motioned her to turn again, then went back to join her. 'Thanks. I'm Cass.'

'Mariama.'

I couldn't see the opening into the Røna from here, but I knew the shape of Vementry Isle, and set our nose to the left of it. For a moment I wondered about returning to Papa, but with this wind and building swell it would be a slog under engine; and besides, Roberts was there. He and Stevie, working together. Let them think the women were dead. I'd keep them safe until they'd given the police all the evidence they needed to nail the pair of them good and proper. I gritted my teeth at the thought. I'd been right that an unsupported allegation of a hazy childhood memory wasn't enough to account for Moon's death. She was like a child, Kirsten had said; curious, but not yet putting her knowledge together. She'd been focused on her own childhood, on Jen, not realising she held even more dangerous information against him. She'd heard him phoning about the *Dorabella* on board the *Swan*, and she'd been awake

274

to see him coming back that night. Stevie couldn't afford any investigation; couldn't risk anyone asking how he afforded his expensive motorbike, his foreign holidays, his share in a fishing boat. Women were commodities, expendable, even his niece.

We had six nautical miles to go before we were in the Røna. I glanced at the log. In spite of the reefed sail, in spite of the people aboard, my tough little boat was doing 5.7 knots already. Just over an hour to go.

It was a long, anxious hour. We were only a mile closer when the wind hit with a bang that heeled *Khalida* over until the waves were washing her lee windows. I knew she didn't care, but I heard a shriek from the passengers squished below in the warm. 'Tell them it's okay,' I said to Mariama. 'She won't capsize.' I gestured below us. 'There's a big lump of lead a metre below us. She wobbles but she won't fall over.'

I rolled half the jib in, and saw with satisfaction that though we were more upright her speed had fallen only to 5.5 knots. The mast creaked, and the wind whined in the rigging, the sails strained, but my *Khalida* was going like a champion, tracking straight over the waves and surfing down their backs. I could see the entry into the Røna now. The red cliffs of Muckle Roe were hazed by spray, and great white waves were washing up them. We'd make it. We'd make it. Mariama came back out in my spare jacket and sat by the cabin, waiting to help. Five minutes later, kind hands passed up two mugs with rice, a meatball in sauce, and a spoon to eat it with.

It was a rollercoaster ride home. The rain came suddenly, drenching, so that we were paddling in the cockpit as the drains struggled to clear it. The wind kept increasing, and it was dead behind us, so that we were running goosewinged, with the boom tied on one side and the jib on the other. It was her most unstable point of sail, so I couldn't leave the tiller for even a second, and I had to watch the sails for any hint of a windshift, of the boom trying to go aback on me. The waves built up as the wind increased, glinting coal-black, streaked with foam. They towered above *Khalida*'s cabin roof when we were in the troughs, and turned into vertigo-inducing hills as she came up to the crests. I rolled away another quarter of jib, leaving just enough to keep her steering steady, and we forged onwards through the blown spume, through the sudden bursts of rain, until we came at last between the Muckle Roe light and the Vementry gun. Now we were in home waters. Not home and dry yet, of course, with the wind still rushing us forwards, but almost there.

I had to think what to do. Most of all I wanted to keep these women safe. I'd planned to head straight for Brae, hot food, friends with clothes and warm houses, but someone would see them all coming off *Khalida*, and word would be round Brae in seconds, and the rest of Shetland in minutes. The men who'd left them to drown would find out that they were alive to testify against them. I bit my lip, thinking. My schoolfriend Inga could put up several of them. She was absolutely trustworthy, and she could pick up a carload from the marina but even if the sharp eyes of marina watchers missed a carload of people leaving, her neighbours would see them coming in with her. That wouldn't do. No, I'd take them to the Ladie, the cottage Gavin and I were going to live in together. It wouldn't be as safe for *Khalida*, stuck on the end of the jetty in this wind, but nobody would see them disembarking there.

I bore away slightly, carefully, my eyes still on the mainsail, heading for the gap between Papa Little and the new set of mussel buoys that had appeared there last summer. The light was beginning to thicken around me, making the exact point where land became sea harder to distinguish. I was sailing by the lee now, with the main liable to fill backwards at any minute. As soon as I could, I'd get the main down and the engine on. I kept going for another five minutes, until we were

276

level with Dad and Maman's house, then explained to Mariama what I was going to do. I started the engine, rolled the jib away, brought *Khalida* round into the wind and dropped the main, bundling it into its bungees for the moment. Done. I gave Mariama a thumbs-up and we chugged into the shelter of Papa Little, around the bay with the rocks we'd christened the Hippopotomi, and towards the jetty.

Even though the wind was hitting the far side of Papa Little, it was still rolling over the top and coming down on this side with a thump that flattened the waves around the Blade and made vicious cat's paws on the water. It was half-dark now, but this was my childhood back garden. I could see well enough to get us in. 'Nearly home,' I said cheerfully to the crowded cabin, and pointed through the window at our blindingly whitewashed cottage gleaming in the dusk. 'That's where we're going.' They all peered with oohs of interest. There wouldn't be nearly enough beds, or bedding, or food, but we'd manage somehow. I suddenly hoped, with a cold feeling at the pit of my stomach, that Gavin would be okay about it all.

I put Mariama on the tiller while I rigged ropes, fenders and board, and then we chugged gently in, and she leapt onto the pier with the rope, and followed my hand signals until *Khalida* was safely attached. I fastened my gangplank and went below to motion my passengers upwards. Relief and tiredness were flooding me like the great Atlantic swell we'd come through. We'd made it. I gave my *Khalida* a caress on the cockpit rail with one hand. She'd brought us all safe home.

Chapter Twenty-five

The cottage looked very small and old-fashioned, with its sit-ootery porch projecting towards us. Never mind; it had a shower, and blankets, and a Rayburn ready to light for warmth. I got my guests onto the pier, huddled in pairs and threes under all the jackets I had, let Cat and Kitten out of their basket, closed up the washboards and cabin hatch, and then we bolted together through the black rain up the pier, up the short piece of road and along the grassy path to the back door.

It was Cat who warned me of danger. He was running ahead towards warmth and shelter when suddenly he stopped, bristled, turned tail and bolted back towards *Khalida*. Kitten leapt out of my arms, hit the ground with a squeak and followed.

A black shape detached itself from the dark doorway. A light switched on in the cottage, and for a moment my dark-accustomed eyes were dazzled by it. Something jabbed my back from behind. I felt the hardness of it and realised incredu-lously that it was a gun. These weren't amateur murderers, half-horrified by what they'd done. This time I'd tangled with professionals, the sort of people who'd left ten women and children to die on the Ve Skerries.

I should have called the lifeboat. I saw with splitting, sham-ing clarity that I'd got too clever, too keen on myself as Cass the fixer, the action-movie heroine who foiled the baddies and rescued the innocent. My vanity had endangered us all. Of course Stevie had seen me heading for the Skerries before he'd got on the ferry, all nice and innocent. Of course he knew where I lived. He'd have driven around to the viewpoint at the Loch of Gonfirth to watch us coming home. If the storm got us, well and good. If not, action would have to be taken.

It was Stevie standing in the kitchen, and we were met by a flood of friendly French. He ushered the women in with gestures. 'Come in, come in. You had a cold journey of it, but with the Coastguard on watch all the time sending Cass to get you off was the best we could come up with.'

The gun jabbed in my back again at the mention of my name. Instinct kept my face blank. Stevie didn't necessarily know about Maman; maybe he was telling lies he thought I wasn't able to understand.

'Did she manage to feed you on board?'

Mariama nodded. 'We have eaten a little.' She showed no surprise at him being there, and the others were looking at him as if he was a familiar face. He must have been their contact in France, the one who'd sold them this perilous journey to Britain. I risked a glance over my shoulder, and got another jab in the back with that hard muzzle. It was Paul Roberts, of course, his partner in this enterprise, as he'd been his partner in the child photographs, standing right behind me, my body shielding his hand with the gun from the women. I tried not to stiffen or show my fear in my face, but the bullet-scar on my cheek tingled. If I had my way, every gun on the planet would be at the bottom of the sea.

'Great, great.' Stevie was leaning forwards towards them, working hard at being convincing. 'Then you're all ready for the next stage of your journey. The van's all ready, it's parked just above the cottage. Can you explain to them, Mariama, that it will be another long time of waiting for you, because we've missed tonight's ferry, so you will need to be in the van for two nights, tonight and all day tomorrow, and then to-morrow night on the ferry, until you arrive in Aberdeen in the morning. You will be given more food, of course, in the van.'

Business as usual. Keep them quiet, get them on board that van without any fuss, to be delivered as promised or disposed of. I glanced quickly across at Mariama, with all the warning I could put into my eyes. *Don't trust him.* I had just time to make my face bland again as he turned to me with that same over-bright smile, and spoke in English. 'Thanks, Cass, for delivering them to us. We'll take over looking after them from here.' His eyes were hard in his cheery face. There were no stupid jokes now. This was the real Stevie. 'You didn't contact anyone on your way in, I hope?' His voice sharpened, and the gun at my back gave a warning jab. Out of the corner of my eye I saw one of the children sidling over, looking, then going back to her mother and tugging her down to whisper in her ear. Quickly I moved my gaze back to Stevie's face, so he wouldn't turn around to see what I was looking at. 'We have enough to do this evening without more loose ends to deal with.'

'No,' I said. 'I didn't contact anyone.'

'Which pocket is your mobile phone in?'

Moving carefully, I took it out and held it towards him. A hand from behind me took it. I heard it snick on. 'No,' Roberts said. 'She hasn't made any phone calls.'

'Now,' Stevie said, looking out into the howling night, 'you'll likely want to go down and secure your boat while we get everyone on their transport.' His voice hardened. 'You understand of course that if you say anything, the police will separate the children from their mothers and dump them in separate grotty immigration holding camps instead of them joining their husbands like we promised them. Illegal, yeah, but who's it harming?'

If I'd believed that was really where they were going, I might

280

have thought about agreeing. I shoved thoughts of forced service in brothels or labour gangs away, and did my best to sound naively convinced. 'You're delivering them to family here?'

'To Aberdeen. After that they make their own way. We don't want to know where.' He turned on the full-steaming-light smile again. 'So you're going to be a sensible girl and say nothing.'

I tried to sound wavering. 'Well, of course, I wouldn't want to get them into trouble . . . and those camps are awful places . . . and if they all have family here, well, I wouldn't want to stop them joining them . . .'

Mariama couldn't understand what I was saying but I knew she'd caught the tone: reluctant, empty-headed conviction. I hoped that that voyage together in *Khalida*'s cockpit, with the wild sea snatching at us, had let her know me better than that. Her dark eyes flicked upward at my face, then lowered again.

'You just need to go down to your boat with Paul and stay there until the van's gone. Forget the dramatic rescue from the Ve Skerries.' He made it all so reasonable, and then spoiled it by a salacious leer. 'You just sailed straight home from Papa to join your policeman boyfriend for a romantic reunion.'

I couldn't do anything right now, but once Roberts got me on *Khalida*, on my own territory, with weapons to hand, I'd do my best to turn the tables. These two, I reminded myself, for all their plausible threats of detention centres, had left these women and children to drown. I hoped that Mariama was remembering that too. As if she'd read my mind, she flicked a look at me. I understood what she was saying, clear as words: *Danger.* I nodded, and hoped she could read my mind too: *I'll deal with this one. You take Stevie.*

Stevie switched back to French. 'Well, friends, let's get you into the van.' He cast a quick look over them, still wearing obvious sailing jackets and Shetland jumpers. 'There are warmer clothes in the van. Leave anything that's Cass's here.'

281

'I still think we should send her with them,' Roberts said, over my head.

'We've discussed it,' Stevie replied. His voice was cold. 'It's not worth the risk.' He gave Roberts a warning glance. 'She's said she'll keep quiet. Get her down to her boat.'

'Gather up your gear,' Roberts said. 'Slowly. Don't try anything.'

A glance showed me that his gun hand was casually in his pocket, the line of the barrel pointing towards me. I hoped Mariama would get the significance of me picking up all the jackets. Nothing was to be left to show that I'd ever arrived home.

The gun jabbed in my back. I flashed a last glance at Mariama and turned slowly, arms filled with jackets, then stepped back out into the night.

Those minutes in the light had lost my dark-vision. I stumbled on the doorstep and was grabbed round the upper arm by a strong hand. Roberts jerked me up again. 'We're in no hurry. Take it carefully, and don't try to be clever.'

They were in a hurry, though. They'd have seen, as I had, the signs of Gavin's presence: his green rucksack dumped in the kitchen entrance, a *Scotsman* on the table, a used plate in the sink, a pan on the stove. Cass's policeman boyfriend who'd be home at the end of the day.

I walked carefully ahead of Roberts along the grass path, wondering if I could turn quickly enough to fling the jackets over him before he fired. A white van glimmered in the dark on the gravel parking place. As we got nearer, Roberts's torch flashed across it, and through the blown rain I spotted the familiar supermarket logo. What could be more everyday, a supermarket delivery van going down south for repairs or to collect orders for delivery? Thinking they were going at last to their destination would keep the women quiet inside, and by the time they realised they weren't going to be released – *I still think we should send her with them* – it would be too late.

282

We'd reached the gate. I opened it, went through. My feet crunched on the gravel of the road down to the pier. As we turned to walk downwards the wind came full in my face. The rain ran down from my drenched fringe into my eyes and stung on my cheeks. Roberts swore, and the gun wavered for a moment as he pulled his hood up, but before I could throw the jackets at him and leap sideways into the night it was back in position.

I didn't believe for a moment he'd let me go. There was nobody to say I'd ever come home at all, and my little *Khalida* wouldn't have been seen from shore coming through those waves in the half dark. A woman coming home singlehanded through that storm, well, if she'd listened to them she'd never have set out in it.

If she'd listened to them. I had that in my favour: this pair looked down on women, just as Asquith and his government had ridiculed what women could do. Just like that War Office official who had told the Dr Elsie Inglis Jen had mentioned to go home and be still, I thought crazily, but she hadn't listened. She and her unit must have used guts and guile and determination and ingenuity to substitute for mere physical strength, just as I'd done all these years afloat. Their little Ford ambulance vans had followed the retreating army, picking up wounded men as the Germans snapped at their heels. I had my own wits and the darkness of the night to help me. I'd outwit this thug or die trying.

The gun wasn't jabbing in my back any more, but it was only a foot behind me. Wait, Cass, wait. He thought I'd believed his promise of safety for silence. The more cowed I acted, the less he'd expect me to fight back.

We'd reached the containers now. *Khalida*'s mast gleamed in the air only fifty metres away. I had the advantage of surprise, and I had the advantage of knowing my boat. How was he planning to dispose of us? Not here; the water was too shallow and too clear. Even if he burnt her to the waterline, risking a blaze that would be seen from the Muckle Roe houses, her remains would be spotted as soon as the gale subsided. Cole Deep was the place, either by driving her out and scuttling her there – in which case he'd have an uncomfortable journey back in my little rubber dinghy, if he made it at all in these waves, which I didn't think he would – or he'd start the engine, turn her round, hole her and lash the tiller to send her straight out there. Two hundred, three hundred metres; the wind might just send her sideways to the shore before she sank, but I didn't expect I'd be still alive at that point. Either he'd shoot me once I'd walked to the boat or he'd rely on his gun and superior wits to keep me quiet until I'd started the engine for him. I walked steadily down the gravel of the pier and prayed it would be the latter. The decks had been cleared for sea; I needed to get below for a weapon.

When we reached the gangplank the wind was whistling round *Khalida*'s mast and thrumming in the rigging. The waves jolted between her and the pier, and she tugged at her mooring ropes like a restive horse, making the gangplank tilt to one side, then to the other. The gun jabbed me in the back again; a torch shone its white circle on the gangplank from over my shoulder. 'Go onboard and wait in the cockpit. Put the jackets down then keep your hands where I can see them.'

I obeyed. He followed me, but remained on the side deck, a metre above me, light trained on my face. 'Open up the cabin.'

I slid the hatch back and took out the washboards, then stood upright again.

'You're going to start the engine for me. No tricks. I can do it myself if you make me shoot you. I just don't want to waste time tinkering with a fifties relic. Take each stage slow and easy. Tell me what you're doing.'

Just how stupid did he expect me to be? 'Why do you want the engine on?' I asked.

He hadn't thought that one through, but he recovered

quickly. 'It's cold and you're drenched. The heat from the engine will dry you off and keep you warm while you wait for us to go.'

'Oh,' I said, as if I was pleased by his consideration, and gave him a tentative smile. 'Well, that's thoughtful of you. I have to turn the starter battery on first.' I gestured towards it. 'It's by the engine, in the engine box.'

His torch was on my back as I bent over and reached into the cabin, but he couldn't see what I was doing from that angle. I felt *Khalida* shift as he stepped forward onto the cockpit seat. Now the light was directly on my right hand as I undid the catches and lifted up the top step to get at the battery switch. My left hand was in darkness. I shifted my feet under me, as if I needed to reach down further, and while I turned the red lever with my right hand, my left was silently pulling the pin out of the heavy fire extinguisher, and easing it from its bracket by the cabin steps. I thought of Kirsten fighting down what he'd done to her as children, of Moon who'd died falling from a thousand-foot cliff, of Kenny's tenderness with Jen, of Mariama and the others, and let the anger fill me. I braced my feet and then leapt up at him in one fast move, swinging the metal cylinder straight for his groin. It hit him square on, and hard. He screamed. The torch dropped into the cabin and the world went dark. I kept swinging upwards, hoping to get his gun hand. Something connected with a metallic crack, and there was the sharp bang of a shot. I could barely see him now, just a darker outline in the pouring dark. I pulled the fire extinguisher back to me and pressed the trigger.

I'd always wondered if these things would actually work in an emergency. This one had come with the boat and was way out of date, but it outdid all my expectations. A great stream of white powder gushed out of the nozzle, and the wind slammed it against his face. He gave a furious yell and clawed at his eyes with his free hand. The gun fired again, wavering and wild. I leapt back onto the opposite cockpit seat to get myself level with him and swung the extinguisher at his head with all the force I could manage. He slumped down, and I leapt for him, shoving him down onto the seat. He wasn't out cold but he was stunned enough for me to wind a rope around his arms and torso, which held him long enough for me to do a proper job on his hands and feet. I found the torch on the floor, checked the ropes were tight, and then had a look round for the gun. It had dropped onto the side deck. I picked the thing up with finger and thumb, holding it well away from me, negotiated my way across the shaking gangplank, and dropped it in the nearest salmon bin.

Being hit hadn't stopped Roberts's tongue. He was cursing me in an ugly monotone, and the wind was blowing towards the house. I went past him into the cabin and found a clean dishcloth to use as a gag, then went back for water to pour over his eyes. 'Shut up,' I said, as he yelled against the cloth. 'I'm getting the powder out of your eyes.' I threw a jacket over him as protection against the rain, then headed up to see what was going on.

The cottage lights had gone out. There was light spilling out from the white shape of the van, up above it. The wind blew the engine noise away, but the headlights wavered through the rain. I caught a glimpse of dark figures climbing into the back of it, then there seemed to be a kind of scuffle. A door slammed. There was silence for a moment, then the soft clang of fists thumping against the inside of the van. Had the women caught on, too late, that they were being tricked?

There was silence for a moment except for the thumping, and muffled yells, then the van lights went out. The locking system snicked. A torch shone briefly on the side of the van then became a bright circle, wavering through the darkness towards me. Stevie, wondering why Paul Roberts was taking so long? He'd find him quickly enough when he got down there, and release him, and then there would be two to deal with.

There was more than one set of feet moving softly on the gravel. Maybe the van had had a driver? The torch beam wavered and shone down towards the pier, but it wasn't powerful enough to reach *Khalida*. I crouched in the dark, not sure what I should do. If I followed the men down unseen I'd find some kind of weapon, a plank or fence post, down at the pier, but how well I'd get on tackling two men – and then I remembered the salmon nets drying. If I could find some way of spreading them into the road as a trap – and then, suddenly, there was someone beside me in the dark, my height, catching at my arm. I gave a startled exclamation, and she called out my name.

The torch swivelled towards us, catching us both in its white light. It was the woman who'd come aboard first, hair and face streaming with water. Now there were footsteps on the gravel all around us, and the person holding the torch broke into a run. It was Mariama. 'Are you okay, Cass?'

I nodded. 'Roberts is tied up down there. Is Stevie locked up in the van?'

'Yes.' Her face was grave. 'I couldn't understand why he was saying they'd sent you to get us when you hadn't said it. Then one of the children said he'd seen the man behind you had a gun.'

One of the other women said something, laughing.

'We talked quickly, in Arabic, and decided not to trust him. We pushed him in and slammed the door on him, and tied it shut.'

'Will it hold for long?'

She nodded. 'It will hold.'

'Okay.' I motioned them towards the house. 'I think we have to phone the police. Roberts is tied up, but we can't let Stevie loose. Only – ' I bit my lip, looking uncertainly round them all. 'If we do, what will happen to you?'

Mariama spread her hands. 'It can't be helped. Without us,

287

you can't explain why you have these two men here. We can claim asylum, I think, and that will let us stay for some time.'

'Inga,' I said suddenly. 'My friend Inga. Come back into the house, and I'll phone her.'

I was in luck; Inga was at the house, and answered the phone herself straight off.

'Inga, it's Cass. This is urgent and top secret.'

Inga was my oldest friend. We'd been together through primary and secondary school, we'd survived first discos, first boyfriends, first Saturday jobs. There was nobody I'd trust more in a crisis. 'Cross my heart and hope to die,' she responded promptly.

'I've brought six women and four children to the cottage. The bastards who own that trawler that went on the Ve Skerries left them to die there, and I'll see them pay for it if it's the last thing I do.'

Inga had a family, as well as running various protest groups, the mother-and-toddlers and the hockey league. Organising ten total strangers was easy for her. 'What do you need? Food. Clothes. What size of children?'

'Upper primary.'

'Right. Leave it with me. I'll get a veggie takeaway and be over as fast as I can.'

'Hang on. We'll talk about it later, but we've got the men responsible tied up here, and we're going to have to phone the police. Only, what's going to happen to the women, as illegal immigrants? Can they claim asylum?'

'Victims of people trafficking,' Inga said promptly. 'Listen, I'll do food first, then as soon as I get to you I'll phone Laura of Women's Aid Shetland. There might be room in shelters, or folk who can put them up, rather than them having to be sent to detention centres.'

'My understanding is that they have family on the mainland.'

'Leave it with me. See you in half an hour.'

By the time I'd finished phoning, two of the women had got the Rayburn roaring up the chimney and radiating heat into the room, and another had organised tea all round. It was all so domestic, so normal, with the children coaxing Cat and Kitten in, that it was hard to remember we'd left a man tied up down on the boat, and another locked into his van. I couldn't leave Roberts down there, he'd need to come into the warm, though well tied-up. If Stevie was secure then he could stay in the prison he'd intended for the women.

I explained to Mariama that we'd need to get Roberts, and she nodded. We'd taken only two steps back into the darkness when there was a gleam of light on the horizon that turned into two headlights, wavering through the rain, then jolting down the track towards us. The cavalry had arrived.

Chapter Twenty-six

Gavin was astonishing. He listened to my explanation with only a quirk at the side of his mouth, greeted six strange women and four children in our house with unruffled calm, and then got on the phone for backup.

'We have two alleged people traffickers who need to be transported. Yes, both male – injured?' He gave me a quick look.

'One got a bump on the head from a fire extinguisher,' I conceded. 'And some powder in the face.'

'Yes, get the doctor to check them on arrival. Okay, great. See you in half an hour, then.' He turned to me. 'We'd better check on your prisoners.'

'Stevie first,' I said. 'Roberts isn't going anywhere. I tied the knots.'

We found a decent torch, put full waterproofs on and headed up to the van. A furious thumping came from inside, but the women had made sure that Stevie wasn't going anywhere either. I made a mental note of the usefulness of a hijab for tying two door handles together in difficult circumstances.

Gavin untied the two knotted scarves that went over the roof to keep the front doors locked, and unlocked the driver's door. There was a metal slats screen rolled down behind the front seats, but we could hear nothing from behind it. Gavin called out 'Police!' and rolled it up.

Stevie was loose in what was visibly a custom-built cell; no internal handles, a firmly-fixed mesh with a pull-down metal screen between the front seats and the back, a bucket toilet fastened in one corner, and the side doors welded shut. He was spitting with rage and burst instantly into furious speech, protesting his innocence and demanding a lawyer. Gavin read him his rights, agreed that he'd get a chance to contact a lawyer once he got to Lerwick, asked for his phone, which Stevie gave up reluctantly, and told him he would remain there until more police officers arrived.

We went down together to retrieve Roberts. Gavin read the rights again, swapped my ropes for handcuffs and took his phone too. Roberts called me for everything all the way up the drive, but Gavin simply said that he could make a full statement in time, as would I, of course, and in the meantime where had I put the gun I alleged he'd threatened me with? I let Gavin fish it out of the salmon bin I'd dropped it in, rather damp but still, I hoped, with plenty of Roberts's fingerprints. He put it in an evidence bag fished out of his sporran and continued to escort Roberts upwards. He bundled him into the front of the van and handcuffed him to the steering wheel. 'No need for you two to be talking to each other either,' he added, and scrolled the metal screen down again.

We'd just locked the van door when the next set of car headlights came bumping down the track. It was Inga, with a heap of bedding and Peerie Charlie in the back of the car, a black bag of clothes in the passenger footspace, and three bags of Chinese takeaway on the seat. I hoped the women wouldn't mind that it was from completely the wrong continent.

Peerie Charlie came running towards me, then fell silent at the sight of so many strangers. 'The girls are at football,' Inga explained. She didn't waste any more time with words, just dumped the food bags on the table and began unwrapping: special rice, chow mein, several vegetable dishes and something chickeny. The smell was wonderful. Plates were beside it before she'd finished opening. We all squished ourselves into the sit-ootery and wolfed it down.

'You arrived at the wrong time,' Inga said to Gavin. 'I was going to make them vanish into the Shetland women's network.'

He gave her a startled look, thought about it for a moment, then gave his shy, unexpectedly charming smile. 'I've called for backup too.'

Inga gave an exasperated sigh, and turned to me. 'Right. You'll have to be the sacrifice.' She gave a sympathetic grimace, then continued briskly, 'Since we can't sneak them all into houses across the isles and work them unobtrusively into the system, we've got to make a big fuss. Blaze it all over the newspapers, "Rescued from certain death – no, abandoned to the storm – "' She paused, frowned and waved it away. 'A big splash, anyway. We need our MPs on board. Interviews – ' She looked around at the women. 'Can any of you speak English?'

They caught the word, and gave that 'not very much' look. One of the women nudged her daughter, who squirmed and nodded. 'I can little.'

'Mariama speaks French,' I said. I gave her a quick resumé of what was going on, and she relayed it to the other women. There was a brief, animated discussion, hands gesticulating, then Mariama came back to me.

'Is your friend's idea that publicity will mean a public outcry that will make it harder for the Home Office to send us back?'

I nodded.

'Then we will do it.'

'My partner's in the police,' I said apologetically, indicating Gavin. He was looking particularly unlike a police officer, a plate of food balanced on his kilt lap, and his russet hair curling as it dried.

'It means I can't help hide you,' he said in French. 'I would lose my job.'

'We can perhaps pay more,' Mariama said tentatively.

I held a hand up to stop her. 'Don't even say it! This country is very different.'

'No,' Gavin said honestly. 'I wish I could say so, but I'm different. I'll help you all I can but I won't lie about having seen you. I think Inga's is the best plan.' He smoothed a hand down my arm. 'Sorry, Cass. *Longship girl in dramatic sea rescue.*'

I made another face.

The child who spoke a little English chattered excitedly to Mariama, who nodded. 'If she's to speak to the papers, she needs you to teach her some words. She wants to tell them that she was very frightened, and she never thought we would all get aboard before the big ship sank. She thought the little boat might get eaten by the waves on the way to land.'

I covered my eyes with one hand. Gavin laughed, and translated to Inga, who nodded approvingly. 'That's the stuff. How can we possibly send a child who's had an ordeal like that back to a French camp, especially if her father's legally here in the UK waiting to clasp her in his arms again? What do all the husbands do, by the way? I don't suppose there's any working in the NHS?'

I gave up, and began dishing out more food, while Gavin found out that yes, indeed, there was a husband in Bradford who was an orderly and another who was a hospital porter in Sheffield. 'Good,' Inga said, and headed off into the sit-ootery to make phone calls.

I looked glumly at Gavin and Mariama. 'She doesn't like the press,' Gavin explained.

I had a sudden awful thought. 'Here, I'm not likely to be charged, am I, like that German skipper who picked up refugees from a small boat?'

'I hope not,' Gavin said.

I set my jaw. 'It's the duty of every seafarer to go to the rescue of others in distress.'

'I'll send you a file in a cake,' Gavin promised. 'Seriously, Cass, I'd be very surprised.'

'So was the German skipper.' It gave me a new worry; Home Office officials were mad enough for anything. I hoped Inga's plan would work.

We ate till the food was all gone. I was just putting the plates in the sink when blue lights flashed across the dark hill-side. I put my head out to look. Three vehicles were rolling down the hill, two squad cars and a van, all filled with police officers. DS Peterson was among them; I supposed she'd be doing the interview with me. I hoped they'd accept wielding a fire extinguisher as a defence against a pointed gun. *Had you any reason, Ms Lynch, to think he was actually going to use it?*

Kenny's death fell into place now. Jen had been right; after Roberts and Stevie had split up coming home from their trip in the dark out to the Skerries, he had gone after Roberts. After him, though, because he'd gone back to see what they were up to, watching from the hill. If he'd been following Roberts, Kenny couldn't have been hit from behind by him, but Stevie could have looked back from the *Swan*, and seen that Roberts had a shadow. He could easily have slipped across the fields, a direct line to Roberts's house passing where that fence post was lying so handy. Kenny wouldn't have been expecting him; he was focused on Roberts. Stevie had struck, and Kenny had fallen. Roberts had turned around, shone his torch on the stranger and found a dead man.

They'd argued about it: Ruby's ghosts. Roberts could have told the police he'd been attacked by someone following him and struck the man in self-defence, but it was a pretty weak chance he'd be believed, made weaker by his record. No, he wasn't going to hold his hand up to this one; but nor was Stevie. There was too much at stake: a clever, lucrative supply line with friendly Stevie hooking desperate people and promising them safe delivery in Britain. I wondered if they'd get the chance to find the hidden compartment on *Dorabella*. Mariama would be able to tell them where it was. Women, children to be landed in Shetland, where nobody was looking for them, and taken in the supermarket delivery van down to Aberdeen to be shipped on to their destination on the mainland.

It made me angry. A century and a half since woman had first asked for the vote, thirty years since Betty had burned herself to be able to leave her husband, and a dozen advances in laws for our protection, yet still women were a commodity for exercising male power. Thirty years ago Stevie had taken videos of his nieces, and Roberts had photographed Jen. Now they were dealing in real people. I remembered Stevie speaking on the phone, the night the boat had gone on the Ve Skerries. *The cargo can stay put for the moment.* I thought of the terror those women and children must have felt when the ship hit the rocks, the hope as each new party of possible rescuers came on board and the despair as they left again; the determination that had got them out of their prison onto the deck, to signal for help in a wilderness of rocks and water.

And Moon? It had to be Stevie. Roberts couldn't have known that she was going to climb the Sneug alone; and besides, he was the canny one, I reckoned, not going to put his neck in a noose. Stevie had killed already; if Moon needed to go, that was Stevie's problem. Her cockiness on board *Swan* that morning, announcing to Stevie that she'd got a backup witness, must have sealed her fate. I imagined him going ostentatiously in the other direction, climbing a bit and watching where she went, then hurrying along the far side of the Neuk until it joined the Sneug, and climbing up the side, unseen, to meet Moon higher up, and kill her. I hoped Gavin could prove it. All he needed was a tiny scrap of DNA under Moon's fingernails, the imprint of one of Stevie's boots on the far side of the Sneug, away from where they'd gone up to search.

As for cutting me loose, that made sense now too. Stevie had already been made suspicious by my asking him about a night attempt to tow the trawler off. Now I was cosying up to Jen, Moon's backup witness. Once the police started asking Roberts about what he'd been doing that Saturday night, he'd remember I asked him, and the fat would be in the fire. Wrecking me wasn't a certainty, any more than pushing Moon overboard had been, but it was worth a try.

'Wake up, Cass,' Inga said.

'Long day.' It was true the warmth of the fire, combined with last night's excursion, and tooling around Papa most of the day, and then coming home in the storm, had wiped me out. The children were drooping too, though their mothers were still upright, alert, very conscious of the police activity all around us. I tried to assess beds. Two in the guest room. The sofa in the sitting room, and there was a reclining easy chair there too. Another sofa in the sit-ootery, and a couple of comfy chairs. Four berths on *Khalida*. If the children could share the two beds, we'd manage. It had to be more comfortable than wherever they'd been on the fishing boat.

Then, suddenly, the Press arrived: Radio Shetland, the *Shetland Times*, followed by our MSP in person and our MP on the phone from London. I had to wake up and tell them how I'd seen the distress signal from the boat, then I passed the story on to Mariama and the little girl, with Gavin acting as translator. They got photos of the whole group of women and children, squashed into the sit-ootery, with Peerie Charlie and me in the middle, and if it hadn't been dark and soaking outside they'd have had us all back on *Khalida* posing for them.

DS Peterson coming into the house at last was a welcome release. At least she knew all about the murders and understood my suspicions of Stevie, and she was very pleased to have one set of traffickers handcuffed, if not behind bars yet. 'All the same,' she said, eyeing up the reporters warily, 'I think I'll come back tomorrow for your statement. Gavin said that one of the women was French-speaking.' She shot a glance at him, talking amicably to the press, and shook her head admiringly. 'He's a star at giving them the minimum of information in a way that makes them feel they're getting the inside edge. Tell you what, I'll talk to her now, if you'll stand by to translate any bits I don't get, just so that I can get the outline of the women's story. That means I can set enquiries in hand, and then I'll do another interview with an accredited translator once they've had a chance to recover.'

I relayed that to Mariama, and we took cups of tea through to the sitting room. DS Peterson leaned forward, and said in slow, careful French, 'Please tell me how you came to be on the boat.'

Mariama nodded, and was silent for a moment, as if she was thinking how to explain. 'It's always difficult,' she said at last. She spoke slowly, looking directly at DS Peterson as she spoke, and pausing at the end of each sentence to let her nod understanding. 'When you're in the camps at Calais, there are always rumours, you know, of people who will get you over. But you have to be careful. You never get to speak to them directly, it's through someone who knows someone who knows one of the guards, or a local person who works in the camp. You never get to see the transporters for yourself, so it's a real leap into the unknown. Some will offer you a boat, but many of the boats aren't seaworthy, and the people drown on the way. The transporters don't care about that. They got their money up front. Then there are others, you know, with lorries, but stories come back that they take you to people who will use the men for forced labour gangs, or put the women in brothels. We agree among ourselves that those who make it will send word back. There's a route and a code.' She held up her hand as DS Peterson's mouth opened. 'I won't tell you it. We were suspicious of Franck at first.' She saw our reaction.

'That's not his name? The man who met us here, the one we locked in the van. That was what he told us to call him. We were told about him through one of the camp workers. We were suspicious because his boat would take only men or women and children, not mixed loads, and not more than ten of us, but then word got through from someone who had gone with him that she'd arrived safely.'

'A tub to catch a whale,' DS Peterson said unexpectedly, in English, then translated. 'Getting one group through to reassure others.'

Mariama nodded. 'The journey was difficult, she said, the boat and then the van, but Franck had delivered what he'd promised. Also, he didn't ask for money up front. Once he'd got us to Britain, he said. That made us decide we'd trust him.'

'How did the journey work?' DS Peterson asked.

Mariama bit her lip. 'I won't tell you how we got out of the camp,' she said. 'You'll have seen photos in your papers of what it's like.' Her jaw set. 'It's indescribable, no way to treat human beings. I won't give away our escape routes. We were told the day and time, and we got out and waited in the dark at the pick-up point. We were all so frightened, but excited too, that at last we might make it out of there and into safety. A new life. Franck drove up in a van, not like the one he had here, just an ordinary Citroen 2CV. One of those little grey vans with the rounded bonnet and the corrugated bits on the side, and a local numberplate.' She saw DS Peterson's head lift and made an apologetic face. 'I just got a glimpse of it as we climbed aboard. I couldn't tell you the exact number, but it was local, Pas-de-Calais, 62.' The crispness of her voice made DS Peterson look at her with extra attention. Mariama smiled wryly. 'I was your rank at home, a sergeant.' She raised her brows at our surprise. 'The poor can't afford to escape. You have no idea how many surgeons, architects, staff nurses, teachers are stuck, wasted, in those camps.' I remembered the way she'd marshalled the others on the deck of the trawler, and nodded. She waited while DS Peterson made a note of that, then continued. 'He reassured us straight away. He was friendly and helpful, and he joked with the children. He wasn't sinister at all. He was like a friendly uncle.'

I thought of Moon and Kirsten, two little blond girls dancing round the living room for their uncle. He'd been a teenager then. Like Gavin's way with the press, his friendliness had been honed as a professional asset.

'Well, we all packed into the back of the van, and Franck drove us to the boat. It wasn't in Calais, it was a little harbour well out of the town, with no customs or anything like that. I don't know the name of it. There were no windows in the van, so the first we saw of it was coming out at the quayside.'

'You'll find it using AIS,' I said to DS Peterson. 'The ship's track, on the internet.'

'It was the middle of the night, and there was nobody about, not even anyone on watch, but it was such a little place you wouldn't have expected that. He took us aboard and we went down, down, right down in the ship and into the hold. There was a false bulkhead, a wall within the hold, with a small door in it.' She made the size with her hands. 'So small we had to wriggle in. When he opened it first there was a panel of switches and sockets, a dummy, and he took that out for us to crawl through, and closed it behind us once we were all in. He put the panel back, and locked the door.'

She wrinkled her nose, remembering. 'It was a strange space.' She stretched out both arms. 'It was this wide. I could touch both sides at once. And it was as long as the width of the boat, and as high as the hold, so we could stand comfortably, and we could all lie down to sleep – there were those flat mattresses, like campers have, you know, that roll up, and duvets. The duvets were a bit smelly, but they had clean covers. It was warm. There was a sink up in one corner, and a toilet that discharged straight into the sea. And a little cupboard with food, lots of packets of those noodles that you add hot water to, and an electric kettle. Franck said we might be there for up to ten days, until they'd filled the hold and taken it to where it was discharged, and then we'd be landed in Britain. We'd be safe as soon as they caught fish, he said. The door would be under the cargo, so a customs search wouldn't find us. But nobody on the ship knew about us, so we had to talk as little as possible, and keep the children quiet. He'd come to get us off once it got to port. We just had to be patient.'

'Ingenious,' DS Peterson said. 'Is there any chance, Cass, that we'll be able to get on board, even just to get photographs of it?'

Outside, the wind howled round the house. I thought of the waves battering the Ve Skerries, and shook my head.

'We had three days motoring. It was fine, just noisy, but none of us was seasick at first. Then they caught fish, and filled the hold with it, and it stank. It was colder too, because they'd turned on the refrigeration. We were glad of the duvets to huddle in. And then,' Mariama said, shuddering at the memory, 'then we felt this jar, and there was a horrible crashing, scraping noise, and the whole ship shuddered and stopped, and we knew we'd hit something. We were terrified. We thought it might sink, but it seemed to settle, on those rocks, the way you saw it when you came to get us, Cass. We heard other ships about, the noise came through the sides of the hull, and we felt the movement as they tried to pull our boat off. There was nothing we could do, you see, because even if we shouted for help, well, we were under the catch. Nobody could get us out until the hold had been emptied, so it was a huge relief when we heard more machinery, and realised that was what they were doing. We knew they were still trying to save the boat; the electrics were still on, and we'd heard some sort of engine running.'

'The refrigeration for the fish,' I said.

'Then after they'd emptied the hold they shut that off, and then our lights went out. That was when we began to be afraid again, but we couldn't quite believe that Franck had abandoned us like that. We didn't know where we were – for all we knew, we might be on a beach, or even have rammed a harbour wall and be in port. We didn't know anything, except that the boat seemed to be sitting on the ground. He might be coming to get us as soon as it was safe.'

Friendly Stevie, who was good at getting people to trust him.

'There was another attempt to get the boat off, but then after that, nothing, just the dark and the sound of the hull grinding on the rocks. We gave it another night, and then we talked about it, and decided we'd have to get out, and risk being caught. So we set about getting ourselves out.' She spread her hands. For the first time I noticed that there were several cuts on them, and one fingernail was half torn away. 'The dummy panel was held on from the other side with bolts, and then the door was locked. We had to batter and batter at the metal until it buckled. I don't know how long it took us. We took it in turns, hammering at it with the kettle. It bent at last, and we were able to pull it out, and then we had to do the same with the door, and that was harder, because you couldn't get a proper swing at it. I thought we were never going to do it. I was hitting it when it gave at last, and I kept going for several more thuds because I didn't believe it. Outside there was this greyness, light at last, after all that time in the dark, and we waited, and listened, and then we crawled out, so scared.' Her eyes were dark pools, remembering. 'There was only the sound of the waves, much louder than we expected, all around us. We came slowly, slowly up the stairs, but there was no sound anywhere, and we began to see that the boat had been stripped. Every machine, every movable bit of furniture. We got as far as the bridge, and there were just holes where the instruments had been.' Her face was bleak. 'And then we looked out, still keeping out of sight, to see where we were, and saw we were on rocks in the middle of the sea, and the nearest land, the island you came from, Cass, well, even that was miles away, too far to swim, and there were no houses on it. No houses, no boats, nothing. They hadn't left even a box of matches for us to light a fire on the deck. And I can't read your skies, but that black cloud looked like bad weather coming.'

She paused, her face reflecting that moment of hopelessness. Then she looked at me, and smiled. 'And then we saw your boat coming around the corner of the island. Just a little sailboat, but you were coming towards us. I found a bit of metal to flash at you, and Leila waved the brightest jacket we had, and then you signalled that you'd seen us, and we knew we were going to be saved after all.' Her face lit up. 'If they let us stay, will you take me sailing again?'

I held out my hand. 'Gladly.'

Our two hands met and clasped, as though we were sisters.

'Okay,' said DS Peterson. 'I've got that scribbled down. Looking back, Mariama, was there any sign that the man you call Franck was working with anyone else?'

Mariama shook her head decisively. 'He came alone in the French van, and the boat seemed deserted when he took us aboard. He told us that nobody knew we were there. The other man who was here with him tonight, that was the first time I've seen him with someone else.'

DS Peterson sighed, and closed her notebook. 'And he had his phone on him while he was locked in the van. He had time to warn his contacts.'

'Maybe not,' I said. 'The signal's lousy here. And you have Roberts's gun.'

'Fingerprints,' DS Peterson said with satisfaction. 'You gave him a good thump with that extinguisher. He's got a lovely bruise on the temple. I got the police doctor to photograph it here, so that we wouldn't be charged with police brutality.' She rose. 'That'll add to his sentence.'

The black rage filled me again. 'Attempted murder. Murder of ten women and children. If real murderers get only fifteen years, out in ten, what will they get? Ten, out in five?'

'The gangmaster of the cockle-gatherers who died in Morecambe Bay got twelve years for manslaughter. Six months per person.' Her voice was bitter; her green eyes looked straight into mine. 'We do what we can. You'll learn that, with Gavin.' Then her face brightened. 'But don't forget Moon and Kenny. Both of those were murder, and even if they try for self-defence with Kenny, Moon was pushed off that hill by someone stronger than her. I got some hopeful leads from your friend Uncle. I'll tell you tomorrow.'

She turned away, then, on a thought, turned back. 'Consider the lecture on reasonable force for dealing with thugs with guns read. You'll probably hear it again from the judge.'

It was nearly eleven before the circus died down. The van was taken away with police escort. As soon as the news hit the internet, three of the Shetland hotels phoned to offer accommodation and taxi transport. Inga accepted on the women's behalf, and once they were all bundled into taxis, with hugs and promises to let me know how it went, she rounded up an over-excited Peerie Charlie and went off too. Gavin and I were left alone in the chaos of what was now our home: chairs from all over the house around the table, a sinkload of mugs and a strong smell of special fried rice.

'Leave it for now,' Gavin said, putting an arm around my waist. 'You've had a long day. Bedtime. They'll surely allow us a couple of nights together before they put me back south, now the case is solved.'

'Bedtime,' I agreed.

VIII

The Calm After the Storm

Chapter Twenty-seven

Thursday 24th October

Tide times Aith
HW 06.14 (1.8m); LW 12.35 (1.0m);
HW 18.33 (1.9m); LW 00.01 (0.9m)

Moonrise 01.15, sunrise 08.03; moonset 16.58, sunset 17.30.

Waning crescent moon

I spent most of the next morning recovering. I lay in bed till long after Gavin had left for the station, then got up and trained an extra-hot shower on the aches and bruises I seemed to have developed overnight. Inga phoned mid-morning to tell me that the women had all been delivered safely to their hotels, and every agency she could think of was on their case. They'd been able to speak to their husbands, and the children had been taken down to the school to see around. 'Getting the children in school here is a great step forward. Then you can argue moving them would be disrupting their education. The story's on all the news bulletins this morning, with the photos they took last night.' She laughed. 'Peerie Charlie thinks it was all about him, of course. He went off to nursery full of himself.'

'He would,' I agreed.

Cheered, I headed down to *Khalida* to see what chaos had been left aboard. It was still windy, with white horses racing down the sound and crashing on the beach. My gangplank had shifted in the night. Cat sniffed at it doubtfully, then leapt across the gap. I grabbed Kitten before she could follow, and set her aboard, then I retied the gangplank and crossed it.

There were few signs of last night on the deck. The wind and rain between them had washed off the foam from the fire extinguisher. My mainsail was sodden, but the bungees had held it in place. I picked up the ropes I'd tied Roberts with, re-coiled them and put them away. The extinguisher itself would need to be refilled. The jacket I'd laid over Roberts was soaked. I set it on the pier to go up to the house.

Below was impressively neat. The berth the children had huddled in had been re-made, the mugs had been washed and returned to their places, the tins rinsed out and stacked neatly in the sink. I put them in a bag and was just about to start making a list of new supplies when I heard a car coming down the road.

It was DS Peterson, with the young officer, Shona, behind her. I considered the temperature of the boat, with the gale flying in the hatch, and decided the house would be a kind option. I made them tea and we sat in silence for a moment in the sit-ootery, watching the waves in the sound and the clouds still flying past, then I took them through it all again: the movement on board, rescuing the women, arriving here and finding Stevie and Roberts waiting for us. The gun prodding my back.

'Threatening behaviour using an illegal firearm,' DS Peterson said, with satisfaction. 'Sheriffs don't like guns, and there's no licence registered for either of them. That'll up his sentence nicely. Luckily it's not just your word for it. One of the children saw him holding it to your back, and told his mother. She couldn't see the gun herself, but she saw that you were standing stiffly, and that he was standing very close to you. His prints are all over the gun.'

'What are they saying about it?'

'They both asked for a lawyer immediately and have been saying "No comment" ever since. I interviewed them in turns all morning, and Gavin's taken over now. But we'll get them. The evidence is piling up. They can't get out of the people-trafficking charge, not even if their lawyers tell them to go for the humanitarian rescue service line, reuniting separated families and making a bit for themselves out of it.'

'But how about the murders?' I asked. 'Kenny and Moon? Can you get them, Stevie, whichever of them it was, for that?'

'Stevie Shearer for both, for my money. We're closing in on him. The case for him for killing Kenny's clearer, though it's still all circumstantial. You saw two men, and identified one as having come out of Roberts's house, and those two children identified Stevie coming off the *Swan* and meeting up with Roberts. You saw Kenny out at night, Jen thinks he didn't go home, Geordie, Betty, Tammie, Uncle all knew he was angry enough about Roberts to go and tackle him. We've got his footprints lurking round about the byre, on the other side of the track from Tammie and Ruby's house. Roberts wouldn't have seen him from there, but when Stevie came down to the *Swan* after the visit to the *Dorabella* he would have seen Kenny waiting for Roberts. Assuming that Kenny didn't pick up the piece of wood which killed him, and I think that's a reasonable assumption, because if he'd been fighting mad, Roberts wouldn't have got it off him without a struggle that would have left traces on the body, then it was picked up to hit him with by someone coming from the direction of the *Swan*. In fact the post was lying in a direct line between the pier where the *Swan* was moored and Roberts's door.'

She paused and smiled, grimly. 'Better still, we got Forensics onto the ground that hadn't been trampled on. Visitors had been over the stile by the toilets and down on the beach, and among the sets of footprints were one lot by where the post had been lying, and nice ones too, as someone had bent to pick it up and pushed himself up again. Shearer's boots. The wear pattern's obviously the same. Even better than that, it was a rough post and Forensics is hoping to find DNA from skin behind the splinters. That'll clinch it; juries love DNA. I think too that Roberts will be keen to distance himself from the murder charge. He may tell us all about it. As for Moon . . .'

She paused for a moment, marshalling her facts. 'Moon was like a child in some ways; I've got that impression from all of you. She got obsessive about things, and her preoccupation during the weekend was his part in what she believed was child abuse. She wanted to get her sister to back her up, and he overheard at least part of a conversation in which Kirsten was denying anything ever happened. So far, so good. It's a toss-up whether she'd get as far as court with it, given she insisted they'd been filmed together. The shove off the RIB in the cave was either a long-shot at murder or a warning – like cutting you loose. Then, on Sunday morning, Moon came out with having found Jen. From your account, she was gloating over him.'

'Yes,' I said. 'She made it far too clear she thought she'd got the upper hand of him.'

'She wasn't afraid of him,' Shona said. 'Cheery Uncle Stevie with his bad jokes. He'd only taken videos of her when she was laughing and thinking it was fun.'

I thought of Jen's visceral reaction to seeing her father again, and nodded.

'That was a mistake,' DS Peterson said. 'Because more importantly, Moon had the opportunity to see him going to the fishing boat in the middle of the night, and from your account Moon heard him keeping quiet about him being there. I think she'd have talked about the murder if she'd actually seen it, but you didn't tell them about it, did you?'

I shook my head.

'So she didn't know there had been a murder at the time her friendly uncle Stevie was out roaming the hills. But she would, when she got back to the mainland and heard the news. At the moment she was taken up with her triumph over Jen, but when she stopped thinking about that she might come out with something about the fishing boat. He didn't want any investigation at all, but he definitely couldn't afford any questions being asked about his links with the *Dorabella*. That gives him a motive to silence her, which pleases a jury, but it's not enough to convict him. Okay. Excluding you, Magnie and the locals, we had only four possible suspects: Stevie, Amitola, Kirsten, Geordie. If it wasn't Kirsten, it had to be someone who'd gone up the side of the hill and returned that way, because otherwise Kirsten would have seen them coming down as she walked back to the boat. The local man who saw someone going that way thought it was a man, and he wouldn't have thought that of Amitola, because of her colourful clothes, so I was inclined to rule her out, and she'd have been pushed to do it in the time. There's another reason too, which rules out Kirsten as well: Forensics reckoned the handmark bruises on Moon's back which proved she was pushed are a size more likely to be a man's. Both Amitola and Kirsten have neat hands and feet. We did consider Geordie seriously, simply because he had a motive for killing Roberts, and Moon could have seen him do it.'

'Tammie?' I said. 'Was the RIB his?'

'He was delivering two sheep there,' Shona said. 'He had a yarn with the person buying them, and that person walked him back to his boat. Alibi.'

'And it took two days of officers crawling over the Sneug,' DS Peterson said, 'but at last they found some footprints in soft ground. If Stevie keeps to his story of having climbed the Noup he'll have difficulty explaining his footprints halfway up the Sneug.'

'His own niece.' I shook my head 'It's hard to imagine someone who's so . . . so detached from other people. All that cheery jokiness, it was just a front.'

'I think we'll get him for Kenny, with a not proven for Moon, but juries are funny things.' She gave a wry smile. 'They don't like men killing women who aren't their wives. Being female may at last work in her favour for Moon. And we've been hard at work unravelling their shared past. Mr Kratter, on Papa, your Uncle, he spoke to us . . .'

I lifted my head up. She let the pause hang, tantalisingly, then shook her head. 'No, let's go right back to the beginning, because that's where it started, with Sky and Moon. No, earlier than that, with Roberts.' Her eyes hardened. 'I've seen a few like Roberts. I got all his pedigree from an officer with Burra connections. Father a fisherman, apt to drink at weekends, bit of a temper, mother and son under the thumb. When her husband wasn't around, the mother doted on her son – he was the only child – and he twisted her round his little finger. He was bright at school, but lazy. Thought the world should be his without having to work for it. Charismatic; he managed to convince everyone else that whatever he did was cool. Expected to take the lead in everything and wouldn't play if he couldn't be the star part. Well, he got an adequate set of exam results, the world wasn't sitting up and taking the notice he deserved, so he set up his own little world on Papa. King of his little fiefdom. There were even children born in the colony.'

'Sky and Moon,' I said.

'In between getting stonewalled by that pair, I spent the first bit of this morning talking to a retired officer who'd been here in the seventies and early eighties. He knew straight off what I was talking about. They'd been aware of photographs in circulation, two pretty little blond girls photographed naked against backgrounds of a beach, or the sea, or grass, nothing to pinpoint where, except that it felt like Shetland. His officers made discreet enquiries all round the primary schools, but nobody recognised them – until one got to Papa, when the teacher knew them straight off as two of the children from the hippy colony. There was nothing actionable about the photos, my informant said, especially given that those hippy folk tended to do the "natural" thing and let their bairns run around half-clad in summer. Parents those days did photograph young children naked, and they weren't in sexual poses. If they'd found them in a family album it wouldn't have raised an eyebrow. What made them uneasy was that a number of copies seemed to be circulating.'

She paused for a sip of coffee, then continued. 'I've got someone on to tracking down how he could have printed them. It's a side issue from long ago, but it links with his later activities. Make-weight. Maybe the photographic club had a darkroom at Islesburgh, or maybe a friend let him use a darkroom. I don't suppose we'll ever find out how he got into distributing. The folk in the archives found a catalogue of one of his exhibitions for me, well, a printed sheet, from the days when the gallery and museum and library were all in the Hillhead building, and there are several photograph titles that could be of them. *Childhood Innocence*, *Exploring the Beach*, that kind of thing. Maybe somebody approached him and offered him money for reprints. He'd be glad of the money. His dream colony lived cheaply, but they couldn't be self-sufficient.'

'Was he interviewed at the time?' I asked.

She shook her head. 'They asked a bit more, and found out that Roberts was the photographer, and they were planning to interview him about it when the colony broke up. The two little girls and their mother came to Lerwick, and Roberts went off south to college. There was an investigation of the baby's death, of course, but no autopsy.' She frowned.

'I know,' I said. 'Times were different then.'

'They were all interviewed. They agreed the baby had been born dead. Amitola got a slap on the wrist for not declaring the birth and death, and the case was closed. There didn't seem to be any harm done, so they let it lie.'

'He wrecked the colony,' I said. 'He killed Amitola's baby, he nearly killed her, and she broke free.'

DS Peterson nodded. 'A real kick to his ego. Not his fault, of course, it never is. So he looked around him for a different way of making himself a kingpin, decided he'd outgrown the hippy thing anyway, and picked on teaching. He was apparently good at it. He was genuinely musical, his charisma attracted his pupils, and he had a sarcastic tongue that flattened anyone who dared to disagree with him. My informant about the photos had been transferred, and when the occasional photo surfaced, nobody linked them with one of the teachers. Particularly not with the enthusiastic probationer in the music department. The officers warned the school jannies to keep an eye open for men in macs.'

'And he teamed up with Stevie.'

DS Peterson nodded. 'Naturally Roberts knew Stevie as Amitola's peerie brother – don't forget they were all classmates in Lerwick and friends after school before they high-tailed it to Papa. Through Stevie he could get at Sky and Moon, and pay off his score against Amitola for, as he saw it, having broken his colony up. He probably enjoyed the power of being at the centre of the distribution ring too, but he wouldn't have used his own children for the photos, or not yet. Men like him are protective of their own children, over-protective often, another way of asserting their authority. They create an atmosphere of tension and then say they're keeping them safe from it.'

I thought of the way Roberts had come out to us when we were anchored off in *Khalida*.

'The abuse is focused on the wife, with the children encouraged to agree how stupid Mum is. The focus changes when the children start to rebel.'

It was after Jen had started to be argumentative, preferring her teacher's word to her Daddy's, that Betty'd found the photos.

314

'Not,' DS Peterson said, 'that I think that Stevie Shearer is anything but a very nasty piece of work. He's the violent one of the two. But Roberts turned the charisma on him when he was still at school and gave him a way of making money. I'd put at least part of the way he is now at Roberts's door.' She glanced at her notes. 'Well, Roberts's marriage broke up in a blaze of bad press for him. Not his fault again, of course. He got a job in Leeds under the name Roberts, which is where, just at that time, Stevie Shearer went off to University. On the motorbike he'd bought with the kind of money I'm sure his parents couldn't have given him.'

'And they kept up their . . .' I wasn't sure what to call it. 'Association?'

She gave a satisfied nod. 'That's where Mr Kratter, Uncle, became aware of him. He was a doctor there. He couldn't give us details because of medical confidentiality, he said, but he suggested we talked to the Leeds police about child photographs in the late eighties and nineties. That turned out to be a treasure trove. I spoke to an officer who'd been there. That had been his first case. There had been photographs of girls from University age downwards, soft porn, suggestive rather than explicit, and one of the girls had subsequently gone missing after a row with her parents. Roberts had been one of the men they'd interviewed, since four of the girls came from his classes. Vulnerable girls, the sort that if you had an unscrupulous teacher, they would be the ones he'd point at to be easily influenced. The girls themselves insisted he had nothing to do with it. They described another man, student age, dark and friendly, always joking, who'd got chatting to them in a bar or on a bus, took them out a couple of times and coaxed them into a room he'd fitted up as a studio. The descriptions they gave could have fitted half the male students in Leeds, and the name was different each time. The police kept digging, but nothing came up, except that the school had a darkroom which

315

Roberts used from time to time. He showed them his photos, arty shots of buildings and cranes, all nice and above board.'

She paused for breath. I waited.

'Then a new set of photos began circulating. This was where Mr Kratter got involved. They were much nastier, and of foreign-looking children they couldn't identify – children who weren't in any of the schools, or known to any of the medical practices. They thought the photos must have been taken abroad, until they raided one of their brothels and found a concealed room with three terrified children in it. They'd each been brought there, separately, by a friendly man who told them jokes and offered them a ride on his motorbike. He'd stopped the bike in a side street, and two men had come out and grabbed them.'

She paused to consult her notes. 'I'm trying to give you this in time order. Also picked up in the brothel was a girl who had been reported missing, not the one I mentioned, another fifteen-year-old runaway. Roberts had taught her too. Well, that put him back in the frame, and he was interviewed again, but there was nothing to pin him to the brothel, and though a picture was beginning to emerge of him working with someone else, he didn't seem to have a student-age friend with a motorbike.'

'Being careful,' Shona said.

DS Peterson nodded. 'Mr Kratter treated one of the children. They all turned out to be from illegal immigrant families who hadn't dared report them missing. The other two families were deported, but this family managed to stay. The child got to trust him, and the police sat him with her and her mother behind a two-way mirror while they interviewed Roberts. The child was terrified. That, she told him, was the man who took the photos. Naturally the police confronted Roberts with that, but he breathed injured innocence at them and asked for a lawyer. Nobody at the brothel admitted to knowing him.

The only evidence they had was the child, who would never have been believed matched against a well-respected teacher with no criminal record. In those days they put a child on the witness stand, and his lawyer would have torn her to shreds. They put the case into Holmes, added some libellous comments on the paper notes and kept an eye on him thereafter, without any result, and no pretext for investigating why his teacher's pay seemed to run to several exotic foreign holidays a year.

'But . . . over the last seven years, across the Midlands, they've been turning up trafficked women. Not the usual Eastern European – Arabic and African, and there's been mention in several of the cases of the Calais camps, and what the women thought was a boat journey to safety. What rang bells was the man who'd taken them aboard, smiling and friendly, telling jokes with the children. The officer I spoke to was intrigued enough to pay a call on Roberts and found him retired, and talking about moving back to his home town in the Highlands.'

'Oh, yeah?' I said. 'Near Inverness, that'd be?'

'The officer was quite surprised to hear we were calling from Shetland. Roberts missed having bairns around him, he said. He wanted to get back and spend more time with his grandchildren.'

'Missed having people to dominate, more like,' I said. 'He was planning a new fiefdom here in Papa. Patriarch of the tribe, with Betty to scare and his children and grandchildren to influence.'

DS Peterson nodded. 'I wouldn't be surprised. Keeping with the Midlands line, I've never been so glad for a lack of signal. Stevie wasn't able to warn his contacts. He'd spent his time in the van clearing his phone of all but friends and family, almost suspiciously clear, but thanks to you tying him up Roberts's phone was untouched. I gave the Leeds officer a list of numbers and he recognised a couple straight away, from the raids I was speaking about that turned up the trafficked woman. They're having a busy time down there tracking the rest, and I hope that'll give us more links in the chain.

'Meanwhile, jumping back thirty-five years, Stevie returned to Shetland after University. I went round to his firm this morning to apologise for his absence and find out more about him. "Such fun in the office, aye ready wi' a joke" was the general verdict. The most interesting thing was that he goes off to France every holiday, touring round on that motorbike of his. There were several postcards on the office noticeboard, the cheery sort, you know, donkeys with hats, that kind of thing. We've got his computer, and there may be something in that. The bank manager's dragging his feet a bit but he said that he wasn't aware of anything odd about the account, in terms of payments. That's a drawback. We need to trace the money they've been making.'

Her phone rang. She picked it up, listened, and her face changed. 'That was quick. Yes, put him through.' A heavier voice followed, and her face clouded. She spoke in French: 'Yes, sir . . . yes, I am in charge of the case . . . That is very good. Yes, please.' She listened for a minute, her face getting increasingly annoyed, and then she shot a glance at me, bit her lip, and said, 'Excuse me, sir, I will need to give you to someone who speaks better French.'

She handed the phone to me with a wry twist of her lips. 'Good day, sir,' I said.

I caught the tail-end of a wine-fuelled chuckle. The minute he launched in I understood why she was having bother. He had a north-of-France accent you could have cut with a knife and served up for dinner, and I'd have been stuck myself if I hadn't had practice with my equally-country cousins.

'Now, then,' he said, at a speed that made absolutely no concessions to a non-native speaker, 'you were asking about an Englishman perhaps in my département with a grey French van, registered here, and perhaps with a motorbike too. I thought of this man straight away, and the photo confirmed it. He's called Georges Oude here, and he has a restored cottage just out of Wissant, to the south of Calais. He bought it, oh, probably thirty years ago, when you could get an old house to refurbish for two sous. Now I tell you straight, I thought he was as frank as a donkey moving backwards. We see plenty of *anglais* here, and they're a funny lot generally, keep themselves to themselves, would you believe there are ones here who've lived here twenty years and don't speak a word of French? He wasn't like that at all. Schoolboy French that he was keen to try out and joking all the time, far too friendly with everyone. The habit doesn't make a monk. I kept an eye on his comings and goings, but I didn't see anything to put my finger on. I tried to find out more from the bank, he'd opened an account here, but it's like pedalling in semolina to get anything out of a bank. The best I could get was that his reference was an English bank in Leeds, he'd had an account there since his student days and he'd bought the house outright.'

'Hang on,' I said. 'Let me just pass all that on.' I covered the phone and looked at DS Peterson. 'This officer knows him. Recognised the photo. A cottage near Wissant under the name of George Wood, had a bank account in that name since his student days, and bought the house outright.'

Shona began tapping rapidly into her phone. I went back to the French officer. 'Okay, go on.'

'You're Poitevin, huh?' he said. 'They're a funny lot down there, I have a cousin married one. Who're your people?'

'Delafauve, from Savigny. My cousin Thierry works the farm there.'

'Thierry Delafauve?' I could hear his mental card index ticking round. 'Yeah, yeah, the singer.'

'Maman,' I agreed.

'So that's who you are.' He chuckled again, sounding just

like Papy in a mischevious mood. 'Well, back to your chicken. He did the house up himself, made not too bad a job of it. The van he keeps here, and he arrives on the motorbike. He comes for holidays and occasional weekend visits, and he has a local woman who keeps an eye on the place for him. He hasn't caused any trouble, exactly.'

'Oh?' I said.

'Just one incident. He'd been here, oh, five years by then, so that makes it twenty years ago. A photograph that surfaced, a very nice one of a local girl. Soft focus, a practised hand. Pity she hadn't any clothes on at the time. Small stuff, but a colleague in England thought she looked French and under-age and sent it over. It got distributed round, and I recognised the girl. Thirteen, she was, and dumb enough to swallow snakes. Both the mother and the girl had hysterics, and the girl clammed up, and the mother made a whole cheese about spoiling her good name. Well, I'd heard she'd been seen on the back of a motorbike, so I took it upon myself to have a word. Nothing since.'

Across the table, Shona gave a triumphant 'Yesss! The power of the internet,' she said. 'An ancient photo on Facebook.' She turned the phone so that DS Peterson and I could see.

'"My flatmates back in my Leeds student days",' DS Peterson read. 'Posted by someone called George Wood.' She put forward one manicured fingertip. 'Stevie Shearer.'

'Easy enough to nick your mate's matric card and a flat utilities bill and open an account in his name for stashing dodgy money.' Shona saved the photo and whizzed it off.

'The name he's using is very useful,' I told the French officer. 'A long-standing faked bank account.'

'What're you after him for?'

'Picking up women and children from the Calais camp in that grey van,' I said, spacing my words like hammer blows. 'Putting them in a hidden hold in a fishing boat and leaving them to drown when it went on the rocks off Shetland.'

He whistled and was silent for a moment. 'Good evidence?' he said at last.

'If I put DS Peterson back on, will you behave, and speak to her so she can understand you?'

His accent modified to BBC, and slowed to half the speed. 'I'll pretend I'm talking to my own boss. He's from Paris. But you actually have him in custody, and the other man whose photo you sent? Nobody knows him, by the way.'

I dug out a couple of cousin Thierry's favourite phrases. 'He's in beautiful sheets. Unless his backside's surrounded by noodles, we've got him this time.' He chuckled appreciatively as I passed the phone back.

Chapter Twenty-eight

Friday 25th October

Tide times Aith
LW 01.09 (0.6m); HW 07.29 (2.0m);
LW 13.32 (0.8m); HW 19.37 (12.2m)

Moonrise 03.17, sunrise 08.08; moonset 17.25, sunset 17.27.

Waning crescent moon

It was mast-down day, and my world was bleak.

Gavin took a last mouthful of coffee on his way out of the door, set his cup down and made a sympathetic face. 'Must go. Good luck. I'll see you in Brae.' He kissed me and headed off in a swirl of kilt pleats.

I poured myself another cup of coffee and brooded. I was tired and dispirited. Inga and our MPs would do their best, but the women would still be subject to detention. The children might be separated from them. They'd see their husbands only under practically jail-visit conditions. I wished there was a magic wand to set the world to rights. There wasn't, though; you just had to do your best in the bit you could influence.

I looked at Gavin's abandoned plate and knew this was my bit. I was lucky; we were together at last. I had to give this my best shot. Gavin hadn't exactly burnt his boats coming up here, he still had his Inverness flat, but his job was here now because he wanted to be with me. I had to be wholehearted too.

I sighed and contemplated the dancing water outside gloomily. 'Mast down, Cat.'

He gave his silent miaow, which I took as sympathy. 'You're not going to like it,' I assured him. 'In fact, you and Kitten should probably stay home.'

I put the breakfast dishes in the sink, and headed down to *Khalida*. I knew that my idea of leaving her still intact down below wouldn't work. It was no good going into this relationship with another house to step back to. He had his work, and I had mine, and apart from that we had each other.

It was miserable work, dismantling my boat. Cushions first. I went back up and fetched Tamar's wheelbarrow, loaded them on it, added the blue and yellow curtains which hung each side of the heads compartment, and loaded my sailing jackets on top. The wind tugged at them as I trundled the barrow upwards. I stored all the cushions in the spare room, put the curtains by the washing machine, hung up the jackets and trundled back down again. Books. My clothes. Bedding. With each load, my *Khalida* looked less like my home.

Cat was obviously perturbed by the vandalism. He went back onboard between loads, sniffing in exposed corners, plumed tail swishing ominously. Once I'd finished I set the engine going and he jumped aboard as soon as I began working with the mooring lines. Kitten promptly followed him. Ah, well, they could sit on the pontoon while the actual deed was being done, and then come back by car. I retrieved the basket and Cat's harness, and stowed them below.

It was a bleak sail up Busta Voe. The gale had died away to a good sailing breeze, and every wave slapping against *Khalida*'s hull, every time she dipped to the wind or speeded down the back of a crest, seemed to say *last time, last time*. There'd be *Sørlandet*, of course, with her white wings spread to fly, but my *Khalida* would be amputated until April, a whole six months. I tried to convince myself that I'd sleep the sounder for knowing her halyards weren't rattling against the mast and fraying on the pulleys, but I knew I was clutching at straws. The long and short of it was that I'd be grounded for the winter.

When we got in, Cat trotted off along the shore, and Kitten rolled on the warm pontoon, showing her white belly. I half-lowered the mainsail, got a bucket of soapy water from the Boating Club, and gave the sail a good wash, then re-hoisted it to dry in the last of the wind. The jib wasn't too bad, but I scrubbed along the stitching anyway and left it to dry too. 'You're taking it down then?' Magnie enquired from behind me, making me jump and splosh drips of water over Kitten. She sneezed indignantly, shook herself and retreated with hauteur.

I gave Magnie an eloquent look.

'You'll be glad come the winter gales,' he said soothingly.

'Likely.' I scowled at my scrubbing brush and dropped it back in the bucket.

'It's a good day for taking masts down. That gale blew itself out nicely. No wind to speak of.'

'There is no good day for taking masts down,' I grumbled. 'Come aboard. It's a bit damp.'

'Don't stop for me, lass. What needs taking off?'

'Everything. The other halyards, and the kicker, and the sheets.'

We got on with dismantling my boat. Magnie undid the halyards, pulling them down from the masthead, then coiling them neatly while I tackled the cat's cradle and pulleys which passed for a kicking strap. Naturally one shackle was seized, and would have to wait until the mast came off to be soaked in oil.

My spirits rose slightly with being busy, and I recovered my manners. 'How did the *Swan*'s voyage round to Scalloway go?' I asked.

'Oh, good. We'd barely reached Vaila Isle when the volunteers had got a list of winter maintenance going, and begun to strip the berths and scrub the kitchen.' Magnie gave me a sideways look from his pebble-green eyes. 'I think you'd have a good chance for either skipper or mate, if you were thinking to apply for it when the post's advertised.' He straightened up. 'There, lass, that's your ropes done.'

'Thanks.' I put them in a bucket, ready to be washed, and went aft to get the mainsheet.

'You could put your sails and boom in the shed if you wanted, up in the loft bit,' Magnie suggested. 'They'd no' get walked on up there.'

It would be dryer than aboard *Khalida* if she wasn't being used. 'That's a good idee.' I gave the mainsail an experimental touch. 'I think this is dry now. Could you give me a hand to fold it?'

We bundled it down and spread it out on the pontoon to flake it small enough to go into its never-used bag. 'You had an exciting time o' it on Wednesday, then,' Magnie said, as we eased it into the bag. 'I even saw a clip o' you all on the news yesterday, and a chopper shot of what's left of the *Dorabella*.'

'Much?'

'Breaking up. By Monday there'll be nothing but her engine on the rocks. Jib next?'

We folded and bagged the jib, and I envisaged the *Dorabella* being pounded by the waves, knocked onto one side, the water flooding in, the rivets that held her being forced apart, the bulkheads being torn out. The women and children could have been there still, as the water flooded in. I thrust the thought away and lifted a sailbag and the bucket of coiled ropes. Magnie shouldered the other bag, and we headed round to the shed. It was filled now with grey Pico dinghies clustered around the RIB like chicks round their mother hen. 'Come spring,' I said, passing the bags upward, 'we'd need to go through these Picos and make sure every single one of them has the gear it needs.'

'I made a list when we put them away, and I've put in for a grant to cover a couple of new rudders and sails for all o' them.'

'About time,' I agreed. The sails were getting on for twenty years old, and had all the aerodynamics of a sugar bag. 'Thanks to you. Tea now?'

'I'll no' say no.' He paused to give a look across at *Khalida*, already diminished without her sails. 'Dinna fret, lass. At least when she's no mast up you can probably keep her by you at the pier at Houbansetter, and only put her back up here when forecast's looking dodgy.'

I shook my head. 'Not without sails as a backup to the engine. And no decent VHF coverage, with no aerial.'

Magnie gave the sort of grunt that acknowledged the truth of that. 'O' course you'd need to tie it down well in the gales, but if you really canna do without sails, maybe you could borrow one of the Picos, though sooner you than me sitting to the waist in water at this season.'

'It's a thought,' I agreed, 'but it would just be too cold. I'll have *Sørlandet*.'

'With sixty teenagers running riot all over her.'

'We don't let them run riot,' I said austerely.

The marina was busy now with all the other owners aboard their boats. Most of them had taken off their sails before the storm, but there were always last bits of unfastening to do, unscrewing the stays to the last inch, and squirting WD40 on every part that needed to move. Magnie undid my careful wire belt-and-braces fastening while I sprayed and unscrewed, then he helped me thread electric wires through behind the cabin wood and up the holes beside the mast while the kettle boiled. I fastened the wires into a plastic bag and taped it to the mast, then we sat in the cockpit to drink the tea. There weren't even any chocolate biscuits to cheer us up.

'Never leet that, lass,' Magnie said, when I apologised. 'You did a good day's work that afternoon. Those bairns needed them then far more than we need them today.'

'Surely they'll let them stay with their mothers while they're here in Shetland, at least.'

'Lass, they're no' going to be forced to leave Shetland. Are you no' heard? There's an online petition wi' over twenty thousand signatures already that they're no' to be taken to detention centres, a fund started for them, offers o' accommodation, and our MP's making statements all over the place. It was all on the lunchtime news on the wireless.'

My heart lifted slightly.

'Mind that Thai boy, that worked to the leisure centre in Lerwick?'

I gave him a blank look.

'It was maybe when you were out o' Shetland. Saakchi Makao. The Home Office decided to deport this boy and did a dawn raid on him. Didn't read his rights or anything, just bundled him to the airport, and it was only because he was about to be someone's best man and asked to be allowed to phone him that anyone realised what was happening. Well, there was a fuss straight away, petitions, funds for a lawyer for him, his boss speaking up for him, all that. They let him go again and he's here yet.' He clapped me on the back. 'So cheer up, lass. You saved those folk from drowning, and your man's come home to stay. Now all you need is a job here in Shetland, then you'll have nothing more to wish for.' He glanced upwards at my stripped mast. 'And never tell me your old Mirror dinghy, what did you call her, your *Osprey*'s no hanging in your dad's garage at this very minute, with almost-new sails, all ready to go, so long as you pick your day and wear plenty of ganseys.'

'And tie her down within an inch of her life against the gales,' I said, but my heart rose a little more. It would be fun to sail *Osprey* again.

Magnie gave the slip a glance. The water was halfway up now. 'You'd likely get in there now, lass, if you want to be ready to get it over with first.'

I put the cups below, started the engine and loosed the ropes. Kitten leapt aboard and looked round for Cat with a plaintive squeak. 'He's over at the shore,' I told her soothingly, and put her back on the pontoon. 'You stay put for fifteen minutes. We're not going far.'

She wasn't happy as we pulled away without her and put-putted over to the pier. We got *Khalida* secured, and I'd just taken off the pair of outer stays on each side and tied the three together when a clanking and rumbling announced that the crane had arrived. The other boat owners gathered round as the crane put out its four supports, one by one, with a hydraulic hiss for each one, and lifted its nose up. The driver fetched the sling from the side compartments and I looped it around the mast. As soon as the driver took the strain, we all scurried round undoing the footbolt, the forestays, the stays, the backstay, not without a bit of bother, and then my mast was rising upwards. I scrambled onto the pier after it, and joined the team of folk guiding it to the trestle tables. In it went, I tucked the dangling wires after it, and went back to my boat.

She was strange and small, my *Khalida*, my love, with only a horseshoe bit of metal where her mast should be soaring skywards. I dropped back into the cockpit, caught the ropes flung down to me and returned her to her berth, where Kitten immediately leapt aboard, purring loudly as if she thought she'd been deserted. I left her in charge and ran back to the pier to help with the next boat.

It was a busy afternoon. We had near two hours of leaping on and off boats and stowing masts. The truck folded its legs and trundled off, and after some tidying up, most of the boat owners went off to drown their sorrows. I was just doing a last spray of Pledge round the wood in *Khalida*'s cabin when there was a knock on the side of it, and a call. I came out and saw Kirsten standing on the pontoon.

'I hope you don't mind me visiting,' she said. 'DI Macrae said you'd be here.'

She looked as if she hadn't slept all this week. Her mouth drooped in a tired line, her skin was mottled under the careful make-up, and there were dark circles under her eyes.

'Come on board,' I said. I gestured at the cabin. 'She's been dismantled below, but I still have water and coffee.'

'If you're sure you don't mind me joining you.' She gave an uncertain shrug. 'We're on opposite sides now.'

I gave her a long look and she shrugged again. 'Sort of,' she added.

I shook my head. 'I'm not anything to do with it. They don't need my evidence against your uncle.' I tried to say it gently. 'They've got the women he brought from Calais. Come aboard, sit down.'

I went below while she was thinking about that and put the kettle on to boil. By the time I came back up with two mugs of coffee, she'd regained control of herself. 'How's your mum doing?' I asked.

'Shattered. Her own peerie brother . . . she's trying to force herself to accept it. She blames the other man, Roberts, Renwick, she calls him Cheveyo, for leading him astray. Once the shock's over she'll come out fighting. Years of undue influence, since Stevie was a teenager.'

I nodded. 'I heard you and Moon talking, at the Guns,' I said.

'I wondered if you had.' She swirled the coffee in her mug, looking at it. 'I don't know what to do. If I came forward to back up what Moon remembered, that would help Mam's case, that he was influenced by Roberts that early. But she doesn't believe he did that. She thinks Moon was misremembering.'

Her eyes were haunted. 'That would break her, that he'd used us for his photos.'

'If it helps,' I said, 'Jen says she doesn't remember. She doesn't want to remember.'

Kirsten's voice was so soft that I could barely make out her words. 'I don't want to remember either.' She looked across at me, eyes wet with tears. 'But maybe that's my punishment for not listening to Moon. If I'd gone with her, if we'd made a statement together, she'd still be alive.'

'No,' I said firmly. 'No.' I set my mug down and tried to think how I could explain. 'Roberts and your uncle, they'd moved on from that long ago. Photographs, I mean. There's a whole long line of nastiness that DS Peterson's untangling, going back to when your uncle was at university. If you ask her, she'll maybe tell you about it. What they were protecting was their current enterprise.'

'The women.' Her face was still torn. 'There was still time for him to have gone back for them. That's what he says. He was waiting for you to go. He had his motorboat in Sandness. He was going to go across for them as soon as dusk fell.'

I wasn't sure whether she believed it, or just wanted to.

She looked at my face. 'But you don't believe that. You didn't think anyone was coming for them.'

I couldn't meet her eyes. 'I can't help you,' I said. 'Your lawyers will tell you what'll help him, if that's what you want to do.' I stood up and took her mug from her. 'Only . . .'

She rose too. 'Only . . . ?'

I gestured with the mug and tried to articulate how I felt. 'You were speaking on the *Swan* about how the world's been designed for men. What they were doing was the worst, the very worst way of men exploiting women. I don't care how he was influenced, or how young he was. He's not an impression-able boy now. He's an adult who knows what he's doing, and he's been involved in exploiting vulnerable women for nearly

330

thirty years, and making a packet out of it.' I heard my voice rising and stopped there. There was a long silence. 'And he killed your sister,' I finished. I looked directly at her. 'And you were listening to him talking, that first night on the *Swan*. I saw the white of your t-shirt. All Moon's clothes were colourful. If he knew you'd been listening, if you'd gone up the Sneug with Moon, he might have killed you too, and made up some story about one of you having slipped and grabbed at the other one.' I thought of the waves pounding the *Dorabella* into pieces. 'You were women. Expendable.'

At last Kirsten nodded. She sketched a wave, and clambered off the boat. On the pontoon, she turned. 'He's nice, your DI. I hope you living together works out.'

'I hope you make it to Convenor,' I said. 'Even if the council men only let you start small, women freezing in too-cold offices need you.'

She gave a half-smile and walked away.

I was ready and waiting on the pier bench, looking gloomily across the mastless marina, when Gavin arrived. He dropped beside me and put an arm round my shoulders. 'Did Kirsten come to see you?'

I nodded, and his arm tightened in a hug. 'Nobody ever believes someone in their family can commit murder, especially not of another relative. The closer, the harder. His lawyer's doing his best to put up an ingenious defence for the women and children in the *Dorabella*.'

'Kirsten told me. He said he was coming back for them.'

'Aye. Well, we'll put up the best case we can, and see what a jury makes of it.' He paused, then repeated the advice he'd given me in the Longship case, 'Write your statement down now, while it's fresh in your memory. Get your times off pat.'

'The time I left Papa will be in the ship's log. I didn't manage to write in it after that.'

He smiled at that. 'You didn't keep up your log? Were you busy doing something?' His hand was warm on my shoulder. He turned to look out at the rows of diminished yachts. 'It's not the same, of course, but I was thinking we'd need a boat. Something small and tough, to give us a way out of the cottage when the road's blocked with snow in the winter, even for a 4x4. How about a Pioneer? They're pretty rugged.'

'With a decent horsepower of engine,' I agreed.

'If you came into town with me tomorrow, we could order one from Thulecraft.'

'New?' I said incredulously.

He nodded firmly. 'New. I won't have time to mess about doing up an older boat. They'll probably be able to get one up here within a week or so.'

My spirits lifted. It would be fun having a power boat. I could easily zoom up to Brae to do all the work *Khalida* needed, and down to Aith or up to Voe for the errands.

His arm tightened, then released me. He stood up and held out his hands to pull me up. 'Shall we stop at Frankie's for tea?'

'A peerie haddock supper.' I glanced down at Cat, good as gold in his harness, and Kitten, sitting upright in the open basket, all ready to go home. 'And an extra battered haddock.'

Acknowledgements

As always, so many people helped in the creation and writing of this book. Thank you to Peter Campbell and the *Swan* Trust for letting me use the *Swan* as the setting for this story. That particular 'three island' voyage was great fun: thank you to skipper Thorben for the trip through the caves and around the back of Foula, and to engineer Ian Nicolson of Tresta, who recounted all of Magnie and Geordie's stories. The *Swan* is now funded principally by paying passengers, so if you fancy seeing Shetland under sail, do please check out her website, https://www.swantrust.com.

Thank you to Hilde and Pete Bardell for letting our writers' group use their cottage on Papa Stour for a wonderful, peaceful and productive weekend. Given that it's the cottage I've featured as 'Uncle's', overlooking the ferry, I'm still not sure how we missed the ferry coming in and leaving again on Sunday evening, but as the next one was Wednesday morning, we were very very grateful to the ferry crew for turning back for the frantically-waving folk on the hillside.

Papa Stour's beautiful little kirk is one of Shetland's older churches. It's now in community ownership, and the fund-raiser Music Day I attended was great fun, even without Cathy's band. 'The Song o' the Papa Men' is a popular one with Shetland bands. It's on several albums, including the North Ness Boys' album *Sea of Life*, under its other title,

'Rowin' Foula Doon'. The Papa Stour Sword Dance almost died out; suffragist and folklorist Christina Jamieson helped rescue it in the early years of the twentieth century, and more recently Papa-born teacher and author G. S. Peterson was another supporter. There are several performances on YouTube. The invitation to come outside is my insertion, not part of the original.

Another inspiration was the loss of the trawler *Coelleiria* on the Ve Skerries in August 2019. Naturally there were neither black fish nor trafficked people aboard.

The final inspiration was my interest in the story of women's fight for equality, and the sections of the book reflect this: that early court case, the first attempts to get women on committees and as officials, the fight for education, the link between socialism and suffragism, and women's work in the war. Kirsten's comments on the world's default setting being male were inspired by *Invisible Women*, by Caroline Criado Perez, a real eye-opener. The section headings are the stages of a storm brewing up.

Thank you to my wonderful agent, Teresa Chris, for her encouragement and critical eye. Thank you to all the team at Headline, particularly to Celine Kelly, my copy editor, whose clear, constructive comments are every author's dream, to my main editor, Toby Jones, for his constant support and encouragement, to Emily Patience for all her work with publicity, and to all the people I never meet who do such a great job on the printsetting, cover and production values of the finished book.

Thank you to my supporters here in Shetland: Karen Fraser and all her team in the Shetland Library, and Karen Baxter and her team in the Shetland Times Bookshop. Local praise is the best, so thank you to the readers here who made my last book top of the library's 'Most borrowed' league table.

Finally, thank you to my husband, Philip, who is always my greatest source of support.

A Note on Shetlan

Shetland has its own very distinctive language, *Shetlan* or *Shetlandic*, which derives from old Norse and old Scots. In *Death on a Longship*, Magnie's first words to Cass are:

'Cass, well, for the love of mercy. Norroway, at this season? Yea, yea, we'll find you a berth. Where are you?'

Written in west-side Shetlan (each district is slightly different), it would have looked like this:

'Cass, weel, fir da love o mercy. Norroway, at dis saeson? Yea, yea, we'll fin dee a bert. Quaur is du?'

Th becomes a *d* sound in *dis* (this), *da* (the), *dee* and *du* (originally thee and thou, now you), *wh* becomes *qu* (*quaur*, where), the vowel sounds are altered (well to *weel*, season to *saeson*, find to *fin*), the verbs are slightly different (quaur <u>is</u> du?) and the whole looks unintelligible to most folk from outwith Shetland, and *twartree* (a few) within it too.

So, rather than writing in the way my characters would speak, I've tried to catch the rhythm and some of the distinctive usages of Shetlan while keeping it intelligible to *soothmoothers*, or people who've come in by boat through the South Mouth of Bressay Sound into Lerwick, and by extension, anyone living south of Fair Isle.

There are also many Shetlan words that my characters would naturally use, and here, to help you, are *some o' dem*. No Shetland person would ever use the Scots *wee*; to them, something small would be *peerie*, or, if it was very small, *peerie mootie*. They'd *caa* sheep in a *park*, that is, herd them up in a field – *moorit* sheep, coloured black, brown, fawn. They'd take a *skiff* (a small rowing boat) out along the *banks* (cliffs) or on the *voe* (sea inlet), with the *tirricks* (Arctic terns) crying above them, and the *selkies* (seals) watching. Hungry folk are *black fanted* (because they've forgotten their *faerdie maet*, the snack that would have kept them going) and upset folk *greet* (cry). An older housewife like Jessie would have her *makkin* (knitting) *belt* buckled around her waist, and her *reestit* (smoke-dried) *mutton* hanging above the Rayburn. And finally . . . my favourite Shetland verb, which I didn't manage to work in this novel, but which is too good not to share: *to kettle*. As in: *Wir cat's just kettled. Four ketlings, twa strippet and twa black and quite.* I'll leave you to work that one out on your own . . . or, of course, you could consult Joanie Graham's *Shetland Dictionary*, if your local bookshop hasn't *joost selt* their last copy *dastreen*.

The diminutives Magnie (Magnus), Gibbie (Gilbert) and Charlie may also seem strange to non-Shetland ears. In a traditional country family (I can't speak for *toonie* Lerwick habits) the oldest son would often be called after his father or grandfather, and be distinguished from that father and grandfather and probably a cousin or two as well, by his own version of their shared name. Or, of course, by a *Peerie* in front of it, which would stick for life, like the *eart kyent* (well-known) guitarist Peerie Willie Johnson, who reached his eightieth birthday. There was also a patronymic system, which meant that a Peter's four sons, Peter, Andrew, John and Matthew, would all have the surname Peterson, and so would his son Peter's children. Andrew's children, however, would have the surname Anderson, John's would be Johnson, and Matthew's would be Matthewson. The Scots ministers stamped this out in the nineteenth century, but in one district you can have a lot of *folk* with the same surname, and so they're distinguished by their house name: *Magnie o' Strom, Peter o' da Knowe*.

Glossary

For those who like to look up unfamiliar words as they go, here's a glossary of Scots and Shetlan words.

aa: all
an aa: as well
aabody: everybody
aawye: everywhere
ahint: behind
ain: own
amang: among
anyroad: anyway
ashet: large serving dish
auld: old
aye: always
bairn: child
ball (verb): throw out
banks: sea cliffs, or peatbanks, the slice of moor where peats are cast
bannock: flat triangular scone
birl, birling: paired spinning round in a dance
blinkie: torch
blootered: very drunk
blyde: pleased
boanie: pretty, good looking

breeks: trousers
briggistanes: flagged stones at the door of a crofthouse
bruck: rubbish
caa: round up
canna: can't
clarted: thickly covered
cludgie: toilet
cowp: capsize
cratur: creature
crofthouse: the long, low traditional house set in its own land
croog: to cling down to
daander: to travel uncertainly or in a leisurely fashion
darrow: a hand fishing line
dastreen: yesterday evening
de-crofted: land that has been taken out of agricultural use, e.g. for a house site
dee: you; du is also you, depending on the grammar of the sentence – they're equivalent to thee and thou. Like French, you would only use dee or du to one friend; several people, or an adult if you're a younger person, would be you.
denner: midday meal
didna: didn't
dinna: don't
dip dee doon: sit yourself down
dis: this
doesna: doesn't
doon: down
drewie lines: a type of seaweed made of long strands
duke: duck
dukey-hole: pond for ducks
du kens: you know
dyck, dyke: a wall, generally drystane, i.e. built without cement
eart: direction, *the eart o wind*

ee now: right now

eela: fishing, generally these days a competition

everywye: everywhere

faersome: frightening

faither, usually faider: father

fanted: hungry, often black fanted, absolutely starving

folk: people

from, frae: from

gansey: a knitted jumper

gant: to yawn

geen: gone

gluff: fright

greff: the area in front of a peat bank

gret: cried

guid: good

guid kens: God knows

hadna: hadn't

hae: have

harled: exterior plaster using small stones

heid: head

hoosie: little house, usually for bairns

howk: to search among: I *howked* ida box o auld claes.

isna: isn't

just: just

keek: peep at

ken, kent: know, knew

kirk: church

kirkyard: graveyard

kishie: wicker basket carried on the back, supported by a *kishie baand* around the forehead

knowe: hillock

lem: china

Lerook: Lerwick

likit: liked

lintie: skylark

lipper: a cheeky or harum-scarum child, generally affectionate

mad: annoyed

mair: more

makkin belt: a knitting belt with a padded oval, perforated for holding the 'wires' or knitting needles.

mam: mum

mareel: sea phosphorescence, caused by plankton, which makes every wave break in a curl of gold sparks

meids: shore features to line up against each other to pinpoint a spot on the water

midder: mother

mind: remember

moorit: coloured brown or black, usually used of sheep

mooritoog: earwig

muckle: big – as in Muckle Roe, the big red island. Vikings were very literal in their names, and almost all Shetland names come from the Norse.

muckle biscuit: large water biscuit, for putting cheese on

myrd: a good number and variety – a *myrd* o peerie things

na: no, or more emphatically, nall

needna: needn't

Norroway: the old Shetland pronunciation of Norway

o: of

oot: out

ower: over

park: fenced field

peat: brick–like lump of dried peat earth, used as fuel

peerie: small

peerie biscuit: small sweet biscuit

Peeriebreeks: affectionate name for a small thing, person or animal

piltick: a sea fish common in Shetland waters

pinnie: apron
postie: postman
quen: when
redding up: tidying
redd up kin: get in touch with family – for example, a
   five-generations New Zealander might come to meet
   Shetland cousins still staying in the house his or her
   forebears had left
reestit mutton: wind-dried shanks of mutton
riggit: dressed, sometimes with the sense 'dressed-up'
roadymen: men working on the roads
roog: a pile of peats
rummle: untidy scattering
Santy: Santa Claus
scaddy man's heids: sea urchins
scattald: common grazing land
scuppered: put paid to, done for
selkie: seal, or seal person who came ashore at night, cast
   his/her skin and became human
Setturday: Saturday
shalder: oystercatcher
sheeksing: chatting
sho: she
shoulda: should have, usually said shoulda
shouldna: shouldn't have
SIBC: Shetland Islands Broadcasting Company, the
   independent radio station
skafe: squint
skerry: a rock in the sea
smoorikins: kisses
snicked: move a switch that makes a clicking noise
snyirked: made a squeaking or rattling noise
solan: gannet
somewye: somewhere

sooking up: sucking up

soothified: behaving like someone from outwith Shetland

spew: be sick

spewings: piles of sick

splatched: walked in a splashy way with wet feet, or in water

steekit mist: thick mist

sun–gaits: with the sun – it's bad luck to go against the sun, particularly walking around a church

swack: smart, fine

swee: to sting (of injury)

tak: take

tatties: potatoes

tay: tea, or meal eaten in the evening

tink: think

tirricks: Arctic terns

trows: trolls

tushker: L-shaped spade for cutting peat

twa: two

twartree: a small number, several

tulley: pocket knife

unken: unknown

vee-lined: lined with wood planking

vexed: sorry or sympathetic: 'I was that vexed to hear that.'

voe: sea inlet

voehead: the landwards end of a sea inlet

waander: wander

waar: seaweed

wasna: wasn't

wha's: who is

whatna: what

whit: what

whitteret: weasel

wi: with

wife: woman, not necessarily married

wir: we've – in Shetlan grammar, we are is sometimes we have

wir: our

wouldna: would not

yaird: enclosed area around or near the croft house

yoal: a traditional clinker-built six-oared rowing boat